# SAM BINNIE

# *The Baby Diaries*

**AVON**

AVON

A division of HarperCollins*Publishers*
77–85 Fulham Palace Road,
London W6 8JB

www.harpercollins.co.uk

A Paperback Original 2013

1

Copyright © Sam Binnie 2013

Sam Binnie asserts the moral right to
be identified as the author of this work

A catalogue record for this book is
available from the British Library

ISBN-13: 978-0-00-747710-4

Set in Sabon by Palimpsest Book Production Limited,
Falkirk, Stirlingshire

Printed and bound in Great Britain by
Clays Ltd, St Ives plc

**MIX**
Paper from
responsible sources
**FSC** **FSC˘ C007454**
www.fsc.org

*For M and F,*

*Singers in every weather*

## October 31st

Have you ever had that feeling you've forgotten something? Something nagging away at the back of your mind – until just the right movement in your memory triggers something else, which knocks another thing down, and like some Indiana Jones death trap, you can feel the clank-clunking of motion in the hidden rooms of your brain, gradually bringing the forgotten memory swinging like a battering ram into your conscious mind. You know that feeling?

That's what I had yesterday.

I've been so busy since the wedding. Tony, my boss and head of Polka Dot Books (purveyors of fine supermarket fiction and glittery celeb books) was as good as his word with my promotion, promising me four new authors before disappearing off on a three-month 'travelling sabbatical' to God Knows Where, declaring he needed a break to 'replenish his business strategies'. Of course, I was delighted that he'd kept his promise – even though that was more his mother Pamela's doing – but soon realised why things had played out that

1

way when I started trying to get details about them. Two were new, so their failure was liable to blow up in my face, one was an author I'd dealt with briefly and reluctantly and the final one I couldn't get any details on at all.

Thom's been settling into his new life as a trainee teacher: to no one's surprise, he's loving it. But as his enthusiasm has spilled over into our evenings, we've spent a great deal of time together marking papers – him, clunky essays on *Wuthering Heights*, me, swathes of mostly unreadable fiction: thirty-somethings who always dreamed of writing, aiming for Heathcliff and hitting Cliff Richard. So we've been dog tired, and when we've had time off we've been with my parents (with half an eye on my dad to check he was taking care of himself after his heart attack earlier this year), my nearly-new niece Frida, or our friends (those we hadn't had to un-invite from the wedding). It was still great to be spending *any* time together where we weren't arguing about money, or the importance of decorative accessories, or the social rules of such a complex endeavour as a wedding. But something kept nagging at me. Did we pay the register office? Had we thanked everyone? Was anyone still locked in the primary school reception venue? None of these nudged anything, although I worried at it like a tongue at a wobbly tooth. It would give eventually. And when it did, I just had to hope I didn't have a huge apology to make to anyone.

Then, yesterday morning, Thom and I were comparing our weeks. Thom said he had me over a barrel, since I spent my time lunching authors and picking my favourite colour for a book jacket, while he was at the coal-face, earning every penny trying to hammer basic English in the heads of his students.

Me:     You love it really.
Thom:  I might love it, but I'm a hell of a lot more tired at

2

                    the end of the day than I ever was making spread-
                    sheets all day. Surprisingly.
Me:        Can it really be that hard?
Thom:    Kiki. I dare you to try dealing with a room full of
                    hormonal teenagers.

    That was it. Clink, clunk. Brrrrrrrrrrrrrrrrrr. Click. Click.
Ka-dunk.
    *BOOM.*

I must have just frozen while my brain went into its noisy
activity, because Thom stopped laughing at the mental image
he'd conjured and looked at me, puzzled. 'What's up?' he said.
    I stood completely still, calculating over and over, mentally
flicking through the pages of my pocket diary – dates, dates,
dates. Dates. When I managed to reconnect my brain with
my voice box, I just said, 'I think we need to go to the
chemist.'
    Thom got it immediately. We rushed out, no coats, no
scarves, into the freezing October afternoon, hurrying to the
chemist around the corner. Outside, it felt like Before for a
moment – we teased one another about who would go in
and buy it, until I remembered what the whole thing was
about, and my face collapsed. Thom went in while I read
the notices in the window again and again. A Great Time To
Give Up Smoking! the sign read. Or indeed, start, I thought.
Then he was out, and we were hurrying home again, and I
thought, Is this time included in the three minutes you have
to count off? If I walk home slowly will I know the result
immediately? Then we *were* home, and Thom was bustling
me upstairs, and I went into the bathroom and locked the
door. When I took the little test out of the box, the adrenaline
was coursing through me and my hands were shaking so
much that I couldn't read one word of the instructions.

3

Me: How does this even work?

Thom: [through the door] Haven't you ever watched TV? Piss on the stick, then we can find out who the father is later.

Me: *Please*.

Thom: [quiet] Sorry, Kiki. Pass the instructions under the door.

Me: [hands shaking, takes several goes]

Thom: OK. It's the bit on the end. Then stick the lid back on and leave it three minutes. Do you want me to come in?

Me: Come in? In here? I don't really know. I don't know. I don't *know*.

Thom: It's OK, Keeks. I'm right here. We can do this later if you want. We don't have to do it right now. We can talk about it first, if you want.

And just for a moment, I thought: 'we'? *We*? If a little plus sign appeared in this window, it wouldn't be Thom squandering his recent promotion. It wouldn't be Thom who was the only one of his friends changing his name to 'Mummy'. It wouldn't be Thom pushing a large ham-weight through his tiny little birth canal. We? Me me me me me. Then I thought: oh, fuck it. Just take the test.

So I did.

I was still shaking, so managed to wee all over my own hands, but I clicked the cap back on and let it sit. I opened the bathroom door, and Thom rushed in.

Thom: How are you doing?

Me: You're holding the hand that's covered in my urine.

Thom: I'm going to take that as a 'good'.

4

He hugged me for a long time, not even commenting on how much the bathroom now stank, then we went over together to check the result. A giant glowing plus sign greeted us.

Me:     Well.
Thom:   That's unambiguous.
Me:     Best of three?
Thom:   It was a two-pack. I don't think you'll need me to go out again.
Me:     Oh. Shit?

Thom took me into the living room, where we sat for ages in silence.

Thom:   But . . . when?
Me:     Our honeymoon.
Thom:   How?
Me:     Remember that night? We'd been walking under the Eiffel Tower? And we agreed to start trying because it could take years? The night before we sobered up and realised our mistake. That one.
Thom:   Wow. Honeymoon baby.
Me:     [breaking down sobbing] It's so taaa-aa-aa-ack-y-y-y-y.

I cried for half an hour, then calmed down into a state of steady shock. Pregnant. I'm pregnant. As if reading my mind, Thom said in a ridiculous over-the-top voice, 'I can't believe we're pregnant already!' which managed to get a laugh out of me; it's an all-time Worst Phrase, and my laugh stuck around until I remembered that it was, at least in one sense, true. My catatonic state returned.

Me: How did this happen?

Thom: Oh Keeks. When a man and a woman love one another very much –

Me: Thom, please! *Really*!

Thom: I don't know, Kiki, these things sometimes happen, don't they? I do love you very much, if that helps.

Me: I just don't know what to do. I don't know what to do. [whispering] This is ridiculous.

Thom: Shall we go to bed? Sometimes these things feel better in the morning.

Me: [staring at him]

Thom: Sorry, I don't mean it like that. I know it's not going to go away, and I know that no matter how much I say I love you and I support you and I feel for you, I know that it's your body and I can only begin to imagine your panic and your fear. But I do love you, and loving you also involves knowing that sometimes you deal best with things by vanishing in a cocoon of sleep to work out what you have to do. Is that true?

Me: Yes.

Thom: Right. So let's do one decision at a time. Would you like me to make you a drink before bed?

Me: Whisky.

Thom: Uh . . .

Me: OH GOD I CAN'T EVEN DRINK. Oh God! How much have I drunk in the last month? The last two months? OH GOD I DO NOTHING BUT DRINK.

Thom: Kiki. It's fine. Let's forget about the drink and just get into bed.

So we did just that. I amazed myself by falling straight to sleep – as Thom said, it's how I cope with most things, but it meant it was an extra struggle this morning, having a mini version of the click-clunking remembering all over again. Pregnant. Pregnant. Pregnant. It still doesn't make any sense. Yes, we both want kids very much, and yes, we look forward to having them, but now? Right now? I have *just* got my promotion, Thom has just started a mind-bogglingly poorly paid job, and we're not ready for this. I feel so strange.

At work today, Alice noticed something was wrong, but only asked me once. She kept her distance for the rest of the day in the nicest possible manner, her excellent breeding (or lesbian superpower) knowing exactly when to press me and lavish me with attention, and when to leave me in peace. Alice, my best friend in the office, is head of Publicity here at Polka Dot Books and a far nicer, better and more capable person than the company deserves. Since Tony began his ridiculous absence, his mother Pamela (who also happens to be the founder of Polka Dot and its major shareholder) has tried to keep out of the office most of the time, wanting to believe her son knows what he's doing. But we can all tell she's worried the company will go down, even with people like Alice working here. Thankfully, this not being one of Pamela's rare visiting days, I managed to get my head down and do work for most of the day; at lunchtime I had to get out of the office, so took my sandwich round the corner to window shop, and found myself in front of the giant Topshop on Oxford Street, facing the maternity wear entrance.

They had some lovely clothes. Gorgeous slim-fitting jeans with fatty pregna-panels in the sides, fabulous tops to show off pregna-busts and delicious high-waisted dresses. Not to mention the mini-me baby clothes: t-shirts and sweaters with the wildlife of the season embroidered on the front, so the infant can be just as sharp as the mother. Could I live like this? Is there hope? I started walking back to the office feeling better, feeling hopeful. Maybe we could do this. It's not the seventies anymore: I wouldn't have to wear huge frilly tents and give up my job. I could be like Rachida Dati, returning to work at the French government five days after having this baby. Only, not the French government. And not five days. Women do this all over the world, all the time. And this wouldn't just be my baby. It would be Thom's as well. And who's going to make a better baby than me and Thom?

So I went to the beautiful stationery shop below our office and bought this diary. I had a sudden urge to keep a record of everything, all our decisions and mistakes and joys. It felt like the first good step in a long road ahead. But I felt good.

Then I left the shop and almost tripped over a woman screaming at her child.

| | |
|---|---|
| Woman: | Didn't I tell you, Nicholas? Didn't I say no? |
| Boy: | [incoherent screaming] |
| Woman: | No, don't keep crying. Pull yourself together and answer me. |
| Boy: | [screaming, but down a notch or two] I . . . want . . . |
| Woman: | Nicholas, if you don't behave right now, not only will Daddy be hearing about this, but you can forget about your skiing lesson with Joshua on Saturday. |
| Boy: | [silent for a moment, weighing up the options, screams recommencing even higher and louder than before] |
| Woman: | [crouching down next to him] Please, Nicholas, please, darling, just calm yourself down. What it is you'd like, Nicky? |
| Boy: | [sensing his advantage, ups the screaming again] |

Woman: Calm down, darling. You know Mummy loves you. Calm down. Shall we go back to the shop to get you the little car?

Boy: [pulling back the screams a little] Ye-ea-aah – [hiccupping sob]

Woman: Alright, darling. You were very good last night, weren't you? You only got out of bed four times! I think you deserve a nice little treat, don't you, darling?

Wait. I'd forgotten. OH GOD I hate children.

So my mood overall was unchanged this afternoon, and when I came home. Thom saw my face and pulled me into another big hug as I walked through the door, and took me to the sofa where he sat me down and smiled at me.

Thom: Do you know what I thought today, as I tried to convince a room full of thirteen-year-olds to not show one another photos of women's breasts while I talked about *Jane Eyre*?

Me: Nope.

Thom: Whether it's now, or whether it's in a few years: our kid is going to be brilliant.

Me: Ha! I thought the same thing today. Just before I stumbled over a woman being emotionally blackmailed by her four-year-old.

Thom: You know we don't have to be like that, don't you? You can pick your parenting style: we can be Aloof Edwardian Parents. Or Distant Army Parents, who only see their children once a year. Or Caveman Parents, who feed any spare kids to their pet dinosaur.

Me: That's the Flintstones.

Thom: I hardly think the Flintstones would feed a *child* to a *dinosaur*.

Me: [silence, thinking] We could be alright as parents. Maybe.

Thom: Maybe we could. But maybe . . . you're too *chicken* to have a baby.

Me: [laughing] If ever that ploy was going to work on me . . .

Thom: Kiki, we will do whatever you like. For now, I'll make us something to eat.

I sat, and I thought. God, if we can deal with Thom's redundancy and Dad's heart attack and my previously-very-badly-paid-and-very-high-stress job, all while planning a wedding that took over our lives, we should be able to manage a baby. Thom's baby. And we might just be OK parents.

Me: [calling to the kitchen] Go on, then. Let's have a baby.

Thom: [running back in] Wooohoooo!

Me: You can't make noises like that in a labour ward. And *I'm* not telling my mum.

Thom: Christ. We have to tell people about this, don't we?

Together: *Shotgun*!

Me: I called it. You can tell them.

So I'm happy. But I still blame you, Paris. I don't know how this is your fault, but it is.

TO DO:
Grow baby
Have baby
Raise baby

10

## November's Classic Baby

Mrs Darling was married in white, and at first she kept the books perfectly, almost gleefully, as if it were a game, not so much as a Brussels sprout was missing; but by and by whole cauliflowers dropped out, and instead of them there were pictures of babies without faces. She drew them when she should have been totting up. They were Mrs Darling's guesses.

Wendy came first, then John, then Michael.

For a week or two after Wendy came it was doubtful whether they would be able to keep her, as she was another mouth to feed. Mr Darling was frightfully proud of her, but he was very honourable, and he sat on the edge of Mrs Darling's bed, holding her hand and calculating expenses, while she looked at him imploringly. She wanted to risk it, come what might, but that was not his way; his way was with a pencil and a piece of paper, and if she confused him with suggestions he had to begin at the beginning again.

*Peter Pan*
J. M. Barrie

## November 2nd

I've spent the last two days at work doing internet searches for pregnancy, then shutting my screen off whenever somebody comes near my desk. Even Carol – our terrifying but secretly incredibly sweet senior Commissioning Editor, who, after a sordid and very exciting office affair, is now with Norman, our reserved head of accounts – has started giving me concerned looks. But I've discovered that the 'classic wedding' emails I signed up for during the wedding planning also come in a 'Pregnancy and Babies' version too. Which . . . is . . . something, I suppose?

What's so strange is how much this new reality is in my thoughts *all* the time. I can't put anything in my mouth without my brain suddenly doing a stop-and-search which makes me keep retching on what I'm eating, either because it *might* be dangerous or my tastebuds have suddenly banded together to bar certain foods. The radio plays nothing but songs about babies: *Papa Don't Preach*, *Hit Me Baby One More Time*, pretty much anything from Phil Spector's Wall of Sound, almost any pop song ever. Adverts are saturated with babies; pregnant women are everywhere; I've gone over my calendar again and again with my sketchy dates to try and work out at what stage I'll be for everything we've got planned. And I'll need to avoid Susie (my sister, and mother to seven-year-old twins Edward and Lily and baby Frida) – my vocabulary has suddenly shrunk to just a few phrases: the number of times I said 'They're such babies/why is he being such a baby/don't be a baby' at work today was absurd. Did I see Alice sniggering at one of those?


November 3rd


A baby. Pregnant. I'm still not used to this. I don't even know where to start. New clothes? A cot? Thom said: 'Maybe go and see a doctor.' I'm glad I'm not doing this on my own.

At the doctor's today, I looked around the waiting room at the other patients with new, wiser eyes. What could they be here for? A teenage girl looks nervous, and plays with her phone the whole time. Pregnant? A woman with three young children looks exhausted and keeps putting her head in her hands. Number four on the way? Then my name was called, and I saw my new doctor for the first time: a black woman a couple of years older than me, standing in the doorway, resting her hip against the frame and rubbing her pregnant stomach. In her office, we each tried to make the other sit down first. She said, 'On three?' and I laughed and sat down.

| Dr Bedford: | So, how can I help you today? |
| Me: | [suddenly nervous] I think I might be . . . [indicating her] |
| Dr Bedford: | Black? |
| Me: | No! No, not . . . no, I mean – |

13

Dr Bedford:     I'm just kidding, Katherine.

I like her.

Dr Bedford:     You think you might be pregnant?
Me:             Haha, ha. Yes, I think I'm pregnant.
Dr Bedford:     And what makes you think that?
Me:             I've missed two periods, I did four pregnancy
                tests in the end and they were all positive.
Dr Bedford:     Just wanting to make sure?
Me:             Exactly.
Dr Bedford:     And how do you feel about this preg-
                nancy?
Me:             It wasn't exactly planned, so I freaked out a
                bit to begin with – we only just got married
                this summer –
Dr Bedford:     Congratulations!
Me:             Thank you – so I wasn't really sure how to
                handle it all, but I'm really happy now. I
                think. We both are.
Dr Bedford:     OK, congratulations for this too, then. You
                say you've missed two periods – do you think
                that's how far along you could be?
Me:             [suddenly feeling like I've made an embar-
                rassing mistake] Ye-es. Is that a problem?
Dr Bedford:     [laughing] Of course it's not a problem,
                Katherine! We're not going to send you away
                because you're a little later noticing than some
                mothers! Now, I'll give the hospital a ring to
                get you booked in for your twelve-week scan
                – obviously these things are often booked up
                a while in advance, but of course we'll find
                space for you. How are you feeling in
                yourself?

14

| Me: | Fine, thanks. |
|---|---|
| Dr Bedford: | Any tiredness, or aches? Any pains around your womb area? |
| Me: | I did feel completely wiped out about a month ago. I kept coming home from work and falling straight to sleep. But I thought that was delayed trauma from everything that's happened this year. Do you think it was related to this? |
| Dr Bedford: | I think it almost certainly was. So you're getting lots of rest now? Anything else, any aches? |
| Me: | Some aching, but I thought it was just period pains. I assume that's why I haven't realised. I kept getting stretching, achey pains, then forgetting that the period itself didn't actually show up. And my appetite has gone crazy – either I'm trying to eat everything, or there's nothing I can eat without feeling sick. I actually kept meaning to come and see you about it. |
| Dr Bedford: | That's quite normal, I'm afraid. And how have you been taking care of yourself, generally? Do you smoke or take drugs? |
| Me: | [triumphant] No! Neither! |
| Dr Bedford: | [laughing again] Well, that is something. How about drinking? What's your weekly intake? |
| Me: | Average? |
| Dr Bedford: | What do you think we're talking; a bottle of wine a night? |
| Me: | God, no! Actually, it has been *way* less recently. That's weird. |
| Dr Bedford: | As long as you're cutting back now, that's all that matters. What's done is done, yes? |

| | |
|---|---|
| Me: | I suppose so. |
| Dr Bedford: | I'll sort out that scan, and give you this booklet [hands over giant A4 folder]. It will hopefully answer any questions you've got, give you some idea how to take care of yourself, and let you know all the check-ups and scans you'll be having. You might also want to think about joining one of the antenatal groups around here, to meet some other mums. |
| Me: | [choking sound] |
| Dr Bedford: | Are you alright? |
| Me: | Mums. *Other* mums. Other *mums*. Is it hot in here? |
| Dr Bedford: | It could help you, Katherine, if you want to talk about this with people who might know what you're going through right now. Do you have any other questions? |
| Me: | Doctor. |
| Dr Bedford: | Yes, Katherine. |
| Me: | Is this all going to be OK? |
| Dr Bedford: | I can't tell you that, Katherine, but you're a sensible girl. If you're eating well and taking care of yourself, I don't see that there should be any reason to worry. But it's the scan that can really tell you what you're looking for. Anything else? |
| Me: | Can you tell my parents? |
| Dr Bedford: | Do you think they'll be upset? |
| Me: | No. I think they'll be delighted. I'm just not sure I can cope with it. |
| Dr Bedford: | Well, Katherine, I'm always here if you need support or guidance, but do bear in mind [leaning in, conspiratorial] I've only two months |

|  | to my maternity leave and I do have quite a few people to see before I can go. So . . . |
| Me: | I see. Thanks, Doctor. |
| Dr Bedford: | [smiling] You'll be fine. |

She is a great doctor. Maybe we'll bond over our babies and become the best of friends, and we'll bring our kids up together and have loads of hilarious misadventures as a gang. But maybe I won't mention that yet. We'll just see how it goes.

Some things that, with hindsight, were possibly caused by me being pregnant:

1. Sleeping fourteen-hour nights for two whole weeks
2. On three separate occasions, eating Thom's portion of dinner when he was fifteen minutes late home
3. Crying uncontrollably during a debate with Thom about funding cuts hitting vulnerable women and children
4. Crying uncontrollably at an old *Gilmore Girls* episode
5. Crying uncontrollably at a bread advert on TV
6. Being sick in my mouth when Alice brought me coffee at work two mornings in a row, after which she stopped doing it
7. Suddenly finding none of my bras fit properly
8. Going off booze (I *thought* that was odd)
9. Only wanting oranges for breakfast for an entire week
10. Finding Mum even more annoying than usual

Yes, I may have been ignoring some major clues there. But in my defence: I've had other things on my mind. Dad's officially recovered from his heart attack, but I still worry about him. He retired early and happily from a boring senior job at a law firm years ago, and became a Jewellery Making

17

teacher at the local college, to our surprise, all in an attempt to slow his life down and keep himself well. But he was never in one of the high-risk groups before the heart attack, which makes it harder to predict how he'll fare over the next five, ten or twenty years. I have to admit: every time the phone rings and it's Mum, my hearts dips. Is something wrong? But it never is (if you discount the neighbour's noisy driveway, Gillian from her old work's daughter's new house, plastic bags, the price of petrol, the shoes she only bought last summer but are already falling apart) and I should be returning to pre-heart attack levels of stress. But I'm not. Every time she reports Dad's got a cold, headache, or – heaven forbid – episode of heartburn, my adrenaline levels go through the roof. And Mum seems worse than usual at the moment – panicking, worrying, even forgetful. So I've been distracted. But how were we going to tell them about this baby? Would they like it? Would they think it was too fast?

At work, before Tony did his Business Strategy Sabbatical Disappearing Act™ he'd been on my case about my new position, pushing me to bring in some money to Polka Dot with my own books. I know his mother Pamela is on my side, since she actually forced him to honour the promotion he'd offered me, but she's barely around. And Jacki Jones, the actress/popstar whose bestselling wedding book originally got me the promotion, is busy going through a very painful divorce, but Tony had still been nagging me to find out if there's a second book in her. She signed up for a two-book deal, as Tony obviously imagined there'd be babies soon enough, but the state she's in at the moment, I can't bring myself to ask. We still see each other regularly: once a month we pick a bar and spend an evening laughing at the terrible coverage her divorce is getting. Our favourite so far is the story that she's divorcing her husband for Pedro, one of her best friends and horrific ego-ridden monster-slash-celebrity photographer who snapped our wedding at Jacki's incredibly kind request (and God knows how much of her own money). He's truly awful (to me, anyway, accusing me of being a social climber at Jacki's cursed wedding), but he is just her friend, and I believe he cares about her. She laughs at these dreadful stories, and the headlines illustrated with pap-snaps of her looking 'tired', 'drawn' and 'emotional', but she's so sad. The more I know Jacki, the more I love her, and it's awful to see this funny, smart, ambitious person being crushed just a little more every day. So I don't know where I'm going to get that money-spinner.

For now, I've got the Four Authors of the Apocalypse to be dealing with.

Hilary Taylor – producer of Aga sagas. I've had brief dealings with her before, when Tony was trying to poach her from her last publisher. He won her over with a glossy presentation and proposed rejackets for her back catalogue, but we all suspect this is going to be one of those terrible triumphs of sales figures over blind optimism: she hasn't sold well for years, and no amount of extra laminate on the jacket is likely to change anything about that. *Favourite fact*: In our email correspondence, she was unbelievably bitter and rude about her then-current publisher. Can't wait until we receive that treatment too.

Matthew Holt – a brand-new author, of truly dire Scandi-crime. I have a horrible suspicion that he's been no nearer to north-eastern Europe than watching Eurovision, but the crowbarred-in geographical references are the least of my complaints. His book is really, truly, very bad, but my only hope is that people will assume they're genuinely Scandinavian and blame the translator. *Favourite fact*: Matthew Holt believes that you can walk directly from Denmark to Norway.

Jennifer Luck – another brand-new name, this time of

trashy, shopping-and-handsome-bosses fiction. Magically inspired by completely current cultural reference point *Sex and the City*, she's given us four books, all of which we've signed up: *Nude in New York*, *Filthy in Finland*, *Hot in Hong Kong*, and my personal favourite, *Bonking in Brazil*. *Favourite fact*: These books make me wish I'd never learnt to read.

Stuart Winton – a complete unknown. The manuscript I have is a very ropy erotica novel set in the eighties, under the pseudonym Tara Towne. But I can't find any details on our systems to even contact Stuart, nor can I find any evidence of the contract. *Favourite fact*: This *may* be an elaborate prank Carol is playing on the rest of the office. I can't even begin to say how unlikely this is.

And all of these I'm responsible for making sure they're insanely successful.

TO DO:
Find out if it's possible to change my career before the baby is born
Also: Eat some fruit
Don't take up horse-riding, cross-country skiing or trampolining
Stop looking up 'dangerous pregnancy activities' online

November 4th

Alice has been great over the last few months. She had to suffer my wedding ups and downs; then a week of Tony pacing the office, sweating profusely and muttering, 'When is she back?' like I'd just nipped out for the antidote to his snakebite, so desperate was he to go on his ridiculous sabbatical. And on my return from our brief Paris honeymoon, she had to witness slight hysteria on my part as I realised Tony's five-minute meeting with me was the only handover I'd be getting before he vanished for who-knows-how-long.

Alice is also still having to live with her 'boyfriend' despite the fact that everyone besides her family knows she's gay. She does the work of three people here (a normal situation for publishing) while always keeping a smile on her face. As I thought over and over about breaking the news to my colleagues, I wondered for the first time in ages how *she* actually is, so took her out for drinks this evening, at our favourite little bar round the corner.

Alice:   What's this for? What are you up to?

Me:   I'm not up to anything!

Alice:   Are you about to set me up with someone? Is there a beautiful woman just waiting to spend the evening being entertained by me somewhere in this bar?

Me:   Only me, I'm afraid. What's your poison?

Alice:   No one actually says that. 'What's your poison?' What *are* you up to?

Me:   Alice! Fine: it's my round.

Alice:   [browsing the menu] I . . . will have . . . a Slutty Horse, please.

Me:   One Slutty Horse coming up, Madam. [to the barman] One Slutty Horse, one . . . Elderflower Handshake, please.

Alice:   Are you making me drink alone?

Me:   Oh no, I'm so sorry – I'm on these antibiotics –

Alice:   [mouth agape]

Me:   What?

Alice:   [whispering] You've been married *three months*.

Me:   [nervous] What?

Alice:   [shakes head]

Me:     *What?*

Alice:  Kiki, Kiki, Kiki . . .

Me:     *Alice!*

Alice:  Don't make me say it, Kiki.

        [silence]

Me:     Alice, please don't tell anyone. It wasn't even supposed
        to happen – we didn't even mean it – but we did
        mean it, but only for one night, and we were drunk,
        and it just – please, you please mustn't tell anyone,
        [almost sobbing] *please*.

Alice:  Kiki, does this face look like it tells secrets?

We talked for a long time. We talked about how I was
feeling, and how Thom was feeling, and how Tony and
Pamela might take it, and what the maternity package may
or may not be at Polka Dot (for some reason we haven't
had anyone go on maternity leave while we've been there).
And some more about how I was feeling. She also told me,
after her fourth Slutty Horse, that everyone knowing about
Norman and Carol's office romance doesn't seem to have
quenched their passion – she caught them snogging in
Carol's office after work the other evening. At the end of
the night, as we stumbled to the tube station and down to
our platforms (Alice stumbling after taking on all the Slutty
Horses, me stumbling after taking on Alice), I realised we
still hadn't talked about how Alice was. 'Plus ça change,
my darling,' she smiled, as I put her on her train home. Is
she OK?

TO DO:

Start carrying around a hipflask filled with apple juice, for
    when someone next needs to see me drinking
Check Alice is OK tomorrow

November 9th

*Body.* Didn't we have a deal? Didn't we agree that enough was enough? That you would stop this nonsense? Yes, it's probably hard work growing another human being, but do you need to make such a fuss? Women do it all over the world. Every day. And they've done it since before even my *mum* was born. So can you just stop? Please?

The last few days, the mild queasiness I've had on and off the last month or two has burst into something far worse. I just feel *rotten*. Tired, aching, and sick, sick, sick. It just doesn't let up. And I don't want to be one of those frail Victorian pregnants, hobbled by confinement and sent to rest until the baby is ready to go to boarding school, but I just can't function like this. It ambushes me at moments throughout the day, but the worst thing – the meanest trick in the whole nausea book – is that this isn't morning sickness. Oh no. In the morning, I wake feeling perky and wholesome, hoping that this might be the day this sickness has slung its hook. So I enjoy a good breakfast with Thom, and we talk, and we make plans, and behave like civilised, happy humans. Then at work, I might feel a bit odd, but it's OK, I just need to get on with work. By lunchtime, my mouth tastes gross, and nothing seems that tempting, but I can normally find something to fill the gaping, ever-increasing black hole in my appetite (because, of course! – it wouldn't be truly funny unless this nausea coincided with a huge increase in appetite!) and I'll be fine for a few hours. If I get hungry in the afternoon, I've stocked my desk with fruit and nuts, plus a huge bottle of water. So I just about make it through the day. I start feeling hopeful. Maybe Thom and I can have a conversation tonight! Maybe *I* can make *him* dinner, to thank him for all his recent kindness and consideration! Perhaps we can even do some of that stuff we're probably contractually obliged to do, post-wedding ceremony!

That would be great! But even as I'm waving goodbye to everyone, I can feel it starting. My mouth-taste is switching from weird to bitter, from Status Normal to What The Hell Is Going On Here? By the time I've got a seat on the tube, I'm desperately praying that no one near me smells of anything, or, heaven forbid, dares to eat anything. And by the time Thom and I meet at home, all I can do is lie down, slipping tiny slivers of whatever arbitrary foodstuff I can handle that day into my mouth. I am not fun company right now.

## November 10th

I'm sure morning sickness is supposed to *fade* around now, not get worse every day. This is something hatching in my brain and stomach, where Thom can't even *say* particular foods to me without bile pooling in my mouth until I have to go and lie with my head on a really cold pillow, sipping water like an idiot. The first night I had this, Thom was thrown.

Thom: What's . . . *wrong* with you?

Me:   I don't know. That morning sickness I was so delighted to have missed? I think it found me.

Thom: It's seven pm.

Me:   Thank you. I'll just swallow your watch to let my stomach know and we should have this sorted in two seconds.

Thom: Sarcasm? This does sound serious. [sitting tentatively next to me on the bed]

Me:   OH GOD don't lean on me.

Thom: [leaping up] OK, no problem. Is there anything you can stomach eating?

Me:   What have we got?

Thom: Um . . . pasta? Salad?

24

| Me: | [gulping] Nonotpastatalkaboutsomethingelse – |
|---|---|
| Thom: | What would you like? Name it, and I'll find it. |
| Me: | Mm . . . Maybe . . . Do we have any salt and vinegar crisps? And a melon? |
| Thom: | You're depraved. |
| Me: | I'm sure I'll feel alright tomorrow. I'm just tired. Tomorrow I'll be back to eating – |
| Thom: | Don't. Don't say anything. I can't risk you being sick on our bed. I'll go and fetch your gourmet feast, then we sleep. |
| Me: | Deal. Thank you. |

And it's just got worse since then. I avoid being sick all day, but what I can't do is stop the feeling that I *want* to be sick, pretty much all the time now. I can't tell you how angry it makes me to be reduced to that movie pregnant cliché, and to feel so bad with no purpose. This isn't something that needs medicating – it's just my body launching a full-on civil war. Well, Body, I shan't forget this. You just remember that. This isn't over.

November 11th

Christ, I still feel so terrible. The fact that there are some women who feel like this every day of their nine months I think is a pretty reasonable explanation for only children. I just about manage to stay upright at work, but I come home and just lie, with a downturned mouth, either on the bed or the sofa and try not to smell the food Thom is doing his damndest to cook and eat in a secretive manner. Then I eat as many mouthfuls of cornflakes and cold, cold milk as I can before my rebellious stomach sends reinforcements and the refuelling party is over. The enemy has realised my plan

25

and all I can do is retreat to the sofa again, trying not to groan out loud and wishing so very, very hard that the feeling of being on a whirling roundabout would stop. Any time now. Like, now. Or now. Or now?

I'm sorry to feel so sorry for myself. As long as this baby is growing, and healthy, and all that jazz that pregnants say to one another like a mantra, then I can stomach this stomach.

Unless I wake up tomorrow and it's still like this. In which case, I will *not* be happy.

OK, I can do this. Millions of people – women, I suppose; millions of women – get pregnant every day, and they just get on with it, don't they? I mean: there will be frightened girls and women who don't want their babies and don't know what to do, and women who want babies so much and can't have them, and here I am, happily married (for *less than three months*) with a supportive husband and family, so what am I worried about?

Yet the reality of this pregnancy rattles around my head. I can actually hear it: rattle rattle rattle, all the time. Are these sound-effect thoughts also a symptom of pregnancy? I'm delighted, then I'm terrified. I think of the fun we shall have with our own child, then I think of my body, and my social life, and – oh GOD – my *career*. Tony's hardly a dream boss, but I love Polka Dot. What am I supposed to do? I've had this new position for even less time than I've been married, and I've got to somehow get a carrier pigeon to Tony in distant lands to let him know that he took a punt on me and it backfired? How am I going to face any of them? And Pamela too! She championed me against her son, and now I'm dragging the Polka Dot offices back sixty years, into the dark days when young women married, bred and vanished into a life of baking and school fêtes. Not that that's even what I want – I don't want to watch my career dissolve while I stay in the

26

kitchen, weeping while my kids pelt me with Lego. But that's definitely the assumption Pamela and Tony will make.

But then I get excited again. A baby, with Thom. Not that I even like babies – I really don't, not at all – but it's exciting, to be doing something so different, so wonderful, so creative, and to have this massive responsibility and to be sharing it with Thom. What an honour. This is the most wonderful thing. And then I think: a baby. Jesus. Not a baby Jesus, but a baby nonetheless. And one that I imagine will do a hell of a lot more crying than the one we have to thank for Christmas. How the hell are we going to cope with that?

And then the nausea comes back.

We spent tonight watching some belated fireworks from a pub window with Jim (a session musician and source of great kindness, and my oldest friend besides Eve) and Poppy, the girl he brought to our wedding and who seems like a keeper. I sat sipping an apple juice ('Sorry, I've been feeling rough all week') and trying to steady my stomach and absorb the letter from Dr Bedford this morning, confirming the date for the twelve-week scan. Thom's got permission from school to go in late, and I'll tell Polka I'm editing from home that day. I can't stop thinking about it. Something about that scan will make it real, rather than just a distant To Do. And I'm sure it's going to be much harder to keep up my heroin habit afterwards. *Joke.*

TO DO:
Start reading any of those pamphlets Dr Bedford gave me


November 14th

I got a letter today from the local team of midwives. Ah, the things you never thought you'd find out: who even knew there was a local team of midwives? A *team* sounds good, though. Like a team of crime-fighters. I hope they have cool uniforms, at least. The letter said that I had an appointment with them next week at the local hospital, and came wrapped around six different leaflets – what I should be eating, how I should be feeling, what's going to be taken from me (blood and urine) and what's going to be given (more information). I find it's most helpful to write the appointment in my diary, tuck the whole thing safe at the back of my drawer, and just not think about it again. Note: this may not work when the actual baby is born.

Mum came over tonight to drop off some photos from our wedding (oh, how recent that seemed) and I thought she'd guess instantly when I was lying on the sofa, grey-faced and sipping water with a lemon in.

Mum: Hello darling, are you ill?

Me: My stomach. I think it's a bug.

Mum: Oh, that's awful. Have you had some plain toast?

Me: [trying not to retch at the thought] No, I don't really . . .

Mum: Well, it's the best thing for you.

Me: I know, but it's not what my stomach wants right now.

Mum: Kiki, I think you're being very silly; a nice piece of dry toast is exactly the kind of thing you should be eating if you want to feel any better. Is it something going round?

Me: [burping, a precursor to vomiting]

Thom: She's been a bit sick all day, it might be better if we let her rest for a while.

Mum: [voice almost cracking] You're being ridiculous! If you don't want to feel better –

Thom: I'll get her some toast later. I think she's just a bit tired at the moment.

Mum: [grumpily] Well I shan't kiss you, in case it's catching
and I give it to your father.

Thom: [sniggering]

Me: [faintly] Alright Mum. Thanks for the photos.

Mum: That's perfectly alright. See you soon!

And she was gone. We both felt such relief, even though
she is incredibly kind (sometimes) and did do a huge amount
towards saving our wedding from disaster: but her attentions
*can* be a little much, and if she'd kept saying the word toast
I would definitely have been sick in front of her. And she
seemed even more tense than usual – surely she wouldn't
care that much about my toast intake normally? Plus, we
definitely don't want to tell anyone until we've had the first
scan. It still doesn't seem real.

November 15th

Ah, crazy hormones. Yesterday I got home from work and,
in a brief respite from nausea, *pounced* on Thom, then fell
straight to sleep to a night of the *filthiest* dreams I have ever
had. I can't even name some of the people who featured for
fear of this diary ever falling into the wrong hands, but it
was . . . well, I'm not surprised I was more tired this morning
than when I went to bed.

November 16th

Thom remembered the Diary today – last Christmas he'd given
me a diary for the year, with trips and treats every month.
Last month he'd dug me out a perfect Marion Ravenwood
costume (wicker-basket-Marion, not Nazi-tent-Marion) for

Halloween, and in return I found him a Captain Sharpe costume (yes, I know, Thom Sharpe, Captain Sharpe, I am exactly that imaginative); the combination of which resulted in us arriving slightly late, but very cheerful, to the party.

This month, the treat was simply *Tickets*. November seemed so far off when Thom arranged it all last Christmas that he couldn't book anything, leaving it instead up to our whims of the moment. Right now, I didn't know what I wanted – a gig? Theatre? A film? An exhibition? That is, until Thom suggested a swap.

Thom: You don't have to go for this. But you know you're only allowed the treat within the month – there are no rollovers.
Me: Where was this written down?
Thom: [taps side of his head] So, here's your alternative. I go out, right now, and get you six ice-cold bottles of ginger beer, a jumbo bag of salted vegetable crisps, aaaand . . . [holding up his hands]
Me: A can – no, make it two; two cans of corned beef.
Thom: [shuddering] Whatever milady requires. So what do you say? Is it a swap?

We agreed to the swap, as I'm in no fit state to be going anywhere at the moment. But I did enjoy my strange, protein-heavy meal this evening *immensely*.


November 17th

Drinks with Eve tonight, my oldest, most difficult, but potentially-most-reformed friend (since meeting wonderful baker Mike, she's developed a taste for not being a terrible human). Or rather, it was supposed to be drinks, but I changed it to a trip to the Wellcome Collection as I couldn't face Eve giving me suspicious side-eyes when I wasn't drinking. So we met outside, hugged, and headed in.

Me:     [narrowing eyes at her, suspicious] You look *very* well.

Eve:    [narrowing eyes too] So do you.

Me:     My goodness, is Mike still making you incredibly happy? Goodness. He is, isn't he? You *love* him.

Eve:    I might. Do you know what it is, though? I just don't see good-looking men anymore.

Me:     Maybe it's because you're so in love.

Eve:    [mock-concerned] No, I think my eyesight's getting worse. I really need to see a doctor.

Me:     Optician. And I don't imagine they'll be able to help with what you've got.

Eve:    Syphilis?

Me:     Wow. You old romantic.

Eve:    But speaking of which . . .

She was right. We were right in front of a huge display of sexually transmitted diseases, complete with moving structures to illustrate the ravages of each one.

Eve:    You sure know how to show a girl a good time.

Me:     You just wait. There's a mummified woman upstairs.

Eve:    Woop!

As always, we linked arms and strolled around; Eve telling me about Mike and her work (particularly her terrible new boss, Joyce: 'She couldn't manage a ball downhill') and me mostly listening, asking questions, and telling her a little bit about my family. *Family.* The whole time we were talking, I was just thinking, 'Don't mention you're pregnant, don't

31

mention you're pregnant,' to the point where I was amazed she couldn't read it behind my eyes whenever she looked at me. I even forced myself to loiter by the cabinet upstairs filled with tiny ceramic models of pregnant women with detachable stomachs, revealing miniature ceramic babies inside, just so Eve wouldn't suspect anything in my avoidance of it. 'That'll be you, soon,' Eve whispered in my ear, coming up behind me. I laughed manically, trying to turn it into a fake laugh, but only succeeding in sounding even more suspicious.

Eve:   Are you pregnant?
Me:    Are *you* pregnant?
Eve:   No.
Me:    [apologetically] Oh, I am. [taking the hand of a suit of armour] Don't tell my husband, but this suit of armour loves me in a way Thom will never understand. I'm due to give birth to a beautiful toaster any day now.
Eve:   Alright, alright. Tell me how Thom's enjoying the teaching life.

So I think I managed to shake Eve off the trail. But why would she ask that?


November 18th

First meeting with Hilary Taylor today. She was exactly as delightful as I'd expected, constantly looking around the room during the meeting with me and Alice to see what she could have.

Alice:   So we're looking at promoting you within the super-markets – we think that we can get you a placement in some of the weeklies, which should lift those sales.

32

Hilary: Can I have a copy of those ones? [pointing at a pile of Jacki's books]

Me: Yes . . . of course. [passing her over a copy]

Hilary: No, I'll need three – for my girls, you see.

Me: Right.

Alice: We also thought that you might like to start talking to your fans online –

Hilary: Do you have those flowers changed regularly?

Alice: I think someone just brought those in.

Hilary: They're lovely. Can someone wrap them up for me?

Eventually Alice kicked me under the table and I called the meeting to a close before we were forced to donate our clothes to Hilary too. She hasn't even submitted her new book to us yet. I should set her and Monica Warner up together – Monica's one of our most successful authors, but she's loaded beyond all imagining, and an absolute monster of a snob. I don't know which of them would make it out alive.

TO DO:
Talk to Alice about whether we could make that meeting happen

November 21st

My midwife 'booking-in' appointment this morning. I've been allocated 'Linda', who took an hour to slowly, slowly scroll through a hundred screens, painstakingly filling in every possible detail about my physical and medical history.

'Linda': Have you ever had any piercings?

Me: Just my ears.

'Linda': Nowhere else?

| | |
|---|---|
| Me: | No. |
| 'Linda': | Not your nose? Or your tummy button? |
| Me: | *No.* |
| 'Linda': | How much do you drink? |
| Me: | How much do *you* drink? |
| 'Linda': | I'll put over four units a week. We recommend you keep it to under two, if you can. |
| Me: | [meekly] OK. |
| 'Linda': | Do you smoke? |
| Me: | [triumphant] No I do *not*. |
| 'Linda': | Have you ever taken recreational drugs? |
| Me: | How long ago would it have to have stopped for us to just be able to say 'no'? |
| 'Linda': | Before your pregnancy? |
| Me: | *God* yes. |
| 'Linda': | Right, I'll just put 'no' for that. |

She was OK, really. It just took forever, with her insisting on reading out every option on every page to me, even though I could see the screen and read it faster than she could say it; I felt impatient, claustrophobic, wanted to just get my jabs (or whatever I had to do there) and get out.

But then she wanted to weigh me, take my height, my blood pressure and Thom's and my family medical history, and to talk me through every possible permutation of giving birth: at hospital, at home, in a midwife-led ward, on a boat (maybe – I might have stopped listening after a while). I must have been sweating a bit when she kept talking about labour and choices and things, because eventually she said, 'Are you alright, Katherine? How are you feeling about this pregnancy?' but I just smiled at her, biting back my panic, and said I had a meeting to get to and was it OK if I went now? She waved me off with even more paperwork, plus a handful of blood forms for Dr Bedford. *Blood forms*. Ugh.

I know that she was trying to help, and I'm so grateful that care like this is free (Jesus, the thought of what this all could be costing us has brought me out in a sweat again) but does it have to be so – babyish? Do we have to keep talking about how it grows, and when I'll feel it, and how it's going to come out of my body? I'm sure in the next six months science will have invented a laser to just zap it right out of there. Like *Innerspace*, only backwards.

Even though I arrived mid-morning, I took Alice to lunch today. I was determined to try and see if she really was OK. As we settled over our bowls of bibimbap, I asked how everything was.

Alice:  Honestly?

Me:     Yes please.

Alice:  Do you remember my ex, Simone? I saw her a couple of weeks ago.

Me:     Did she look dreadful?

Alice:  [sighing] No. She looked fantastic. She'd just been on a fantastic trip to her parents' house in Italy with her fantastic new girlfriend and a whole bunch of brilliant power lesbian couples.

Me:     Did you look good?

Alice:  [scornful] Kiki. Need you ask. But I was thinking about how Simone never hassled me about telling my family about us, which was one of the things I liked about her. But . . . maybe it *is* getting ridiculous. Maybe I'm too old to still pretend. What am I doing?

Me:     Only you know when you feel ready.

Alice:  I'm almost thirty, for God's sake. Look at you! Married, a child on the way.

Me:     Hold on, don't let me be a catalyst for anything. I *tumbled* into this kind of responsibility. This wasn't

35

a life choice, this was too much red wine in a Parisian café.

Alice: Whoah, hold *something* back for your child's wedding speech.

Me: Alice, you'll know when you want to talk to your family about it. But don't look at me – or anyone – to see how to do things better. I can just about manage to be married, I'll hopefully come to terms with having a baby, but I don't think I can ever take the responsibility of being someone's example.

Alice: You're right. I should tell them.

Me: That . . . wasn't exactly what I said.

Alice: Shhhh. Eat your bibimbap.

As we get closer to the scan date, the days crawl by. I snuck into a bookshop around the corner from the office today, and, sweating like I was buying the worst kind of porn, paid for and stuffed hastily into my bag a glossy, hardback *Guide to Pregnancy*. I've been going through it this evening, and my brain, freshly fed with dangerous information, has now started imagining all the things that can be wrong with the six-centimetre shape inside my womb. Thanks, Brain.

Thom says I should try to relax. He's offered me baths, food, even a foot massage with a face that screamed his reluctance for me to take him up on it, and insists that we won't know anything until the scan, and I should just take care of myself. He tried to say, Let him take care of me, but I think he could see a Force 10 Suffragettes Lecture building, and changed it to how I could look after myself. I know he wants to help, and heaven knows he's seen enough of my panicking this year, but I can't help it. There's something in there, and all I can think of is *Alien*.

November 22nd

We were in bed last night when I suddenly rolled over.

Me:     Oh my GOD!
Thom:   [half asleep] What? What's happened?
Me:     Zoe's pregnant too!
Thom:   [mumbling] I don't know who Zoe is, but I'm very
        pleased.

I let him get back to sleep, but stayed up for ages trying to
work out her possible dates. Surely if she'd seen me twig about
her pregnancy at our wedding but hadn't told us, she wouldn't
have been more than three months? So that meant . . . she was
at the very most three months ahead of me? I was so excited
that I called her this morning, to ask if she wanted to catch
up. She's been away working in New York with her nightmare
boss, horrible celeb photographer (and Jacki's alleged new love)
Pedro, since just after our wedding, so I've had no chance to
see her, but heard from Jim that she and her boyfriend Zac
had just got home again recently. She didn't pick up when I
called, but left a return message for me later to meet her at a
Goth pub off Tottenham Court Road after work tonight, if I
was free. I was so pleased to be seeing her, I didn't really think
twice about the strange espionage nature of the set-up, particularly since I already knew about her pregnancy. And it *was*
nice to see her, as she came into the pub and rushed straight
over to give me a hug. I beamed at her.

Me:     So how have *you* been?
Zoe:    Well, I have a little news.
Me:     [laughing] Oh, I know your news.
Zoe:    Nope. This news. [holding out her hand, with slim
        wedding band]

37

Me:     Oh, you two did it! Congratulations!

Zoe:    Thank you! I didn't want to talk to you on the phone because I knew I'd give it away. I'm so happy.

Me:     Please, tell me *all* about it.

It seems that, because it was such a long stay in the US, her super-handsome American boyfriend Zac stayed out there too, and her parents and sister came to visit for a week in the middle. With Zac's family living right around the corner, they figured it was an opportunity they may not get again for a while; the day before, Zoe asked Pedro for an extended lunch hour and that was that. Only – and this is the most surprising bit of the whole story – somehow Pedro found out what she was doing, and not only cancelled their whole afternoon schedule, but followed them to City Hall, swept both families off to a top restaurant, paid for everything and took photos the whole time.

Me:     But he took it out of your wages, right? Or he had you deported that night? What was his punchline?

Zoe:    If he's got one, I'm still waiting. He's been . . . he's been *human*, Kiki. Believe me, I'm as baffled as you are, but I'm enjoying it while it lasts. Oh! Do you know – he wouldn't let me travel economy, either way? He upgraded me to First Class, saying it wouldn't be good for the baby.

Me:     And how *was* First Class?

Zoe:    It was *very* good for the baby.

Me:     Ah. Speaking of which.

Zoe:    Ye-ee-es?

Me:     Zo, I'm slightly knocked up. I don't know what to do.

Zoe:    [biting back a woop] OK, let's take this step by step. Can I ask if it was planned?

Me:     No. Yes. No, I mean yes you can ask, and no, yes, it
        was and wasn't planned. It was planned at the time,
        but it was a one-night error which we realised in the
        morning. It really isn't planned. I haven't thought
        about how it would fit in with my promotion, or how
        we'll look after it, or how we'll afford it, or what
        we'll do with it. What am I going to do with a *baby*?

Zoe:    Right, and how pregnant do you think you are?

Me:     Entirely.

Zoe:    And in weeks?

Me:     Maybe . . . eleven? It's all fairly approximate at the
        moment.

Zoe:    And have you seen a doctor or had any scans?

Me:     Yes doctor, no scans. Day after tomorrow.

Zoe:    And how's Thom?

Me:     He's pleased, I think, but worried about me. He's
        OK.

Zoe:    How are you feeling? I've just been talking the whole
        time and not even asking about you.

Me:     Ugh. I don't know how I am. I feel sick almost all
        the time, although actually that's improving. I don't
        know what to think about this, but I don't know
        how to think about anything else.

Zoe:    Everything makes you think of it, and nothing feels
        real?

Me:     *Exactly*.

Zoe:    This one wasn't exactly planned either. Well, it wasn't
        a full accident, but we were just . . . trying it. Seeing
        how it played out. And it's worked out brilliantly, so
        far. If it helps you at all, Kiki, I was so freaked out
        when our plan actually worked. Hugely freaked out.
        I couldn't speak for three days.

Me:     And then?

Zoe:    [shrugs] Then I could.

39

She said she realised that this was something happening to both of them, and it would be a hell of a lot more manageable if she shared it all with Zac. She didn't want to be alone, and she didn't want him to feel alone either, and if they loved each other enough to marry in the face of Pedro's insistence on twenty-hour working days, they could certainly manage growing a baby together. We stayed for a couple of hours, nursing our non-alcoholic cocktails, then were both so wiped out that I was home by 9, although I agreed to keep her posted with our scan results.

I think she's right. I need to share this properly with Thom, not carry it all on my own and keep him at a distance. And I'm so glad to be going through this with a friend, too. And she might be only a month or so ahead of me, if my dates are right.

November 23rd

I couldn't sleep last night, thinking about the scan today. I'm a giant emotional pendulum, elated one minute and excited to see our baby, terrified and frozen by the thought of actually seeing it the next.

But we had a slot first thing, and got to the hospital just in time so we didn't have to hang around waiting. We completed the forms and had barely sat down in the waiting room before my name was called by the receptionist, and a friendly woman was welcoming us into the little room, filled with wires and screens.

Sonographer: Hello, I'm Clare. Katherine?
Me:         [staring at the equipment] Yes, hello.
            [silence]
Thom:       I'm Thom. We're hoping I'm the father.

Me:      [not really listening] Sorry, yes, this is Thom.
Clare:—Hello, Thom. Katherine, there's no need to be worried. Nothing I'm using today will harm your baby in any way, it's perfectly safe equipment just to check everything's going well, OK?
Me:      OK.
Clare:   Shall we get started? I just need you up on this bed, please, and you just need to lift your top up, that's all. [I clamber on] Great, that's perfect. I'm just going to put some of this gel on your stomach, to improve the contact, OK?
Me:      OK.
Clare:   Right, I'll just have a look around. Yes, we've got the head here, can you see that?
Me:      OK.
Thom:    [quietly] Wow.
Clare:   And you can see the spine following down, here. See that bit there?
Me:      OK.
Clare:   That's the stomach, and all the internal organs.
Thom:    Kiki, isn't that amazing!
Me:      OK.
Clare:   I'm just going to take some measurements now, to check everything's on schedule and growing as it should.

She worked in silence for a while, moving the wand around and marking points on the scan.

Clare:   Mmm. [concerned] *Mmmm.*
Me:      What what is it what's wrong?
Clare:   I'm just . . . is it?
Me:      What can you see?
Clare:   No, I . . . No, I think it's fine. I just watched *Alien*

41

for the first time the other night, and I can't stop thinking about it. Just checking your baby has all its limbs and no tentacles. Hang on, is that . . .?

Me:     *WHAT*?

Clare:   [cheerful] No, nothing. Have you seen that film?

Me:     [wide eyes at Thom] Yes.

Thom:   No.

Clare:   [to Thom] Don't. Not for at least . . . a year, I'd say. OK, we're all done here! Everything looks fine. I'd say you're just over fourteen weeks at the moment, which makes your due date the 21st May, and your baby's growing well so we don't need any further scans at the moment. We'll see you in six weeks for your twenty-week scan, then. I've sent your pictures to reception to collect.

We stumbled out of the room to get our pictures.

Thom:   She was amazing. And now I'm curious: I really need to see *Alien*.

Me:     You really, really don't. And she really, really wasn't.

We agreed to disagree, but I shall have to keep an eye on Thom. I suppose I'll know if he's watched it on the sly as he'll suddenly come nowhere near my stomach.

It was so strange to see the baby really there. It sucked its thumb and rolled around, and I really believed for the first time that we were going to be parents.

TO DO:
Find out what babies do, and need, etc.
Ask Suse?

42

November 26th

Today was the day we'd agreed to break the news to our families. As with our engagement, we – by which I mean Thom – told his parents in Australia over the phone, just prior to telling my family over here. Aileen and Alan were delighted, shrieking down the phone and checking over and over that I was looking after myself, that Thom was looking after me and the baby, that we were happy, that we were well. It was so nice to talk to them and so nice to hear how glad the news had made them, but I also felt exhausted by it, and nervous about having to do it all over again with my family actually in front of us, where I'd be unable to draw my finger across my throat as a signal for Thom to draw the conversation to a close when it all got too overwhelming. My hands were shaking so much as we left our house that Thom had to do my coat up for me, saying, 'It's all practice for when you can't do this yourself in a few months,' to which I sighed, 'I'm only going to have a bigger stomach, I'm not having my hands cut off.' Thom tugged an imaginary forelock at me, and we headed over to Susie's.

When we got there, I'd barely got my shaky finger onto the doorbell when the door opened to reveal Susie, husband Pete and all the kids in the hallway, all wrapped up in coats and scarves. I asked them whether their heating had broken again, but Susie told me that Dad's birthday lunch was now at Mum and Dad's house rather than theirs; she didn't think I'd mind if we moved venues. 'Come on, Sour Puss. I didn't have to buy any supplies. Free food!' 'Is it, Suse? *Is it*?' I said, but we were flurried out with their family. Thom and Pete took the twins Lily and Edward between them, walking in a wide line together, and Susie gave me Frida to carry.

43

| Susie: | So what's new with you? |
|---|---|
| Me: | Nothing! Why do you say that? |
| Susie: | Jesus Christ, you're pregnant. |
| Me: | [wailing] How does everyone do that? |
| Susie: | OH MY GOD I WAS ONLY JOKING. [doubles over laughing] Oh my GOD. I literally could not be more pleased with myself right now. |
| Me: | Susie, you absolutely cannot tell Mum and Dad. |
| Susie: | [wide-eyed, serious face] Oooh yeah, they'll totally ground you and you'll never get to go to the end of term party. |
| Me: | Susie, *please*. |
| Susie: | Alright. Do you want me to do it? |
| Me: | Tell them you're pregnant? I don't know how long that story will hold. In about six months' time my hospitalisation with Swollen Stomach is going to seem reeeeeally suspicious. |
| Susie: | That wasn't what I meant, but actually . . . |
| Me: | We'll all pretend we're pregnant! Like Spartacus! |
| Susie: | You're hormone-addled. |
| Me: | And you have to stop saying that stuff. |
| Susie: | Alright, spoilsport. But I think you should know . . . |
| Me: | God, *what*? |
| Susie: | Mum's actually really good at all this stuff. Looking after us in pregnancy. If she's anything like how she was with me; she was brilliant. Asking all the right things. Providing great food. I think you're going to see a new side to our mother. |
| Me: | Hang on – Mum, who can barely remember our names at the best of times? Mum, who never quite manages to listen to what we're saying when we're in front of her? Mum, who reacted to news of your pregnancy with 'Is it definitely yours?'? |

Susie:  Mum who single-handedly catered and decorated your wedding? Trust me. She's good at this. She always preferred us when we were *in utero*, so she gets really excited about pregnancies.

Me:  I'll believe it when I see it.

We settled on Susie and Thom tossing for it. When we got to Mum and Dad's, we took a coin from the pot in the hallway and all three of us squeezed into the downstairs toilet.

Susie:  Call it.

Thom:  Heads.

Me:  No, tails.

Susie:  Which one?

Thom:  I don't care.

Me:  Tails! No, heads. HEADS.

Susie:  [flips coin] Ha ha! It's tails. [sing-songing] I get to tell them.

Thom:  Oh, thank God.

Me:  Just . . . do it. Don't gloat, Suse. Get it done with.

So we filed back out, Dad giving us an odd look, and came into the kitchen where Mum was plating up our lunch.

Susie:  Mum, Dad, Pete, children. I have an announcement to make.

Pete:  [crossing fingers]

Susie:  Your daughter's knocked up – and it's not me, for once!

Pete:  Oh, thank God.
[silence]

Mum:  Fucking *hell*.

Me and Susie:  *Mum!*

45

I actually love it when Mum swears. It's like Johnson's walking dog – we're not concerned so much how well she's doing it, but that she's doing it at all.

Mum: Sorry, darling, I just . . . well, I was surprised. Sorry. I just thought . . .

Me: What?

Mum: Well, I'm just surprised you're having children so soon! I just thought you'd want to wait a little while. You two are both so young, and I thought you'd want to settle into your careers a little bit more . . .

Me: Susie had had two kids by the time she was TWENTY-FIVE!

Susie: [pulling a *Question Time* face] I *hardly* think *that's* the point.

Me: [pleading] *Mum*.

Mum: Oh, darling, of course we're excited. You do spring this on people, don't you?

Me: [indignant] Would you prefer a blow-by-blow –

Thom: Don't.

Me: [understanding] – mm.

Then Dad and Pete and the Twins were excited and gave us both hugs, and Mum came and gave me a lovely hug too. She asked lots of questions (all the right sort, for once), and Susie caught my eye and winked at me. Mum stayed excited for the rest of the afternoon, although she did occasionally repeat herself, which I can forgive in the name of her excitement.

Sometimes, I really love this family. Now it's just telling everyone else we know. Gulp.

TO DO:
Find out if Susie's available to tell all our friends

November 28th

Alice hasn't so much as raised a conspiratorial eyebrow at me since she guessed the news. She's been as friendly as ever, sweet and funny, but she's too tactful to make hints or whisper questions to me in the office. She shows her me her neutral face, the face that's meant she's managed three Christmases with her handbag Gareth and her family, and never even looked at me when Carol reported that Tony had bought a baby book. In our weekly meeting, Carol asked if we had any thoughts yet on Lucie Martel's *A Womb of One's Own*.

| | |
|---|---|
| Me: | Her what? |
| Alice: | A what of her *what*? |
| Carol: | Tony bought this just before he left. It says here Kiki's handling it in his absence. Didn't he tell you? |
| Me and Alice: | [blank faces] |
| Carol: | Bloody hell. Right, it's an American import, obviously, but we'll publish in March, the same time as them. Lucie's an incredibly wealthy New York journalist, mainly working in the US but with a few things published over here. Her piece on arranging a prostitute for her super-rich-CEO husband went down a storm last year in the *Mail*. |
| All: | Oh, *her*! |
| Carol: | Quite. She's written the book already, but we won't bring it out until the baby is actually born. |
| Me: | But what *is* it? |
| Carol: | Looking again at the submission notes, it's 'a unique look at pregnancy, labour and the early years through the fresh eyes of someone |

47

| | appreciating the beauty and purity of the experience'. |
|---|---|
| Alice: | I've heard about Lucie. If her eyes are fresh it's only because she's had them injected with dolphin endorphins at some million-dollar spa. |
| Carol: | We're all thinking it, Alice, but I'm afraid you must learn to love this book. Tony's spent enough on it that we must make use of the month we'll have her for. |
| Me: | But how can she have finished it if she hasn't even had the baby yet? |
| Carol: | Because when you have that much money, you can guarantee that life will turn out how you planned. I'll send you the latest version; she's over next month for a meeting with us. Did Tony really not tell you any of this? |

All I could think was: Christ, I really hope Tony doesn't buy a How to Cope with Everyone You Know Dying book, or I'm going to have to keep a closer watch on my loved ones. Why does he keep predicting my life? What the hell is going on? And why the living hell would he not tell us he'd bought it?

But it felt like the right time to tell Carol about this baby, after the meeting. She took it so well, giving me a hug and asking me for all the details. She said she'd email Tony – not that he responded with any real frequency – and get all the information to me about my leave and maternity pay. Her enthusiasm was quite infectious, in fact, and for once I didn't mind telling people. Alice pulled out one of the bottles of prosecco that always seem to dog this place, and we had a tiny toast. I even saw Norman raise his glass to Carol before he drank, that old romantic. It wasn't so bad, after all.

A *Womb of One's Own*'s publication date is in March, four months away, a month after Lucie's baby is born. As long as there are no complications, I'll be happy to assist Alice with Lucie's publicity; at seven months pregnant, I'll be delighted to be on the phone for them while I sit in comfort in the office. Who knows, maybe she can actually give me some tips. And I can practise holding another baby, too, one that, unlike Susie's kids, it *does* matter if I drop. Maybe I'll start feeling maternal.

Although that seems unlikely.

November 29th

This morning, I remembered the times we'd visited Heidi and Rich, Thom's best man, and their new baby Megan since our wedding. I liked them both very much, and found Megan wonderful to hold, like a kitten. But I'd always been quickly bored of that little animal warmth, and was happy to pass it back to Heidi so she could uncover an udder and feed the squirming creature. I never felt broody when we saw them – ha! In fact, last time we went, we even talked on the way home about how we hoped our feelings about babies would change before we had them ourselves – and never looked forward to seeing the baby, rather than Rich and Heidi. Yet there we were tonight. Pregnant, and on their doorstep again for another visit. We had a nice enough time, but I couldn't wait until we were driving home again.

Me:     Did you see the face they made at one another?
Thom:  What face?
Me:     The 'Didn't we say' face.
Thom:  Didn't they say what?
Me:     Have you really not noticed that when we've told people? The second you're married, everyone starts

waiting for the womb on legs in the relationship to get knocked up.

Thom: [laughing] I can't say I have noticed that, I'm afraid.

Me: No! I know you haven't! And do you know why? Because –

Thom: I'm a man. I know. And I can't tell you how sorry I am about that fact right at this moment.

Me: [laughing] Thom, I'm not blaming *you*. I'm just saying it's another one of the countless things which exposes the idea of pregnancy being some kind of partnership as completely and utterly false. *We* are not pregnant. *I* am pregnant. I am the one everyone is watching. If something happens to this baby, whose fault do you think people will think that is?

Thom: [stopping the car] Kiki. If anything – heaven forbid, times a million – if anything happens to this baby, I couldn't give the slightest shit what anyone else says. My only concern is loving it, and loving you, and making sure that even if it's a tiny contribution, I do whatever I can to make your lives better.

Me: [crying] I'm just so hormonal. You don't know what it's like.

Thom: [pulling me into a hug] I know, Keeks. I know.

TO DO:
Investigate how long these crazy hormones are supposed to last
On second thoughts, maybe don't
Do something nice for Thom


November 30th

Pamela came in for one of her infrequent visits to the office today, so I thought it was a good idea to tell her about the pregnancy: I owe my promotion purely to her and won't ever give her an excuse to be disappointed in me. But she was as nice as Carol, checking I felt well and wasn't exhausting myself, asking how the check-ups had been and whether my parents were excited. 'I hear grandchildren are one of the greatest gifts one can receive,' she explained, 'but I've long since abandoned any hope of Tony giving me such a blessing.' She shook my hand and congratulated me again, and I reassured her that she wouldn't be able to keep me out of this office for long.

Drinks with Jacki tonight. I was so excited, since I missed our last drinks in October and I haven't told her about this pregnancy yet. I have so much to thank her for – my promotion (it was the success of her book that sealed it), my wedding (she offered to bankroll it), and the fact I had a husband at all (she reminded me what really mattered when her marriage to a gold-digger broke her heart) – but even if I didn't, seeing her always makes my day. We met at one of our favourite snug bars in Soho, underneath an erotic bookshop, and clacked downstairs to a booth. We were talking over one another before we'd even ordered our drinks.

Me:     Jacki! I can't believe I haven't seen you for so long.
        It's been the craziest few months.
Jacki:  I know, me too, darling. I've been filming two videos
        back-to-back for singles from the bloody *Love Songs*
        album, and I don't think I've slept for a month.
Me:     Well, you look well, Jacks.
Jacki:  Do I? I'll give you some advice that you won't ever
        need: Don't get divorced. [seeing my face] Sorry, love,
        I don't mean you. Don't let anyone you know get
        divorced either. It's not the money – I always knew

I'd be worse off after marrying Leon one way or
another – it's everything else . . .

Me:     Jacks, I'm so sorry. Come and sit next to me. [putting
        my arm around her]

Jacki:  I'm sorry, I'm not a complainer, you know that. But
        this is . . . knackering me. It really is. Leon, his girl-
        friends, the rumours, the public judging us both, and
        waking up on my own every day . . . Ugh. [shaking
        herself] Tell me about your life, Kiki. [swallowing
        hard] Is married life good for you? You look amazing
        on it, anyway. Glowing!

And with that, I lost my nerve. I told her all about my
new role, about how her book was still selling, about Thom's
new job and Mum's increasing anxiety over Dad, and Susie's
battles with the icing bag for yet another school event. As
ever, Jacki listened so attentively, asking all the right questions and remembering everything I'd ever told her about
these people. She asked about guests from our wedding too,
Eve and Mike, and lovely Jim and Poppy.

Jacki:  And wasn't your best man's girlfriend due any day?
        What did she have?

Me:     They had a little girl, Megan. She's . . . wow, almost
        three months now.

Jacki:  And are they happy?

Me:     I think so. Heidi doesn't get much sleep, though.

Jacki:  And Ped told me all about Zoe, too.

Me:     [not looking at her] Yeah! It's amazing, isn't it? I hear
        he's treating her really well. First class all the way,
        these days. Maybe I *will* work for Pedro, after all.

Jacki:  That only works if you're pregnant, though.

Me:     Ha! Hahaha! Haha! Yes! Haha!

52

Jacki:   But at least Zoe and your friend Heidi have someone
         to care for, and to care for them, Kiki. They're very
         lucky, and they should remember that.
Me:      Would *you* like another *drink*?
Jacki:   Ooooh, yes please. Isn't it my round?

But I had to go and order the drinks so she wouldn't
realise that I was having Virgin Mules and Shirley Temples.
Poor Jacki. As if she needs to hear from me how I'm
happily breeding with my loving husband when she's so
lonely and hurt from that conniving horror Leon. I made
a useless resolution that if anyone else I know ever seems
to be marrying someone who appears to be a feckless
greedy gobshite, I will *definitely* tell them. For now, I will
continue to support Jacki in any way I can (or until I start
showing).

## December's Classic Baby

'You may, perhaps, be prepared to hear that Mrs Micawber is in a state of health which renders it not wholly improbable that an addition may be ultimately made to those pledges of affection which – in short, to the infantine group. Mrs Micawber's family have been so good as to express their dissatisfaction at this state of things. I have merely to observe, that I am not aware that it is any business of theirs, and that I repel that exhibition of feeling with scorn, and with defiance!'

Mr Micawber then shook hands with me again, and left me.

*David Copperfield*
Charles Dickens

December 1st

Oh, advent calendar joy! When we were very little, Susie and I had a fabric advent calendar each which Mum had made, and which she and Dad would then fill with all sorts of gifts. When Dad had to travel with work, the calendar would include little German Christmas decorations, American sweets or even just miniature hotel jars of jam, while Mum would provide pound coins, lip glosses, single chocolates and hair clips. Despite the fact that we are far too old to indulge in such things, Mum still delivers the bags of twenty-five gifts each November 30th, with each tiny parcel numbered, so Susie and I don't spoil one another's surprises, although now the calendars are obviously filled with gifts for Thom, Pete, the Twins and Frida too.

Thom and I had spent last night diligently filling each pocket with the numbered parcels, and I was allowed to string the fairy lights around the bookshelves (but not turn them on). This morning, I leapt out of bed to open the first one.

Me:    A hair clip!

Thom: [grumpily] Yours.

Me:    Ahh, is someone feeling left out of the widdel advent caw-endar?

Thom: I hope you're not going to talk to my child like that.


I always hug myself when he says something like that. If all goes well – a phrase I think to myself a hundred times a day – we'll be celebrating next Christmas with three of us here. Three! Our baby! Wait. I got too excited too quickly. Won't it just pull down the tree? Eat all the presents? Mmmm. Still not ready for this.


December 2nd

So I've finished *A Womb of One's Own*. Wow.

Wow.

What a mixture of preachy, hippie garbage and self-congratulatory smugness. Here are some of my favourite bits:

On discovering the news:

> It was a moment I shall never forget. As Bill and I looked at the doctor's report telling us that our great blessing had arrived, we held hands. 'Our souls are fused together forever,' Bill's eyes seemed to say. 'This is a child of love,' mine replied. Bill started to cry, then I joined in, and even the doctor wiped his eyes. 'I've been doing this job for thirty years, and I've never been so moved when I told a couple the good news,' he exclaimed. 'Thank you. Thank you for reminding me of the magic of this job.'

On going into labour:

It was a swelling wave, a jungle noise that I rode, crested, becoming stronger and more powerful than I ever could have considered possible. I reached inside my soul, and found myself as a small girl, a teenage beauty, a handsome woman, a wise old crone. We stood in a circle holding hands, and they guided me to the place I needed to be, delivering me strength and love. I knew my child was being born, and that it was a journey only I could go on. I could hear my doctor: 'One more push, Ms Martel,' and my selves nodded at me, smiling. With one final effort, I could feel myself doubled, grown, as the love Bill and I created became a person, a name, a life. It was Creation.

On feeding the baby:

I had watched others around me struggle with breast-feeding, discovering pain and bleeding. Others had simply given up, and turned to a plastic bottle for their newborn wonder. Blessed as we were with our child, so was I blessed with his feeding. He took to it like a natural – as that's what it was, the most natural thing in the world. We stared into each other's eyes, and I could feel the love flow between us. I knew that no pain could ever touch me, as I was giving him the greatest gift in the world – mother's milk, which would be with him for the rest of his life, bettering him and lifting him among his peers, wherever he went.

On the baby's toys and clothes:

Bill and I agreed from the start that we wanted only beauty for our child. We had no plastics in the nursery, which our own interior decorator had redone completely for us, in shades of dove grey with a yellow accent. The cot was made from an old altar from Brazil, with wood which was hundreds of years old. The changing unit was fashioned from a table Bill's family had kept for generations, while the baby's wardrobe was an heirloom from my grandmother, shipped from France in the eighteenth century. We carpeted the room in the softest New Zealand wool, with a feature rug from Morocco. The toys were handmade – an artisan in upstate New York made a whole family of wooden animals, and an Italian craftsman designed an original light fitting in a giraffe shape. All the bed linen and blankets came from handcrafters across the country when I'd sourced throughout my pregnancy. We even had a film prop-maker fashion us the baby's name in lights, to go on the wall – Bill and I both knew how important it was for this baby to feel at home the second we brought him in.

I cannot wait to meet this woman. Orrrr . . . not meet. One or the other. Probably the latter.

TO DO:
Find out if Thom will repaint our living room in dove grey and accent yellow. That actually sounds lovely.

December 3rd

My final treat from Thom's diary of treats: a trip to the local garden centre, choosing and buying a Christmas tree, plus as many Christmas decorations as I could carry. We both got slightly giddy, sniffing the needles and displaying the baubles to one another in very, very mature ways, but eventually we left with a tree that was, of course, slightly too big for our living room, and an enormous box of extra fairy lights, baubles, bells, bead ropes, robins, ribbons and a golden, glittering star tree topper.

We blew the rest of the afternoon getting the tree positioned and decorated (Thom: 'I think we need to soak the base first.' Me: 'Do it later! Let's get it up first!'), with me tying bows everywhere while Thom kept us supplied with tea and mince pies.

Thom: Do you ever worry you might peak too soon?
Me: Nonsense. *Carpe diem*. And the *diem* I *carpe* is Christmas Day.
Thom: I didn't know one could pick.
Me: One can and one does. If Scrooge resolved to keep Christmas every day, I think starting at the beginning of December is the very least we can do. It's not like I'm making us eat turkey and all the trimmings every day for the next month.
Thom: Don't. I know you. You start off joking about these things . . .
Me: [pulling him down beside me] I promise. No turkey until at least the 17th. But thank you, for all these things over the year. It's been lovely. And I think next year might be lovely too.

TO DO:
Double check which foods I'm allowed to eat, before Christmas kicks in properly


December 4th

Time to tell Eve. Why was I nervous? This wasn't the Eve of old, this was new Eve. Nice Eve. Thoughtful Eve. Normal

Human Being Eve. Since she'd tried to seduce Thom at her last birthday party, met someone she'd actually cared about for once (the lovely baker Mike) and faced my half-hearted wrath, Eve had changed. I loved seeing her now – she no longer made me feel guilty or inadequate. Yet, still so nervous.

She'd come over to mine for lunch, and was loitering in the kitchen doorway while I got everything together.

Eve:   I brought some wine – shall I open it?
Me:    Yes please. Just a bit for me, though, thanks.
Eve:   Late night last night?
Me:    [brightly] No, it turns out I'm pregnant! Oops. Didn't mean for that to happen. Not that I'm an idiot or anything. Just . . . statistically unlikely. But it's fine. I'm fine, and the baby's fine, although I'm still not used to it actually being a baby – I just like to think of it as a thing I'll have to get round to dealing with sometime next year. Ha!
Eve:   Oh right. Cool.

And that was it. She didn't ask any more, and I didn't volunteer it. We ate lunch, and talked about work and our families, then she left. I felt flat.

When Thom got home from the pub, I was still lying with my face half-pressed into the sofa, watching something dreadful on TV with my open eye.

Thom:  Eve back on form?
Me:    No! She was fine. It was nice to see her. She just didn't really . . . care.
Thom:  Wasn't that what you wanted? Better that than her telling you how to name it and where we should live and what clever little vintage items it ought to wear, isn't it?

60

Me:     I suppose so.

Thom:   Keeks, I know she's been different these last few
        months, but a leopard can't change its spots entirely.
        Just think about all the other people who do make
        you happy: Suse, Zoe, Alice – have you seen Greta
        recently?

Me:     No! That *will* be nice! You're right. It's just habit
        with Eve. But you're right.

TO DO:
Stop having high hopes for Eve
Start enjoying the rest of our friends while I can
Remember I'm not dying, just having a baby


December 6th

An evening to try again with Jacki. She'd emailed me this
time, asking if I wanted pre-Christmas cocktails at the
Dorchester after work, even though we've only just seen
one another. I knew I had to get there before her, to order
my soft drinks again, so I left the office at 5; walking up
Oxford Street towards Marble Arch, admiring the
windows, but hurrying. I got there almost half an hour
early, bursting into the bar in a sweat, and grateful that
I'd have time to compose myself. But Jacki was already
there.

Jacki:  [waving] Woohoo!
Me:     Jacki! Hello? Didn't we say six?
Jacki:  I thought so. Thirsty?
Me:     I *am*, yeah.
Jacki:  [gesturing to a barman] Here, it's coming over now.
        [taking two drinks from the waiter]

Me:      [smelling it] Oh . . . lovely. Thank you. What is it? [lifting it to my mouth]

Jacki:   It's called a Belladonna.

Me:      [wetting my lips with it] Mmm, what's in it?

Jacki:   Gin and rum. And apricot liqueur.

Me:      [still holding the glass to my lips] MmmMMMm.

Jacki:   And a double whisky.

Me:      [putting glass down] Alright, enough. [wiping mouth] Oh, that is *good* though. How long have you known?

Jacki:   I had an email from Polka Dot telling me they were looking for my replacement editor and would let me know as soon as they could.

Me:      *What?*

Jacki:   Which is exactly how I felt. Why the hell didn't *you* tell me, Kiki?

Me:      Well, partly because I only found out really recently –

Jacki:   So you didn't know last time I saw you?

Me:      Um.

Jacki:   Was this a pity silence? Was I so sad that you couldn't even tell me you were pregnant?

Me:      No, of course not!

Jacki:   So what was it, then?

Me:      It wasn't pity, it was just tact. You were sad, because of course you would be, because your husband . . .

Jacki:   He's not my husband.

Me:      I'm sorry, Jacks. You know what I mean. Of course you would be sad, and we were talking about that, and I didn't think it was appropriate to say, 'Hey, guess what! I'm having a baby!'

Jacki:   [quiet] OK. Alright, Keeks. What a pair we are, hey?

So Jacki drank both the Belladonnas, and I drank some amazing ginger and apple things, and we stayed there for a while. I told her about the scan, and how my family and Polka Dot were taking it.

Me:      Hey, Jacks, do you want to be godmother to this baby? Well, not *god*mother godmother. Non-godmother. What do you say?

Jacki:   Did you just think of that?

Me:      Nope.

Jacki:   Kiki?

Me:      Please? It's all so medical I could do with a little laughter and colour in the mix. As long as the colour isn't flesh pink or wound red.

Jacki:   Oh, you do know how to sell it, Kiki. Can I think about it?

We kissed and said goodbye, and I headed home to collapse on the sofa and tell Thom the good news.

Thom:   Jacki *Jones* Jacki?

Me:      Yes.

Thom:   As the baby's godmother?

Me:      Non-godmother. I'm not dunking my baby for *anybody*.

Thom:   Jacki *Jacki* Jones?

Me:      Yes, Thom.

Thom:   [thinking] Sure, that sounds nice.

December 7th

Thom woke me up this morning.

Thom: Uh, Kiki?

Me: Unnnnn. *What*?

Thom: What was the last thing you got in the advent calendar?

Me: Nnnnidunno. Mm. Maybe . . . oh, a lip balm. Why? What did you get today?

Thom: Look.

I finally opened my eyes to see what it was. Thom was holding up a slightly chewed stumpy pencil, the kind of thing Dad always keeps behind his ear at college. I felt baffled, then I realised that Susie had finally excelled herself.

Me: Oh my God . . . it was Susie!

Thom: How do you work that out?

Me: When she was over the other night, she had me rooting around for ages, trying to find a top she'd lent me. That bloody crafty wolf.

I roared with laughter, and we agreed that Susie deserved to be congratulated on her effective sabotage. I also determined to swap one of her parcels for her own little surprise before she got our congratulations. I was pretty amazed neither of us had had this brainwave before, to be honest. But if she wants to play mean, we can play mean.

At work today, I asked Carol about the email Jacki had got.

Carol: Jesus. Well, I assume that means Tony is checking his emails. I only told him last week, but he's clearly back to meddling, wherever he is. Was Jacki OK?

Me: Yes, thanks Carol, she was, but I think if she'd been slightly more nervous this could have tipped her over the edge. Why would he do that?

Carol:  It's a refrain I've been singing for the fifteen years I've been here, Kiki, and I'm no closer to finding a satisfactory answer. It was an ignorant, trouble-making thing to do and I've not got the slightest clue how he thought it could benefit anyone. But let me know if you get any hassle from your other authors.

Lovely Carol. How rotten to be second-in-command to someone with such a deadly combination of laziness and cluelessness. Tony can be relied upon to get involved in something just long enough to muck it up, then he'll get bored and require someone else to do the actual work. Going on leave seems such a distant future event, like having the baby: something I know I'll have to deal with eventually, but nothing I need to think about anytime soon. But this talk of cover has made me realise that within six months, the office won't have me in it anymore, and I won't be in meetings, and I won't have books to work on, and someone else will be doing all of my jobs.

I feel incredibly strange about all of that.

The Christmas cards have started arriving in the office, from authors and agents. The very first one was from Clifton Black, Polka Dot's military fiction specialist – and by specialist, I mean 'someone who's spent his career trying to convince us he has previously served in the army, while writing books like *Bullets and Bravery* and *Serving Under Fire* with an entirely straight face' – who I may have accidentally sexted slightly before our wedding. *It could happen to anyone.* Since then, he doesn't come into the office anymore, a fact which, if we'd known earlier, any one of us would have been willing to send all manner of inappropriate texts to him. But he sent a lovely card, albeit one which omitted my name entirely. God bless us, every one.

TO DO:

Come up with a few items to scatter into Susie's calendar: a boiled egg? An empty M&Ms bag?

Find out if romantic text messages can scare off all the difficult authors

Make my peace with someone else doing my job for a little while


December 9th

Polka Dot's Christmas party tonight. I had such a nice time, but definitely felt some sadness at being stone-cold sober throughout. Having said that, it *was* completely hilarious to see Alice, Dan (my favourite of Polka Dot's designers), Carol, Norman and the rest of the team drunk beyond all comprehension and actually be able to remember it for once.

As is tradition, Pamela joined us for the first course, laughing gamely at our rising spirits, then bidding her goodbyes as the plates were cleared. As she came over to leave her company credit card with Carol, she checked that I was keeping well, and not working too hard. I'm so glad I've got to know her – not only is she a good person to have on one's team, she's also hugely inspirational, a capable woman running this company solo for years before Tony got involved.

After she left, the nice dinner rapidly descended into plate-sharing, drink-spilling, name-calling bunfight (in the best possible way) which I think will result in a) Dan waking up with a very nasty bruise on his left thigh, b) Norman being grateful he has no social media presence, and c) no employee of Polka Dot books ever being permitted back into that restaurant again.

Funny to be so sober. Funny how things change.

December 10th

If that's how she wants to play it, that's how we'll play it. After finding a half-used box of floss in today's calendar, I resolved to sneak over to Susie's at 7 tonight, knowing – with Pete away on some travel agent job somewhere around the world – it would be the most frantic time for her. Between helping her bath the Twins and Frida, finding their pyjamas, telling them stories, brushing their teeth and getting them down, I managed to swap tomorrow's parcel out of her calendar, replacing it with a similarly wrapped burst balloon. I would be the worst poker player – I could barely contain my glee when I went back downstairs to find Susie putting all the toys away and tidying up the kitchen.

Susie:  Thanks so much, Keeks. When Pete's away this part of the evening is always so unbelievably exhausting.
Me:     [feeling slightly bad] But practice makes perfect?
Susie:  More like familiarity breeds contempt. Oh, not for them, you shocked face, just for this bloody life. I'm *so tired*. Yes, they all sleep well and eat well and I love them dearly, but I'm going mad, Keeks. When I wave Pete off on another trip these days, my blood boils. It *boils*.
Me:     Do you tell him?
Susie:  Tell him what? That I wonder if we married too quickly? That I wonder what I'd be doing now if I hadn't got knocked up that night?
Me:     [feeling a bit sick] Do you regret it?
Susie:  [looking at me] Oh, no, of course I don't regret it. And your life isn't my life, and my decisions aren't your decisions, and *you* aren't married to *Pete*. I'm glad he loves his job, but I wished he loved a job slightly closer to home, so *he* could put *his* children to bed more than

67

twice a month, and tidy the house, and remember their
school projects and the new socks they need.

Me:     [putting an arm around her] Are you happy, Suse?
Susie:  [silence] Not really at all, these days. I'm so tired and
        bored and angry that my emotional resting state is
        permanently somewhere in the red. Sometimes I just
        think – maybe *I* could just go, one day. Just go on
        holiday and come back after a few months, and see
        how Pete had got on. He knows what to do. If he
        had to, he'd be absolutely fine.

I'd not heard Susie talk like that before, although I've
suspected for ages that's how she felt. I *almost* had a guilty
twinge for sabotaging her advent calendar.


December 11th

To try and begin to thank Thom for how supportive and
thoughtful he's been over the last few months, I took us to
the new production of an Alan Bennett play at the National.
It was fantastic – funny and clever, moving and sparky, and
we talked solidly in the interval about how we both wished
we came to the theatre more often.

At the end of the play, I felt Thom nudge me.

Thom:   Were you . . . were you *asleep*?
Me:     No. [wiping drool from side of mouth] Do you have
        any water, please? My mouth is a bit dry.
Thom:   Well, I really enjoyed it. Thank you for the kind
        thought. And for not snoring.

It's literally the least I could have done for him, *and* I
managed to stay awake for dinner afterwards. Also, for

the after-dinner treat at home. Which was very much worth it.

## December 13th

Pre-Christmas Christmas drinks with Greta. She's so utterly fantastic – an unexpected surprise when I signed up to be a bridesmaid at a hideous wedding last year, and a woman I would almost certainly have married instead of Thom if she'd been a man.

Greta: Hello there! I haven't seen you since the early Halloween party. Nice costume, by the way. And Thom looked . . . *good*.

Me: Thank you, and tell me about it. I'm debating making him wear that every night in.

Greta: Alright, get a room. Did you manage to get the pumpkin off that guy in the end?

Me: No. He said it had his medication in. Spoilsport.

Greta: So tell me something from the world of publishing. Tell me a celebrity scandal. Make it up if you don't know any. But don't tell me you've made it up.

Me: I'm pregnant?

Greta: No no no, the tabloids will never care about that. Something about someone actually famous.

Me: I . . . am?

Greta: No – are you really? Well that, Katherine Carlow, is a nice treat.

Me: Thanks. Do you want to deliver it?

Greta: Noooooo. No, I do not. Do you want me to ask you lots of things about it?

Me: No, I don't really. But is it going to be a wedge that will come between our new friendship? Are we going

to grow apart because the baby has come between
us? Is it going to be weird?

Greta:  Only if you make me catch it in the maternity ward.
Otherwise: couldn't care less. In the nicest possible
way. But I'm pleased for you.

Me:  Understood.

So we didn't talk about it, and I was happy. See? A relationship undefined by this pregnancy! I don't need everyone
to sing and dance about it. Joy!

Which means it *is* just Eve's reaction that bothers me.

TO DO:
Pump Greta later to find out if she really doesn't care, or if
she just doesn't care because she totally hates babies, like
any sane person, and will thus never want to see me again
after May

December 14th

Seven months pregnant, Lucie Martel has defied her
weeping doctor's advice to fly over for some pre-publicity
stuff, and to meet with all of us. For that alone, I suppose,
I have to respect her. I'm already feeling slightly nervous
just being away from my bed, but Thom says that's a latent
tendency that's purely been verbalised with the pregnancy.
Rude.

I met Lucie over breakfast at the Charlotte Street Hotel,
where she ordered a decaf espresso. I must have been staring
at her a little, because she laughed and said, 'Pathetic, isn't
it? Like ordering a meat-free steak. But it helps to cling to
these little things somehow.' She seemed nice, by which I
mean normal, by which I mean she acknowledged that

pregnancy seems to be just a desperate battle to cling on to life as it was beforehand.

Since Tony had already negotiated her contract earlier this year, we were free to talk about her publicity, any marketing we might offer, the bookshop deals we were looking at and how long she'd be over in the UK after the baby's birth.

Lucie: I'm afraid I can only offer you four days for any publicity.

Me: Oh, OK. We thought you were over here for a month . . .?

Lucie: Well, three weeks, but I don't think it's fair to be working all that time when the baby is so young.

Me: No, OK, that's great! So the baby will definitely be with you?

Lucie: [shocked] Absolutely. He'll only be five weeks old when you publish over here, and I don't think Bill will be ready to deal with his son for, what, eighteen to twenty years?

Me: [laughing] Of course, you know it's a boy. That's nice.

Lucie: Yes, Bill insisted on all the scans – we have a beautiful 4D scan of little Bill Jnr, that some nights I just watch over and over again. Do you have children?

Me: [choking slightly on my tea] Nope, no, no children. No children.

Lucie: Tick tock tick tock, you know! I see you've got a ring at least – how long have you been married?

Me: [gritting teeth] A few months.

Lucie: Well, don't leave it too long. Do you know, Bill Jnr has already cost us almost $500,000? That's because we were 'waiting for the right time'. And that's not including redeveloping his nursery, costs for the nanny, and any of his education.

Me:     Jesus, I'd be hoping he comes out covered in gold for that money.

We both clearly had a mental image of exactly what I was suggesting and got very quiet. I suddenly thought, 'If she walks out and refuses to do anything for us again, how I am going to tell Tony that I scared off my new author by encouraging her to push a metallic infant through her birth canal?'

Lucie shook her head and blinked, and said, 'OK! What kind of publicity do you guys have in mind?' I ran through the options we were chasing, women's glossies and the weekend supplements, gave her the latest jacket options we were looking at and asked her to think about any pieces she might be writing for the US that we could use over here. Then I got the bill and got out of there, before I offered to cut her umbilical cord with my butter knife, or something.

And oh. Came home tonight to find a beautiful letterpress card from Eve, saying how pleased she and Mike are for us, with a tiny lobster holding hands with two huge lobsters on the front. Oh, Eve. I will really stop thinking the worst of you one day, *really*.

TO DO:
Consider whether I'm actually safe company for any antenatal group if I keep saying my grotesque birthing nightmares out loud

December 15th

My stomach has suddenly popped out. From spending ages each night standing in front of the mirror smoothing my

72

t-shirt over a small curve (only there if you were looking), with Thom saying, 'Stop bending your back,' it has now – somehow *overnight* – become indisputably that of a pregnant. And I love it. I really do. For one thing, it means all those maternity clothes are finally beginning to fit a little better; for another, I now get a seat on the tube; for one more, it is just lovely. It has somehow lent my body proportions which suit it much better – with a small stomach curving out, I fit together perfectly, and my body just makes sense. So while I can't grow a plant to save my life, I can grow a whole other human being. Amazing.

And yet, and yet . . . it's novel, like wearing makeup for the first time, and I feel grown up. But when I consider what's in there, what's required of me both in that hospital room and for all the years of my life following, I can't . . . breathe.

Me:      Thom, what are we going to do?

Thom:  About what?

Me:      [patting the bed next to me] This baby.

Thom:  [lying down beside me] I don't know, Keeks. Is there anything that could make you feel better? Do you still feel sick?

Me:      Hey, I don't actually. That's nice.

Thom:  Why don't you do some of that 'get in touch with yourself' rubbish you'd normally scoff at? Pregnancy yoga, or something? You can make some friends, lie in a quiet room and fall asleep . . .

Me:      Well, that does sound nice.

Thom:  And *if* I had been keeping my eye out for that kind of thing, I *might* have found out that there was a class round the corner every Thursday night, and I *might* have discovered that they have spaces and I *might* be willing to get those classes as a Christmas present if it's anything that would make you feel better.

Me:       My God. You're such a . . . flower child.

Thom:    [rubbing my head with fake soothing motion] I just think someone needs to do a little swimming in Lake Me?

Me:       [laughing] No way, I know where you've been.

Thom:    Katherine, you just need to connect to the life inside you.

Me:       [serious] Oh. Don't. Thom, this is so hard. I'm sorry to be ill, to be tired, to be hormonal –

Thom:    Is it OK to say I quite like some of your hormones? [wiggling eyebrows]

Me:       Yes, I liked those ones too. But it's horrid for me to feel so at the mercy of this thing I don't even know, or understand. I'm still me, I'm still Kiki, but now I'm this vessel being pummelled and slugged and lectured.

Thom:    Who's lecturing you?

Me:       [mumbling]

Thom:    Christ. Have you been looking at forums again?

Me:       I was just curious!

Thom:    What, bloody UninformedMumsSpeculate dot com? Kiki, if those places upset you, why would you look at them?

Me:       It's just . . . one of the people mentioned that if you don't bond with your baby while it's . . . you know . . . in there, it can really affect how you get on with it when it's born.

Thom:    [putting his arms around me] Kiki, that sounds reasonable. I'm sorry.

We just lay in bed for a while, not talking, and I hoped that something would change, to stop swinging wildly

74

between finding a positive and being suddenly petrified by it. I didn't want to be quite as certain as Lucie Martel, but I wouldn't mind just a little piece of that.

Optimism, I suppose I was after.

December 16th

Before Christmas swept us up in Publishing's usual month-long shutdown, I thought I'd better get in touch with my other new authors. Jennifer Luck, rather bafflingly, wrote back to say how far she'd got with Tony's notes (Tony writes notes?) and would resubmit in January, as they'd agreed. Matthew Holt, meanwhile, seemed delighted to have a new editor, as he hadn't quite 'clicked' with Tony. I've no way of knowing whether that means Matthew saw straight through him, or whether Tony pointed out that most parts of Sweden don't have three months of continuous daylight each summer. Can't wait to read his updated manuscript too, next year. Still no clue to the contact details for Stuart 'Tara Towne' Winton, though. I'll look into this properly in January.

Back at home, I've no idea how she's done it, but she's done it again.

Me:    Has Susie been round here while I've been out?
Thom:  No. Why?
Me:    [holding up a tampon]
Thom:  This is a bit too abstract even for me. What's the connection?
Me:    It was today's calendar gift.
Thom:  Oooooh. Ooh, that's good. No, she hasn't been round here for ages. You haven't done something foolish like give her a key, have you?

75

Me:    [thinking] Oh, I bloody did, as well. For *emergencies*.
Thom: We need to raise our game.

TO DO:
Come up with a full blueprint for Susie Revenge


December 17th

We went to Susie's last night, before heading out with them
for drinks for Pete's birthday. Mum and Dad stayed in to
babysit the kids, and I managed some quick advent calendar
manoeuvres before we left. 'What are you grinning about?'
asked Susie as we wrapped up for the walk to the pub, and
Thom just mouthed exaggeratedly, 'DID YOU DO IT?' over
her shoulder. I nodded to him but just smiled at Susie, saying,
'Gosh, nothing! Aren't we suspicious?' She narrowed her eyes
at me, but we went off nonetheless. I had a great time tonight,
and Susie's so much happier when Pete's around. I'm sure
she didn't mean all that stuff she was saying the other day.
I can't imagine how exhausted she must feel all the time, or
how much she misses him. I'm sure they know what they're
doing, though.


December 21st

Susie rang tonight.

Susie:  Have *you* been meddling with my advent calendar?
Me:     [sniggering] No. I don't know what you're talking
        about.
Susie:  You little bastard. Those calendars are sacrosanct.
Me:     You started it!

| Susie: | What do you mean, I started it? |
|---|---|
| Me: | You put the pencil in mine! |
| Susie: | What? |
| Me: | What? |
| Susie: | What pencil? |
| Me: | Don't try that game with me. The pencil . . . in my . . . advent calendar . . . Didn't you? |
| Susie: | I did no such thing, you horrible brat. How dare you. |
| Me: | Well, who did then? |
| Susie: | [silence] Dad? |
| Me: | I got a tampon last week. |
| Susie: | [longer silence] Mum? |
| Me: | [even longer silence] She has been really stressed, Suse. I think Dad's heart attack shook her more than we realised. And you know she always goes crazy at Christmas. |
| Susie: | So you're blaming your mother, are you? That does not seem like the actions of a grateful child. Your poor, aged mother. |
| Me: | Don't, Suse. |
| Susie: | Alright, alright. Poor Mum. Don't mention it to her, OK? |
| Me: | OK. And Suse? |
| Susie: | What? |
| Me: | Don't let the kids open tomorrow's calendar parcel. |

Poor Mum. She does seem pretty stressed at the moment.


December 22nd

Final day in the office before Christmas. Contracts all taken care of until January, publicity all wrapped up – Alice,

Carol and I will be on the phone should there be any emergencies – Secret Santa gifts exchanged (gave: a woolly hat to Norman; received: a pack of fake moustaches, obviously), plans gone over and seasonal farewells said. There's such a holiday mood over all of us, even though we're a small office: I wonder how much of that is Christmas, and how much is how well we've done these last few months in Tony's absence. Anyway, it's nice to have these almost-two-weeks stretching ahead of us.

TO DO:
Check I've actually done everything?

December 23rd

Drinks with everyone tonight, bliss. Eve and Mike, who brought fresh boxes of stollen for everyone, Alice, Designer Dan, old pal Jim and Poppy, Zoe and Zac, Greta (my bridesmaid-buddy), Thom's new teaching colleagues Liz, George and Robin, and even Susie and Pete (Mum and Dad had the kids). It was great, the first time I'd seen everyone together since our wedding, and reminded me and Thom both that we didn't want to give any of this up when the baby arrived. It was always a pleasure to see these people, and for every friend we'd lost touch with over the years, there were new ones: Zoe, Greta, the teachers. This was a nice life, and we're grateful for it. Eve's stopped being a frenemy and is just my friend again, Mike brings us baked goods, Zac's really handsome and Greta and Alice are hilarious – what more could one want from life?

TO DO:
See if this baby can be postponed a couple of years

December 24th

Christmas Eve. I have all my presents bought, wrapped and ready to go, I have my mocktail ingredients in Mum's fridge (I've got everything for several jugs of mock-itos, but I'm pretty sure I'm going to just end up on the dusty Buck's Fizz as usual) and our flat looks like a grotto explosion, every available surface covered with fairy lights, paper chains, snowflakes, Christmas cards, flocked reindeer, tissue paper snowmen (from the Twins' school), weathered metal stars and little festive wooden decorations. Our tree was festooned with gold bows and red baubles, and with tiny decorations made by Dad. It was beautiful.

I made us both some mulled wine (so thoroughly mulled I'd be lucky if there was even a breath of booze left in there) and brought two mugs of it through. Thom was sitting on the floor, staring at the tree.

Me:     You OK?
Thom:   [slightly surprised] Yeah. I am. Are you?
Me:     Yes. I like how much this baby moves. And I like you.
Thom:   My *God*, Christmas makes you emotional.
Me:     You say that like it's not fact number one about me.
Thom:   Do you like it today?
Me:     I do. More and more.
Thom:   You're going to have a baby here next time we do this.
Both:   – All going well.
Me:     We will. Are you going to cover it in 'Baby's First Christmas' bibs and babygros? Will you get it tiny baby antlers?
Thom:   I don't think they exist.

79

Me:     Well, now we know what we can pitch to *Dragon's Den*, don't we?

We stayed up late tonight, mostly just resting against the sofa, looking at the tree, until suddenly at 11.59 Thom said, 'Right, get to bed. Father Christmas won't come otherwise.' Quite right, too.


December 25th

Oh, a lovely day. Thom woke me up with such wonderful treats, gifts from under the tree and a tray of Christmas breakfast in bed: buttery scrambled eggs and toast, fresh orange juice and tea, and a little mince pie. 'I'm going to look nine months preg by New Year if you keep this up,' I warned, stuffing the mince pie in my mouth first. 'Ah, the beauty of Woman in bloom,' Thom countered. 'Plus, blooming woman, we need to be at your mum and dad's in an hour. Shall we open something here first?' My mouth still full, I grabbed the nearest gift and thrust it at Thom, nodding, wide-eyed.

Here's what we got one another:

From Thom:

A new MAC Ruby Woo lipstick (mine's run out)
Four paperbacks, none of which were about babies
Plants for the window-box
*To Catch a Thief*, my favourite Cary Grant film

From me:

A boxset of Paul Newman films (maybe a little bit for me too)

A tie (of course)
Two poetry books
A jar of homemade chutney (annual ritual)

We thanked one another, then I said with mock casualness, 'Oh. What's *that*? Is there something still in the tree?' Thom looked at me quizzically, then pulled out a gold envelope from within the branches. His face lit up. 'It's not what you think it is, I think,' I warned, 'but have a look anyway.' He pulled out a little card, similar to the one he'd given me last Christmas (and yes which we still used, *thank you very much*).

Thom:  'For a night off.'

Me:     Ah, but don't you know how these things work? Turn it over.

Thom:  'Definitely redeemable more than once.' Thank you, Keeks, but a night off from what?

Me:     From everything. I may regret this once the baby actually arrives, but I don't want to you to feel that your every waking hour away from work has to be spent here, with your baby. Or with me.

Thom:  Where else am I supposed to be?

Me:     With your friends! Wherever you want! I know that you want to look after me, but I want *you* to know that you're allowed nights off too. To be a pal to someone other than us. I know we don't need to give one another permission, but if you ever want it, it's there. OK?

Thom:  You're going to be a nice mother.

Me:     I do hope so. I've already bought a card with that message for you to give me on Mothers' Day.

As we wrapped up to go over to Mum and Dad's, Thom said, 'By the way, there were other things I wanted to get you but I thought they might be pretty depressing as special gifts, and I didn't want you to think that you were just a breeder to me now. Maybe you can have them another time.' He widened his eyes at me mysteriously, as is his wont, and we headed off.

When we got there, the house was strangely quiet, Susie and Pete and the kids not having arrived yet. While Thom went to give Mum a kiss, Dad took me to one side.

Dad:    Listen, love, I think your mum's a bit overworked at the moment, so be gentle on her, alright?

Me:    Overworked? She's been retired two years.

Dad:    Katherine, I mean it. I think she's too worried about all of us – my heart, your pregnancy – and we need to go easy on her. Tell your sister.

Me:    Dad, I will, and we will. We'll be model daughters. Susie and I were worrying about her only the other day.

Dad:    Why's that?

Me:    I got some . . . odd things in my advent calendar this year.

Dad:    [something flickering across his face] Did you, now? Alright, love, don't mention anything about this to your mum, alright? Just . . . be a good girl.

He gave me a kiss and a hug, but I felt worse, rather than better. I can understand how Mum would be so shaken by Dad's heart scare, but it had been six months now, and she seemed to bounce back so quickly at the start. Is it a delayed reaction? Is it just Christmas stress taken up a notch?

When I followed them all into the kitchen, Thom gave me a quizzical look – are you OK? – so I smiled and nodded at him and gave Mum a long, tight hug.

Mum:   What's that for?

Me:    For letting all of us ne'er-do-wells into your home every Christmas. What a nice time we have. Thanks, Mum.

Mum:   [surprised] *Well*.

Me:    Now, what can we do to help?

But the one time I was offering to help, she wouldn't hear of it, insisting that I must relax and stay off my feet, while I still could. I liked the first half of it, but the thought – even if this wasn't what she intended – that next Christmas I would be jogging around like a maniac after a crying, stinking baby, planted me firmly on the sofa with my feet up. Dad turned the carols up and brought me a heavy tumbler of Buck's Fizz (one part champagne to one hundred parts orange juice), and handed me a long, thin parcel. 'You can open it now, if you want, before the hordes arrive,' he said.

Inside was one of Dad's little mobiles. Oh! I'd forgotten about this tradition. As I pulled it out, I saw what was hanging from each wire: tiny little books, no bigger than my thumb, wired open so the tissue-paper pages flapped as the mobile went around. Looking closer, I saw that the books were actually printed, in a tiny font: *Little Red Riding Hood, Goldilocks, Puss in Boots, Cinderella, The Gingerbread Man, Hansel and Gretel*.

Me:    Dad! This is lovely.

Dad:   Oh, I'm glad you like it. Some of my kids may have helped with the printing inside – extra grades and all that.

Me:    Thank you, Dad.

Dad:   You're more than welcome, Kiki.

Me:    Thom! Come and see this.

Thom was as delighted as I was by the gift, and I felt overwhelmed for a minute by how lucky I was. This kind man, determined to make my life better in any way, and two parents who had bent over backwards for the last thirty years to make their children's lives happy, secure, fulfilled. I choked up, and Thom pulled me into a bear hug. 'She does this about six times a day,' he explained to Dad.

Just then, Susie and co. arrived, banging through the front door in a wall of scarves and noise, bags of presents, bottles of wine and kisses, with the Twins and Pete singing Christmas carols as they kissed everyone. As they went through to the kitchen, I grabbed Susie in the hall, just as Dad had caught me.

Me:      Dad says we have to be extra nice to Mum.

Susie:   But we're *always* nice to Mum.

Me:      [moving my hands into Chinese burn position]

Susie:   God! Alright! You have my word that I will be nice to my mother. Why did Dad say that?

Me:      I think he's worried about her. I hadn't even told him about the advent calendars until then. He says she just seems really stressed and . . . well, that's all, actually.

Susie:   *Calendar*, singular. The only rotten surprises in mine were from you, thank you very much. Nothing else, though? Just that she seems stressed? That's pretty normal for Christmas.

Me:      Shouldn't we be making more of an effort for her? Aren't we old enough to be making Christmas dinner ourselves?

Susie:   I'd like to see you try to get all of us in either of our places.

Me:      No, I'll always want to come here for Christmas, but maybe we ought to be doing slightly more than just turning up?

Susie:   Thanks, Mother Teresa. When you've got a newborn next Christmas, remind me to check how eager you are to cook turkey and all the trimmings for nine of us.

Me:      Ten, Suse.

Susie:   [looking at me as if I'm mental] At seven months old, your baby probably won't need its own turkey leg. God, you have *so* much to learn about parenting.

Me:      I hate you.

Pete:    [poking head round door] Suse, where's Frida?

Susie:   Oops. Asleep in the car, I assume.

Pete:    Was she asleep when you put her in?

Susie:   [staring at him] I didn't put her in.

Both:    [grabbing the car keys, rushing outside]

I heard the engine wildly over-revving as they sped back to their house round the corner. Dad wandered in from the kitchen, saying, 'Where've Susie and Pete gone?' I smiled sweetly. 'I think they forgot something at home.'

When they came back in a few minutes later carrying a sleepy-looking Frida, Susie came over and whispered in my ear, 'If you mention this again, I will destroy you.' I took her hand and said, 'I know, Suse. I have so much to learn about parenting.'

The rest of the day was good fun, although occasionally Mum did seem really tired. But the food, as ever, was wonderful, and everyone seemed pleased with their gifts. We put the kids to bed upstairs and stayed up late, eating and drinking and watching *Casino Royale*. Merry Christmas, you foetus.

December 26th

Home again, home again. For once, we (I) didn't leave Mum and Dad's in a flurry of repressed fury – it was one of the nicest Christmases I've ever had there. Maybe Susie's right about Mum; maybe pregnancies do bring out the best in her. Once all the cooking was out of the way, Mum was just funny and relaxed, giddy and happy with her family all around her. And rather than the usual gross and/or useless gifts (dear GOD this baby better not be as ungrateful as I am), she'd bought me a beautiful maternity top and a set of the most fabulous nail polishes ('Because nail polish always fits you, darling,' she said, giving me a hug). Pete was around for the whole thing, Thom wasn't stressed about his job, Dad romped with the Twins and I could not have been happier. Thanks, everyone.

Later, back at home, I reminded Thom about the twenty-week scan next month.

Thom: Do you want to know?

Me: If something's wrong?

Thom: No. Well, yes, but I meant the sex. Do you want to know about it?

Me: [Groucho Marx voice, waggling imaginary cigar] Wasn't not knowing about it what got us into this whole mess?

Thom: The way I recall, you seemed to know exactly what you –

Me: Yes, I did, didn't I? Hehehe. Anyway . . . I don't know. Lots of people say they don't want to find out so it gives them a reason to push. But I do tend to think that there're enough unknowns, cheers, and I'd rather know everything I can.

Thom: So you would like to?

Me: I think so. But would you?

Thom: Sure, why not? Do you have any preference?

Me: [screwing up face] Mmm, not really. I don't know. I suppose I'd quite like a girl – look how brilliant

Susie's Lily is. But I don't really mind. But a girl would be great. But I don't mind. Although a girl would be really cool. All the stuff we can show her! We can make her into the world's best girl! But I don't mind, really.

Thom: Well, as long as you've got no preference at all either way, then.

Me: No, really! I don't mind. Our baby will be amazing whatever.

So we agreed: we would find out the sex. Which I can definitely stop thinking about some time before the scan. Any minute now. I'll definitely stop dwelling on it. Any . . . time . . . soon . . .

December 27th

Back to the doctor again, for my twenty-four-week check. Dr Bedford was (naturally) even bigger than last time, and she didn't wait for me to sit down this time.

Me:             How are you feeling?

Dr Bedford:     [laughing] I believe that's my line. I'm well, thank you. Counting the days, a little bit. Your turn now: are *you* feeling well?

Me:             I am. I think I'm beginning to get used to the idea of having a baby. And my morning sickness came and went, leaving only a few lingering cravings and repulsions, so it's been good.

Dr Bedford:     Well, that *is* good. For this check-up I'm going to need some blood and urine from you –

| | |
|---|---|
| Me: | Sounds like a typical Saturday night on the town. |
| Dr Bedford: | – so if I give you this cup, I'll get everything for the bloods ready. |

I wondered briefly while I was in the surgery bathroom whether Dr Bedford was calling security to have me escorted from the building for my inappropriate attempt at humour, but when I came back she'd laid out the syringes and rubber strap on her desk. I sat back down and she lifted my sleeve, wrapping the strap around my upper arm.

| | |
|---|---|
| Dr Bedford: | Still getting Saturday night flashbacks? Ah, memories of a misspent youth. |
| Me: | [agape] |
| Dr Bedford: | [laughing again] Just kidding. |

I turned away, unable to high five her due to my tethered arm and unable to keep watching as the blood filled up the syringe. After a minute or two, she released me and put a tiny round plaster on the hole, packing up the bloods and dipping a testing slip into the urine sample.

| | |
|---|---|
| Dr Bedford: | Right, this sample looks fine, and I'll send the bloods off today. We'll let you know if there's anything we need to look into further. How are you doing with antenatal classes? |
| Me: | I will definitely book them next year. |
| Dr Bedford: | That's less than a week away. |
| Me: | At *some* point. |
| Dr Bedford: | OK, I'll leave that with you. We've also got a whole new range of leaflets for you: flu jabs and whooping cough vaccines, which we can give you at your next check-up, plus these |

|            | about hospital tours, and this one about Vitamin D in pregnancy. Now, is there anything else you'd like to talk to me about? |
|------------|----------------------------------------------------------------------------------|
| Me:        | I don't think so. Did you have a nice Christmas? |
| Dr Bedford: | I did, thank you. Lots of lying around, making the most of it while I can. |
| Me:        | Mmm, that's the best way, isn't it? |
| Dr Bedford: | Well, we shall see you again in eight weeks. You'll have a midwife appointment before then – they'll be in touch if they haven't already – and next time you'll be seeing my locum. |
| Me:        | Oh! I hadn't thought about that. Good luck, I suppose. |

TO DO:
Book jabs
Start taking Vitamin D
Stop taking After Eights like they're an essential foetal
  medicine


December 31st

Oh, how wild our lives are now. The only people we could think of who would share this sobriety pain are Zac and Zoe, who came round this evening for dinner and a film (*Die Hard 4.0*). The dinner was excellent (though I say so myself, etc.) but the film did not go down so well.

Thom: If you ever make me watch such a bad film again, I
  will leave you.
Me:  Hold on – that one wasn't even my choice! I blame
  Zac.

Zac: You have got me sorely mistaken if you think I would ever choose a Bruce Willis movie.

Me: [aghast] Zoe, are you sure your wedding papers are all legal? Sure it's not too late to annul?

Zoe: [sighing] It's his only real flaw. We have to let it slide.

Zac: We do. Particularly since Zoe was responsible for choosing the film tonight.

All: Booo! [throwing things at her]

Zoe: Honey, you need to get used to Bruce Willis's pretty face. Your kid isn't going to look too different.

Zac: [narrowing his eyes at her] I knew it was a mistake to leave you unattended on these celebrity shoots. I can see it now: 'Big Bad Bruce Put His Fifth Element in My New Wife'.

Thom: I would read that article.

Me: Have you thought about doing a book? Because I know the perfect editor for you.

Zoe: And my tell-all: 'Wily Willis Was Unbreakable'.

Me: 'It's like he had a Sixth Sense.'

Zac: 'He gave me the Whole Nine Yards.'

Thom: [laughing] 'Bruce was a real Hudson Hawk.' [silence]

Me: What does that even *mean*?

Zac: I never really liked that film.

Zoe: Too far, Thom, too far. We're *pregnant*, for crying out loud.

Thom: You're all bastards.

We sent them on their way with a doggy bag of leftover dessert and were in bed by 12.30. Hardcore.

January's Classic Baby

She hoped for a son; he would be strong and dark; she would call him George; and this idea of having a male child was like an expected revenge for all her impotence in the past. A man, at least, is free; he may travel over passions and over countries, overcome obstacles, taste of the most far-away pleasures. But a woman is always hampered. At once inert and flexible, she has against her the weakness of the flesh and legal dependence. Her will, like the veil of her bonnet, held by a string, flutters in every wind; there is always some desire that draws her, some conventionality that restrains.

She was confined on a Sunday at about six o'clock, as the sun was rising.

'It is a girl!' said Charles.

She turned her head away and fainted.

*Madame Bovary*
Gustave Flaubert

## January 1st

Happy new year, all. If all goes well (there's that phrase again), this is the year we'll get a –

Oh man.
A baby.

Ridiculous. I will get used to this idea eventually, really.
Wow.

TO DO:
Only a few months to go; get all those things a baby needs


## January 3rd

As Thom and I headed up to the maternity wing late this afternoon, I knew we were both sharing one thought: If Clare is our sonographer again, we'll just walk straight out and cross our fingers that this baby's intact. Yes, fine, Thom might actually have liked Clare, but I'm sure he *would* have been sharing that thought if he'd actually seen *Alien*.

But it wasn't. It was a lovely scan technician called Sunita, who made us laugh throughout by telling us about some of the things she's scanned for in the past when she was on the X-ray unit. Heavens alive, labour suddenly doesn't seem so bad.

Me:     But why would you do that with a bicycle pump?
Both:    [staring at me]
Me:     OK, not why, but . . . *why*?
Sunita: It takes all sorts, Katherine. Speaking of which, shall we finish looking at this little one? Now, do you want to know the sex?
Thom:   I think . . . [looking at me]
Me:     We do, if that's OK? [looking back at Thom]
Thom:   Of course! This is exciting.
Me:     I bet you're wishing you'd organised that sweepstake with your classes, now.
Thom:   [nodding ruefully]
Sunita: OK . . . [examining, making notes] Alright, it looks like you're having a healthy and growing baby boy!
Me:     [trying to smile] Oh, good.
Thom:   But the baby's healthy, everything in the right place?
Sunita: Yes, he's exactly where he should be on all the charts, just right. [looking at me] Are you alright, Katherine?
Me:     [fixing a smile on] Yes, just – surprised! That's all. There's really a person in there.

She put her hand on my arm and said our pictures would be at reception if we wanted to collect them, then left us to it. It wouldn't have taken a rocket scientist to feel our changed mood. We managed to get back to the car before I started crying, but once I started, I couldn't stop. I howled all the way home, up into our flat and as Thom tucked me into bed.

Me: I don't [hic] want a boy! I h-[hic]-hate boys! They stink and they make a mess and they don't want to learn [hic] dancing!

Thom hugged and hugged me, and towards 9ish, I calmed down.

Thom: Listen Keeks, I hate it when you're upset, you know that, and if I could do anything, I would. But here are some things it may or may not help you to think about: one. You don't have to be such a sexist pig about it, do you? Who says boys don't want to dance? This is *our kid*, remember. He'll do whatever we brainwash him into doing.
Me: [still hiccupping, laughing]
Thom: Two. All children are smelly. Fact. And three. You know what the world needs more of? Feminist men. Imagine what an amazing man we can make him! He'll be able to recite the poetry of Sylvia Plath, and critique . . . I dunno, some woman philosopher –
Me: Simone de Beauvoir?
Thom: Yes! Exactly! And he'll be able to give reasoned arguments for equal pay, and equal parenting leave, and all that other feminist jazz.
Me: [hic] We've still got some work to do on [hic] you, haven't we?
Thom: Yes, we do. But think of all the worlds we can open up to him. Our healthy, wonderful, brave, funny, smart, egalitarian baby.
Me: [crying again]
Thom: Isn't that a nice thing to think about?

Me:     [crying harder] Yes. You're just so nii-iiiii-iiiiiice.
Thom:   I know. I know.

Once my hiccups had subsided, he showed me how I could thank him, but I said my belly wouldn't be comfortable so we'd just have to do it the normal way. Which was still very nice, thank you.


January 4th

Back to work this morning. Alice looked like I felt, having had to sit through a Christmas where her entire family took turns to bully Gareth into proposing to her. She said she felt more sorry for him than for herself, but I know our discussion about her life is still playing on her mind. She's not herself.

When I woke up today, I'd remembered again about the boy in here. I was so happy when the technician said it was whole and growing well, so it feels awful – awful – to be sad about this, about his boy-ness. Sad in the way that followed me around all day, a feeling in the pit of my stomach, a tiny regret that said maybe if we'd waited, our first baby would have been a girl. What a horrible feeling. And I was sorry to this baby, to everyone who would love any baby, of any sex, and sorry, truly, that this bothers me so much, at all. It ate into my day.

And then, suddenly, I wasn't. Not sorry at all, not sad. When I got home and saw Thom again, and remembered his pep-talk about the feminist we shall brainwash him into being, I felt – for a moment, but I'll feel it again, and keep feeling it – excited, amazed, to be meeting our son soon. To have a son!

Yup. Still not really taking it in. But some switch has been flipped and I'm ready, now, to have our child. Just about. No, I am.

It was strange to be at work today, though, suddenly feeling like my leave was only round the corner. Carol was talking about books that I'll never see through to publication, and others where both hardback and paperback will be out before I'm back in the office. Although I know I need to talk to those four new authors (if I can track down the mysterious Stuart Winton), I do feel it's harder when I won't get to see them printed, won't follow their sales with quite the same day-by-day fascination as I would if I was still in the office. I'm not disengaging in any way – I've got too much on to do that – but I do wish Tony would magically appear once more so I can actually talk to him about the maternity cover he saw fit to email my authors about weeks ago, my finishing dates and my return dates. These months are going to speed by, and then I shan't be in any of these meetings to sort out jackets, or schedules, or contracts. And I feel strange about that.

TO DO:
Throw away old name list
Start coming up with some boys' names

January 6th

Mum called after work to find out whether we knew the baby's sex yet. I told her that we had the results in an envelope, but weren't planning to open it unless we got really desperate, closer to the time. It took all her self-control not to ask where we kept the envelope, but eventually she let me go, content that I didn't know more about the pregnancy than she did. Oh Mum, I'm sorry to fib, but Thom and I agreed that everyone else could just wait until the baby was born to find out.

Eve's birthday party tonight. I just couldn't face it; work is suddenly making me absolutely knackered. Was it the Christmas break, getting me into lazy habits? This will be the first time I've missed her party in – God – fifteen years? Oh, that makes me feel even worse about missing it. I sent her a beautiful card and ordered flowers to her office, but the thought of not being able to raise a Band on the Run with her makes me feel rotten. Although . . . her last birthday party hardly passed without incident. Thom didn't even ask if we were going tonight; I think last year's drunken public slow-dance with Eve still haunts him. I tried to call but she wasn't picking up.

January 8th

Mum and Susie turned up on my doorstep today, to take me shopping. Apart from my last-minute wedding dress, we hadn't been shopping all together for at least a decade, usually because it would end in one or all of us having an argument and requiring a strong drink – not that easy to get when you're a very fresh-faced teen.

But that was then, and this is now, and they had Thom's collaboration to get me away from the weekend papers and into town. On the tube, Mum and Suse made some recommendations about the kind of thing I might want – what the hell is a belly band? – and it felt exciting, like getting camping equipment ready for a jungle adventure.

Me: Mum, this is a tent. I'm not wearing this.
Susie: It's not a tent, you little brat. It's a really nice dress,

that, with some chunky heels and a good cardi, will look the bee's knees.

Me:     Stop trying to dress me for the school run! I'm only twenty-eight, for fuck's sake.

Mum:    Language, Katherine.

Me:     She's trying to make me into a mini-me.

Susie:  Maxi-me more like, you pregno-whale.

Mum:    Girls, girls, stop being *silly*. Kiki, you will get much bigger over the final months, and you'll want to be comfortable. When you've got a big stomach, something like that will be much more flattering – but if you don't like it, we shouldn't get it, and we'll find something you do like. [looking meaningfully at Susie] After all, it's you who's got to wear it.

Me:     [a bit ashamed] Thanks, Mum. [poking tongue out at Susie]

Susie:  [pokes her tongue into her cheek, lifting her curled hand up to it]

Mum:    [not even looking at us] *Girls*.

In the end, they did help me get loads of stuff: not only dresses and trousers and tops, but belly bands (which are apparently to cover the gap between trousers and tops when your stomach is SO LARGE) and shoes and body creams (Susie: 'It is a rite of pregnancy that your bathroom shall become full of useless but delicious-smelling creams. The prophecy is: you shall never finish them') and even an absolutely gorgeous, huge handbag, that Mum somehow spotted and declared perfect as a nappy bag.

Me:     Really? Don't I need one with special bottle-warming compartments? And wipe pockets? And muslin . . . zones?

Susie:  No. They're all super ugly anyway. Just get a normal bag – like this. As long as it's roomy, and not made of velvet or angel hair or something. If you like it, it makes a hell of lot more sense. Unless . . . [pulling realisation face] Ohhh, you *want* to look like a mum. You want people to look at you walking down the street and say, 'Hey, that woman's definitely pushed a baby from her womb!' Don't you?

Me:    [to Mum] I will *take* it. Thank you.

It was a lovely day, the first day in ages I hadn't seen a single hint of Mum's tiredness or stress. And since Susie bought me one of the dresses, and Mum got me the bag, this shopping haul doesn't feel quite so profligate.

When I got back and showed Thom, he complimented everything. 'Hey, nice bag,' he said. 'Not mumsy at all.'

Me:    Thank you, Gok Wan. But I didn't have to pay for the dress or the bag.

Thom:  Shoplifting? [mouthing] Is it a fake bump?

Me:    No! Mum bought me the bag, Susie, the dress – they said they were delayed Christmas gifts.

Thom:  Speaking of which [gets out chequebook] how much was the rest?

Me:    Alright, Daddy Warbucks.

Thom:  No, that was the Christmas gifts I thought would be a bit grim. I didn't want to just get you Pregnant Clothes for Christmas, but I did want to be able to get you some. So. How much?

Me:    Stop asking me that with your pen poised over your chequebook. I feel like you're trying to pay me to leave your wholesome son alone.

Thom:  Has that happened to you before?

Me:    [shiftily] No.

Thom:  Can I pay for anything?

Me:     If you would like to pick one thing from this haul, that would be incredibly kind and it would mean a lot to me. But if you keep saying, 'Can I pay for anything?' like a sweaty Richard Gere in *Pretty Woman*, then I'm afraid, sir, this pretty woman ain't for sale.

Thom:  Mmm. Well, I do like that dress. And those Rosa Klebb shoes. How about those?

Me:     I will ignore your Rosa Klebb comment because I am the bigger person –

Thom:  Hem hem.

Me:     – and thank you for your most-kind generosity.

Thom:  Do I have to wrap them?

Me:     No. Our transaction here is complete.

What a lovely day.

TO DO:
Send a card to Mum and Suse to say thank you
Start making a list of what we might need for the baby?

January 11th

Still no word from Eve since I missed her birthday. I left another message and even tried Mike's number, but no response. Maybe they've just fled the country. Maybe they're busy having crazy, hungover, unpregnant sex. I just can't bear the thought that I coud be losing her, since I told her about the baby.

Whatever wild fun they're having, I've booked my place on the yoga course. If you've always made fun of people who do yoga, is it OK to suddenly be looking forward to this? Well, motherhood just changes you, doesn't it? as I insisted sarcastically to Thom. I do look forward to it – the new course starts in a couple of weeks.

It feels like the office is taking longer to warm back to work than usual this year: I don't know if it's Tony's absence or my subconscious withdrawal from Polka Dot, but we're all getting in late each morning, and titles are being pushed back in the schedules again and again. I'm spending what little energy I've got on *A Womb of One's Own* for March; it's unfortunately spent almost entirely on conference calls with Lucie, during which she panics about what coverage we'll get her, what angle the British press will take, and how we'll take care of her when she comes over for the UK launch. Goodness, she makes me hate publishing. But I suppose she has got only a month until her due date – I'll be panicking when my time rolls around too, no doubt.

TO DO:
Try once more, then let Eve call me
Any more maternity clothes?
Try to smuggle in a mattress as a yoga mat. And a duvet.


January 14th

Mum and Dad came to ours for lunch today. Mum wouldn't let me lift a single finger the whole time: she and Dad set the table, brought the drinks, and she offered me cushions and footrests and blankets. I kept laughing at her solicitousness, protesting that I wasn't an invalid in any way. 'I went for a run yesterday,' I explained. 'No! You didn't!' Mum gasped. It took reassurances from all three of us to convince her that I wasn't going to jog the baby out of my vagina (not in exactly that language), but that had triggered something in her memory. 'Oh, Kiki, I've brought you the cushion that my mother gave me when I was pregnant with your sister. It's got lavender in – I just freshened it up – and it's

101

wonderful for when you can't sleep. Susie had it with her pregnancies and loved it.'

I was touched, and cuddled it until Thom announced lunch. Thom told us all about one of his GCSE classes, containing a girl so far ahead of the rest of the year – really, the rest of the school, he confessed – that he felt embarrassed to be teaching her the GCSE syllabus. He's just so happy, though. He rarely ever talked about his work before, and if he did it was only with a weariness and bitter humour to disguise the awfulness of it. To see him talking eagerly, excitedly about the stuff he does every day, to hear him say explicitly how much he loves it, how his days fly by as he sees those kids learning more and more – that makes *me* happy.

January 19th

I don't know why, or how she got my number (cough, *Mum*, cough), but Annie called me this week. Annie and I were friends when we were eight or so, but grew apart when she wanted horse riding lessons and I wanted alcoholic lemonade and snogging. But last year, equally out of the blue, she invited us to her wedding, and we, whether in a spirit of generosity or schadenfreude, went. It was as bad as I had feared – not so much the bizarre, silver holographic foil decorations, or the fact that the top table had an entirely different meal to everyone else – more that Stephen, the groom, vanished upstairs for a bath half an hour into the reception and wasn't seen again for the rest of the night. Poor Annie. But not so poor that I wanted to rekindle our friendship. I had nothing against her (besides inviting us to what was effectively a Dry wedding) but five minutes in her company at that wedding reminded me why our friendship hadn't continued through the years – we hadn't even invited her to our wedding, although at least we had the excuse of having to cut vast swathes of the guest list at the last minute. So why has she started calling me? I'd had the sense to let it go to answerphone – I'm not yet prepped enough to have a conversation with her again. She just left a rambling message about keeping in touch, and something about the top table's last bottle of wine (oops – maybe someone did notice our theft at her wedding after all) followed by some nervous laughter.

I nearly asked Mum at her birthday dinner yesterday, but I didn't want to ruin the night if she *had* been spilling all my secrets.

## January 21st

Back to the big department store today, for the next stage in our lists there; Wedding List, Nursery List, Funeral List. Maybe not the last one. And really, not the second one either. It was only ghoulish curiosity leading us back there, and the need to get some idea of the things we'd need; as broke as we are, neither of us intends to put a list online for our friends and relatives to browse and buy from. But we were curious, had a tonne of vouchers for the store from our wedding, and we do need to think about a buggy and cot eventually. We toyed with the idea of sleeping it in a drawer, or – like my grandmother – in a suitcase with the lid pinned to the wall, thus handily doubling as a carrying-unit too, but social pressures demand that these purchases are made, eventually. We booked an appointment for first thing this morning, with the hope that the baby department would be at its quietest and we could slink in and out without even a splash.

Oh, we of misplaced faith.

Even at 9.30, the floor was full of smart mothers with slim hips and glossy hair, distracted fathers tapping at their phones, and little Oscars and Rubys begging for toys, a Hogarthian vision of the twenty-first century. Thom squeezed my hand.

| | |
|---|---|
| Friendly sales assistant: | Hello, may I help you two? |
| Me: | Oh, hello, we've got an appointment for the nursery . . . um . . . thing. [gestures to stomach] |
| Assistant: | Are you my nine-thirty? What's the name? |
| Me: | Carlow. |
| Assistant: | Hello, was it Katherine? [shaking hands with us] |
| Me: | Yes, hello. |
| Thom: | Thom, hello. |
| Assistant: | Lovely to meet you, Thom and Katherine. I'm Gordon. Now, is this your first baby? |
| Me: | Yes, first one. We have no idea what we're doing. [nervous laughter] |
| Assistant: | Don't worry, we'll take care of that! |

We then spent an hour being shown things that I didn't even know existed before, and things I cannot imagine why they exist. Cot bumpers, Moses baskets, girls' sleeping bags and boys' sleeping bags (because obviously a creature which has been out of your womb a few days definitely needs to be reassured about its gender by sticking pink fairies/blue dinosaurs all over its clothing, its lying-around-asleep area, and its lying-around-awake area). Plus the technical stuff, reminding me what I'm really here for: breast pumps. Postnatal 'cushions'. Nipple cream. *Maternity pads*. Shudder.

The buggies alone took forty minutes. Every possible

colour and shape, and with sizes and prices ranging from 'Mmm, where shall we keep it in the house?' to 'Christ, we're going to have to sell the house for this'. There was a 'Pushchair Travel System' there for almost a *grand*. Now I'm sure we all want to show our barely conscious offspring how much we care for them, but bloody hell. That's . . . a lot.

Lovely Gordon showed us everything, and we felt bad for him, all his efforts in vain, so we pretended to make notes of things and we scanned things and I put on a doe-eyed face and pretended it was making me so giddy, and I realised Thom was worried I was getting carried away with my role.

Me:     Thom, pleeeeease can we get the good buggy?
        [pointing to a £800 model]
Thom:   Haha, we'll think about it.
Me:     Pleeeeeeease? You have got that nice bonus coming
        in a few months.
Thom:   Kiki?
Me:     [out of the side of my mouth] I. Know.
Thom:   [out of the side of his] Ohhhhh. [normally] Alright,
        I suppose so. Anything for my little buttercup and
        the little flower inside her! They're just so precious
        and I'll get them anything they could *possibly* need.
        [patting me on the head]
Me:     [out of the side of my mouth] You need to stop that
        right now.
Thom:   What's your most expensive breast pump?

As Gordon turned away for a moment to show us, I shoved Thom as hard as I could onto one of the display beds next to us.

Me:     Thom! Are you OK? Gosh, I hope our baby doesn't
        inherit your clumsiness.

We left shortly after, giggling, although I was slightly dazzled by all the buggies and recited their various merits to Thom all the way home (Me: 'But who knew I could ever be so obsessed with the weight of buggies?' Thom: [raising hand]). We got back and deleted the list from their website, before swinging round to Susie's to pick up her hand-me-downs. We found Mum and Dad there: Dad was outside with Lily and Edward, climbing the tree, and Mum was in the kitchen with Susie, going through an *Elle Deco* with her.

Me:     Oh, can I join in?

Susie:  You may. I'm just educating our mother in the beauty of patterned wallpaper.

Mum:    This is the stuff we had in our houses in the seventies.

Susie:  [taking a deep breath] It's not *exactly* the same, Mum.

Mum:    We had to strip it all off when you were children, when it went out of fashion. We should have just left it there, and we'd be the most trendy house around.

Susie:  Yes, Mum.

Mum:    Ah, Kiki, I've been meaning to come and see you. I've been wanting to give you the cushion that my mother gave me when I was pregnant, but I can't find it anywhere. [a bit upset] Susie, you don't still have it, do you?

Susie:  [indignant] No! I gave it back ages ago.

Me:     Mum! You gave it to me last weekend.

Mum:    [confused] No, I didn't.

Me:     Mum, you did. When you and Dad came over, do you remember?

Susie and I looked at one another.

106

Susie:  You did say you were going to, Mum.
Mum:   [not looking at us] Yes, right, I remember.

Then Susie asked what I was there for, and took me upstairs to get the clothes.

Susie:  What was that about?
Me:     She gave it to me a week ago. In our house. Did she really mention it to you?
Susie:  No. Did I make things worse?
Me:     No, I don't think so. Is this still post-Christmas forgetfulness?
Susie:  We're all going to get like this, Keeks. We don't need to panic. They're just getting old.
Me:     But I don't *want* them to.

She gave me a big hug and a bag of her maternity clothes, ranging from (she said), 'good quality smart stuff to soft shapeless garbage you'll live in after eight months'. As I was leaving, I asked Susie if she'd really had the cushion from Mum in her pregnancies.

Susie:  Yeah, it was really good, actually.
Me:     Why didn't you mention it?
Susie:  Why would I?
Me:     Why wouldn't you?
Susie:  Don't take this the wrong way, but you weren't pregnant. Why on earth *would* you care?

After Mum's memory lapse I didn't have the energy to be upset by this too, so I took another hug from her, thanked her for the clothes and went home.

As Thom made us sandwiches, I put on a fashion show of the maternity clothes. Susie was right: some of the

107

clothes were really nice. There was a blue and white striped dress that I could wear now, but most of the rest had baggy stomachs where Susie's pregnancies had stretched it out, so I'd need to wait a while before wearing those. And I saw what she meant about the other stuff; flabby, floppy tops and sweaters, and sagging tracksuit bottoms that I can't personally imagine ever sporting, although I do remember Susie in them for a few weeks. With the Twins, she'd stayed in great shape throughout, keeping her work clothes on-trend and sharp as a tack right up until she went on maternity leave, at which point she collapsed into this stuff. With Frida, she 'dressed for comfort' for the last six months, eating what she liked and gaining three stone. As long as I don't start an all-Haribo diet and have to be lifted by crane to hospital, I'm not so fussed about what happens to my weight. And I have no intention, either, of undergoing the Broccoli Diet and starting workouts when this kid is two days old. My bikini body has always been more Poundland than Pacific anyway, so I don't think I'll be troubling the tabloids with my baby body: 'LOCAL WOMAN HAS BABY, BODY SHOWS SIGNS SHOCKER'.

Yoga taster tonight. It was bliss. There was – unsurprisingly – one fool who insisted on showing us all how bendy she is, exactly the reason I've never wanted to go to a yoga class, but otherwise the teacher saw straight through us, and just gave us all gentle 'stretching exercises', which in reality just meant lying on our sides while we wiggled our toes. For the last fifteen minutes, she just lit candles and did that, 'Imagine you're on a beautiful beach, warm sand beneath you, waves lapping nearby' thing that gave me a flashback to all the slumber parties of my youth. Thankfully, she didn't then want to know in return who I'd been snogging at the

108

disco. But it was lovely. The room was dim enough that I didn't have to talk to anyone else beyond a 'Hello, yes, hello,' when we all grabbed our yoga mats. And it's interesting to see the differences between us: teeny weeny eight-month-pregnant women with perfect beach-ball bumps, and six-month-pregnants who clearly *have* adopted an all-Haribo diet and look pregnant from all sides. More strength to 'em, I say, if they're enjoying these things. I know it's a sweeping generalisation, but I bet those skinny-min pregnants will *not* be fun mothers. I bet their houses are all-white and their husbands will have affairs with the nanny.

Better stop before I lose my post-yoga-class-good-karmic-buzz.

TO DO:
Breathing exercises
Stretching exercises
Eat a bit of fruit?
Stop eating Haribo?


January 22nd

Sunday lunch at Mum and Dad's. When we came in, Dad kept me back in the hall again, and I thought of Christmas.

Me:    Is this about Mum? Is she OK?
Dad:   [shaking his head] I don't know, Kiki. I'm going to take her to the doctor's. I'm sure it's nothing, but . . . it's better if we get it checked out. Maybe it would have been better if I'd taken a bit more care of myself before the heart attack got me. And now I need to make sure your mum is taking care of herself.
Me:    Has something happened?

109

Dad:   No, not really. She's just . . . not herself so much. I really wanted to believe that there was something on her mind over Christmas, but . . . she's still the same. Most of the time she's fine, but sometimes . . . Ach, you know. It's something and nothing. Sometimes she's a bit repetitive. Or she makes odd mistakes around the house, gets cross at herself.

Me:    Isn't it just – isn't she just getting old?

Dad:   [smiling] I'm sure it is, love. That's why I'm going with her to see Dr Sanderson, so he can check her over. Maybe he'll just prescribe a long holiday, somewhere hot.

Me:    [hugging him] Thanks, Dad.

I felt sick as I headed into the kitchen, suddenly frightened at what I might see, but Mum was exactly as she always is, friendly and bossy and nagging and not listening to anyone. The four of us sat down at the table and started on Mum's delicious roast.

Me:    Mum, this is lovely, thank you.

Mum:   You're welcome, dear. Now, have you thought about where you're going to put the baby? When Susie came home with the twins she didn't have a bed ready for them at all! I hope you'll be a bit more organised than that.

Thom:  Well, we've ordered the cot now, to arrive in April. We won't put it up straight away –

Me:    I'm too superstitious.

Thom:  – but that'll take five minutes when the baby's actually born.

Dad:   And I can always help with that, while you two are at the hospital.

Mum:   And are you driving there?

Thom: Depends on the time of day, and how fast the contractions are. If it's rush hour, I might encourage Kiki to walk. It's meant to be really good for speeding up contractions.

Me: [nodding sagely]

Mum: Well, I hope you're going to be more organised about the whole thing than your sister Susie. Do you remember when the twins came home, they didn't even have a bed to sleep in!

Dad caught my eye then, and I put my fork and knife down on my plate and closed my eyes for a second. What was going on here? Thom carried on the conversation as if nothing had happened.

Thom: We've got the cot on the way, so I think we'll be alright. Fingers crossed.

Mum: Are you alright, Kiki?

Me: [opening eyes] Oh, yeah, sorry Mum. Just a really big kick. It's really squirming in there. Mum, I'm so sorry, do you mind if I just lie down for a minute? My stomach's shrinking every day. Only from the inside, obviously.

Mum: Of course, love. Do you want to go upstairs or on the sofa?

She fussed around me in her Mum-ish way, and wouldn't sit back down to her meal until I was safely stowed on my bed upstairs, the embroidered blanket she'd made for me when I was little tucked up to my chin. I didn't know what was wrong with her, but I was frightened when I imagined all the things it *could* be.

Thom came up after they'd finished their main course, and I told him what Dad had told me. 'We don't know what's going on, none of us. I think your dad's being really sensible taking her in. Then you'll all know, and if anything needs doing, everyone can start doing it. Come and have some pudding, Keeks. It's crumble. With your mum's custard.'

Since he was right about Mum, and since it *was* crumble and custard, I leapt out of bed (stepped gracelessly) and raced downstairs (slowly) to find Mum serving me, smiling. 'Feeling better, darling? Poor thing, you must be tired out by that baby by now.'

Lovely Mum. I wish I could appreciate you this much all the time.

February's Classic Baby

And, please God, just let me stay out of trouble until June!

Only till June! By that month Scarlett knew she would be forced to retire into Aunt Pitty's house and remain secluded there until after her child was born. Already people were criticizing her for appearing in public when she was in such a condition. No lady ever showed herself when she was pregnant. Already Frank and Pitty were begging her not to expose herself – and them – to embarrassment and she had promised them to stop work in June.

Only till June! By June she must have the mill well enough established for her to leave it. By June she must have money enough to give her at least some little protection against misfortune. So much to do and so little time to do it! She wished for more hours of the day and counted the minutes, as she strained forward feverishly in her pursuit of money and still more money.

*Gone with the Wind*
Margaret Mitchell

February 1st

First proper yoga class; lying down and breathing in a warm, dimly lit room. But my calm spirit has been bludgeoned to pieces on checking my email.

Of course. Of course this would happen. Of course it would. Why would I not have expected this?

A message from Annie.

From: anniehearts2000@hotmail.com
To: Kiki Carlow
Subject: GREAT NEWS!!!!!!!!

Hi Kiki!

Your mum told my mum that you're pregnant, due in May! Guess what! Us too!! I'm SO SO SO excited, Kiki – let's meet up next week to have a lovely baby chat about everything! We can compare dates and sizes and movement and everything!!!!

114

Lots of lots of baby dust,
Annie ; )

I rang Mum immediately.

Me:     You *did* tell Annie's mum that I was pregnant!

Mum:   Oh dear, was it a secret? I rather think people might
        have noticed soon, particularly when you turned up
        to events with a baby.

Me:     Are you . . . Is that sarcasm?

Mum:   You children think you invented it.

Me:     Mum! You're being . . . *funny*.

Mum:   It does happen from time to time.

Me:     Fine. But please don't tell Annie's mum anything
        about my life. Annie's pregnant too and now she
        wants us to Share The Journey together. She'll prob-
        ably try to make a website about it.

Mum:   She already has. Her mother gave me the details, I'll
        dig it out for you.

Me:     Please don't. At least this way I can plead
        ignorance.

Mum:   And next time I see Judy, I shall plead the State Secret
        Act.

Me:     Who are you and what have you done with my real
        Mum?

Mum:   Have a nice day, Kiki.

I love it when Mum's like that. And I know it's ridiculous to expect her not to talk about her daughter's breeding
– what else are mothers going to talk about? Politics?
Global warming? Their hopes and dreams? – but the
thought of Annie now being yet another thing I have to
crowbar into my life because of this pregnancy – along
with yoga classes, getting fatter, antenatal classes and

having to raise a child – makes me feel fractionally less welcoming to this foetus. Sorry. But it does.

Speaking of which, the antenatal classes are now all booked, starting in March. I've had another of those growth spurts, so I'm suddenly so utterly, unmistakably pregnant that I'm glad to have them so soon, but for the amount they cost I'm kind of hoping they include childcare for the first six months. The woman I spoke to reassured me that I would find them incredibly useful, and they were worth every penny; I bet she would say that, though, while she rolls around in used fifties in their head office. She kept calling it a 'Mums' Group' too, which curdled my enjoyment of my efficiency too. When I think of modern mothers, I picture Elle and Stella and Gwyneth and Gwen. But the term 'Mums' Group' makes me feel like I'm becoming . . . well . . . *Mum*. And no one needs that when they're twenty-seven.

The class is only around the corner from us, so hopefully anyone we meet will be easy enough to stay in touch with. Although . . . God. I've just realised the flipside of that. I'll have to see these people *all the time* afterwards. Maybe I can just send Thom to the classes.

February 4th

The Noses over to dinner tonight – Nick and Rose; the former, my good friend from uni, the latter, his now-wife who joined our circle later. We'd somehow booked the date before I realised it was Susie's birthday, too, so missed drinks out with her and Pete. We hadn't seen the Noses since their wedding last year (which was beautiful but soulless) because they'd been one of the casualties of our busy-ness the last few months, and didn't even know if news of my pregnancy had reached them. I was looking forward to catching up on everything. When I opened the door in one of Suse's shape-less preg dresses, I saw that Nick had put on around two stone, and he didn't look happy.

The four of us exchanged handshakes and hugs, and we brought them in from the cold.

Me:    It's been so long since we saw you, not since your wedding!

Rose:   Yes, that's – how long now?

Nick:   [immediately] Eight months and two weeks.

Me:    [nervous laughter] And our wedding too, of course! Sorry!

Rose:   We were working out our anniversaries earlier.

Thom: Right, what can I get everyone to drink?

Rose:   Do you have any white, please?

Nick:   Whatever, thanks Thom.

Me:    Just a soda for me, please. Thanks, Thom.

Nick:   Not drinking tonight, Kiki?

Me:    [always hating this bit] I . . .

Thom: She's pregnant, would you believe it? So I'm afraid we've had to cancel the MDMA main course.

Rose:   Pregnant? [looks at Nick, who looks back at her, with frozen faces]

There was a beat or two as they looked at me properly for the first time, before Rose recovered and came over to me, hugging me and congratulating us both. Nick followed.

Nick:   Well done, well done! That was . . . [faltering] quick.

Me:    Is it gross to say it was slightly accidental? Not that we'll say that to the baby, obviously.

Rose dropped my hand and moved across to the armchair opposite me and Nick, and Thom disappeared to get the drinks. Nick stayed beside me, chatting determinedly about his work and their new house. They moved from a flat to a house shortly after the wedding (Rose's dad had provided a huge deposit) and are having the worst time with plumbers and builders as they redo the whole downstairs (also on Rose's dad's bill).

Sitting down over food, Thom asked Rose if she looked forward to the house being finished.

Rose:   Well, I look forward to all those workers being out of the house, but I don't know if it'll ever be really finished. I can already see how I'd like things to have been done differently.

Nick:   [trying to make a joke] Rose knows what she likes!

Rose:   [silently staring at her plate]

Nick:   She's worked really hard on the house, haven't you? I don't know where we'd be without her!

Rose:   In your old flat?

Nick:   Hahaha! Haha! Yes, back in that old flat. But we've both worked hard, haven't we? And I can work harder, if that would help?

Rose:   [slowly drawing with her fork on her plate]

Nick:   Would it? Would that help, Rose?

Rose just shrugged, and I wanted desperately to lock myself in the bathroom. But when I announced that I'd just be back in a minute, Thom's narrowed eyes fixed me where I was. 'It's OK, it can wait,' I muttered.

Thom:   How's your work at the moment, Rose?

Rose:   Terrible. I really want to leave, but . . .

Nick:   Well, hopefully I can keep Rose in the manner which she deserves! I keep telling her to just stop, but she sticks at it. She's no quitter, are you, Rose?

Rose:   [staring at the table again]

Nick:   Rose? Rose, you're not a quitter, are you?

Rose:   Is that all you think it takes?

Nick:   Well, we can both keep trying, can't we? I can work harder. I can do whatever you think would help. But you don't just give up, do you?

Rose:   [to us] Excuse me, I need the bathroom.

The whole meal was a nightmare, with Rose refusing to speak for the final half hour, and I felt as exhausted as they both looked by the time they left at 11.

Me:     We *really* need to stop having those guys over.

Thom:  I think they were just upset.

Me:     I think you mean horrified.

Thom:  No, I mean upset. Couldn't you tell? Maybe they want a baby.

Me:     [laughing] Ah, bless you Victorian Husband. Not everyone wants to get knocked up on their honeymoon.

Thom:  No, but some people do. We did.

Me:     For ONE NIGHT.

Thom:  Well, anyway. I think it was just a shock, and they were a bit sad.

Me:     Even if you're right, do you think that's all it was?

Thom:  How on earth would I know?

Apparently he can turn those mind-reading super powers on and off. I hope they're OK, though. What a crummy time.

February 6th

Thom and I started going through some of the things we'd need, and trying to work out what we wouldn't. Even being as brutal as possible – no bouncers or walkers or baby baths – our flat is still going to be overwhelmed. It's a one-bed that fits us perfectly. How we're going to get in a cot, buggy, and entire child's wardrobe is beyond me.


February 7th

Susie and I were over at Mum's tonight – Dad was at an Open Evening at the college – and while they were making drinks and some kind of Healthy Fruit Dish for us in the kitchen, I was flicking around the TV and stumbled across an old episode of *One Born Every Minute*, the Channel 4 documentary featuring different births every week. I was immediately sucked in by the woman I saw, panting and wincing as her husband larked around the birthing room, but gasped aloud when her son joined them for the birth.

Me:     [calling through] Mum, if you had another kid now, would you want me or Susie in the room with you?
Mum:   [calling back] What on earth are you talking about?
Me:     Alright, if we were boys, would you want us to see you giving birth?

For a moment, I could just hear them muttering in the kitchen, then suddenly Susie was next to me.

Susie:  [trying to wrestle the remote off me] Mum! Quick! She's trying to watch *One Born Every Minute*!
Mum    [rushing in, standing in front of the TV] Kiki, darling, you don't want to watch that do you? I'm sure we can find something much nicer.
Susie:  [to Mum, out of the side of her mouth] I think this is the one with the . . . *tearing*.

120

| | |
|---|---|
| Mum: | Come on now! Shall we watch something a little more fun? Oooh look, there's a new *Top Gear* on the other channel! |
| Me and Susie: | *Mum!* |
| Mum: | Sorry, you two are making me panic. Not that – shall we watch a film? Something a little more . . . gentle? |
| Susie: | Something with a lot fewer people putting their forearms into other people? |
| Me: | Well, there go all my suggestions. What's wrong with this? It's going to happen to me, you know. |
| Mum: | Yes, but . . . you don't want to see it like this, do you? |
| Me: | I'm not sure I want to see it from any angle, but this will at least prepare me. |
| Mum: | I don't think you want to watch other women giving birth this close to your own dates. |
| Susie: | These women scream. They cry. They spill blood and deliver placenta and demand pain relief before they've even booked in. Believe me, you do NOT want to watch this. |

Two hours later, Thom came to pick me up to drive me home. He found the three of us sobbing on the sofa, holding hands and watching the TV through our tears.

| | |
|---|---|
| Me: | Thom. Birth is *so* beautiful. |
| Susie: | It's a miracle. I think I want another one. |
| Thom: | Have you three just been watching this all evening? |
| Me: | It was a whole night of old episodes. |
| Mum: | You're a very lucky man, to be experiencing |

121

this amazing marvel. To think of these two as babies in my arms, all those years ago. How magical that time was.

An hour after that, Dad arrived back to find me on Thom's lap, all four of us still on the sofa, all crying.

Dad: What's happened? Are you all OK? [looking at TV] Oh, it's this! Sorry, can't watch it – I cry every time.

We finally managed to get home, driving with puffy eyes, and we were filled with excitement for what was ahead of us. Although we might need a camera crew and experienced editor to fully replicate the magic.

February 8th

Yoga again tonight. A special treat for everyone, as a stand-in teacher decided to give us some breathing exercises to help us with the 'strong sensation' of labour. She made us balance our whole weight just on our flattened toes, and challenged us to see how long we could stay in that position for. When one of the others asked if she'd found the exercise useful in her labour, she smiled sweetly and said, 'I've not had children of my own, but working as a doula for many years now, I've seen time and again how this preparation can help the spirit and the body ready itself.' I wanted to throw my shoes at her. I'll show her 'strong sensations'. If this class doesn't revert to lying around, I'm going to want my money back.

TO DO:
Practise some lying around at home until normal classes resume

February 14th

Valentine's day. In what might be the cutest thing I've ever seen, Carol and Norman were glowing at one another, all winks and repressed smiles around the office.

Alice: [smiling] Those two are unbearable.
Me: You don't even mean that.
Alice: No, I don't. But saying how adorable they are will utterly destroy my image as a heartless vixen.
Me: Ah, I thought I saw you going through our bins last night.
Alice: [raising an eyebrow] Yes, I was after the secret of your happiness.
Me: I'll give you a clue: it involves a *lot* of equipment. And most of it we had to order on the internet.
Alice: You're disgusting.
Me: Am I still disgusting when I give you . . . these? [pulls out a bunch of anemones and a box of chocolates]
Alice: Oh! Keeks! Are these Pity Valentines?
Me: [indignant] No they are not –
Alice: Because I could not be more delighted!
Me: Well. I just wanted to say that I love you too.
Alice: I didn't say I loved you. No offence, but married pregnants just aren't my type.

But she was pleased, and I was pleased too, since she'd got me a tiny little heart-shaped gateau. I'll miss my office-wife so much when I'm on leave.

Meanwhile, back in my real marriage, I planned a meal for Thom. I'd got all the ingredients, prepped them to within an inch of their lives, set the duck and potatoes to roast, the chocolate to melt over simmering water, and sat down to rest for a second.

Like a perfect magic trick, I opened my eyes a moment later to find Thom standing over me with a smoking fire extinguisher, saying, 'Kiki? Kiki? Can you hear me? Keeks!'

Me:     I'm awake, I'm awake. What are you doing?

Thom:  Saving your life.

Me:     How did you get in?

Thom:  With my key. It's me, *Thom*. Did you hit your head?

Me:     No, I didn't, I sat down for two seconds to catch my breath. What's that smell?

Thom:  The hot contents of this fire extinguisher. How long ago did you sit down?

Me:     A second ago, I just said. Are you drunk?

Thom:  No, but I'm beginning to wonder if you are. What happened to dinner?

Me:     Nothing, I'm just waiting for you to get home.

Thom:  Are you awake yet?

Me:     Not really. I've still got absolutely no idea what's going on.

Thom:  Hang on. [goes away, comes back with glass of water and a biscuit] Don't look at me like that, it'll do for now. Right. It's now 8 o'clock. I got home at 7.45, half an hour earlier than I'd been expecting. I came through the front door to find a house full of smoke and neither hide nor hair of you. I grabbed the fire extinguisher that I can't believe we actually have, or that it really works –

Me:     Worked.

Thom:  Quite. And turned it on the oven. It seems we may need some new roasting tins and a saucepan.

Me:     Oh no! Did you ruin dinner?

Thom:  Yes, Kiki. *I* ruined dinner.

124

Me:    What would you say to a takeaway instead, my
       romantic partner in crime?
Thom:  I would say as long as I don't have to find the plates
       in that kitchen, that sounds like a very good idea.

It seems I might have nodded off a little, and the duck
and the potatoes and the simmering pan of water may have
slightly . . . blackened. But nothing was actually on fire! So
there's good news! The flat stinks, though, but because the
hall window was open I didn't actually breathe anything in.
Hurray! Happy endings all around.

TO DO:
Plan something utterly safe for next year's Valentine's
Probably only dare to cook Pot Noodle once there's a tiny
   infant in the flat


February 17th

Matthew Holt came into the office today, to go through
the latest manuscript of *The Ice Dragon*. It's definitely
getting better, I have to give it to him, although there are
still some fairly hefty inaccuracies popping up here and
there. Which is more than I can say for Jennifer Luck's
first book to be published, *Nude in New York*. It's charm-
less, boring and implausible; I can't even begin to fathom
why Tony signed her up for four books, nor what kind of
notes he must have provided her for this updated version
to be somehow worse.

TO DO:
Go on maternity leave now?

February 22nd

Hurray! Last night's yoga was back to the good old days, and relaxed me so much that I *even* agreed to meet Annie. Oh yoga, you have so much to answer for in the world.

She's sent me four messages, with ever-increasing tones of desperation and hurt, so I thought if I finally met her for a coffee she'd realise she's knocking at a long-boarded-up house and leave me alone. I just don't see why I should have to share the most intimate details of something that's still curled around my internal organs, just because I once went to school with her. It's psychological torment.

I chose somewhere neutral, a coffee shop sort-of equidistant between me in North Finchley and her in Gerrards Cross. She bumbled in shortly after I arrived, all comfortable shoes and fun necklace, and gave me a big hug, our gently bulging stomachs bumping against each other.

Annie: You look fantastic! How do you feel! Have you felt little Baby move yet?

Me: [uncomfortable] Yeah, yeah, it's really moving now.

Annie: And do you have a name for it?

Me: Oh, Thom and I've talked a bit but haven't really settled on a name. I think we'll wait to see how it looks when it's born.

Annie: Oh no! I meant a name for while it's inside you! We've named this one Buglet.

Me: W – oh, that's nice. [clenching fists under table] No, no, it's just That Baby, I suppose. I didn't think we needed to come up with something else already. [trying to make a joke] Have you got the outfit picked for when it's born too?

Annie: Well, of course it depends what colour it is! We've

got a beautiful pink outfit for a girl Buglet, and a lovely blue and white one for a boy Buglet.

Me: Oh, you really do. Oh, that's so nice to get so excited and make these plans, isn't it? I feel like Thom and I have just been so busy, with the wedding and my new job, and Thom's new job, that we just haven't had much of a chance to think about this kind of thing. I know we need to!

Annie: [concerned] Yes, you do. What'll happen when the baby's born and you haven't got anything for it to wear? What would it sleep in?

Me: Oh, we've got a couple of my old t-shirts and some well-ventilated drawers in the wardrobe. I'm sure we could find something.

Annie: [shocked] You wouldn't really put the baby in the wardrobe, would you, Kiki?

Me: No. No, I'm sure you're right, Annie, that's probably not best.

And so the long, long hour continued. As we'd agreed, Thom rang with An Emergency, so I had to leave sooner than I'd have liked, and Annie was disappointed (again) but understanding. With her final hug, she giggled, 'Well, now we know where to meet, it'll be so much easier next time, won't it!' Then she looked at me a bit oddly, which must have been my eye starting to twitch, but I was at least allowed to leave.

I got home at five, completely exhausted and feeling entirely uncharitable towards Annie and her foetus. Thom was sitting merrily marking essays, without a care in the world.

Thom: How did it go? Are we going to rent a hologram birthing tub for two?

Me: [hissing] *Oh God does that exist?*

Thom: I'd imagine not. What *happened* to you there? Did she make you look at photos of her birth canal?

Me: Stop saying these things! You'll only give her ideas.

Thom: Uh . . . I don't think she can hear us.

Me: Yeah. That's just what she wants us to think.

Thom pulled me onto his lap without winding himself, and promised me that I wouldn't have to see her again if I didn't want to. He swore that he'd tell her I'd been sent to Guatemala for work if she kept calling.

Me: But why do I have to see her at all? No one's calling you up out of the blue to say, 'Hey, someone's carrying my baby – we should hang out now!' Why isn't anyone doing that to you? Why is this something I would want to do just because we have functioning wombs in common? Can that be all? I mean . . . Quick, name a female dictator.

Thom: Mrs Hitler?

Me: No.

Thom: Um . . . Oh, Lucrezia Borgia.

Me: Controversial. But my point is, I wouldn't want to share an iced bun with Lucrezia Borgia just because she's due to push a baby out in three months' time. Don't you agree?

Thom: Yes, Kiki. I agree it would be monstrous to expect you to have tea with Lucrezia Borgia.

Me: [narrowing eyes] Are you humouring me?

Thom: One wouldn't *dare*.

But if even Thom says I'm excused from Annie, I should just be able to relax. Shouldn't I?

February 23rd

Eve, at last. I was on my lunch break, rushing to pick up a present for Alice's birthday, when I bumped into her. She was chatting to a man as they came out of a restaurant, and she looked like she'd seen me and tried to pretend she hadn't.

Me:     [hackles up] Eve.
Eve:    [turning round] Oh, hi Kiki! [giving me huge hug] I'm sorry I haven't got back to you, it's been crazy. [turning to man] Hasn't it? Listen, John, do you mind if we move the meeting this afternoon? I'm afraid I must attend to this. Tell them it's some kind of charity emergency?

The man she was with smiled at us and nodded, as Eve bundled us back into the restaurant they'd just left. She bought us a jug of something non-alcoholic and apologised again for her silence, keeping us there for an hour after I'd texted Alice to please cover for me.

Why do I want to assume the worst about Eve? Haven't I learnt my lesson yet?

TO DO:
Stop feeling guilty. That's the whole joy of New Eve.

February 29th

Someone actually went into labour in tonight's yoga class. Well, their waters broke. But it was nothing like in films – no one ran about panicking before we all had to decide who was going to deliver the baby, born mere moments later. She just looked a bit surprised and confused, until the teacher said, 'I think your waters have broken, Jilly.' But she seemed fine – no contractions, no pain. She made a half-gesture of trying to mop up the puddle (again, hardly the seven litres splashed around in a soap opera) before we all shooed her on her way; the teacher gave her a towel to sit on, and she drove herself back home to meet her boyfriend and drive on to hospital together.

And that, ladies and gentlemen, was our drama for the night.

When I told Thom, he said, 'Hey, if it starts in your yoga class, does that mean one of them will just go with you? Will you just call me when it's done?' I had to break it to him that we'd sent that poor woman on her way solo, so his responsibilities would, sadly, not be shirked.


I can't wait for someone to explain to me why I still feel uneasy about *A Womb of One's Own*. It's not just the terrible writing or the hideous message – nothing can possibly be as important or creative as pushing a baby out – it's something else. But until that something else reveals itself, I shall just enjoy vicariously living the life of a super-wealthy mother.

TO DO:
Don't look too closely at how much cashmere Bill Jnr will
   be wearing

## March's Classic Baby

Later, when the time for the baby grew nearer, he would bustle round in his slovenly fashion, poking out the ashes, rubbing the fireplace, sweeping the house before he went to work.

Then, feeling very self-righteous, he went upstairs.

Now I'm cleaned up for thee: tha's no 'casions ter stir a peg all day, but sit and read thy books.'

Which made her laugh, in spite of her indignation.

'And the dinner cooks itself?' she answered.

'Eh, I know nowt about th' dinner.'

'You'd know if there weren't any.'

'Ay, 'appen so,' he answered, departing.

*Sons and Lovers*
D. H. Lawrence

March 1st

Alice is very careful to keep her family out of her life as much as possible. She lives with Gareth to hide the fact she's gay, and she avoids big Hamilton parties to hide the fact she's a secret liberal. Seeing her these last few months, saddened by her ex and questioning the quality of her life as it is now, has broken my heart. She reassures me regularly that she's just saving up to tell her parents – or at least one of them, she reassures me – although with her deadpan manner, it's really hard to tell.

Sometimes, that time just comes.

This afternoon, Alice and I had just come out of a meeting with Raff Welles, a TV star of yesteryear whose *AutobiogRaffy* had done surprisingly well last year, so whose paperback launch in May we were giving renewed attention to. We were giving him his usual reassurances and praise after the meeting when we heard what seemed like a familiar clattering up the stairs of our building.

Me:            Pamela's not due in today, is she?

| | |
|---|---|
| Alice: | [staring at the stairway, frozen] Mum? Dad? |
| Mrs Hamilton: | Alice, darling! Come and give your mother a kiss. |
| Raff: | [looking between Alice and her parents] Right, many thanks, I'll . . . I'll see myself out, shall I? Goodbye, my darlings! [shuffles downstairs] |

I'd never seen Alice like this before. She was completely at a loss.

| | |
|---|---|
| Mrs Hamilton: | [becoming insistent] *Alice*, *come* and *kiss* your mother. |
| Mr Hamilton: | [stern] Alice. |
| Alice: | [quietly, turning to me] Kiki, you cannot leave me alone with them. |
| Me: | Are you OK? |
| Mrs Hamilton: | [starting to whine] Come on, darling? |
| Alice: | Hello, you two. |
| Mr Hamilton: | Hello, Alice. Now, I won't take no for an answer, I'm taking you to Harvey Nicks for lunch. Come on, my girl. |
| Alice: | Oh, Dad, that's really kind, but I've got a lot to cover with Kiki and we were planning on a working lunch today. I'm so sorry – are you around later? |
| Mr Hamilton: | Nonsense, she can come along too. The more the merrier. You come along too – Kiki, was it? Come along, we've got a taxi waiting outside. |

Alice nodded at me, so we both grabbed our bags and coats and followed them back down the stairs to the taxi, and sat in silence all the way to Knightsbridge, Mr Hamilton looking triumphantly out of the window while Alice's mother searched her handbag for something. Outside Harvey Nichols, I was the last to step out of the taxi and Mrs Hamilton suddenly noticed my pregnant state, worrying that maybe I shouldn't have ridden in a cab, or that I should be sitting down again, or that maybe I wouldn't be able to eat anything on the menu. 'Nonsense,' Alice's father reassured her. 'She's as strong as an ox, aren't you, my girl.'

At the Fifth Floor restaurant, he took our coats fussily and made a great show of demanding the very best table as he bundled our coats into the greeter's arms. When we were seated at a perfectly good table, he looked about him, dissatisfied, and Alice squeezed my hand under the table. Her father ordered us the most expensive red wine on the menu and laced his fingers together, resting them on his stomach as he surveyed the surroundings.

| | |
|---|---|
| Mr Hamilton: | Well, girls. How's the work? |
| Alice: | Kiki's actually off on maternity leave soon, Dad. |
| Mr Hamilton: | Are they sad to lose you? |
| Me: | Well, it's only for eight months, so I think they can survive without me for that long. |
| Mr Hamilton: | Oh, right, I *see*. What business is your husband in? |
| Me: | Teaching. Secondary English, to be precise. |
| Mrs Hamilton: | And does he think he'll do that . . . forever? |
| Alice: | [jumping in] Mum, Dad, sorry to interrupt. I just wanted to let you know that I'm gay. [silence] |
| Mr Hamilton: | Nonsense, my girl, what's all this really about? |
| Alice: | [quietly] Dad, it's about me liking women. I'm sure you've heard of that kind of thing before. |

134

| | |
|---|---|
| Mrs Hamilton: | Don't be rude to your father, dear. |
| Alice: | I'm not being rude. I thought it was rude not to tell you. |
| Mr Hamilton: | Why are you trying to ruin this perfectly nice lunch, Alice? |
| Alice: | I'm not. I just thought maybe you would like to know a little bit about your daughter, that's all. |
| Mr Hamilton: | [to waitress hovering over us] Just *leave the bloody wine*, we're not ready to order. |
| Mrs Hamilton: | [loudly] Well, I don't know if *she'll* be getting a tip. |
| Mr Hamilton: | Where's all this come from? Is this something to do with your friend here? |
| Me: | [opening mouth] |
| Alice: | Yes, my friend is pregnant so I thought I'd be gay for a while. |
| Mrs Hamilton: | Alice, do *not* be cheeky to your father. |
| Alice: | I'm sorry, Mum, but do you not want me to say this? Would you rather not know? |
| Mr Hamilton: | I've rather lost my appetite. Tamasin, we're leaving. Now. |

They pushed themselves from the table, loudly demanding their coats. I saw Mr Hamilton grab the coats from the waitress, pluck his and his wife's from the pile and drop ours onto the floor, before shouldering his way into the lift.

I gave Alice a hug and brushed her hair out of her face, pouring her a large glass of red.

| | |
|---|---|
| Me: | Drink. How are you feeling? |
| Alice: | I'm so sorry, Keeks, I didn't mean for it to play out that way. I had that teenage feeling, that if I had a friend with me they couldn't be as cross as they would |

135

otherwise. I was just suddenly so . . . tired of them not knowing. Sorry. I'm feeling relief. Anger. Relief. Disappointment. Relief. Guilt.

Me:      Relief?
Alice:   Yeah, let's hit the town and pick up some hot dames!
Me:      Really?
Alice:   No. But let's at least eat while we're here.
Me:      That sounds lovely.

But she was quite quiet for the rest of the meal, and it didn't last long. She asked me to just talk at her, while I did reluctantly in case it kicked off the full-blown transformation into *my* mother, but had a flash of enormous gratitude for my own lovely parents. From the little Alice did say, she's so happy that she's told them, but feels crummy about every other aspect of it. And she insisted on paying for lunch before they cut her off. 'There's only so much gold a girl can keep in her bank vault, Kiki,' she warned. 'I'm going to have to actually find out where my wages are paid into now.'


March 2nd

Alice seemed OK this morning, but still quiet. Was there something I could have done differently, something I could have said to make her feel better? She looked after me so well when she found out about me being pregnant, and I don't want to let her down now. Oh, poor Alice. And those silly, foolish Hamiltons.

Lucie Martel arrives with her new son Bill Jnr and their entire support staff tonight. Alice is meeting them at the airport – I offered to go for her, but she just looked at my stomach and flared her nostrils – before showing them to the apartment we've rented for them, for her fortnight's stay.

Besides Bill Jnr and his nanny, she's also bringing her own assistant, her personal doctor, and her dietician. Which sounds fun.

We'll have breakfast with her tomorrow to settle her schedule and check any last minute details.

TO DO:
Go and see Mum and Dad, hug them
Work out how to lessen the weirdness of me being pregnant but not having mentioned it to Lucie before

March 5th

Breakfast with Lucie Martel was exactly as much fun as I'd been hoping. In the middle of our breakfast of mango and granola in her apartment, she had to leave us for a call from her husband. She closed the door to her study, but we could still hear her raised voice. 'No, I'm sorry Bill, that's unacceptable. No. Well he's your son too! . . . Jesus Christ, Bill, you couldn't even make the birth and now you're away for his christening? . . . No, *you* need to think very carefully about this. I'll call you later.' There was the sound of a smashing cup, a moment's silence, then the study doors drew back open and Lucie was striding towards us, smiling peaceably. 'Sorry, ladies, just some crossed wires with my husband. All sorted now!' She turned to me.

Lucie:  Kiki, I see you're pregnant! Have you made all your plans?
Me:     Well, some, but not much. We've chosen the hospital. And we're thinking about names.
Alice:  Oh, are you? What have you got?
Lucie:  No no no, Kiki, you'll need to do better than that,

137

I'm afraid! If you aren't prepared, if you don't know exactly what you want – well, that's when things go wrong.

Me: Really?

Lucie: Trust me. Go back to the drawing board, and plan everything out. It's the only way to get the birth you want.

Really not sure what kind of advice that is, but we managed to wrap up the meeting fairly quickly and Lucie's pleased with everything Alice has set up. I was able to leave them to it, and head back to the office. As well as working on further edits to *Nude in New York*, I've *still* got to track down erotic genius Stuart Winton.

## March 6th

I know Eve's got such a busy time at work at the moment, so was really pleased when the phone rang today and it was her.

Eve: Kiki?

Me: Eve! How *are* you? *Where* are you? How's work?

Eve: My mum just called. Dad's dead.

Me: *Your* dad?

Eve: Yup.

Me: Are you OK?

Eve: Yup.

Me: How did he die?

Eve: Pancreatic cancer.

Me: Do you want me to come over?

Eve: No, it's OK, Mike's here. But thank you.

Me: Will you go to the funeral?

Eve:    I suppose so. Will you?

Me:    If you want me to, of course.

Eve:    I'll send you details. Talk later.

And that was it.

Eve's dad was always a class-A bastard, hence her apparent lack of grief. He'd left her and her mum when Eve was six, and shacked up with a new wife almost immediately, so I'd only ever known him from photographs; as far as I knew, Eve hadn't had anything to do with him in the intervening years, and her mum never mentioned him either. But poor Eve. I'll be glad to go with her, and at least I know her and Mike are still together (my major concern when it comes to Eve).

## March 7th

I've been worrying so much about Alice these last few days. Coming out to her parents seems to have really knocked her, but she came into work this morning beaming and bouncing.

Me:    What's happened to *you*?

Alice:  Gareth and I broke up.

Me:    Hey! That's great news!

Alice:  I know. It was *amazing*.

Me:    How did he take it?

Alice:  He was delighted for me. I do adore him – if only he was a bit more of a female, I'd be made. And he was always very cooperative about moving his stuff around when my parents visited. I suppose I shall miss him.

Me:    Well, then I'm a little bit sorry about your break-up. Will he stay there?

Alice:   He will for a while, until he finds something else. But there's no hurry – I've grown so used to his company, but I've got no rent worries when he's off either. Thank *Christ* I had the sense to insist Daddy put the deed in my name, though, or Gareth and I could both be homeless.

Me:      Well, this calls for a toast.

Alice:   I'll get the teas in.

Me:      Can I ask, though – have you heard from your parents?

Alice:   Ugh. No. Well, I had a call from my cousin Richard, congratulating me and telling me that he had a civil ceremony with his partner last year, which none of our branch knew about, so I assume at least one of them is broadcasting the news. His wing of the family always have been a lot more fun. [to herself] I bet that was a bloody *brilliant* party. Dammit.

Me:      Well. If you want me to post them some Jeanette Winterson or something, just let me know.

Alice:   [widens eyes] Yes. I'm sure that's what they need.

But she stayed happy all day, smiling and sunny.

She's worked her magic again on *A Womb of One's Own*, too, getting amazing coverage. We've got a piece in *Grazia* ('Motherhood, Manhattan-style'), while the *Daily Mail* has gone with a 'How modern women don't take childbirth seriously enough' headline. The *Guardian* has got an interview with her, with the journalist bravely wondering whether Lucie is particularly representative of most women's pregnancy experience, and even *Woman's Hour* is involved, doing a piece with her this morning on 'Can you buy a good pregnancy?' This is some of the best coverage since Jacki's wedding book – there's something about Lucie and her book that really pushes the media's buttons. So we can't complain:

pre-orders have been fantastic and even the supermarkets have ordered over ten thousand copies. Hopefully her success might cancel out any forgettable performance from my other new authors.


March 10th

I would like to phone the police, but I'm unsure how I'd really phrase my complaint.

Well you see, officer, what happened was, I was sitting at home this evening, editing a manuscript and hoping Thom (my husband) was having a nice night out with his teaching pals, when my house phone rang. It rings approximately once a week, officer, and it's always either my mum, Thom's mum (my mother-in-law, you see), or cold callers, and since Thom wasn't there to be amused, there was no point in putting on any kind of ridiculous voice to scare off the cold callers (always a gamble when it might be one of the mums). So imagine my bafflement to find that not only was it neither of the mums, but it was also not a cold caller – instead – and this is where you might need to make notes, officer – instead, it was a girl I once went to school with, many years ago, but have only seen twice since then, at her own wedding and over a recent coffee. No, we didn't invite her to our wedding, officer. Because – well, if you'll just allow me to continue, you'll understand that our decision was entirely understandable.

So it was this girl – woman – on the phone. Let us call her Annie, since it's her name. Annie was on the phone, saying that, Could I believe it, but she was in the area, and she had my number – no, I've no idea how she got it, officer – and she was wondering if I was around for another cup of coffee? I'm sure you are ahead of me in one key matter: since it was the house phone she called me on, I couldn't even say I was out somewhere and not free. Instead, I had to admit that Yes, how lucky! I was home tonight, of course I'd be free for a coffee, and confirmed my address for her.

Within seconds, officer – seconds – my doorbell rang. There I was hoping that perhaps my husband had returned early from his night out, but imagine my horror when the door creaked inwards – no, you may not actually have noticed the creak when you came in, it only really does it for particularly unwelcome guests – and Annie was standing there, with a basket on one arm and a bunch of flowers in the other. Yes, officer, they were for me, and no, officer, they didn't contain any concealed weapons. Although they *were* sunflowers. Yes. Exactly.

On letting her into our place of abode, she then proceeded to 'make herself at home', putting the flowers in a vase she found, and setting out the contents of the basket on the sofa, while I made her the hot drink that had been requested of me. As we drank our hot drinks – no, she didn't throw it at me, officer, can I just get to the end? – she then showed me all the baby clothes she'd brought for us, that they'd been given but thought they already had so much, and maybe we, who were apparently so wildly underprepared, could use instead. Yes, it does seem very kind of her to bring those things over. No, officer, she didn't seem to want anything in return. Or at least – she didn't *seem* to.

Now we get to the heart of the matter. For it was indeed the fact that she wanted something. Many things. She wanted my time. She stayed at our home until 11 pm. *11 pm.* That's got to be some kind of misdemeanour. She wanted my attention – to stare and coo and marvel at these horrible pink and blue clothes like fabric blood-flow diagrams. And, sir, she wanted my friendship. And *that* she *shall not have*.

Yes, I know it was very kind of her. No, I'm sure she hasn't committed any actual crime. But she was in my house!

For hours! An entire evening I won't get back! And now I've got sunflowers in there! *Sunflowers*!

Yes. Yes. I understand, officer. Yes, I shan't call you again unless there's a genuine crime that's been committed. And no, not just a crime against good sense. No, or fashion. Yes, officer. No, officer. Well, if you think she sounds so lovely, I'm more than happy to hand her your details. No, officer. No, I won't do that. Thank you, officer.

So you see my predicament. What if she does it again? Which, now she knows she can, she will. Am I just going to stop answering the phone? Will I be sneaking into my house, in case she's waiting at the end of the street? What am I going to do with all the hideous baby clothes she's (with infinite kindness and generosity, I admit) given us? And why doesn't Thom ever have to deal with this kind of thing?

TO DO:
Change phone number
Move

March 16th

Eve, Mike and I drove up to the funeral together today. Eve's dad had moved to Forton, a little suburb of Birmingham with his second family, and where the service was being held. It was a beautiful day and we were roasting in our black clothes in the hot car.

Me:     How are you feeling?
Eve:    Hungry.
Me:     Tell me about it. Do you want to stop for a Burger King at the services?

143

Eve:     I said I was angry, you fucking idiot, not hungry.
Me:      [silent]
Eve:     I'm pissed off that we're having to do this. I don't think I owe that dickhead any more of my time than he took from my childhood already.
Me:      [silent]
Eve:     I'm sorry I'll have to face his stupid wife, and that his stupid friends won't even know who I am.
Me:      [silent]
Eve:     And yes, I could really fucking do with a Burger King.
Mike:    O-kay. Unfortunately, this is our exit.
Eve:     *Keep driving.*

Mike turned off his indicator and kept on the motorway until we came to the next service station. We pulled in and Eve jumped out, but was back in the car before we could even lock up, saying, 'No Burger King here. Let's try the next one.' So on we went, twenty-one miles up the motorway until we found what we wanted (eaten at the leisurely pace set by Eve), then twenty-one miles back to our original exit. Needless to say, we missed most of the service, filing into our pew in the crematorium as the last hymn was playing.

Eve:     [whispering] Oh good, time to go.
Me:      [whispering] Aren't we staying for the cocktails?
Eve:     [whispering] *Jesus.* They're not *cocktails*.
Me:      [whispering] What do I say then?
Eve:     [hissing] Kiki, it's a fucking *wake*.

But I had spotted the strangest thing. Sitting on the other side on the back row was an incredibly handsome young man, in his late teens or early twenties. But what was strange about it – besides the way he was staring at us – was how exactly he looked like Eve. Albeit an *extremely* handsome male Eve.

'Uh, Eve,' I said, but she'd already seen him.

| | |
|---|---|
| Eve: | [whispering] Oh shit. |
| Me: | [whispering] Who's *that*? |
| Eve: | [whispering] Well, if I'm going to make an educated guess . . . |
| Mike: | [leaning into our conversation, whispering] Why is that guy staring at us? And why's he got your face on, Eve? |
| Eve: | [hissing] I suspect that's probably my half-brother. |
| Me: | [whispering] Oh. |
| Mike: | [whispering] Oh. I didn't know you – |
| Eve: | [whispering] Neither did I. |
| Me: | [whispering] Oh shit, he's coming over. |
| Mike: | [whispering] Act casual. |
| Me: | [hysterical sniggering] |
| Young man: | [whispering] Are you Eve? |
| Eve: | [whispering] Yup. |
| Young man: | [whispering] I'm Alex. I'm your half-brother. |
| Eve: | [whispering] Nice to meet you. |
| Alex: | [whispering] This is almost finished. Do you want to go outside? |
| Eve: | [suspicious, normal volume] What for? |
| Alex: | [laughing, then looking solemn, whispering] To talk? Come on, let's go. |

We followed him outside while the hymn came to an end, and a voice rose and fell with the closing words.

145

Alex:   Hello.

Me:     [gushing] Hello I'm Kiki I'm Eve's friend.

Alex:   Hi Kiki, nice to meet you. Eve, I'm sorry that we're meeting like this.

Eve:    [not really looking at him] Are you?

Alex:   Dad told me all about you.

Eve:    [silent]

Alex:   Shall we go and get some drinks?

Me:     Yes!

Mike:   Uh . . . [gesturing to my stomach]

Me:     Oh, bloody *hell*. Fine. Mine's a half ahahaha! [laughing hysterically]

Mike:   He's gone, Keeks.

We looked towards the crematorium hall, where Eve had half-raced while Alex jogged to keep up with her.

Me:     [sighing] As if this day wasn't shitty enough for her.

Mike:   She's glad you're here, you know.

Me:     Will she still feel that way when she sees me and her brother grinding on the dance floor?

Mike:   Funerals don't have dance floors.

Me:     Tsk. Stupid funerals.

Mike put his arm through mine and we walked over to the hall.

Me:     How's she been since she heard?

Mike:   Strange. Angry, I think. I don't know everything that's gone on there, but I know she's cross to feel anything about his death. What do you think?

Me:     However cross she was before, she's going to feel a lot worse about having a brother she knew nothing about. Oh CHRIST. What if there's more of them? What if

146

there's a whole army of young Eves in there? What if his widow's got a newborn Eve in her arms?

We made it to the reception just as the service ended, so the mourners filled up the room and I got separated from everyone. I could see Eve standing at the drinks table, with an empty glass in one hand and a full one she was drinking from in the other, apparently just listening to Alex. I watched them there for a while, until some middle-aged woman accosted me and asked how I'd known the deceased. If I'd had any gumption at all, I would have said, 'Oh, he deserted his daughter when she was a child, before I became her best friend,' but one man's gumption is another man's scarring lack of tact at a funeral so I just mumbled, 'Eve,' and nodded over in her direction. The baby kicked at that point, and if there's one thing that's useful about it, pregnancy is one hell of an icebreaker. The woman was suddenly asking me a hundred questions, as if I was the first pregnant to have made it to this little village: was it my first? Did I feel it kick a lot? Had I chosen a name for it? I felt my usual flailing desperation to get away from the small talk, but I thought: what else am I going to do? And besides, this is good practice for when I'm a parent, as I'm pretty sure all parents do is stand around making small talk. So I let her interrogate me, hoping Eve and Alex might be bonding a little bit, but then I noticed he was next to me, offering me a 'very small' glass of wine which may or may not have gone to my very light-weight head, and I found myself enjoying an *excellent* conversation with Alex who was, it turned out, utterly fascinating and hilarious as well as being devastatingly handsome. But suddenly Eve was beside me, saying, 'Take your paws off my fucking brother. You're married, remember?' and bustling me away, waving goodbye to Alex and ignoring everyone else, stuffing me back into the car as Mike started the engine.

| | |
|---|---|
| Me: | [blinking] What just happened there? |
| Eve: | We just left my dead absent father's funeral. |
| Me: | I didn't even get to say goodbye to Alex! |
| Eve: | Jesus Christ. Stay classy, you pregnant booze hound. |
| Me: | I had one glass, Eve. |
| Eve: | Don't tell it to me, tell it to the police questioning you about harassing a minor. |
| Me: | I wish you'd turn around so you can see what I'm holding up. |
| Eve: | Well it certainly isn't the moral high ground. |
| Me: | I'm going to put this down to grief and shock. Wake me up when we're home, please. |

I think Eve and Alex bonded. I've never seen her protective over someone before. It's sort of . . . unnerving?

TO DO:
Find out if Eve can lend me some of her newly-discovered
   maternal instinct


March 18th

It was Lucie Martel's final day in the UK, and she wanted to meet me for breakfast before she flew out. I knew she'd taken Alice out the night before to say thank you, and I was happy to bid a personal goodbye to my author, particularly when she seemed to be doing so well for us. But when I arrived at her apartment, Lucie was crying so hard she couldn't speak.

| | |
|---|---|
| Me: | Lucie! What's wrong? Is Bill Jnr OK? |
| Lucie: | [hiccupping] Yes, he's (hic) fine. It's . . . |
| Me: | Let me get you a drink. What do you want? |

Lucie: A black . . . a black . . . [taking a halting deep breath]
a black coffee, please.

I poured the coffee and took it over to her: just taking
the cup seemed to calm her down a little.

Lucie: I owe you . . . (hic) an apology.
Me: An apology?
Lucie: I haven't been honest with any of you.
Me: [breaking into a slight sweat] How dishonest have
you been?
Lucie: Not *that* dishonest. Bill Jnr is our baby, and he's real,
and I gave birth to him . . . but none of it happened
like I said.
Me: Oh.
Lucie: Yes. I ended up having to have an emergency c-section,
and Bill was in a meeting and missed the whole thing.
Bill Jnr had some trouble with his airways, so we
couldn't even take him home for a week.
Me: But none of that's your fault!
Lucie: No. But it is my fault to tell you – to tell all the
people I've spoken to this week – that my way is the
best way. 'Planning and preparation is the key to a
good birth!' They made my birth a hell. I couldn't
relax for a minute, I was so petrified that someone
might stray from my script. What if I'd gone into
labour early? What if I'd found the pain too much
to bear?
Me: No one knows what it'll be like, first time.
Lucie: No. But once I did know, I shouldn't have kept saying
to you that you were doing it wrong. You're not
doing it wrong. If you and your husband are still
speaking, you're doing a lot more right than I did.
Me: Lucie, is there anything Polka Dot can do for you?

149

Do you want us to say anything to anyone, is there anything we can help with?

Lucie: No. Thank you. Alice knows all this – if you guys are happy not to say anything, so am I. But I don't want to promote this anymore. If that's OK. And please – ignore everything I've said. *Everything*.

I put Lucie in a taxi for the airport, to meet up with the rest of her team, and went back up to her apartment to check everything had been cleared out. In her bedroom I found a cuddly rabbit, and Lucie's wedding rings. I took the rings back to the office, and left the rabbit for the cleaners.

March 19th

Our first antenatal class tonight. We were sent directions to somewhere called the Community Rooms, which turned out to be hidden above the Sainsbury's on the high street. We were the first of the pregnants to arrive, and were greeted at the door by the bright and chirpy leader of the class, a smiling woman named Ros, dressed head to toe in Boden. She asked us to make ourselves name tags while we waited for the rest of the class to arrive, then fired questions at us in the now-familiar way with her head tipped on one side, with a wide, fixed smile on her face the whole time: where did we live? What did we do? How did we meet? Were there any other babies in our wider family? Why, I wanted to ask, is there something about pregnancy that brings this out in people? After a few minutes of this the next couple arrived, and we were released. Thom and I let out a collective sigh of relief.

Me:   I don't think I can do this.
Thom: It's alright, Kiki. I'm here. I won't let the nasty antenatal teacher hurt you.

Me:     What do you think she's thinking about when she smiles like that?

Thom:  The delicious taste of babies? How dreadful pregnant couples are? That if she has to talk about placenta any more she won't be responsible for her actions?

Me:     Urgh, please don't say that.

Thom:  Baby eating?

Me:     [mouthing] Placenta.

Thom:  Come on. Let's go and judge the other people.

So we sat down on the hard grey plastic chairs that Ros had put in a large horseshoe, while she interrogated the new couple. From the number, we were waiting for four more couples; twelve of us altogether, plus Ros. Despite the fact that we'd spend the next three months talking about our pelvic floors and comparing notes on how we wanted our genitals to handle this whole baby-expulsion thing, the couple who had just arrived chose to sit the other end of the horseshoe to us. Thank God. The last thing I wanted was to blow my very poorly-stocked range of chat before this whole thing had even really got going.

By 8.15, everyone had arrived. The last couple reminded me of the Noses – well-groomed and boringly moneyed – but around the circle was a fair mix of people. There were:

Me and Thom

Molly and Craig – the second couple to arrive.

Reiko and Andy – if I had to guess, she's a fashion journalist and he's a computer programmer.

Becca and Joseph – Both in 'natural coloured' cotton and linen clothes. She wears too many rings, he looks suspiciously like he should have a ponytail (but he doesn't, thank God, or I would have been sick all over the floor and blamed it on preg hormones).

Paula and Stuart – both short, dark haired, dark eyed. Alarmingly like siblings.

Sadie and Ollie – I didn't think it was possible, but these two sported more Boden than our teacher Ros. I didn't think Boden even made human fleshsuits, but if they don't then they should. And they should model them on these two.

Ros: Right, everyone, welcome to your first antenatal class. From your details, I can see that this is the first child for all of you, is that right? Good, good. OK, as a warm-up exercise, I'd just like us to go around the circle, and say which one thing we all hope to pass on to our babies. [strokes an imaginary pregna-belly]

Molly: I hope my daughter fights for world peace.

Me: [trying to turn a groan into a cough]

Craig: I hope *our* daughter [meaningful look at Molly] respects others' boundaries.

Me: [whispering] Bloody hell, Thom, we're last. Think of something good.

Thom: [whispering] I've already got something.

Reiko: I would like our baby to be good at languages. [laughs charmingly with partner]

Andy: I'd like our baby to be good at sport.

Me: [whispering] *What is it?* What have you got? You *have* to share it.

Becca: I'd like this baby to have a good soul.

Ros: Right.

Joseph: I hope this baby has our love of music.

Paula: I'd like this baby to be kind.

Me: [whispering] *Shit.* I should have had that one.

Stuart: So do I.

Ros: OK, a repetition, that's fine, let's keep going.

Sadie: I hope our baby is good with money.

152

Me:      [whispering, squeezing his arm] Seriously. Thom. *HELP ME.*

Ollie:   I hope this baby can hold its own at school.

Thom:    I'd like our baby to have a good sense of humour.

Me:      [sweating, panicking] I'd . . . like . . . this baby . . . not to be a pussy.

Circle:  [silence]

Ros:     OK, good, a lot of different dreams there for our unborn children. It's interesting to see *how* different our plans are, and we'll see over the coming weeks how different our labour plans are as well. Right, let's see with some hands up: who's planning a natural birth? [all hands go up around the circle, albeit at different speeds, ours last, hesitatingly] Good. It's nice that you all want to do things as naturally as possible, but let's investigate the process of labour, and see what options you might want to look into, as it draws closer to your dates. OK?

She then proceeded to spend the next forty-five minutes drawing diagrams of what could have been vases, or canal systems, or ghost sightings, but which made me feel consistently nauseous. At the coffee break, I told Thom we had to cancel the whole thing.

Thom:    Aren't you embarrassed to be such a cliché? No one else is trying to back out of having a baby when they're seven months along.

Molly:   [a few feet away, hissing at her husband] You can fucking do it. I'm not pushing that baby out of my vagina until you can give me a fucking signed contract that I'll be knocked out cold and a trained surgeon will go in, fish it out and stitch me back up again without me breaking a sweat.

Me:      [to Thom] *Au contraire.*
Craig:   You don't need to be such a baby about the whole
         thing.

Thom did a 'one point to you' face, then we had to sit down again to talk about episiotomy cuts versus natural tearing. God, my bones were fizzing right out of my body with the horror of it all.

Genuinely unsure whether I can stomach a second week of this.

March 20th

Knowing that we've got one of our own on the way has slightly changed the time I spend with Susie and her family. What used to be entirely carefree and fun has now become a series of lessons, something to watch intently like an Attenborough documentary, to see how the young are reared and fed by their elders. Oh, so that's how you stop a baby crying, etc.

But today's trip to Susie's was so enjoyable, like it used to be: just me and Thom horsing around with the Twins, and little Frida. The Twins are such good kids, and despite Pete's near-constant absence due to his travel work, they've turned out happy, confident and sociable. How can we hope to have such a great child? How can we love someone more than we love that trio? What could we do to ever have a family that was, really, as much fun as this lot?

I do love them so much, and have done since Suse and Pete first brought them home. Their tiny, matching faces; their growing personalities; their growth spurts and habits. Oh, this baby, could you be even better? Is that possible?

154

March 21st

We were stunned. As if someone had released a horrible stale-sweating over-tanned genie from a bottle, Tony strode into our meeting today.

Me:     Welcome . . . back, Tony?

Tony:   Yes, thank you, I'm back, let's all carry on. Right, everyone, I want all of you to take a look at your lists and work out what we can do to sex them all up.

Alice:  [trying to recover from the surprise] You mean, make them look sexy?

Tony:   No, I mean, get some actual descriptions of sex into the books.

All:     [stunned silence]

Tony:   Yes, of course we want the marketing and the publicity to look sexy too – look into getting new author pics from all of them; female authors with an off-the-shoulder thing, men a bit more smouldering – but I've been thinking about all of this while I've been away – a lot of thinking for lots of things – and I want you all to look at the titles you've got, and see if we can put a bit more sex in. Kiki, you've got Clifton Black: can his latest one have our hero seducing some local Middle Eastern girl?

Me:     I think that might be offensive on quite a few levels, Tony.

Tony:   [rolling his eyes] Fine, fine, but think about it. What about Jacki Jones's next one? Can you talk to her about the possibility of a sex book? Some erotica?

Me:     She's famously going through a very painful divorce at the moment, but I'll talk to her. I'm not sure that's our best avenue, though. [barely hidden sarcasm]

155

What about Ann and Charlie – maybe they can do a book about using food in sex?

Ann Tate and Charlie Greer are my absolute favourite authors in the Polka Dot stables. They're a pair of married chefs who usually write the most drool-making cookbooks, but who have branched out with a new series of tongue-in-cheek crime books featuring amateur chefs Steve Mortar and Emily Pestle, who solve crimes with kitchen skills, the first of which – *Dining with Death* – has done surprisingly well since its launch last month (which, hem hem, Tony wasn't even around for), and the second of which, *The Maltese Gherkin*, is due for publication in the autumn.

Carol:  [sniggering] Yes, there's a definite market for that. Alice, what do you think about making Polka Dot the go-to place for food porn?
Alice:  [deadpan] That sounds very do-able. It's also worth bearing in mind that I've heard Salman Rushdie has been touting around a book of erotica. I'll get in touch with his agent.
Tony:  Marvellous! Marvellous! That's the spirit, everyone. Let's go full steam ahead with all the *sex*.
Alice:  [whispering] Is it too late to just swear off sex altogether, forever until I die?
Me:  Isn't it *nice* to have our glorious leader back again?

While he slid off to his office to check no one had touched or cleaned anything, we sat around the table, staring at one another. 'Did that really happen?' said Norman. 'Was that a dream? Am I having a heart attack?'

'Is that your equivalent of heading into the light? Tony coming into work?' asked Carol. Norman acknowledged the unlikelihood of this with a nod, and we all, shell-shocked, headed back to our desks to wonder at his sudden, unannounced return.

Alice whispered to me over our computers, 'Do you think Pamela said he had to come back?'

Me:      I don't know if she'd even noticed he'd gone. Or maybe that was the *problem*. Oooh, unwelcome prodigal son. That's got to hurt.

Alice:   I know the feeling.

Me:      Oh, Alice, still no word?

Alice:   Nope. But I have my flat, and more importantly – my dignity.

Me:      I think you need the wind blowing nobly in your hair more when you say things like that.

Alice:   And I'm not sure it counts if I preface it with a brag of the flat I managed to weasel out of my dad.

Tony:    [from office] A quick word, Kiki?

I hurried in, worried that he'd suddenly twigged my stomach and had a huge surprise.

Tony:    Hello Kiki, yes – I was just having a look at the schedules, and I wondered if I shouldn't take the Tate and Greer books off you now. I know you've got a couple of months yet – congratulations, by the way – but I think it might get a bit clumsy with the timings. Alright?

I was too stunned to say anything as I filed back to my desk. Why would he take them off me now? They were selling well, and I still had plenty of things to do with them for both the latest book and the upcoming one – I'd already started editing the manuscript. Was this a punishment of some sort?

TO DO:
Check that Tony received Carol's details of my maternity leave
Find out who's being given Ann and Charlie


March 26th

Our second antenatal class tonight. We were a few minutes
late, and arrived to a full horseshoe, just two sad-looking
seats left for us. I'm such a stranger there, with these grown-
ups around us: I don't know if any of them are even under
thirty, let alone accidentally pregnant, and I feel like a teenage
mum in a room full of Tory mummies. But I'm sure that's
*my* problem, and they aren't making any judgements at all
about us. I'm sure Sadie and Ollie are definitely liberal,
empathetic people. Even if they do drive a 4x4 and wear
colour-matching Joules gilets.

After Ros's welcome, we got started on tonight's topic.
The labour. She reached behind her into a large box and
pulled out –

Me:     [whispering] Jesus Christ, what's that?
Thom: It looks like a plastic . . . pelvis?
Me:     [sniggering, then realising] Oh.

And it was, much to my un-delight. There was lots of talk
of openings, and softenings, and there many insertions of
fingers into orifices on the model, and more than once I
tasted my dinner in the back of my throat, particularly when
Ros explained why women used to have enemas before labour
in the old days. 'And they still do in Europe!' she chirped.
'Oooh, is it too late for you to teach abroad?' I whispered
sarcastically to Thom.

Ros went on to explain cervical dilation and the hormones

158

responsible, but all I could think was stop saying cervix stop saying cervix stop saying cervix. I had an image in my mind like the transformation in *An American Werewolf in London*, all stretching flesh and bone, and I must have looked bad because Ros called break ten minutes early and came over to me, sending Thom to get us both a tea.

Ros:  Are you alright, Kiki?

Me:  Yes, I . . . my imagination really paints those things vividly, you know.

Ros:  Are you squeamish normally?

Me:  This isn't squeamishness. Squeamishness is not being able to get a splinter out of your finger. This involves body parts I've never even *seen*.

Ros:  Does the sight of blood from your period make you feel faint?

Me:  No.

Ros:  Well, this is just the same. It's just your body doing what it was designed for, even if it's doing it somewhere you don't normally see.

Me:  Ever see. I won't ever see my birth canal.

Ros:  There's plenty of . . . let's say *stuff* involved in a labour, yes, but it's your stuff, and you can deal with it. Didn't you say you didn't want your child to be a pussy? What about you? Do you want to show the world that women can't handle having babies? Do you want them to take this off us?

Me:  [accepting the challenge] No, *sir*.

Ros:  Right. So let's get on with it. Placental fluid and all.

Maybe she's OK after all. We spent the rest of the session discussing delivery positions, and when the time came for a volunteer to manoeuvre a toy baby out of that pelvis, I was over to Ros in a heartbeat. Yes, the baby ended up with a big dent mashed into one side of its head, but Ros says real babies have super-soft skulls that can take a hell of beating in the delivery. So . . . that's fine.


March 27th

After last night's class, I plucked up the courage to text Molly for a drink. She replied straight away, and we spent a great evening in the pub round the corner from the Community Rooms, talking about our jobs (she's a town planner), our pregnancies, the rest of the class and all the other stuff we can't really cover when there's someone at the front of the room holding up a baby with some 'fake waste' in its 'practice nappy'. Ugh. She also told me that before our first class, when she and Craig were trying to park, a huge shiny Land Rover cut them up and nicked their space. Craig gave them the finger, and found another space even closer, but imagine their surprise when the passengers strolled into the class a few minutes later.

Me:     Sadie and Ollie?
Molly:  As if it could be anyone else.

   We covered everyone else in our group (Molly: 'Paula and Stuart? Siblings') and our own major concerns about child-birth and rearing (Me: 'Tearing.' Molly: 'Raising them anything like our parents did us.' She has pretty poor parents as role models). So that was a nice time.


March 28th

I thought it was time to buttonhole Tony and have him formally talk me through my leave, and the company's arrangements. He'd been scuttling in and out of the office since his return, batting us all away when we tried to ask him any of the myriad questions we had in his long absence (although strangely, not as many as we expected when we found out he was disappearing for an indeterminate amount of time). I was reduced to hiding in his office and shutting the door between us and the rest of the office when he finally came in. I felt like a third-rate Raymond Chandler dame when Tony jumped and spun around.

Me:     Tony. I just wanted to talk to you about arrangements for my maternity leave. Did you get the message from Carol about it?

Tony:   Yes, yes, I heard about your . . . [nodding at my stomach] I heard all about it. Haven't we covered this? Are you . . . well? Is there something wrong?

Me:     No, no, Carol's been a great help, confirming my leave dates, letting me go to appointments and things.

Tony:   Oh right, a lot of those, yeah?

Me:     Not really. Anyway, I just wanted to run this through with you, just once, and then my mind's at rest that we're all organised on this. I've given my maternity forms to Carol and we agreed on a finish date of May 4th, with an eight-month leave period. Is that OK?

Tony:   [going through some other paperwork on his desk] Yes, that's fine.

Me:     Right. Good. OK. That's it then.

Tony:   Good, good. Anything else?

Me:     No. Um . . . thanks, Tony.

Back at my desk, I found Alice watching me.

Alice: Are you OK?

Me: Yes. He seems to be incredibly frightened of pregnants.

Alice: That would make sense. At his boys' school they wouldn't have ever seen women – certainly not fertile ones.

Me: Well. As long as that's all it is. Can't it be quite useful having him afraid of you? I ask one who knows.

Alice: Oh yeahhh.

Like I say, as long as that's all it is. What an odd man. He's the one person in our whole office who I'll be glad to be away from during my leave.

April's Classic Baby

TESMAN:
[Following.] Yes, but have you noticed what splendid condition she is in? How she has filled out on the journey?
HEDDA:
[Crossing the room.] Oh, do be quiet—!
MISS TESMAN:
[Who has stopped and turned.] Filled out?
TESMAN:
Of course you don't notice it so much now that she has that dress on. But I, who can see—
HEDDA:
[At the glass door, impatiently.] Oh, you can't see anything.

*Hedda Gabler*
Henrik Ibsen

April 2nd

Our third antenatal class tonight. Everyone is so *round*, already. How can we fit any more baby in? Ros announced as we settled in that this session we'd be focusing on pain relief.

Ollie:   Yes please! Dad would like some of everything! [guffaw]

Me:   [whispering to Thom] I hate him.

Molly caught my eye then, and poked her tongue behind her bottom lip, to which I responded by nodding sagely and trying not to laugh.

Thom:   [to me] Will you two behave?

Ros:   So, can anyone tell me some of the various pain relief methods on offer? Yes, Paula.

Paula:   Epidural.

Ros:   Good, epidural. [writing it down on the big flip-board]

Molly:  Gas and air.

Ros:    Yes, good. Any more?

Sadie:  Hypnotherapy?

Me:     [snorting]

All:    [silence]

Me:     Sorry.

Ros:    Any more?

Ollie:  Water birthing?

Becca:  TENS machines?

Ros:    Yes, good, OK. Those are the main ones, I think.

Having got them all up, she then went through everything we'd heard about them. This being North London, of course all the members of our little circle were thoroughly clued up on every possible detail of each option, some even citing studies they'd read online about benefits and risks. Fun times! But the TENS machine, for some reason, baffled Paula.

Paula:  No, sorry, I still don't get it. It gives you an electric shock, to distract you from labour pains because the machine hurts more?

Reiko:  No, Paula, it sends tiny electric pulses through your system, which the brain recognises as much less than your labour pains, releasing the hormones to block the pain.

Craig:  No, isn't it to do with your spinal column? Some kind of receptors?

Becca:  No, Reiko's right, it's more to do with controlling your body's response to the pain. The machine creates a space for your body to feel pain but not suffer from it.

Molly:  Hang on – does that machine hurt?

Ros:    On the scale of childbirth? Honestly, mixed responses. Some people swear by their TENS machines, others take them off within a minute. Like I always say, every labour is different – I can't tell you whether or not the TENS will work for you.

Molly: I think I might leave it, cheers.

We got home and I was laughing at the whole session, as always. It *is* nice to meet these people (mostly) but it also feels a bit pointless, overall.

Me: Can't I read all this in a book, and save us all valuable time?

Thom: Keeks, it helps me too, you know.

Me: [stunned] *Does* it?

Thom: [laughing] Yes, it does! I know you just take one day at a time, and make choices for your pregnancy and labour – which I can't even imagine how scary it must seem to you – and you make jokes and talk to your sister, but I've just got to watch this happening to you, and I can't do anything. When you're bleeding and screaming in labour—

Me: A pleasant image, thank you.

Thom: —what can I do? Can I help? Can I take away any of the pain? I can't do anything, I can't help you at *all*. Going to these classes at least gives me some information about what you might be going through, and more than that, it allows me to see other men with that same panic in their eyes as they prepare to helplessly watch the women they love screaming.

Me: I'm sorry, Thom. Of course it's helpful. But I don't think you understand how essential you are to this. My worst fear for the labour isn't that I'll have to have a caesarean, or any of those other things we don't talk about – it's that you wouldn't be with me. I don't think I can do it without you, Thom. I'd go

166

mad. Please, Thom, please understand how important you are to this labour. I couldn't do it if you weren't there.

Thom: Really?

Me: Of course! How can you not know that?

Thom: OK. That's nice. [pulling me into bear hug] And I couldn't do this labour without *you*, either.

Me: [muffled] Buffoon.

TO DO:

Get a TENS machine? Anything that might help with the pain has got to be worth it, surely

April 3rd

We've finally started getting the equipment in. The buggy arrived (neither as big nor as expensive as our car), and from Thom's mum and dad, a travel cot and playmat. None of these are ridiculous, unnecessary objects (although I'm sure if I really tried I could find a mother who believed they were) but our flat feels so small. *Bijou* has become *boxed-in*. A few bags from Mum and Susie of baby clothes old and new, and we're struggling to find somewhere to sit in the evening. I just don't know what we'll do.

A lovely invitation in the post, though: a wedding invitation from Fiona and Mark, my brilliant first boss in publishing all those years ago, and her equally lovely boyfriend. Fiancé, I should say, I suppose. 'Short notice,' it said, 'but if you're free on Saturday 12th May, we'd love it if you could join us at Battersea Arts Centre for our wedding and party. Bring booze and your dancing shoes, RSVP.' What joy! It was so nice to see them both at our wedding; what a pleasure to be seeing them again, plus it's only on the overland so we don't even need to worry about a hotel. Or an outfit, come to think of it, as Susie's lovely blue and white striped dress will be perfect. But how to accessorise with this growing lump?

TO DO:
Try to test Thom's feelings on my buying a hat for their wedding
Check that hats are still OK and haven't drifted back into mother-in-law status


April 9th

Tony came over to Alice and my desks today, with a miserable-looking Dan trailing in his wake. 'What do you two think of this cover?' he barked. He flung down a print-out of *The Maltese Gherkin*, Ann and Charlie's new crime-comedy, the front of which was overwhelmed by a black and white photo of a woman's parted thighs.

Me:      I . . .
Alice:   Wow.
Tony:    Good, right?
Alice:   No, not good.
Me:      Tony, this is terrible. God, sorry, Dan.
Dan:     [cheering up] No, that's *fine*.
Alice:   This is wrong in just about every possible way. Although it's a very well-designed piece of misjudged sexism—
Dan:     Thank you.
Alice:   It's still . . . well, it's wildly wrong for the audience.
Me:      Delicate little flowers we may be, but she's right, Tony. This is not a good route to go with this. You'll

|      |                                                      |
|------|------------------------------------------------------|
|      | alienate most of our customers. And can you see this on supermarket shelves? |
| Tony: | [grumbling] Fine, fine. Dan, redo this. [stomps off] |
| Dan: | Jesus, that felt close. |
| Me: | Does anyone else feel like Tony's on the edge? |

I'd love to know what happened to Tony on that sabbatical. He's come back twice as sweaty and half as coherent. But which of us would ever leave him, if it meant also leaving Polka Dot?

It was the final antenatal class tonight. As we gathered in the Community Rooms for the last time, I felt sad. As always, I blamed it on hormones, but it might also be that I'd come to see Ros as an authority, someone who I trusted to give me useful truth about childbirth and babies. Plus, it was nice to have such soft targets as Sadie and Ollie to make fun of behind their backs each week. This week, I thought of Lucie Martel.

| Ros: | Hello everyone. It's our final session this week, so I wanted to cover birth plans, bringing the baby home, then any other questions you might have. Right, so how many of you have written your birth plans already? [everyone puts their hands up except me and Thom, Molly makes apologetic face at us, then sniggers] Alright, well, I'd probably say to most of you that you need to bin them. [I poke my tongue out at Molly, make smug face] 99% of birth plans that midwives see are completely impractical: 'I must not have this, I definitely will have this.' Just try to bear in mind that labour is, generally, completely unpredictable. Something that seems impossible to you now may, when you're in labour, come to be the only thing you want. And since the birth plans aren't |

medically enforceable anyway, the only people suffering here will be you. So try to think: what would you prefer? What would you *like* to happen, if it goes to plan? If it doesn't go to plan, what would you go along with if it meant saving your baby and yourself?

Becca: But I know I definitely don't want an epidural.

Ros: Of course you know that. And you've researched it and read about it, and doubtless heard from lots of people with lots of opinions, but my point is that your labour is yours, and is totally unique from everyone else's. I'm not saying that you should go in asking for one, but if you instead write on your birth plan, 'I'd prefer not to have an epidural, but will consider if it seems necessary', then at least you won't feel like you've let yourself down if you decide you want one.

Becca: But I don't.

Ros: OK, you don't. [sighing] I'd also suggest having a codeword between you and your birth partner, so if you've said you didn't want an epidural, or whatever, but you then subsequently decide you want one, your partner knows that – if the codeword appears – you are to get the best pain medication in modern medicine.

Me: [whispers] Bagsie 'rooster'.

Thom: [whispers] Why?

Me: [whispers] It was the first word that came into my head?

Thom: [whispers] When talking about the miracle of child-birth, the first word that came into your head . . . was 'rooster'?

Me: [whispers] Yeah. Do you have something you'd prefer?

170

Thom: [thinking, whispers] No.

Ros: OK, well you can decide on those words later, but let's keep going with what will happen afterwards.

She then started talking about things like afterbirth and thigh injections, so I had to focus on putting on a face of concentration, rather than revealing the low-level nausea so common when my internal organs are referenced.

At the end of the class, we all said our goodbyes as normal – it wasn't really goodbye for any of us, as we'll see Ros again for our informal postnatal meeting, and the women have already planned to meet up at each other's houses as we start drifting off towards maternity leave.

April 10th

It's been so nice having Zoe through all of this. Although I've been grateful to our antenatal teacher (and the rest of the class, I suppose), it's nice to go through this with someone I knew before. Plus, Pedro's bizarre, continued kindness to her reaffirms my faith in humanity. We met for lunch today to compare further notes.

Zoe: Final day before maternity leave.

Me: Bloody hell. Is it really?

Zoe: How long have you got left?

Me: I'm stopping two weeks before, so . . . 4th May. God, that's not long either. How do you feel?

Zoe: Knackered, but great. Pedro has been so nice, Kiki. I'm almost sick of telling you this, but for the fact that he might suddenly revert at the worst possible time. Do you know what he's done?

Me: I'd like to say killed a puppy or something, but

171

|        | looking at your face . . . given you a diamond cot? |
|--------|-----------------------------------------------------|
| Zoe:   | Oh. You ruined it.                                  |
| Me:    | He gave you a *diamond cot*?                         |
| Zoe:   | Haha, no, you fool. But he did give me a promotion. I shall no longer be his lackey and picker-upper, but I'm moving into his office as his Creative Assistant. It means I'll be able to come with him when *I* think I need to be there, and I'll have more input on the creative side of things. He even gave me a practice shoot, last week. |
| Me:    | Are you serious? That's great!                       |

Pedro had been as good as his word, letting her try her hand with a junior popstar, directing some of the photos while he followed her instructions. What joy! Instructing Pedro! Zoe seems blissfully happy, and even says she feels she could keep working right up until she goes into labour, but Pedro (and Zac) insists that she take it a little easy. I told her that Tony is being pretty good too, happily agreeing to me being off for eight months, getting someone in to cover me, and saying if I got closer to my date and wanted to finish sooner, it would be no problem at all. Admittedly, all that made him sound a lot more human than he really is, but none of it was technically untrue. But I never thought I'd be jealous of anyone with Pedro as a boss.

We also ran through the seven tonnes of equipment we've each collected. Zoe said that because Zac's family are so far away, they compensate by constantly ordering things from UK shops. She said they had parcels arriving every day for two weeks, stuff from every shop that has ever stocked baby items. She also said they clearly aren't consulting with one another, as they now have three rocking chairs in their one-bed flat; we're welcome to have one, apparently, which is awfully kind. Looking around our flat, though . . . I'm just not sure where we'd put it. On our bed?

TO DO:
Find out what we need for hospital
Pack hospital bag
Do pelvic floor exercises
Remember to sleep on left side of body
Find more room in this flat. Somehow.


April 11th

I would just like to say, Brain, that you and I are no longer on speaking terms. After last night's guest appearance from a hugely underdressed Pedro – was it the phrase 'Instructing Pedro'? – in my dreams, I am now busy trying to rinse the taste of sick from the back of my throat. I shall now only be talking to you if I want you to make me a sandwich or call an ambulance when my baby is trying to get out.

TO DO:
Spend today thinking very serious thoughts about instructing
   Daniel Craig


April 13th

Thom had gone out to the supermarket while I cleaned the bathroom (live fast, die young, right?) and returned with a suspicious spring in his step.

Me:    What have you done?
Thom:  When?

Me:     Why are you in such high spirits? What have you done?

Thom:   [high voice] I haven't done *anything*!

Me:     Alright, sorry. Sorry.

A few minutes later, Thom said with mock casualness, 'I saw that woman from our antenatal class today.'

Me:     Which one?

Thom:   The pretty one.

Me:     [silent]

Thom:   [oblivious]

Me:     *I beg your pardon.*

Thom:   Wait—

Me:     I. Beg. Your. *Pardon.*

Thom:   Kiki—

Me:     '*The pretty one.*'

Thom:   Kiki, you know you're the best-looking one in there! I just meant it's the one woman in there who doesn't look roughly equivalent to my mum or your sister.

Me:     What the hell is wrong with my *sister*, now?

Thom:   Nothing is wrong with your sister! But you're so much better looking than any of the others in that group that she just stands out as . . . [faintly] you know . . .

Me:     What? Not quite as much of a sea cow as me?

Thom:   Come on, Keeks. Be fair.

Me:     Be fair! Are you serious? I'm no longer able to move around the flat without knocking things over, and I look the worst I've ever looked in my whole life, and you're reminding me quite how much you're attracted to other women.

Thom:   Jesus Christ, she's as pregnant as you are!

174

Me:     What's that supposed to mean? That she's making a better job of it than I am?

Thom:   [pausing, trying not to snigger] Oh, well done Kiki, you cracked my code. Yes, that's just what I was saying.

Me:     Oh this is funny, now? You think leaving your wife for another pregnant woman is funny?

Thom:   And getting more so all the time.

Me:     [trying to hide my smile] Dad'll be furious at you.

Thom:   I believe he'll come to love whatever-her-name-is like a daughter, in time.

Me:     I'll name the baby Atticus Hawthorn.

Thom:   I don't mind. I'll have another baby to name.

Me:     [thinking hard] Aha! I'll tell the baby that its father was an illiterate heroin addict—

Thom:   Shame.

Me:     —who was also a member of the far right—

Thom:   Oh well.

Me:     AND whose favourite film was *Showgirls*.

Thom:   You wouldn't.

Me:     [arching an eyebrow]

Thom:   You're bluffing.

Me:     Haven't you heard the old adage? 'Angry pregnant wives never bluff.'

Thom:   You just made that up.

Me:     Does it matter?

Thom:   Fine. Fine. I shall pretend to call up the woman whose name I don't know, and tell her that the affair she didn't even know we were having is all over.

Me:     *Thank you.* And it's Molly, by the way.

Thom:   Yes! Molly! The pretty one.

Me:     *And* she's my friend now, so you can't say that stuff.

175

Thom just kissed me on the nose and left the room, forgiven for his indiscretion.


April 15th

The hospital tour today. Slightly nerve-racking, and always unusual to be given a tour of anything other than a Haunted House when there's a background noise of screams and weeping, but (besides the sound effects) it was a lovely place. Reassuringly calm, and clean, and free from all alien lifeforms. The wonderful nurse showed us around the various areas – the reception we would arrive at, the rooms in which we'd be checked, the birthing rooms themselves and the wards I'd rest in afterwards. We'd rest in. Me and the baby. Gulp. The birthing rooms are wonderful: a huge bath in each; balls to bounce on; ropes to pull on; beds to lie on, weeping. They looked so new and fresh that I felt almost an excitement, like visiting a spa, but one where you get to take a whole new member of the family home.

Then it happened. Just as we were leaving, as we were thanking the nurse and making goodbye small-talk with the other couples (see? It's all grown-ups do), I saw her. Just a glimpse, but it was definitely her.

*Annie.*

Her and Stephen – looking more like a young Keith Chegwin than ever – as clear as day, waltzing through the hospital corridors. What could they be doing here? They don't live anywhere near this hospital, as far as I know, and she didn't look like she was in any kind of emergency labour. The second I saw her my fighter-pilot reactions kicked in, and I pushed Thom back into the lift we'd just left.

Only, this wasn't the lift we'd just left. While talking to the group, we must have drifted, because this was not the lift we'd just crowded together in. This was a huge lift, clearly designed for gurneys and staff. And how could I tell that? Because that's who we were stuck in a lift with. And when I say 'staff', I mean three figures in full scrubs staring at us with horror and disgust. And when I say 'gurney', I really mean, 'screaming, bleeding woman in labour on a bed'.

| | |
|---|---|
| Me: | Is this . . . not . . . the maternity tour? |
| Thom: | Look away, Kiki. Look away. |
| Me: | Sorry, I – |
| Woman: | AAAAAAAAAAAAaaaaaaaaaaaaaaaaaaaaaaaa AAAAAAAAAAAAAGGGGGHHHHHHHH. . . |
| Scrub 1: | Mrs Hobbs, we're moments away from theatre, and we can give you something for the pain the second we're in there, OK? |
| Me: | [quietly, to Scrub 1] Gosh, that sounds bad. Is she alright? |
| Scrub 1: | She's having a baby. |
| Me: | Right. |
| Thom: | Kiki, stop looking at them. Look at me. |
| Me: | Yes, sorry. [trying to whisper] That does sound bad, though, doesn't it? Does it always sound like that? |
| Thom: | Is this lift broken? Are we still moving? |
| Scrub 2: | Mrs Hobbs, we're nearly there. Your husband will be waiting for us in theatre, and our anaesthetist will give you something straight away. Can you still hear me? |
| Woman: | [panting] Yes, yes, I can hear you. Who . . . are . . . these people? |
| Scrub 1: | They're just checking standards in the hospital to see we're doing everything absolutely perfectly. And aren't we doing a good job, inspectors? |
| Thom: | [weakly] Yes, brilliant. |

| | |
|---|---|
| Woman: | Oh the baby's coming out the BABY'S COMING OUT. |
| Scrub 3: | Yes, it does look like Baby just won't wait today! OK, Mrs Hobbs, we'll take care of you. You and the baby are going to be fine. |
| Me: | Oh God, the baby is coming, look, the baby is coming right out of her, right now Thom open the door! Now! Now now now! |
| Thom: | [mashing buttons to open the door, doors finally ping apart] |
| Scrub 3: | Clear the way! We've got a crowning in progress! [all sweep out] [silence] |
| Me: | Shall we . . . take the stairs? |
| Thom: | Why even bother with that? Let's just jump from here and end my misery. |
| Me: | Yeah, well that certainly didn't allay my *Alien* terrors. Oh, that reminds me, I saw Annie downstairs. |

Thom understood then, although he said he still wished that hadn't meant we'd had to step into a horror movie sequence. We edged down the stairs like a couple of budget Bonds, and got back to the car without bumping into them.

TO DO:
Take this uterus into Outer Space, as it may be the only way to escape Annie
Check with Mum to see if she knows why Annie would be around here

April 17th

A message from Nick, of the Noses, asking if I would meet him for a drink tonight. I went straight from work to the pub round the corner from the office, and was immediately struck by how many dirty looks I got. When I reached the bar, the barman looked at me warily.

Me:       A lime and soda, please.
Barman:   [relieved] Oh, sure.
Me:       Why does everyone do this? AND A TEQUILA, please.
Barman:   Oh. Um . . .
Nick:     [calling] Kiki, over here!
Me:       Fine, you can forget the tequila. *For now*.

It was nice to see Nick, although he looked like he'd gained even more weight and he didn't look happy. I gave him a sideways hug, turning my stomach out of the way to get nearer him.

Me:     Hey, what's new with you?
Nick:   [miserably] It's more what's new without me.
Me:     [confused] What's without you?
Nick:   Rose. We're getting a divorce.
Me:     God, Nick, I'm so sorry. Are you OK? Well, no, of course you're not OK, unless you are OK which is fine too. Not fine. OK. Sorry. Sorry.
Nick:   Don't be sorry, it wasn't your fault. [rueful laugh] Well, it was a bit. No, sorry Kiki, not really. But your pregnancy –
Me:     What?
Nick:   Kiki, of course it wasn't really anything to do with you. But things had been off since the day we got

179

married. We both wanted a baby – me more than Rose, even. And when we saw you, pregnant straight away, and accidentally, it . . . It was too much for us. I moved out a week later.

Me:     Nick, I'm so sorry. Not from me, but for you. This is . . . oh, Nick. How are you doing?

Nick:   Terrible, really. Her family are furious at me, for some reason – I've no idea what she's told them – and although we saw each other for a while after I moved out, I haven't seen . . . her . . . for almost two months now. I've had the paperwork through, though. I've signed it and sent it off today. I just wanted to talk to someone.

Me:     Where are you staying?

Nick:   An old mate from school's got a spare room until a fortnight's time. I've been crashing there. It's been completely shit, Kiki. Why did it turn out this way? I love her— [voice cracks]

Me:     I know you do, Nick, we all know you do. I wish I could say anything to make it better, but sometimes there just are these shitty situations that no one can make any better. I really, really wish I could, though. Do you want to come and stay with us?

Nick:   [laughing sadly] Yeah, you definitely want me staying on your sofa when you've got a baby coming.

Me:     God, I forgot about that.

Nick:   Did you?

Me:     [silent] I really did. Jesus, I forgot I was having a baby. [silent]

Nick:   I wish I could forget about Rose.

Me:     [taking his hand] Fine, it may not be a great time to come and stay with us, but I do know a few lovely people with spare rooms. Do you remember Jim from our— [stopping]

180

Nick:  Wedding? You can say the word, Kiki.

Me:    [hurrying on] The one on the piano? He's got a spare room and I can tell you from experience that he is great company at times like this. Shall I have a word?

Nick:  [shrugging] Sure. Thanks.

I stayed another two hours until my back felt like it was going to explode, talking about how things had been between them. Nick had thought everything could be fixed, and even when he moved out, thought he'd be moving in again soon enough, but Rose had told him soon after that she'd known since even before the wedding; and the baby had never come along to fix things. She'd married him because that seemed like the sensible thing to do, because she wanted a house, a family, but she'd always known that it was a mistake.

I can't even begin to imagine how Nick must have felt, hearing that from the person he'd loved, that he'd married. To have said those vows in front of everyone you cared about, and to have that person say that they'd not meant it, they'd always known it was wrong. At least – if I can think of a contrast, if not a consolation – at least Leon had always been open with Jacki about his feelings on the matter, even though she'd ignored it. Nick had thought it would be forever. He'd never had any reason to suspect they wouldn't be together with their children as they grew old, side by side.

Oh, poor Nick.

Thom was shocked but not surprised. At least he didn't brag about being right – what a sad thing to have been right about. Poor Nick. And poor Rose.

April 18th

I spoke to Jim today about Nick. He remembered them both from the wedding, and from our reactions at his birthday barbecue to their wedding the day before.

Jim:    I remember thinking I hope any wedding I have doesn't leave my guests feeling like that.

Me:     That's the one. And guess how it's ended?

Jim:    Have they split up?

Me:     Yup.

Jim:    Shit.

Me:     Quite. But he's going to be homeless in two weeks – how would you feel about having a miserable housemate again?

Jim:    How does he feel about zombie films? I'm having a binge currently.

Me:     I imagine he can sympathise greatly. Is that a yes?

Jim:    Sure, the more the messier.

Me:     Is it?

Jim:    My house, my rules.

Me:     Thanks, Jim, you're a nice man.

Jim:    I know. I keep telling that to Poppy, but I don't think she's convinced yet.

Nick was delighted when I told him, if by 'delighted' you mean gave a huge sigh, thanked me, voice cracking again, and hung up immediately afterwards. I wish I could do more, though. It's horrible to feel so powerless when my friend is in such a state, but at least I know Jim will look after him.

TO DO:
Get toys for the baby?
Try to work out where we'll fit everything

182

April 20th

Thom convinced me that there was no point us having been to the antenatal classes if we didn't socialise a little bit, and that maybe we should have at least one lot over before our babies were born. I already knew Molly was great company, and was curious to see Craig out of the confines of the antenatal sessions, so agreed and said, 'Only if it's Molly and Craig, though.'

Thom:  That's only because you fancy him.
Me:    Ex*cuse* me. Did you see how your face lit up?
Thom:  I'm just happy when *you're* happy.

So we invited them over, and they came tonight. I was amazed at what a good time I had: they were both utterly charming and funny. Over a huge dish of chocolate tart (eaten from the dish with spoons) I confessed that this baby had been an accident.

Molly:  Christ, really? We spent almost ten grand on bloody IVF.
Me:     Oh, Molly, sorry . . .
Craig:  Don't apologise. The only person who needs to apologise is the doctor who suggested that we try it the 'natural way' a bit longer.
Molly:  Yuck.
Craig:  Yeah, if I'd wanted to actually *sleep* with my wife I wouldn't have married her, right?
Thom:   So how many rounds did you go?
Molly:  It worked second time, thank Christ, or we might have ended up with a baby but no home.
Me:     And how did you find it?
Molly:  Nerve-racking.

183

Craig: [mouthing] EXPENSIVE. But I *did* get to wank into a cup. Every cloud . . .

Molly: Wow, you're a dream dinner guest, aren't you?

Me: Christ, the science of it boggles my mind completely.

Molly: I'm so happy that the technology exists, but . . . it was a long time coming.

Craig leant over and pulled her head to his, kissing it, and we were all quiet for a moment. 'I'm going to make that kid earn back every damn penny,' he reassured her, softly, which made us all crack up. At the end of the night when we said our goodbyes (non-pregnants pretty drunk, pregnants wearily sober) I was glad Thom had talked me into it. As we closed the door and headed to our bedroom for me to collapse fully dressed on the bed, I said, 'Maybe this "socialising with people" thing isn't so bad.' Thom looked at me. 'Wow. Hark at the social butterfly over there,' he smiled insincerely, then rolled me up in the duvet and turned off the light, giggling, stripping off all his clothes and flinging himself down next to me.

Me: Thom! Let me get ready for bed.

Thom: Shhhhhhhhhhhhhhhhhhhhhhhhhhhhhhh. It's bed time. It's not all party party for some people, you know.

Me: My *God*, your head is going to hurt tomorrow.

It was one small consolation for not being able to drink tonight.

TO DO:
Please please *please* don't go into labour during the night

184

April 25th

The phone rang this morning, at 6 am. I rolled over and groaned, and sent Thom to answer. He shuffled out of bed, returning with the phone to mumble, 'Isfyou.'

Me:      Hello?
Zoe:     Hello! Is this too early – holy shit it's six am! I've called six people and no one told me the time? Kiki, I'm so sorry.
Me:      Hey, Zoe, that's OK. Have you had the baby?
Zoe:     I have! I've had that little monkey, and then some.
Me:      What is it?
Zoe:     It's a girl, Edith Melville Clark. Born around two this morning, seven pounds one.
Me:      Is that good?
Zoe:     It felt good once it was out of me, that's for sure. Her. She felt good.
Me:      Well, congratulations, both of you. All of you! Well done.
Zoe:     Shall we talk about this later?
Me:      I'm sorry, Zo, I'm just not really awake yet. But well done again, I can't wait to see you all. Send my love to Zac, and the baby.
Zoe:     [whispering] OK, go back to sleep, we'll talk soon. Shhh. Bye.

Thom:  [into pillow] Did Zoe have a baby?
Me:      Nnnm.
Thom:  Did she like it?
Me:      Mmmn.
Thom:  We aren't going to go back to sleep again, are we?
Me:      No, goddammit.
Thom:  You know what that means?

Me:     You know all of this is going to have to stop once
        our child is born, don't you?

  But he convinced me.

The cot arrived today. It's been staring at us from its box all
day, but I meant what I said about not putting it up until
the last minute. I'm too superstitious. Plus, I can't really bear
to see what's going to have to be moved out of our room to
fit that cot in here.

Oh Jesus. This is not a three-human flat.

TO DO:
Visit Zoe, Zac and Edith
See if there's any extra room hidden somewhere, like I
    continually dream
Maybe between the kitchen and the bathroom? Or under
    the bed. Usual place in the dreams.

April 26th

Lunch with Jacki today. She insisted we shift our monthly
dates to earlier in the day, as I'm in no fit state to be 'out
on the town' in this condition. But I don't mind when she
says it, because she find the best restaurants rather than the
best bars and slips me sips of her cocktails like a sinister
uncle. She was lit up today, glowing like I haven't seen her
look for ages.

Jacki:  I've decided to get cracking on my next book. I can't
        tell you how much I enjoyed doing the first one –
        even if some bastard decided to do his best to wreck

|        |                                                                                 |
|--------|---------------------------------------------------------------------------------|
| | it for me – and I've realised I need to get on with this one, and move on. |
| Me: | Jacks, that's great! And Tony will be delighted. |
| Jacki: | I'm not doing it for Tony. I'm doing it for me, of course, and you a little bit, because I want you to have nice books to work on, and then me again because I like working with you. |
| Me: | And may I ask what it's going to be about? |
| Jacki: | I'm not . . . sure yet. But I've had a few thoughts. Do you know what, though? I'd love to write something about how much I enjoyed writing that last book. |
| Me: | Readers, we are down the rabbit hole. |
| Jacki: | Not as indulgent as that, Keeks. It's just . . . that stuff was a real blessing for me. A whole new route to go down, that's completely mine and that worm never had a hand in. God, I'm glad I kept him away from that. |
| Me: | Is that what we're calling him now? |
| Jacki: | Yeah, it seems an improvement on 'manipulative pug-faced life-ruiner'. Which I didn't think contained the necessary positivity for me to move on with my life. Which I am, as you can see, doing. |
| Me: | [lifting sparkling water] Cheers! |
| Jacki: | Cheers! Quick, drink some of this martini. |
| Me: | Mmmmm. Cheers. |
| Jacki: | So, I'm thinking about that. But, we shall see. But if I do get something done – would you mind reading it while you're on maternity leave? |
| Me: | I would *love* to! I'd be too sad if I *didn't* read it. I promise I shan't let it wreck my baby bonding time. Promise. |
| Jacki: | Well then. Cheers again. No, put my glass down, you can't have any more. |
| Me: | Boo. |

I'm excited about that, too. A whole new Jacki book to work on, and one that is making her so happy. It was nice to hear her taking it in a completely new direction, too, and not just churning out the sequel Tony believed was so inevitable (baby book if she got pregnant straight away, home decoration book if it took a bit longer) – not that Jacki would have been doing any churning anyway. But I'm so pleased at how happy she seems. And how her book seems to have helped.

April 28th

With her baby only three days old, Zoe invited me over for a full debrief. She seemed great and looked wonderful, little Edith lying snuggled in a bouncer on the floor while Zac made us cups of tea in the kitchen.

Me:     So, you absolute wonder, how was it?
Zoe:    [smiling tightly] Fine.
Me:     Zoe . . .?
Zoe:    It was fine! Fine. Fine. Look at the baby. She makes it all worth it, doesn't she?
Me:     Zoe. How did it go?
Zoe:    Oh GOD, Kiki, don't have a baby. It's SO SORE. It comes right out of your vagina, did you know? RIGHT. OUT.
Me:     [shocked] It does *what*?
Zac:    [from the kitchen] ZOE. I will bar you from having guests if you keep doing that.
Zoe:    [laughing] All I'm saying is, take every single pain option they offer you. Don't be a hero.
Me:     Rest your thoughts, I will be doing just that. I have literally no interest in winning any pain medals. You

don't see those same smug mums refusing pain relief at the dentist, do you?

Zoe:  [relieved] Good. Good. You'll be fine, Kiki.

Me:   So tell me all about it.

Zac joined us then, and they told me all about the labour, from early contractions (Zoe: 'Hey, I can totally deal with this! Labour is easy') to their arrival at hospital (Zac: 'They were doing a shift changeover, so we were put in a room that the new shift didn't know was occupied. Zo was hooked up to a monitor for two hours and was starting to black out from the pain of contractions when a nurse found us') to their move to a delivery suite (Zoe: 'At which point they said I was too far along for an epidural, and offered me some gas and air. Bastards') to the actual delivery (Zac: [mouthing] 'It *was* just like *Alien*.' Zoe: 'What?' Zac: 'Nothing').

Zac:  Have you ever seen an umbilical cord, Kiki?

Me:   Hard to believe, but no.

Zoe:  It's like something from *Alien*.

Zac:  *See*?

Me:   The magic of childbirth really was destroyed by Ridley Scott, wasn't it?

Zoe:  I'm not kidding. It's like meaty telephone cord. It crunched when they cut it.

Zac:  I actually threw up in my mouth a little.

Zoe:  [nodding]

Me:   Well. I can't tell you what a pep talk this has been for me.

Zoe laughed and gave me Edith to hold then, and she is *dear*. Unbelievably small and mammalian, like a fuzzy doll rather than a human. I balanced her on top of my bump and said, 'Edith, meet – I don't know, Steve, or something.' Zac asked if we were really going to call the baby Steve, and I said of course not, but it's a good holding name for the time being. Better than Tadpole, or any of those other gorge-rising foetal nicknames.

And I liked holding her but, as ever, didn't struggle to give her back. In fact, all I could think of was lying on my back, once I'd pushed this baby out and could have my body back again (well, minus the stretch marks and breastfeeding). Zoe's been lucky, really: aside from the healthy baby, of course, and besides the slight hiccup over pain meds, she had no tearing and no complications. Merely the word 'tearing' now makes me cross my legs so tightly this baby might be born through my throat.

April 29th

Thom was making dinner this evening, when he suddenly stopped, facing me and crossing his arms.

Thom: I'll toss you for the surname.
Me: Gosh, I really wish I knew what you were talking about.
Thom: We can rationalise either way whether the baby should have your surname or mine, can't we? I think we should just toss for it.
Me: [thinking] OK, but I get to pick the coin.
Thom: What, because I have such a wealth of weighted coins?
Me: You *never know*. [rummaging in bag] OK. 2p.
Thom: Don't you think our child deserves slightly more than a 2p piece to decide its future?
Me: Sorry, I left all my doubloons at the office. Call or flip?

Thom: Heads.

Me: OK, here we go. [flips coin] TAILS! OH MY GOD.

Thom: Oh.

Me: Oh, Thom. Are you OK? Do you want to flip again?

Thom: No. No, I feel a bit weird, but that's OK, isn't it? It's still my child, isn't it?

Me: Yes. Until the paternity test shows up which declares otherwise.

Thom: [glaring]

Me: OK, not funny yet. Sorry.

Thom: I'm a pretty good husband, right?

Me: [pulling him into a bear hug] Yeah, you are pretty good. Pretty handsome too.

Thom: [looking at me with an eyebrow raised] Oh *really*? Didn't those hormones wear off ages ago?

Dinner got a bit burnt in the end.

## May's Classic Baby

Prince Andrew went again to his wife and sat waiting in the room next to hers. A woman came from the bedroom with a frightened face and became confused when she saw Prince Andrew. He covered his face with his hands and remained so for some minutes. Piteous, helpless, animal moans came through the door. Prince Andrew got up, went to the door, and tried to open it. Someone was holding it shut.

'You can't come in! You can't!' said a terrified voice from within.

He began pacing the room. The screaming ceased, and a few more seconds went by. Then suddenly a terrible shriek – it could not be hers, she could not scream like that – came from the bedroom. Prince Andrew ran to the door; the scream ceased and he heard the wail of an infant.

'What have they taken a baby in there for?' thought Prince Andrew in the first second. 'A baby? What baby . . .? Why is there a baby there? Or is the baby born?'

Then suddenly he realized the joyful significance of that wail; tears choked him, and leaning his elbows on the window sill he began to cry, sobbing like a child.

*War and Peace*
Leo Tolstoy

## May 1st

I was reading at home this afternoon, so was here when Thom came back from school. He slammed the door on his way in, utterly unlike him.

Me:     I'm in here! What's wrong?

Thom:   Rrrr. You know I love my job, Keeks, and I love those kids, and I love that school, but sometimes . . . I just despair.

Me:     What's happened?

Thom:   Nothing's happened, really. But we're a month from their exams and two of the classes have gone on strike. We don't need English, apparently, not with predictive text and spell check. Thank you very much, Alan fucking Turing.

Me:     Bit harsh on Alan Turing? A man who committed suicide because of government-level homophobic persecution?

Thom:   But *he* didn't have to face class 11F, *did* he?

Me:     I think we're getting off the point a little.

Thom: Maybe. But I don't know what to do. Never mind the fact that if these classes refuse to do their exams, our entire school's league table scores are going to smash through the floor; if these kids don't have English GCSE, they're lost. They can't do anything after that. It's essential, and they're all good at it, too. Not amazing, but they could all pass, and have all their options open to them. But without it, almost every door they'd be interested in closes.

Me: Have you told them that?

Thom: Of course, but they don't believe me. They don't always understand that if doing A makes B happen, if *they* do A then B *will* happen to them too.

Me: I'm so sorry, love.

Thom: Me too. It's so frustrating. The deputy head says we should just keep teaching as normal. But it makes me so angry to see whole classes just mess up their chances like that.

I made Thom a cup of tea and started hatching a plan. More when I know more.


May 3rd

I had a midwife appointment at lunchtime today, but Tony insisted I stay at home and only come in afterwards if I felt like it. I did feel like it – the midwife just wanted to check the size and heartbeat, and I'd had a lovely lie-in – so turned up at the office at two, seeing a girl clutching a pile of our books leaving through the building's front door just as I arrived. I asked Alice if we'd been ram-raided.

Alice: No, Tony's interviewing for your maternity cover. I think he's trying to sweeten the deal with some free books.

Me: Finally! I was worried I wouldn't have time for a handover before I went. But why didn't he do it with me? I could have told the interviewees more about this job than he ever could.

Alice: The mind of our glorious leader, as you put it, is not one we shall ever understand. We should be grateful for that.

Me: So what were they like?

Alice: The applicants? Young, actually.

Me: How young? Younger than me?

Alice: Sorry, lady, but yes.

Me: Capable-looking?

Alice: Mmm . . . yes, I think so. There were only four of them, but from what I saw they all seemed nice enough.

Tony came out of his office then.

Tony: Ah, Kiki. How are you?

Me: Fine, thank you, the baby's still in there. How did the interviews go?

Tony: Good, good, all well, thank you.

Me: Will you be letting them know immediately, so I've got time to do some handover stuff with them tomorrow?

Tony: Oh, that's all fine. If you can just leave the details with [looks around] well, me, I suppose, and I can pass it all to them. We don't want to rush these things, do we, and you've got enough to think about!

With a pleased guffaw, he shambled back to his office and shut the door. Alice promised she'd keep an eye on him, and would help out whoever ended up doing my cover. 'It's only for eight months,' she reminded me. 'How badly can they mess up?'

May 4th

So. My final day in the office. It felt pretty odd, although of course it's only until January, it's not forever. But I still had a lump in my throat as I looked around, in between frantically trying to ready everything for my cover. When I shared my strange mood with Alice, she just said, 'Uh, Kiki? I don't think that lump's in your throat. You're having *a baby*.' And of course, I shall miss Alice most of all, even though, as she points out, she'll be round our flat all the time, teaching the boy everything he may possibly need to know about women. Which seems like kind of an odd offer to be making to an unborn child but, hey, one I'll probably really appreciate in seven or eight or eighteen years.

I handed over as best I could to Tony. I explained that Matthew Holt's book was coming along really well, and I thought it would make the publication date in the autumn. *Nude in New York* needed a bit more work, but could hit the autumn pub date too; Hilary Taylor's latest still hadn't appeared in any form, and Stuart Winton didn't seem to have so much as a telephone number in our files. I also filled him in on what I'd done for *Dining with Death* and *The Maltese Gherkin*, for the early draft of the new Clifton Black I'd seen, and the discussions Alice and I'd had with Raff Welles for his paperback. Tony just continued to look shifty throughout, and when I'd finished running through everything and handed over details, I wasn't sure whether he'd taken in a single word. Oh well. For eight sweet, sweet months, Tony is not my problem.

And everyone was lovely today. Norman continued to reveal his previously hidden warm, thoughtful side, making sure I still felt well and could manage this final day. Carol was bustling and bossy, but made everything OK when she took a split-second to wink at me, and the Art team, of course, had designed a beautiful card: a stork carrying a bundle with a little arm sticking out, holding a *Complete Works of Shakespeare*. We toasted with glasses of Appletize and they threw in some last-minute name suggestions: Bartholomew (Carol), Smike (Norman), Kal-El (Alice), Daniel (Dan – people just can't resist, can they?) – then Alice said, 'Hang on – will the baby have both your names? Carlow and Sharpe?' When I confirmed it, she said, 'Then how in the name of all that's good can you resist calling it Major? For its whole school life, it will be . . .' Norman finished it: 'C Sharpe, Major. Oh, that *is* good.'

I really shall miss this lot very much.


May 5th

After a walk through Regent's Park today, we indulged in our most decadent pastime – glaring at the super-rich in Harrods. After a while, we got bored of eyeballing people buying sunglasses costing more than our car and wandered through the food hall instead. 'I miss oysters. And pâté. And liver. Mmmmm, *liver*.' Thom just said, 'You're disgusting,' and took me away from all the things I couldn't eat. Naturally, we ended up in the baby section. A wave of guilt overtook me.

Me:     Listen. I know we're being careful about money, and I know so much of this stuff is ridiculous [Thom slowly lifts a babygro with the Ralph Lauren logo stitched in, what, gold?] but we done so little for this kid. Nothing. I don't want any of this stupid stuff, I don't want something huge, or show-offy, or pointless. But he's got everything from everyone else, and nothing from us. Just because he's a boy, I've got to at least pretend to welcome him! Please, Thom!

Thom: [putting the babygro back gingerly, eyes wide after reading the price tag] Keeks, of course we can. I thought *you* didn't want to. Of course we can get something for him. But first – let's get out of here.

We scarpered sharpish as a pointy-fingernailed assistant came over to see what my wailing was about, and walked a few streets before we found a normal baby shop. In the end, we got a few normal, useful, *sensible* things. None of them are blue (or not solely), none of them have vehicles or roaring animals on, and all of them make me feel like we're making a home for this baby to be born in. Oh, and we also bought an elephant that's bigger than my current torso.

IT'S MY BABY I CAN DO WHAT I LIKE.

TO DO:
Find somewhere to keep both elephant and baby
And my current torso

May 7th

With two weeks to my due date and finally out of Polka Dot for the next eight months, I was hoping to just lie around,

198

building my chrysalis until my baby hatched. But today was the day that I would be trying to save Thom's bacon, in gratitude for him saving mine *all the time*.

So at lunchtime, instead of watching another Ginger Rogers film and groaning at my size, I was picking up a special guest to whisk to Thom's afternoon GCSE classes.

Jacki:  Hello, darling! [huge hug]
Me:     Mmm, that's a nice welcome! You ready?
Jacki:  As I'll ever be, Keeks. Has Thom got everything set up?
Me:     Just as you asked. You'll be amazing.

Jacki beamed at me, and I marvelled again at her generosity and support. She'd had a meeting booked this afternoon with her lawyers, but had ditched it immediately when I proposed the plan, and she'd put together – something, I didn't know what; some kind of presentation? – to show the kids. She'd even rushed straight from another video shoot this morning, some VH1 thing to promote her *Love Songs* album.

She didn't seem nervous at all, and was unfazed by the welcome she got at the school, with the head and all the secretaries hovering around the door to meet her after I parked up. I could tell that they were surprised by her calmness, her wit and her gentleness, because everyone always is with her, and the head himself took us to the school hall, where all the year 10s and 11s had been gathered for a 'special English assembly'.

Me:     Still OK?
Jacki:  You bet. It's an honour, Keeks.

And she behaved like it was. The headmaster announced a special guest to the school, and you could hear the kids fidgeting and shuffling. But when Jacki walked on stage, the kids went crazy – cheering, stamping and whistling, until the head came back on and gave them Stern Face. But Jacki was just Jacki, smiling at everyone and lighting up the room.

Jacki:   Hello, everyone! Thanks so much for having me this afternoon! Now, I've heard from some of your teachers that you don't really think English is an important subject for you to work on, is that right? Can any of you tell me why you feel that way? [forest of hands go up] Yes, hello?

Kid 1:   Because we don't need to learn to spell anymore.

Jacki:   OK, good, any more reasons?

Kid 2:   No one writes long stuff anymore, so why do we need to learn to do it?

Jacki:   Right, anyone else?

Kid 3:   Because it's *boring*. [kids laugh]

Jacki:   OK, that seems to be the most important argument here. Would any of you be interested in hearing my thoughts on all that?

She was greeted with some wary cheers, but she had them back in the palm of her hand in no time. She talked about songwriters and poets, comparing them on the hall's big screen, getting the kids to read out lyrics of chart hits past and present; she talked about writing computer games, and how long and complex those stories were, and compared them to classic literature, asking the kids to guess which was a Shakespeare play and which was a computer game from the storyline alone. She talked about the freedom reading could give you, and if you considered it a chore you would never visit all those amazing worlds. She showed pictures of successful writers past and present,

200

from the adventure and fascinating life of George Orwell to the dripping diamonds and political altruism of J. K. Rowling. She looked at amazing ads with great copy, to which the kids could recite the slogans, and explained how fashioning a sentence wasn't just about writing a long essay on *Jane Eyre*. It could be anything from the curling verbaceousness of Will Self to the acerbic telegrams of Cary Grant and Dorothy Parker. Word play was fun, and it was everywhere, and it was how we communicated all the time.

Jacki ended with her own most recent hit, after talking through the lyrics, backed by the school's ropy sound system, and the hall erupted into cheers and shouts. She smiled and waved, and looked at me as I shook my head in amazement, applauding her in the wings, open-mouthed. After a while, as the noise died down, the head came back on and thanked her, sounding stunned, and she came off with him to the wings where I was waiting.

Head: Really, Ms Jones, that was . . . wonderful.

Jacki: Oh, Jacki, please. I didn't do it *all* on my own, but it was *very* good fun.

Head: Well – thank you, really. And might I be able to request . . . a photograph, for the local paper?

Jacki: Of course!

It was great to see Thom's headmaster so pleased with the afternoon, and even better to see how pleased he was with Thom. The head clapped him on the arm a dozen times, saying, 'Excellent work, Thomas, well done,' and Thom winked at me, straight-faced.

Then I took Jacki to the pub, where Thom met us an hour later, and where we all stayed until closing (even though I was, obviously, still on the lime and sodas [and chips]).

Thom was so grateful for the plan and its raging success that if I hadn't been pregnant already, I definitely would be now.

May 8th

Now that my one project before childbirth is over and done with, I feel I ought to concentrate on the baby part. What is he going to wear? Where will we put his cot? Where will we store his buggy? What do I need to take to hospital? What do *I* need to wear? There's so much to do, and nothing I can do – I can't make it come any quicker, and I can't make our flat any bigger. I wish I knew when this baby will actually arrive.

I love our flat, and I always have done. It's always been perfect for me and Thom, and I love its light, its cosiness. But with a whole extra human on the way, suddenly it seems like a joke: how many elephants can you fit in a Mini? The baby will sleep in our room for a while, but then what? Tucked behind the TV? In the fridge? It was bad enough just trying to manoeuvre everything the baby will need around the flat – the buggy, the cot, the travel cot, the baby bath, the breast pump, the steriliser, the piles and piles of pastel-coloured muslins and babygros and sleep-suits – but having been to Sadie's for coffee this morning, with the rest of the antenatals, I can only marvel at the lack of space we have. Sadie and Ollie had prepped their nursery already, in immaculate shades of cream and soft greens, and *still* have a spare room and study. And a kitchen you can comfortably fit more than one person in. You could probably fit more than thirty people in their kitchen, actually. I couldn't help but imagine those antenatal friends visiting our flat, baffled as they opened cupboard doors in their search for the rest of the property. I don't ask for much in life; just a five-bed, mortgage-free home with a big kitchen and large outdoor space. Oh, and a healthy baby and husband. And a fulfilling job. And the same for Suse, I suppose. Is that *really* so much to ask?

Well. While I wait for those miracles, some new procrastination techniques have arrived in the form of Mum, come for another cleaning session. It's been so nice seeing her so much recently, just me and her and occasionally Susie and Frida. While I don't complain about the lack of space to her – I don't want her to think I'm waiting for them to help us – she does a little concerned-eye-scan of the flat every time she comes in and sees more stuff we've got for this baby (play mat, mobiles, buggy foot-cosy) from Suse, from them, or from Thom's parents, the other side of the world. But I just bite my tongue and enjoy her looking after me.

TO DO:
Keep looking for the secret hidden extra room that must be
  here somewhere

May 9th

Finally, finally got round to one of the NCT sales today. I'd prepared with a wallet full of cash and a list of those things we still needed – I'd have been better off digging out my shinguards and elbow pads.

The doors opened at 10, but the queue was already out of the car park when I arrived at 9.45. When the crowd of (mostly) women were let in at 10.01, there was almost a *howling* as we surged forwards into the big council hall, where fifty or so stalls were laid out with babygros, maternity clothes, soft toys and, around the sides of the stalls, even cots and buggies.

One of the main things I was after was a baby sling, having been told that these sales had some of the best bargains, but they were being snapped up even as I watched. I had never seen money changing hands so fast – it was a series of frantic transactions between panicking buyers and gleeful stallholders – and I felt I couldn't even get one foot on the train to keep up. Just to get myself started, I picked up and paid for a £2 pack of plain babygros at the nearest stall, and felt my adrenaline rising. OK. I could do this.

Three stalls away, I saw exactly what I was looking for. A Baby Bjorn sling, still in its box, as yet ungrabbed. I started shoving my way past shoppers, pulling money from my wallet, ready for the purchase. I was at the end of the sling's stall, reaching across several other browsers, when another hand leant over and picked it up. I put one hand on the table, groaning and clutching my huge stomach, doubling over. I saw the hand put the sling box on its side and take my arm, and I heard someone say, 'Are you alright?' Without looking up, I grabbed the box and thrust my money at the stallholder. 'You bloody cheating horror,' the voice said, to gasps around the table. I looked up.

Me:      Well, if I'd known it was you —
Molly:   You'd have bitten my hand off? Toss you for it.
Me:      No, you take it. I don't know if I even want one – I'm just a thrill-seeking adrenaline junky, and this is how I get my kicks these days.

When the crowds thinned out a little, we found another one anyway, in a battered box but in perfect condition. Then we admitted defeat and sat down to some deep-brown tea and matching walnut cake. As Molly picked off a bit of icing, she turned to me and said, 'I'm getting too old for this shit.' We clinked tea cups.

TO DO:
Pack hospital bag
Get breast pump?
Pick a name


May 12th

Fiona and Mark's wedding was absolutely brilliant. The wedding was brief and beautiful, and the party was filled with a ceilidh band at one end and tables of food at the other. The newlyweds were charming and hilarious, and all the guests clearly adored them. When they made it round it to us, Fiona fell on me, lipstick-smeared but dizzily happy.

Fiona: I'm so glad you two could make it!
Mark: Your wedding quite inspired us.
Me: Oh! Really? That's so nice!
Fiona: The least we could do was invite you, to examine your legacy.
Me: It seems like a very nice legacy indeed.
Thom: Congratulations to you both. I have to confess, this *might* be an even better party than ours.
Fiona: [dismissing him with a smile] Whsht. Kiki, I also wanted to talk to you about *work*.
Me: Now?
Fiona: Yes, but we can do it properly later. I'm setting up a little publishing house with Mark and his brother, and we could do with some more editors. It's only

a tiny publishing house, and the salary wouldn't be much to begin with, but you'd be your own boss and you could order these designer types around. [flicking her head at Mark]

Me:     Oh, Fiona, that's so kind, but I'm [indicates stomach] and I'm not sure that's the right time to join any company, plus I've just had a promotion at Polka Dot. But thank you, though. I hope it goes really, really well. Will you send me some books when you start?

Fiona:  Oh, you're so pregnant, aren't you! Fine, fine, we don't want your big pregnant face around the office anyway. But still, if you change your mind.

Mark:   Don't bully her or she'll never want to work for us.

Me:     Well, congratulations again. Let's do some dancing instead.

I can't imagine how, with a new baby, I could leave the security of Polka Dot to go into someone's new business, but I would *love* to work with Fiona again one day.

We got home at 1 and ate two whole pizzas. Then the baby started squirming, I got the worst heartburn in the world, and the three of us stayed up until 3 playing a very cross-eyed Scrabble.


May 13th

I've had a sudden burst of energy this week, perhaps in a last-ditch attempt to get everything done before the baby arrives. But rather than nesting with floor-scrubbing and cupboard-clearing, I've been out every day and every night, at galleries, cinemas and restaurants. Tonight was the final night out before I thought I probably needed a rest, so we'd planned a trip to the pub with everyone, after a family birthday party for the twins. Sheila the Landlady, boss of our local, had planned an Alvin Stardust night at the Queen's Arms which I didn't quite feel strong enough for, so we'd agreed to meet at a pub closer to town: me, Thom, Susie and Pete, Eve and Mike, Jim and Poppy and Nick (still staying with Jim), Alice, Greta, Rich and Heidi, who had left baby Megan with Rich's mum – everyone. It was a nice pub and the weather had dried off for once, so we all sat outside, chatting and laughing. Greta declared it my baby shower, so they raised their glasses to the baby, and spent a while trying to guess its sex, appearance, and possible names.

Susie: Susie.

Pete: Susan Peter Carlow Sharpe.

Eve: English Language Sharpe Carlow.

Jim: Stevie Wonder. No other surname.

Poppy: Do you mind what it is?

Thom: [squeezing my hand] Nope. As long as it's devilishly good looking.

Me: And has all its toes and eyes and things, etc. etc.

Mike: What about naming it after a trait, Quaker-style? Colin Culinary-skills Sharpe.

Me: Nothing double-barrelled. It's *so* pretentious. Otherwise, I like it.

Thom: No no, Colin Spelling-ability Sharpe.

Me: Hem hem.

Thom: Sorry, Sharpe *Carlow*.

Me: I think we've found our winner. Plus, we'll win the medal for Most Middle Class Name, too.

Eve: [laughing] I think not, what about –

And she suddenly stopped. She was staring at the door, completely white, and we all followed her eyes to see a skinny,

207

handsome, scruffy man standing in the doorway, staring back at her. Louis. Eve's nightmarish, manipulative, bullying, boring, ruinous ex (who did always have great hair). Oh, bloody hell. 'I thought I heard your voice,' he said, and I turned back to Eve. She dropped Mike's hand and stood up, like she was hypnotised. When she started walking over to Louis, I couldn't watch anymore. I looked briefly at Mike, but his face was frozen with embarrassment as the two of them disappeared inside the pub. Suddenly everyone tried to talk loudly amongst themselves about sport, the news, jobs, loudly and merrily.

Mike: Need I ask?
Me: So now you've had the pleasure of meeting Louis. Well, I say pleasure, I mean utterly repellent experience.
Mike: Is he as bad as he looks?
Me: Worse.
Mike: Is it ridiculous that I feel bad for her?
Me: Are you worried about her?
Mike: About her going off with him? Not really. But I'm sorry all of you had to see that. Would Beyoncé do that to Jay-Z?
Me: Is that our generation's What Would Jesus Do?
Mike: No. [sigh] Not really.

We all stayed for another twenty minutes, but when Eve didn't come back out – I didn't think she'd want me following her – the mood had been broken; everyone started trickling away, giving me and Thom good luck hugs and pressing us to keep them posted.

On the bus home, Thom and I talked more about Eve.

Thom:   Back to her old tricks again?

Me:     Mike said he wasn't worried about her running off with Louis, and I think he's right.

Thom:   She might not be banging him right now, but she *did* go off with him.

Me:     Don't be unfair, Thom.

Thom:   Unfair!

Me:     We don't know what they were doing, or why she wanted to talk to him.

Thom:   Mmm. You never used to be this charitable.

Me:     I suppose I've had my faith restored in Eve a lot these last months. She's been different for ages now. Mostly.

Thom:   Since she met Mike?

Me:     Mmm back at you.

Thom:   Then I hope for the sake of your faith, she isn't messing this up.

I didn't say anything but I agreed with him. Oh Eve, what happened tonight? Why did you just walk away from us all? And how long until this baby is born and I can lie on my stomach again? I miss that. I really do.

May 14th

Due date minus one week. I can last seven more days. I can definitely cope with seven more days of heartburn, seven more days of going to the toilet every thirty minutes, seven more days of aching lower back and hips and feeling like the skin across my stomach is actually about to split in two. I can cope with a week of waddling, of making grunting noises every time I stand up and sit down, and of being unable to sleep in snatches of more than a quarter of an hour. What I can't cope with, is the suspense.

Thom came home bouncing in his shoes.

Me:    Did one of the good-looking mums wink at you
       again?
Thom:  The headmaster wants to make me deputy head of
       English in September!
Me:    Hold on, let me guess. Was it the blonde mum with
       the curly-haired boy in Year 9?
Thom:  The head of English is moving to Lancashire, so the
       old deputy head is moving up, and the head wants
       to offer the position to me! He was so impressed by
       Jacki and what I'd put on for the kids . . .
Me:    Hang on. Was it the brunette, then, with the daughter
       in braces?
Thom:  No, but she did give me a special smile today.
Me:    Thom, that's amazing! Not the smiling, the job. That's
       brilliant! Are you pleased?
Thom:  I am, yeah. I'm really pleased. It means the school
       likes what I'm doing, for one thing. I'm very
       pleased. [bellowing into my stomach] IS BABY
       PLEASED?
Me:    [waiting for movement] Yup, the baby is also pleased.
       Well done, you boffin. I'm pretty damn proud.

TO DO:
Eat curries for every meal
Give Thom a son as a congratulatory present
Pack hospital bag


May 16th

Right. Like a good parent, I have finally done my homework, and written my hospital and post-hospital list.

210

Should records demand it, I've wedged it into the back of this book.

Slightly overwhelming: I *literally* take less on a two-week holiday. I am taking the contents of a grocers, a baby shop, a pharmacist and a newsagent, plus some slightly questionable eighties technology. If I actually got all this stuff out, I wouldn't be able to see the bed anymore. How the Jesus Christ are we going to get it all to the hospital? Into a room? But I also can't see a single thing I can do without.

OH GOD and a car seat. Although I suppose at least that doesn't need to go into the ward with us. OK. Thom says, 'Why don't you stop panicking about how much space all the things on the list take up, and actually pack the damn bag?'

TO DO:
Find out if anything can be culled
If not, get a bigger car
And a bigger hospital
Check list over one more time


May 19th


With two days to go, I had a date with Eve at the Serpentine in Hyde Park. It was a gorgeous morning, sunny and hot, so I stuffed my feet into some sandals and rolled down there on the tube, surprised to find Eve already waiting for me at the café.

Me:    What's happened?
Eve:   Nothing's happened. Why would something have to have happened for me to be on time to meet my beautiful model-of-fertility friend?

Me:     Really. What's happened?

Eve:    Mike and I had a fight.

Me:     A fight with *Mike*? *Mike* Mike? [pursing lips]

Eve:    Yes Mike, and no, I didn't have a fight *with* him, we
        had a fight together. Apart. Against one another.
        Whatever. Anyway, we had a fight, and I don't really
        know what to do. Do you?

Me:     I don't even know what the fight was about, Eve.

Eve:    [staring at me]

Me:     [taking her arm] Oh, riiiiiight, *Louis*. I'll get you a
        drink. What do you want?

Eve took one look at me trying to carry a tray with a
huge stomach in the way and suggested that the day was so
nice, we should just get some drinks to go; she said she'd
grab them while I took a brief weight off, and I watched her
chatting with the handsome waiters. She came back with our
drinks, glowing from their attentions.

Eve:    What?

Me:     Nothing. [hefting myself up] Tell me about the fight.

Eve:    Don't make it sound like that.

Me:     Like what?

Eve:    Like it was a . . . bout.

Me:     Wasn't it?

Eve:    No! You're making it sound like we traded blows.

Me:     Eve. [pushing open the café door] What happened?

Eve:    It really wasn't my fault.

Me:     That's an ominous start. Shall we walk along the
        water?

Eve:    Sure. Is it?

Me:     *Eve*.

Eve:    So you were there. You saw Louis just turn up out
        of thin air.

212

| | |
|---|---|
| Me: | Thin *hair*, more like. |
| Eve: | Who are you kidding? His hair is still amazing. |
| Me: | [gritting teeth] Yeah, it really was. How long until you came back out? |
| Eve: | I didn't. |
| Me: | What! Why? |
| Eve: | I didn't want to freak Mike out – |
| Me: | You 'didn't want to freak Mike out'. As you might do by, say, vanishing off with an ex? |
| Eve: | I just thought Louis and I should get all the talking out of the way – |
| Me: | Before what? |
| Eve: | Before I could walk away, back to Mike, and never have to think about Louis again. |
| Me: | Eve – are you completely deranged? |
| Eve: | No, I'm not, and I'm not perfect either, but I think you live in such a tiny little bubble that you can't even understand how normal humans feel. Now I've had to break up with Mike and the last thing I need is you fucking – [to my stomach] sorry – lecturing me on what to do in relationships, like you're soooooo good at that, you would never do something like leaving someone before the wedding – |
| Me: | *You* broke up with *Mike*? |
| Eve: | [suddenly defensive] Yeah. |

I don't know what happened next. I was so utterly exasperated at Eve's stupidity. I could handle her spitefulness, trying to attack me when she felt cornered, but I could not believe that she would walk away from something as good as Mike, and that she would let that error be triggered by someone as awful as Louis. But I blame my actions on hormones. Or at least, I blame my actions on the tiny voice in my head saying *You can blame this on hormones.* We were right by the Serpentine, walking along the banks as we talked, and when she turned to me with her swaggering, defensive, 'Yeah,' I just lost my mind for a moment, shut my eyes, opened them to find she was still there, and pushed as hard as I could. In slow motion, she flailed her arms, slowly, inevitably, falling backwards into the water, but I didn't stay to watch, just walked past all the staring people and waddled as fast as I could out of the park.

I took the tube home, waddled from the station back home, where Thom met me at the door, arriving home at the same time. As he let us into the flat, he said, 'So how was Eve?'

Me:      Fine. [silence] She broke up with Mike. [silence] I pushed her in the lake.

Thom:   What?!

Me:      I *know*! What is wrong with that girl? How stupid must she be to let someone like that go?

Thom:   Bloody hell, Kiki, you can't push people into lakes.

Me:      It wasn't people, it was Eve.

Thom:   [throwing his hands up] Well, was she OK?

Me:      I don't know. I didn't stay to find out.

Thom:   You pushed her in a lake, then walked off.

Me:      You're making it sound worse than it was.

Thom:   Tell me where I'm going wrong.

Me:      You're – you weren't *there*, Thom. She was being ridiculous.

Thom:   Kiki. You need to call her. Now.

Me:      You're not my boss.

Thom:   No, I'm your voice of reason, since yours is clearly being borrowed by the baby right now.

Me:      You're . . . your mum is clearly being borrowed by the baby right now.

Thom: I'm going to blame that on hormones.
Me:   [muttering imitation] Mem-mem-mem-mem-meeh.
Thom: [leaving the room] And that.

It took me a moment to register what Thom was doing while we were talking. He'd got out our two weekend bags, and was systematically filling them with everything on my hospital lists.

Me:   What are you doing?
Thom: Packing our hospital bags.
Me:   No! I've got a system!
Thom: Is your system 'Wait until it's too late and just go to hospital with spare pants in your pocket and a book only if you remember it'?
Me:   [small voice] Maybe.
Thom: If you're going to carry on packing, I will stop right now. Will you do it?
Me:   Yes! I just want to check the list *one* more time –
Thom: Right, the second you finish checking, I'll stop.

The bags were done before I'd finished going through it.

TO DO:
Ensure my child treats me with the utmost respect at all times, despite any foolish behaviour on my part

May 20th

Eve called this morning.

Eve:  Because I am the better man, I am calling to say I would like us to be friends again. I shall blame your

215

savage attack on me as a moment of hormonal madness, and I would like this to be water under the bridge. Much like I was when you left me yesterday.

Me:     Thanks, Eve. I'm so sorry. I tried to make a joke about it with Thom, but what if I'm going mad, and you're my first victim? I'm so sorry. I'm *so* sorry.

Eve:     It's OK.

Me:     But what if this is just the beginning? These hormones can make you do such strange things . . . What *happened*?

Eve:     I think . . . I think *I* just freaked out, seeing Louis again. I didn't have the slightest feeling for him – he made me feel a bit sick, actually . . . but I just felt weird. It just took me back to all that time with him . . . and my head just went a bit weird. I apologised to Mike.

Me:     And how did that go?

Eve:     Much better than I deserved, really. We're OK, I think.

Me:     Well, I'm sorry too, Eve. I might have been judging you a little bit, and it wasn't even the slightest bit my business. I'm sorry. Oh, and I'm sorry for pushing you in a lake.

Eve:     What's a little bit of aquatic horseplay between old pals?

Me:     Thanks Eve. I do love you.

Eve:     Ugh, don't get your hormones all over me. I'm hanging up now.

See? I knew it was worth keeping my faith in her.

But I meant it when I said I was worried. Who behaves like that? What if this is the beginning of something? What if I go all *Yellow Wallpaper* and have to be confined? This

216

just isn't acceptable behaviour, and although I knew at the time I could blame much of this on pregnancy, it still doesn't mean I shouldn't worry. I just miss work. I have to keep an eye on things. Just relax a little.


## May 21st

Oh, my legs. My legs and my back. My legs, my back, my pelvis, my shoulders, my fingers, my feet and my womb. Jesus Christ, it feels like this baby is either going to burst out when my over-full stomach just splits open, or the weight of it is going to push it out of my birth canal while I'm staggering to the kitchen for another Jaffa cake. I hurt all over and am huge. I've just eaten too many buns and almost stopped moving altogether and I miss running and swimming and being anything other than a sofa-based mammal.

As I've hit the golden forty-week point, I had an appointment, back at the doctor's. Since I've been seeing only midwives the last few months, I'd completely forgotten that Dr Bedford had gone on her maternity leave. When my name was called, I waddled into Dr Bedford's room, with a, 'Hell – oh!' Sitting at Dr Bedford's desk was an elderly gentleman with a burgundy bow-tie and an enormous stomach. And yes, I know I'm on shaky ground here. He stood up with a wheeze to shake my hand, and introduce himself as Dr Moore.

Dr Moore:   Now, Mrs Carlow, I can see from your notes here that you're due to deliver very soon.
Me:         Ms Carlow. Yes, due today, but no stirrings yet.
Dr Moore:   Right. And do you feel well – any nausea, dizziness or bleeding?

217

| Me: | No, I'm just very tired. |
|---|---|
| Dr Moore: | [looking at me as if I'm mad] Well, you *are* forty weeks pregnant, so that is to be expected. Is there anything else? |
| Me: | No . . . thank you. Is that it? |
| Dr Moore: | Yes, you have the hospital's number if you go into labour, don't you? No lifting heavy objects, no jumping up and down. And we'll see you back here in a week or two if nothing's happened, alright? |

I couldn't even speak when I left, I was so angry at his laziness. He hadn't even checked the baby's heartbeat – he hadn't even checked my blood pressure! – and certainly hadn't offered me a cervical sweep (although I feel a bit sick at the thought of him performing one) which might have got the labour going. As I stomped home, I rang Midwife Linda, and told her everything. She was equally furious, and sent one of the other midwives round to do a full check on me. When the midwife Joanna came, she checked me over completely and explained that this had happened a lot with Dr Moore – but she reassured me I didn't need a sweep yet, unless I wanted one. I suppose my face said everything, as she just laughed and packed up. As she was leaving the flat, she said, 'You have our number, Katherine. If you need anything else, or you want that sweep, just give us a call. I'm sure Baby will be here any day now – just try to relax.'

Ahahahahaha.

TO DO:
Eat more fresh pineapple
Try some extra-hot curry

May 23rd

Listen, you stupid fucking bullshit baby. You better come out of there or I'm coming in to get you. And you do *not* want that to happen.

TO DO:
Star jumps

May 24th

Oh. Ohhhhh. I'm writing this quickly. Just as I was debating going for a sweep, we were sitting down to a Korean takeaway when there was an audible (to me) pop, and I felt a slow *glug glug glug*.

Me:    Thom. Fetch the carpet cleaner. I think my waters have just gone.
Thom: Are you kidding?
Me:    Yes, three days overdue, these are the jokes a heavily pregnant woman makes.
Thom: [slightly squealing] This is *exciting*!

I don't have time to write more. I'm having a baby!!!!!

[Later]

Home again.

So mid-takeaway, Thom grabbed the overnight bags, checked we had the car seat for the baby, guided me carefully into the car and drove like a maniac to hospital, having me call them to say we were on our way. When we got there, Thom dropped me off right at the doors of the Maternity Wing before he parked the car 'just in case you have it while I'm parking', found me there three minutes later browsing the contraception leaflets and coddled me carefully into the lift and up to the reception. They left us there for about twenty minutes, then a lovely midwife came in to check on me as I tried not to picture the slow *glug glug glug*ging happening out of my birth canal. She led us into a little room where she had to check – like the world's most unlucky plumber – my leaking waters, then left me strapped up to a monitoring machine, with a giant bandage wrapped around my giant gut, printed with little smiling baby faces. We were there for an hour, with Thom occasionally saying, 'Is it coming yet?' After the hour was up, they checked the monitor, said, as it was a first labour it would probably be hours, and if nothing had happened in a day and a half, I should come back for an induction.

So we're home again. IN THE NAME OF ALL THAT IS HOLY, *WHY*?

May 25th

Welcome to the world, Stanley.

This is how you joined us.

About two hours after being sent home by the lovely midwives, my contractions really sped up. Thom called the hospital again, who asked to speak to me. Remembering Ros's excellent training, this time I made sure to sound as 'in labour' as possible, making my previously silent

220

contractions full of groans, which actually made me feel a hell of a lot worse. I suddenly thought: Shit, is this really happening now? Thom fished the TENS machine out and stuck it all over my back, giving me the control button, wrapped me up, grabbed my bag and whisked me back out.

Thom:  Second time lucky?
Me:     [doubling over on the car bonnet] *Ungggggggghh* . . .

When we got to hospital, Thom parked up, stuffed ten pound coins into the ticket machine, found a wheelchair and brought it over, before I'd even registered where we were. Somehow, he managed to get me into it ('Can I put the bag on your lap? No, sorry, forget that') and wheeled me back up to the Maternity floor.

This time, thank God, I was immediately deemed in labour, and taken to an empty room, where the midwife Linda, who I'd been so scathing about at my booking visit but now had the halo of a saint around her, stuck her fingers in my vagina (Me: 'OH MY GOD that's sore. No, sorry, carry on, sorry, you're just doing your job') and said I was five centimetres dilated, and could have the water bath in the corner if I wanted. 'Thank you, Linda,' I shouted, unable to tell how far away she was when she didn't have most of her fist inside me, and also unable to see, having had my eyes closed in pain for the last twenty minutes.

Suddenly I became aware that the TENS machine was killing me. Really, really hurting me. It was like it was tuning in to the waves of labour pains, then turning them up to 11 and digging knives into every nerve in my lower body. I managed to moan, 'Take it off.' Thom said, 'Take what off? Turn the water off? OK! No? OK, take your t-shirt off, right,' and started trying to manhandle my

221

clothing off me, until I summoned every available muscle, reared up and roared, 'TAKE OFF THE MACHINE!' 'Right, sorry, yes, getting it off now, don't worry.' I grabbed Thom's hand to apologise, but the ripping, aching pain riding back and forth in my body knocked my speech away again, so I just rolled over as best I could so Thom could get access to all the sticky pads on my lower back. He started pulling them off, but I became aware (seconds later? minutes?) that there was still one on, and it was still really fucking painful. 'THOM!!' I wailed, '*PLEASE!*' He muttered more apologies and soothing words, but I could sense that he was trying hard to remain calm, and I heard Linda leaving the room. I wondered briefly what he could see that was making him panic, or hesitate, and what she was leaving for. What was – but another contraction arrived then, so I was no longer thinking about anything apart from just not letting my head explode or my teeth grind down to stumps between each gritting jaw. Finally the pads were off, the TENS machine was away, and I could hear Linda coming back into the room.

Linda: I'm just going to have another look at how dilated you are, Katherine, then we'll get some idea of how things are going on with Baby. Alright? It's been a while since I last checked. You might remember that it could hurt a little bit.

Me: Can I keep my eyes closed?

Linda: As long as you stay still, you can do whatever you like. [reaching down] Alright, you're . . . wow! You're nine centimetres already here. You're pretty much done, Katherine, well done. If you carry on at the speed you've been going, I think you'll be fully dilated in another twenty minutes or so, and then we can think about pushing.

Me:      [gritting teeth as another contraction builds] Idon't thinkI'llbepushinnnnnnnnng –

Linda:   Alright, you've got another contraction? Just breathe through it, Katherine, try to take some good breaths in and let the contraction grow. It's your body dilating your cervix to get Baby out, and getting Baby into the right position so you can get it out easily. Just try to let your body do the work, don't fight it.

Me:      Nnnnnnnnnnnnnnnnnnnnnnnnnnnnnnnnnnnnnnnngkay.

Linda:   OK, that's another one gone. If it helps, Katherine, you can think about the fact that you've only got a finite number of these contractions before you're holding your baby in your arms.

Me:      Can the finite number be one?

Linda:   [laughing] It's not one, but it's not far off. Let's get you into this water now, shall we?

Then Thom and Linda were either side of me, helping me into the nice, deep, warm bath.

Me:      Oh. Oh, that's good.

Linda:   Is that better? OK, it sounds like you're feeling a lot better.

Thom:    How are you doing, Keeks? I'm right here.

Linda:   Well, it looks like the labour is progressing really well. You seem calmer, and happier. You're coping with things really well now, Katherine. Is everything OK?

Me:      Yes. Much better. Thank you.

Linda:   Good, good. Do you think you might be able to open your eyes?

Me:      No. [silence]

Linda:   OK, no problem. Try to enjoy the water, move around if you like.

I don't remember what happened for a while – things just kind of telescoped together. I know people came and went, but I don't know who they were; I heard Linda saying to them that she didn't think delivery was too far off; I remember Thom offering me drink and snacks, and me being so thirsty. But just as he headed off to get me a drink, another contraction kicked in, worse still than the last, and I grabbed his arm and wouldn't let him go. I was just wailing, 'WaaaaatttEEEEERRRRRRR!' when I think I in fact meant, 'Get this thing ouuuuuuuuuuut.' Still. Forgivable lapse in vocab there.

Then something shifted; not a sudden pop like the waters, but like a hidden switch had been flicked somewhere inside me, and I just said really calmly, 'Oh. The baby's coming.'

Linda: It is coming, Katherine! Not long now!

Me: No. Now.

Linda: OK, don't worry, Dad! Let's have a look at Kiki. [reaching into water] Right, yes. That baby really is coming, isn't it?

Me: He.

Thom: Heeee heee heeee – slower breathing, Keeks.

Me: *HE*.

Thom: Longer breaths, like this, heeeeeeeeee. Heeeeeeeeeeeeeee.

Me: Not it, *he*. Please.

Linda: Oh, it's a boy! Wonderful, let's get him out, shall we? Something's suddenly happening, I can feel his head down there. Now Katherine, I need you to not push unless I tell you to, OK?

Me: OK. I've got a contraction coming.

Linda: Alright Katherine, I want you to wait until your contraction starts, and then push all the way through, OK?

Me: No problem.

Thom:   Can I do anything?

Linda:  Did you want to get in, Dad?

Thom:   Kiki?

Me:     Please can you not? I'm just – mmmMMMMMMM
        MMMMMmmmm . . . mmMMMMMMMMMMMMM
        MMMMMmmmm . . .

Linda:  Push for me, darling, keep pushing –

Me:     MMMMMMMMMMMMMMMMMMMMMaaaaAAAA
        AAAA –

Linda:  Good girl, well done, push down into your bottom –

Me:     AAAAAAAAAAaaaaaaammmmmmmm . . . [silent]

Linda:  Nearly there, then we'll have a little break, good girl,
        I'll give your back a rub –

Me:     [roaring] *Please don't touch me.*

Linda:  And we'll take a little rest. Well done, Katherine, that
        was amazing.

Thom:   Are you alright, Keeks?

Linda:  Some women love their backs being rubbed, some
        don't want to be touched at all. It's not a problem.

Me:     There's another one –

Linda:  Alright, just like before, push down, push down, good
        girl.

Me:     mmmmMMMMMMMmmmmm – [silent]

Thom:   Is she OK?

Linda:  She's just concentrating, that baby's coming any
        minute. Do you want to feel it?

Thom:   [silent] JESUS. Is that – what *is* that?

Linda:  That's Baby's head out.

Me:     – mmMMMm*gaaaaaaaah*.

Linda:  Just take a moment, and I think the next push we
        might have Baby with us.

Me:     [to myself] I can do this.

Thom:   Keeks, you're doing so well. You're doing so, so well.

Linda:  You are, this has been an excellent labour, you've

really done well. Now we need one more push, OK, one more, nice and gentle, don't force it, just a nice steady push when your next contraction starts, OK?

Me:     It's coming –

Linda:  OK, good girl, just a nice steady push, nice and slow.

And you were born. At 3 am, you were born.

It's so incredibly nice to meet you.

## May 26th

Hey, this baby is still here! Oh, it is so lovely. Anything below my waist is either numb, bleeding or tender, and my breasts have gone mad ('Oh, excuse me, I'm just going to make MILK to feed a HUMAN' and I know that's what they are supposed to do, but it doesn't stop it being completely, totally bonkers). But I am so happy. I was allowed home yesterday evening, since I had no complications and Stanley was feeding well, and was so relieved to be back on my sofa, in my bed, with my bathroom and my kitchen. The hospital was wonderful and I can't thank Linda enough, but it was such a great feeling to come back through our front door, with Thom bearing our son in his arms. And the painkillers they've given me are probably the best things in the world. I'm smiling now as I think of them.

After Stanley was delivered, Linda offered Thom some hedge-shear-looking things, saying, 'Would you like to cut the cord?' But Thom politely declined, insisting he would leave it to the professionals. He told me later it was like watching someone try to cut a garden hose with some children's safety scissors ('I couldn't believe how tough it

226

was') and that he had to bite his lip from screaming a bit when the cord flicked back and splattered him with blood. Ugh. I held Stanley on my bare chest and then tried to feed him, which seemed to go well. Once he'd come off again, I gave him to Thom, who immediately burst out crying.

Me:    He's nice, isn't he?
Thom:  [wiping his eyes] Yup. You grew a nice one.
Me:    Do I get my bonus now?
Thom:  I love you.
Me:    I love you too. And Thom – I want our son to share your name. I already got to carry him for nine months, so it really doesn't seem fair.
Thom:  Stanley Sharpe?
Me:    I like it.
Thom:  I love you, Kiki. I love you so much. I'm so happy. Thank you.
Me:    You're welcome. It was *nothing*.

Then Linda told me I still had to deliver the placenta, which was NOT WHAT I WANTED TO HEAR, but she just gave me the thigh injection and that sucker basically fell out (sort of to my horror). I cannot tell you how horrific a placenta looks, but I imagine anyone who's ever seen their own body part *outside* their body could probably understand. I wincingly climbed out of the pool, and was dried and dressed by Linda and Thom while Stanley lay staring at us from his little plastic cot.

I stayed for a few hours, as they checked on my 'condition' (three of the greatest words known to womankind: 'No stitches needed'), bleeding (yes, fine, thank you), Stanley's feeding (fine, thank God) and how I felt (really longing for my bed, having not slept the whole night).

227

At 7 am, we thought it was finally a decent hour to ring the family; we started with Susie, who just burst into tears. She just wanted to know when she could meet him – as I was hanging up, she suddenly remembered, 'Are you OK? Was it OK? Are you covered in stitches? Was Thom sick?' Mum and Dad were delighted, of course, and we could hear Mum clapping her hands together and her voice getting muffled as Dad pulled her into one of his hugs. Alan and Aileen picked up the phone with, 'Is it here? Thom?' and explained they'd been answering any international call that came in for the last two weeks like that. It was lovely to talk to them, although it felt a bit strange telling my father-in-law about my labour, even if he was the other side of the world. Thom grabbed the phone when he heard Alan ask if I'd delivered the placenta in one piece, and promised we'd give them another call when we got home.

When they let us go at 2ish and Thom drove us home, I went straight to bed, with Stanley tucked up in a sling on Thom's chest. I woke what seemed like minutes later, with Thom cuddling a squawking Stanley, saying, 'It's 4 o'clock – is it hungry?'

It's so funny how none of this seems real yet. It's like we're play-acting at being parents, being grown-ups that can take care of a baby: the baby's hungry, the baby needs a change, I think it's tired, like we have any idea what we're doing, like we're not just guessing. We make our pronouncements like we're waiting for the other one to say, 'What? How would you even know? You've done this job for less than a day!' but Thom says he's in a weaker position than me because at least I've been feeding the baby reliably for the last nine months. He only just saw it. Saw *him*. God, that's a hard habit to break.

\* \* \*

228

Mum and Dad, and Susie and her family all came to visit us this afternoon; in two separate visits, thank goodness, and only for half an hour each. Mum and Dad came bearing meals for the next five days, Mum piling them into the fridge and freezer before she'd even sat down, plus a huge bunch of flowers. 'Now where's my beautiful grandson?' she said, prising him from Dad's arms. But Dad didn't mind, just putting his arm around Mum and smiling down at them both. She was so warm and loving, immediately, and so giddy that she kept asking the same questions over and over, even calling Stanley 'Katherine' at one point. 'I'm over here, Mum,' I waved, and she looked at me, blinked, and said, 'I know that!' almost crossly. She'd also brought over what we have christened the Baby Parcel of Doom – a box full of bottles, formula, a baby thermometer, wipes, nappies, ice packs and teething gel rings to go in the freezer, a pack of dummies, baby Calpol – and which I received with a flash of ungraciousness.

Me: What's this for?
Mum: It's just a few things I thought you might need, darling.
Me: Dummies? Formula? No judgement happening there, then.
Mum: Don't be silly, Katherine. Of course I'm not making any judgements on anything. They're just a few things that, at some point or another, you may or may not need.

I didn't fancy getting into an argument when I still couldn't feel most of my legs, so we just said thank you and let them head off after more kisses for us and for Stan. Thom tucked Stan back into the sling on his chest, and started going through Mum's parcel.

Thom: That is quite a strange parcel, though. Why would she give us bottles?

Me: This preparation for failure doesn't make me feel great.

Thom: I'm putting it at the back of the hall cupboard, OK? We can find it again when we move out in twenty years.

Me: Hahaha, 'twenty years'. You are joking, aren't you?

Thom: Relax. I think it's already fairly apparent that we're going to need a bigger boat.

An hour after that, Susie and the gang arrived. She piled more food into our kitchen, handed me a giant box of chocolate-covered cherries and a bottle of Amaretto, then ignored me for the next half an hour while she cuddled her first ever nephew. 'Oh, he's *lovely*,' she finally breathed, then let Pete and the Twins 'have a go' while she pumped me for every detail of my labour.

Questions included:

1. Did you have stitches?
2. Are you now incontinent?
3. Were you sick?
4. Did Thom cry?
5. [mouthed] Will you ever have sex again?

Reassured that we were all in one piece, and that if she kept interrogating me she would never see Stanley again, she gave us all kisses and bustled everyone out again. Pete gave Stanley back and gave me a kiss, congratulating me again on the baby's excellence. 'He's not that good. He can't even make me breakfast in bed yet,' I sighed, as I fell asleep for another two hours before I'd even heard the front door close. Tough life.

When I woke, we called Thom's parents again. They were still so giddy, asking us questions and occasionally sighing that they couldn't be there with us right now. Alan made Thom promise to send over photographs every day, and Aileen said that they're counting the days until December, when they'll be over for a nice long visit to get to know their grandson.

Oh, and I asked Thom what the alarm was when he was removing the TENS machine from me. He started sniggering. 'It wasn't alarm. The pads stuck to my fingers when I was trying to pull them off. You kept pressing the button in your panic so I was having wave after wave of electric shock through my fingers.' He mimed his hands turning into spasming claws. 'I didn't think you'd appreciate the joke at the time, but I found it pretty funny. And the midwife was laughing so hard she had to leave the room.'

As I doubled over laughing, clutching my spongey stomach as Thom made claw hands at me over and over, I thought, 'Yeah. Maybe not proper grown-ups *yet*.'

May 28th

Molly called this morning to say baby Patrick was born last night. She's being kept in until this afternoon, but they're both fine, he's absolutely huge and Jesus, didn't it hurt? Cannot *wait* to see them both.

Discovered this afternoon that maybe I haven't got this feeding thing quite right after all. The health visitor, an older woman called Deborah, came over to check on us all today. I hope so much that she's just someone on work experience, filling in for the qualified health visitor, as she was unutterably useless.

Deborah:    Right, I'm just going to ask you a few questions, OK? Let me get my forms out. [sorts through messy briefcase] Right. First of all, do you have English as a first language?

Me:         Yes.

Deborah:    OK. Do you have any smokers in the house?

Me:         No. Unless the baby's developed some bad habits already.

Deborah:    [ignoring this] Right, do you suffer from domestic violence?

Me:         [staring at Thom, sitting right next to me on the sofa] No?

Deborah:    Good, OK, how's the baby doing? Has it been feeding and sleeping?

Me:         Has *he* been feeding and sleeping?

Deborah:    Yes, has he?

Me:         Yes, both.

Deborah then got out her scales to weigh Stanley, who was laid on them completely nude, like a little frog. Deborah looked concerned.

Deborah:    Right, I'm looking at what he weighed at the hospital, and what he's weighing now, and it looks like he's lost a little bit more than we'd like.

Me:         How much?

Deborah:    Only a little bit, but I'd like to see you give him a feed, please.

I obligingly got him on, where he started feeding immediately. Deborah studied us, then said, 'Right, that's enough,

232

I can see what's happening here. Your baby isn't getting all the milk he needs because he isn't fully latching on. It's quite common, but your nipples are too small – what you need to do is get some plastic nipple shields, from any chemist, and that will help Baby get all the milk he needs. OK?'

I don't really remember what she said after that, only that I said whatever I thought would make her leave as soon as possible. I smiled and let Thom see her out, then as I heard the door go, I roared. Stanley woke up and started crying like a kitten, but I was so angry that all I could do was pick him up and press him to me.

Me:     Sorry, Stanley pet. That's her advice? *That's* her advice? Your baby's starving because you aren't wearing plastic nipples?

Thom:   God, and if I was beating you . . .

Me:     I know! What was that!

Thom:   'I'm just going to ask you in front of the person you may live in mortal fear of, whether they keep you in mortal fear. OK?'

Me:     Nipple shields. *Nipple shields*. What am I going to do? I'm not getting *nipple shields* to feed our baby. But what if I am doing it wrong?

Thom:   Maybe Suse can help?

And of course, she could. When I rang her and she was able to make sense of what I was actually saying, she was utterly scornful on my behalf. 'Stay there,' she said, as if I'd had other plans. Within ten minutes, she and Frida were at the door, with a bag of grapes and another bar of chocolate. Within twenty, she had me and Stanley on the sofa, with cushions and supplies, and showed me in a no-nonsense manner exactly how best to feed without hassle or fuss. 'I'm so glad we're so comfortable with you manhandling my rack,' I deadpanned. 'Listen, sister, do you know what I would have given to have this knowledge when I'd had the Twins? Since Mum bottle fed us both, she was no use. *Be grateful*,' she ordered. After I'd fed Stanley in this new, painless way, Susie insisted on holding him until she had to go and pick the Twins up from school.

When she gave me a kiss goodbye, she said, 'Don't panic, Keeks. You two will do a great job.' I think that's all I needed to hear.

This evening, Thom brought dinner in as we watched *Butch Cassidy and the Sundance Kid*.

Thom: It's nice to have your sister so close, isn't it?
Me: Yeah, I'm glad she's around. Do you mind having your parents so far?
Thom: [thinking, mouth full of food] I bimt funk . . . [swallowing] Ahem. I didn't think I would, but I do. I feel sorry for them that they're missing out on this, and I suppose I miss them a bit too.
Me: I'm really sorry, Thom. Do you want to call them again?
Thom: Not tonight. Not with *Butch* lined up. But I will in the morning.
Me: Wow. I hope Stanley doesn't grow up with your parental priorities. We'll be at the bottom of the stairs, frantically pushing the Medicaid buttons on our necklaces while he swans off down the 4D picture show.
Thom: Yes. That is just what will happen. Now put the film on.

I do feel bad for Thom. I know how glad I am, over and over again, that Mum and Dad are around to meet Stanley.

And I know Alan and Aileen are still alive, but they haven't even held their only grandchild yet, and I can really see why Thom is sad.

TO DO:
See if we can post Stanley to Australia for a grandparental visit, à la *Flat Stanley*
Find out if we ever, ever need to see a health visitor again


May 29th

An odd card from Pamela today.

**Congratulations on the birth of your son. It's been a pleasure to work with you,**
**Pamela**

Is she selling the company? Is she dying? Did Tony's sabbatical mean he's now going to be the boss? Oh God, that's too terrible to consider. But how nice of her to send a card.


May 30th

Jacki came to visit us today. I realised that she's never been to our house before – but such is life in London that it's all too common to be friends with someone for years and not step inside their home – but she found her way easily enough (most people don't bother her when she takes the tube, partly because everyone wants to be too cool to get excited about seeing a celebrity, and partly because they can't believe it's her, I suspect).

It was amazing to have her in our little flat, although I'd already got most of the weirdness out of the way when I had both her and Pedro at Mum and Dad's house for our wedding. She brought a massive array of gifts, of course, and while she was there a delivery came from Fortnum and Mason's, a huge hamper.

Me:     *Pâté*. Oh you wonderful thing.
Jacki:  So tell me. How was it? Really.
Me:     Like . . .
Thom:   Rainbows and unicorns and soft summer breezes.
Me:     Only with a lot more blood and swearing.
Jacki:  Did you cut the cord, Thom?
Thom:   No. It was disgusting. Do you think I let the team down?
Jacki:  [laughing] No, love, I'm amazed you could even be in the same room.

Thom took Stan out for a walk then, so Jacki and I could catch up. The fact that she barely raised a protest confirmed my suspicions, and when the front door closed Jacki heaved a huge sigh.

Me:     How's it going with you, Jacks?
Jacki:  Oh, love, not good. Why don't I feel better yet? I felt so good about the book – and I felt great helping Thom out – and I thought I was fixed. I thought that was it. So why aren't I happy that I'm *free* of Leon?
Me:     [tentative] Because you did really love him?
Jacki:  I did. And maybe that's why I feel so bad: I'm just furious that I felt that way despite knowing exactly what he was. Why would anyone do that to themselves?
Me:     You do know several billion people would like to

know the answer to that, don't you? It's a pain, but that's how we humans work.

Jacki: But maybe I don't want to work that way. What if I'm just subconsciously waiting for the next manipulative prick to come along and spend all my money? What if it's worse next time – what if we get as far as having kids? Oh, sorry, this is no good for you to hear. [suddenly looking around] Where's yours, by the way?

Me: Out with Thom, we said goodbye to them about five minutes ago.

Jacki: Mmm. But do you know what I mean? What if Leon and I had actually had a baby together: what kind of marriage would that be to bring a kid into? And if that's who I fall for, then who's to say the next one won't be the same – or worse? And I have a kid with them!

Me: Jacki, Jacki, it's OK, you haven't yet. Don't panic. Has this thing with Leon taught you anything?

Jacki: The marriage, you mean? I don't know. I want to be more careful, but I'm also terrified of being so careful I never let anyone near me. But then I feel wide open again, and just keep swinging between those two feelings.

Me: It's barely been a year since the wedding, let alone the divorce. You just need some time, Jacks.

Jacki: And do you know how much harder it is to take time when every move your ex makes is reported in every paper from here to . . . well . . . Newcastle, or something?

Me: Oh, that is horrid. What do you do?

Jacki: What can I do? Try not to see them. Try not to let anyone tell me about them. Ped's been amazing, actually, keeping both the paps and their mags out of my

237

way. I just . . . need to be thinking about something else, Keeks. I need something else to focus on for a while. Oh, don't look like that, I'll be alright!

Then Thom brought Stan back, we had one more cup of tea together and she was off. I know I've only known her for eighteen months or so, but I never thought I'd see her like this.

## June's Classic Baby

A day came – of almost terrified delight and wonder – when the poor widowed girl pressed a child upon her breast – a child, with the eyes of George who was gone – a little boy, as beautiful as a cherub. What a miracle it was to hear its first cry! How she laughed and wept over it – how love, and hope, and prayer woke again in her bosom as the baby nestled there.

She was safe. The doctors who attended her, and had feared for her life or for her brain, had waited anxiously for this crisis before they could pronounce that either was secure. It was worth the long months of doubt and dread which the persons who had constantly been with her had passed, to see her eyes once more beaming tenderly upon them.

*Vanity Fair*
William Makepeace Thackeray

June 1st

A nice day, taking Stan around the parks with Thom, and having coffee with Craig, Molly and baby Bruiser. Alice and Dan came over too after work to meet Stan. They came bearing books and gossip and a whole slab of dark chocolate, which made them very welcome, and Dan held the baby curled up on his stomach for most of the time. It was good to see them, but I felt exhausted after they'd left – I'm looking forward to a good night's sleep tonight (albeit one interrupted every three hours).

10 pm: Stan just doesn't seem himself tonight. He's been a bit grizzly, a bit snotty. Hmm. I'm sure he's fine.

12 am: He's been a bit sick. Will try to feed him, then hope-fully we'll all get some sleep. I can take him to the doctor in the morning if he still doesn't seem well.

2 am: Stan's now been vomiting for the last three hours, and his fontanel looks really dippy. Has it sunk all the way in? Will

240

it eventually pop like a sucked-up bubble? OH GOD WILL I SEE HIS BRAIN? His nappy is dry, and he won't take a feed from me. And there's so much mucus everywhere, pouring out of his nose. OH GOD.

3 am: Right, I made Thom call the NHS emergency number. They put us through to the doctor on call, who asked us a few questions: how long had the baby been vomiting? When was his last full feed? Is he floppy? Does he have a rash? Eventually, reassuring us it was unlikely to be anything serious, she just reminded us to keep him hydrated as best we could, and to take him to our local GP in the morning if we were still concerned. Hydrated? How the Christ am I supposed to keep him hydrated when he won't feed?

4 am: I can't even see properly anymore, I'm so tired and I'm sweating from every pore on my body. Thom fished out a bottle and the formula from Mum's Baby Parcel of Doom, her emergency kit delivered on their first visit.

Me:     Thom, no! If we get him on the bottle now, he'll never get back on the breast. You know that! I'm not going to do that to him, especially not when he's so ill. He needs my milk!

Thom:   Can you express a bit and put it in the bottle? At least it's your milk, then.

Me:     But he'll get *nipple confusion*. He'll never feed properly again, Thom. Is that what you want?

Thom:   Keeks, you need some rest. If you want to give him your milk, if you express it, I'll stay with him on the bottle and tell him very firmly that it's only a temporary measure.

Me:     No! I've got a better idea. Where's that bottle?

Thom passed it to me, and I pulled off the little blue cap, turning it over.

Me: Look! A cup!

Thom: [speechless]

Me: We can feed him from the cup, and he won't get nipple confusion. See! I do still have my thinking powers intact!

Thom: [still speechless]

So that's what we did. I expressed what felt like eighteen pints (since he hadn't fed well on his last try), and we poured it, tablespoon by tablespoon, into the little six-centimetre-diameter cup, raising it to Stan's mucus-smeared face and trying to feed it to him. I don't know if you've ever tried to pour anything extremely sticky into a moving hole that doesn't want anything sticky poured down it at 4 am, but I imagine you probably ended up with a comparable amount of it all over your hands, legs and sofa. But we stuck at it. I'm desperate to not ruin this feeding for Stan. Now if you'll excuse me, I'm going to tense every muscle in my body until my beautiful baby is OK again.

June 2nd

Stan completely fine. What a bloody drama king.

I, however, have hit wall.
So tired.

I've been tired so far, but now, I'm SO TIRED. Stan sleeps 'well' but is up every three hours for a feed. EVERY THREE

242

HOURS. That's basically a huge convention of the Geneva Contravention.

I'm so.
Tired.

## June 3rd

Am still alive today, goddammit.

Someone called earlier. Was so tired I put the phone in the fridge, then spent ten minutes wandering around the flat trying to work out where the person I was talking to had gone.

Can't even remember who it was now.

Thom found me staring at the bath with the oven gloves on.

Very, very tired.

## June 4th

Cant write propely today. Stan a bit il. Up every hour and a hlf.

Not il but up a lot. Susie says growing spirt.

Startd crying when nipples leaked everywher. Me not him. My niples, my cryinge.

Cant stand up. Thom just puts baby on me whil I lye on bed.

Just cry if Thom asks me a qestion.

June 6th

What's this? My eyesight back? My spelling and grammar?
My will to live? The greatest gift I've ever been given: sleep.
Thom and I were both absolutely cross-eyed with tiredness
when Mum and Dad called round last night. They both
looked really shocked, and said they would come back in
the morning and help us. I think I just assumed she meant
bring more frozen lasagnes, but when they arrived this
morning, Mum asked if Stan had just been fed, then they
bundled him up in his outdoor clothes, stuffed a bag full of
nappies and wipes, and said they'd be back in three hours.
They were out the door before Thom and I could realise
what was happening.

Me:     [starting to panic wail] But what if he's ill? What if
        he needs us? Won't he get hungry?
Thom:  They'll be back in time for his feed. We've got three
        hours.
Me:     OH MY GOD MY BED.

So we slept. We didn't even change, we just lay on top of
the bed and pulled another cover over us. Mum and Dad
were as good as their word, and came back three hours later
for Stan to feed. Then, when he was full, they took him out
again. Mum called out as she was leaving, 'You get one more
nap, and then we'll come and make you tea, and then we'll
stay for the evening. OK?'
Thom and I tumbled back onto the bed, but only managed
an hour-long nap this time, then we just read companionably
next to one another, until Mum and Dad returned. Dad
reassured me that Stan had slept for most of this walk, lying
flat on his buggy, but had seemed 'perfectly happy'.
It was possibly the kindest thing they'd ever done for me,

and certainly the thing I've been most grateful for. This isn't fixed forever, but I certainly feel more able to cope with the night ahead. And Mum has said they're going to keep doing that for the next three days, by which time Stan's sleeping patterns might have improved.

I could not be more grateful. Thank you, Mum and Dad. You're amazing.

June 8th

Registering Stan today, back at the register office we were married at just under a year ago. When I thought back to that day, it seemed like the young pair who skidded into the car park that sunny August morning were a completely different couple. Then Thom asked me to close my eyes, and put Stan's directly against my nose for me to decide whether it needed changing, and I knew we were no different at all.

We saw a different registrar this time, and I didn't even need my hackles up for the paperwork (marriage certificates only require the name and occupation of the marrying couple's fathers, not their mothers) as the birth certificate required everything from us short of blood (even though one of the final documents barely even identified Stan, such is its brevity).

But you're formal now, kiddo. You're in the system. Our son, our Stanley. I hope you have a good time.

June 10th

Feeling more human after several days of nine-hour (albeit scattered) sleeps, I signed up for a postnatal group today – Molly recommended it, and said most of our antenatal group are doing it too. This one's just a council-funded one, where we can meet other local parents and have someone to compare notes with. I feel I've got those bases covered with the antenatal squad, but if nothing else it will get us out of the house.

Meanwhile, trying to find a nursery around here is giving me flashbacks to hunting for a wedding venue. Why are they so full? Where are people shipping babies in from to clog up every gated establishment in a four-mile radius? They're all friendly enough when I call, but when I tell them when I'm planning on returning to work they all do that shocked, 'Oh. Well, I'm afraid it's unlikely we'll be able to fit you in for that date. But if you want to leave your details and a deposit, we can certainly keep you on the waiting list' thing. Waiting list! I'm not after heart surgery. Just somewhere I can leave my child for the day without him being savaged by dogs/carried off by a pigeon/picked up by Social Services. One place genuinely asked, 'And what's your due date?' I just panicked and hung up, then laughed hysterically. Slightly worried that this will resolve itself by me trying to keep Stan quiet in my drawer at work, and hoping nobody notices.

In the meantime, a text from Annie.

Beautiful Baby Grace Eva, finally born at 8am this morning on just gas and air, 9lb exactly, Mum and Baby both doing well.

I suppose I should send a card, or something. Is she going to want me to visit? Has Mum told her mum about Stan?

TO DO:
Enjoy feeling rested for a while
Keep investigating nurseries

246

June 11th

R-Day.
Return to work day.

Not for me, but for Thom. He was fine, he says. He would
miss us, of course, he says, but hey, that work needed doing.
He shut the door slowly, with a rueful wave, but I could hear
him whistling all the way down the street, that lucky clown.

So, Stan, just you and me. I stared at him for a while, and
didn't really know what to do. A feed, you say? Fine. A feed.
By 9.15, I was already on the third episode of the *Battlestar
Galactica* boxset, and there was no sign of me washing or
dressing for my day ahead. I remember feeding Stan several
times; I remember bowls of cereal; I remember brushing my
teeth at some point; and then suddenly Thom was home,
and I was in my pyjamas, with bowls of curdling milk around
me, Stan cooing on the bouncer in front of me, and fracking
Cylons on the TV.

Me:     Um . . . hello.
Thom:   I *raced* home. I thought you could really do with my
        backup.
Me:     [clapping my hands together] Good-oh, time for a
        shower!
Thom:   It's four-thirty in the afternoon.
Me:     Or as I like to call it, Shower Time.
Thom:   Is this the example you're setting to our child?
Me:     Well, you *clearly* don't have any idea how much
        galactic history he will have learnt today.

I did feel amazing after that shower, though. Washing is
wonderful.

TO DO:
Wash before Thom gets home
Maybe take Stan out for some air?


June 12th

DAMMIT. Thom somehow managed to get home again before
a) I'd discovered who the Cylon spies were, and b) I'd washed.
Leaving me with that boxset was an irresponsible thing to
do, though, and I would like it on record that I feel I've been
tricked into this slovenly lifestyle.


June 13th

Molly called today, trying to ruin everything.

Molly: Do you two want to come for a walk with me and
Patrick today? He's so big I have to get him out the
front door while I still can.
Me: [coughing faintly] Oh, Molly, I wish I could, but I
just don't feel great today. I think I'm just going to
stay in and nap with Stan.
Molly: What are you really doing? Have you got a lover?
Me: Ewww, no, don't be disgusting.
Molly: So what are you doing?
Me: I'm . . . I'm in pyjamas and I'm watching *Battlestar
Galactica* boxsets.
Molly: I'll be over in fifteen.

When Thom got back at 5, he found me and Molly
slouched on the sofa, her in my slippers and me in his, with

Stan and Patrick lying on the baby mat, staring wide-eyed at the toys dangling above them.

Thom: Evening, ladies.
Molly: It's not evenin— oh.
Thom: Would Craig like to join us for dinner?
Me:   Is that OK? We can whip one of Mum's meals out.
Molly: Really? I would love that. Is that really OK?

So I washed and dressed and put on some clothes that weren't originally designed to be slept in, and Craig came over, and we all had a great time, while the babies slept in our room, Stan in his cot and Patrick in Stan's pop-up travel cot. I even drank wine. It was *nice*.

Having all this adult company and conversation has broken the spell, I think. So long *Battlestar*. You have been a faithful friend in a time of need, but now we need to part ways.

TO DO:
For my own sake, snap those DVDs in half – willpower too
   weak otherwise

June 15th

Ros had invited our group to her house today, for a postnatal catch-up. We all came, bearing our babies slightly self-consciously, like returning to school for a new term with new haircuts and braces, but it was nice to see everyone. Sadie's baby is unbelievably ugly, with a post-box mouth and bug eyes, and when she kisses him even Ros winces a bit; Paula's baby looks simple and Becca's looks like a beautiful doll, all creamy skin and dimples. Reiko's smiles *all the time*. Molly and I looked at Patrick and Stan, one ginormous and one peppered with milk spots and a rash up one side of his face, and we shrugged.

Ros made us a huge pot of tea and asked us to tell our birth stories. Sadie's doula sounds like a dream: she 'facilitated an easy, relaxed birth' (*not possible*, my eyes signalled to Molly) then came to her house every day for a fortnight to do their laundry and bring fresh loaves and cakes to keep up Sadie's strength. Amazing. Reiko and Becca both needed emergency caesareans, which they seem upset by (Reiko a little less so – she says she was just so happy they were both OK that she was grateful in the end), Paula had Hector in a water pool at home, and Molly and I had pretty normal hospital deliveries, although thanks to Patrick's . . . *solid presence*, Molly had needed a few stitches after an episiotomy (at which we all crossed our legs a little tighter).

Ros asked with a wicked gleam in her eye if any of us had thought about a second baby yet, to which we all responded with a horrified roar, except Sadie, who just said, 'Well, Ollie and I want hundreds, so we need to just get on with it, don't we?' I shuddered at the thought of those two at it, picturing every freshly-decorated room in their house being used and abused in terrible ways. I came to when I realised Molly was laughing at me, clearly knowing exactly where my mind had gone.

Despite all my good intentions, we also talked for ages about how the babies were eating and sleeping, and Ros reminded us again and again that the babies were all different, would have different habits and individual ways of feeding and sleeping. But it was satisfying to compare, anyway. (Becca says her doll baby takes an hour and a half to feed. Can that be right?) It was great to see everyone, and I'm glad we have each other. This baby raising ain't no cake walk.

\* \* \*

Greta came over tonight, to meet Stan and have a film night with me. She seemed to like Stan, doing the usual tiny-fingernail-admiration, but was more herself when we settled down to watch *Brazil*. I couldn't care less that she's not fussed about Stan – it's more alarming when people are, partly because I just can't see the attraction, and partly because I'm convinced they *must* be faking to be polite.

It was good to see her.

June 19th

Alice has been begging me to bring in Stan to show him off to the rest of the office (although she and Dan have already been round to visit him at home), so I went in this afternoon. It's the first time I've taken the buggy into central London, and it felt utterly bizarre – like I'd morphed from a normal young woman into a MUM WITH BUGGY, a unit that got either disapproving stares or dismissive glances. And it's not something I'm imagining: when we first got on the tube, a man gave a huge sigh even though there were enough seats for everyone, and made a big song and dance about squee-ee-eezing around us to get to the door even though the route to the equally close other door was completely clear. But I felt much better when the old man next to me leant over and said, 'What an idiot.' Getting out at Tottenham Court Road, I'd psyched myself up to have everyone growling as we tried to get up the stairs, but two people offered to help, and the young guy carrying Stan's end chatted to him the whole way up. But I still felt so strange pushing it around, like I was in costume, or someone was going to stop me and say, 'What are *you* doing pushing *this*? You know this is just for people with real children, don't you?'

But I made it to the office in one piece. It was lovely to

see everyone again – it feels like I've been gone for months, while everything round here continues as it's always done. Carol and Norman seem very happy, and she is positively glowing. It was good to see the rest of the Art team, and even Sales. Tony came out of the office to give Stan a nervous prod to the stomach, then asked if he could 'have a quick word'. I left the baby with Dan, and followed Tony into his office.

Tony:  So, how are things going?

Me:    Good, thank you.

Tony:  Loving motherhood? Found your vocation?

Me:    [laughing] Well, while I am fond of my son, Tony, I have to confess – I'm already looking forward to coming back to work.

Tony:  Are you? Good, good. And when do you think that might be? Couple of months?

Me:    Well . . . no. We talked about all of this. I'm off for eight months. Do you remember us talking about this?

Tony:  Yes, right. And are we allowed to ask you if you can do any work at home?

Me:    I don't think so.

Tony:  You don't think you can do it, or you don't think I can ask?

Me:    Both?

Tony:  Right. Have you met Melissa, who's doing your cover at the moment? Obviously she's not as experienced as you, but she's doing well as an editorial assistant.

Me:    Oh. No, I haven't.

When Tony took me back out of his office and called Melissa along, I looked over at Alice with a 'What the hell?' face. Melissa turned out to be a very sweet twenty-two-year-old; this was her first proper job, but she was passionate

252

about publishing and really honoured to be doing my maternity cover. She made me feel about a hundred.

As phones started ringing and emails started filling inboxes, everyone began drifting away, so Alice and Dan took the two of us down to the café on the corner.

Alice: So how did that go?

Me: It was really nice to see everyone! I'm glad I came. But I miss it.

Alice: But how did it go with Tony?

Me: Fine, I suppose. He was a bit weird, but that's Tony, isn't it? Why?

Alice: He's been nervous all day. He's just been sitting in his office, not even going out for lunch.

Dan: Yeah, he's definitely been weirder than usual.

Me: Maybe he just really doesn't like babies.

Alice: Mmm, *maybe*.

Dan: What did he say to you?

Me: When am I coming back, can I work from home on my leave, that kind of nonsense. Why are you looking at each other like that?

Alice: Just . . . be careful. Stay in touch with him.

I'm not exactly sure what she means, but it's good to know the paranoia and weirdness inherent in the publishing industry hasn't died off in my short absence.

On the tube back, Stan was going crazy with hunger, so I had to juggle him with one arm, undo a bra cup with another, stop the buggy from overbalancing with my foot and keep Stan between my bare breast and the rest of the carriage. When the train suddenly shrieked and stopped, Stan jerked forward and gave everyone around me an eyeful, but I felt great pleasure that my time in the maternity ward had not yet entirely faded: I couldn't have cared less. If anyone was scandalised or titillated (hahaha) by one breast about to feed a baby, it was their problem, not mine, and I stared at the man who tutted at us. My moment of Empowerment was slightly ruined when Stan puked up a little of his milk all over my handsome Zara blazer, but you can't make an omelette without spilling some stomach juices and self-made milk.

When I told Thom about my conversation with Tony, and with those two, he did exactly the same face as Alice. Thom said, 'Mmm. Don't panic about any of this, but it won't hurt to send him a couple of emails, to keep you in his mind, if only for books that are due to come up when you're back. But don't worry about it. You know how important you are to him, with all his work you cover.' Not sure what to make of all of this.


June 21st

I've sent an email to Tony, following everyone's advice, asking him for another meeting to talk through ideas for my return. Now I just wait to hear from him, I suppose.

Also, three of the nurseries have got back to me. Two are vaguely affordable, and the third didn't have their prices up on the website but seems nice. We're going to check them all out on Friday morning, as Thom has no lessons in the morning.


June 24th

A lovely walk with Mum, Dad, Thom and Stan today, through Alexandra Park. Mum pushed the buggy and Thom walked with them, while Dad and I fell behind to talk.

Me: Thanks for the other week, Dad. You were lifesavers.

Dad: Oh, it was your mum really.

Me: Have you been to the doctor with her yet?

Dad: We have. It all looks fine, love.

Me: Oh, I'm so pleased. What did he say?

Dad: He ran lots of tests on her, asked her lots of questions, and she passed with flying colours. He said it's probably just delayed stress from my heart attack, plus just a little bit of getting old. Although he said it a lot more diplomatically than that.

Me: Dad, I'm so pleased.

Dad: I'm sorry to have worried you, love.

Me: No! I'm glad you told me.

Dad: Are you?

Me: Yes! After you not telling any of us about your heart condition, I definitely want to know if any of you have any ailments at all. Even an ingrown toenail. I want to know all about it.

Dad: Well you can tell me all about how you are, then. Recovered from the birth?

Me: Ugh, you don't want to know about that.

Dad: [laughing] Come on, I'll buy you an ice cream.

Mum *did* seem well, completely herself. I can't imagine the stress that nearly losing your partner must put on you, and none of us were much help either, just worrying about my wedding and Susie with her new baby. We haven't helped her enough, at all, but we'll make up for that now. While I'm on maternity leave, I'll visit them more, and help them with cooking and cleaning and whatever they want. I'm just so glad Mum seems back to her old self. Old being the operative word.

June 26th

Took Stan in the buggy to do some shopping this afternoon. It took a little longer than I'd expected, so by the time we got on the bus home it was just tipping over into his feed time. He squawked a bit but was happy enough when positioned near the window. Three stops from ours, he started really crying, but the bus was so full that I knew I had to keep him in to be able to get him and the buggy off at our stop. I held his hand and tried to sing to him, but he was just getting frantic. Two stops . . . one stop away. Stan sounded so cross now. Then, from the front of the bus, came the bus driver's hoarse shout: '*Will you* pick *your baby up?*' I just blinked, stunned. The whole bus turned towards me, watching to see what this irresponsible mother would do. I muttered, 'Ours is the next stop,' and the bus drove on. I pressed the bell. Seven seconds later, I pushed past all the staring passengers to get my screaming baby off the bus, and watched, still stunned, as the doors closed and they drove away. I was shaking so hard. What the living Christ had just happened there? Stan had been crying for – at most – a minute. No more. He clearly wasn't in pain, and the bus ride was short, the bus busy. Had someone who had seen no more of us than a glimpse as I swiped my Oyster felt it was fair to order me about, to humiliate me as a parent in front of his entire bus? And why could I not shake the feeling that the whole thing simply wouldn't have happened had I been the baby's father?

When Thom got home, Stan was cooing on a mat in the kitchen while I scrubbed the oven.

Thom: Jesus. What's happened?
Me:    What does that mean?

Thom: I've never seen you clean before.

Me: We can add a new member to the People Who Think It's Appropriate to Judge Me as a Parent.

Thom: On top of your mum and her Baby Parcel of Doom, the Patriarchy, and the Health Visitors from Hell?

Me: Yes. The bus driver of the 626.

Thom: What happened?

So I told him. He couldn't believe it.

Thom: He was definitely saying it to you?

Me: Stan was the only baby on the bus.

Thom: And he wasn't . . . [grasping] on the phone, or something?

Me: He wasn't on the phone.

Thom: Oh, Keeks. I'm so sorry.

Me: And you know, Thom, you know [voice cracking] . . . You know that he definitely wouldn't have done it if I'd been a guy.

Thom: [looking a little sceptical] Mmm. I'm sorry, love. No one deserves that. Will you complain to TfL?

Me: What for? What would it do?

So we shrugged and I got Stan ready for bed, telling him every story I could think of that would indoctrinate him into not being awful when he grows up. My own personal highlight: *Red Riding Hood*, in which Red rescues herself, her grandmother, and the woodcutter from the wolf, and teaches them all a valuable lesson about making value judgements based on gender or appearance. So that's basically him ready for life, now.

June 29th

I'm drinking the most enormous Band on the Run as I write this. What a day. This morning, Thom and I were such different people: happy, carefree, hopeful, and with enough money to live. Tonight, we are broken shells, with our hope gone and our wallets raided.

We'd left Stan with Mum and Dad to investigate the three available nurseries in our area. The first one seemed nice enough: there were smiley bears all over the windows, and brightly coloured balloon stickers covering the door. We pressed the buzzer and waited to get buzzed in, waiting, waiting . . . waiting. We buzzed again. And again. We waited for over ten minutes, until I called the nursery from my phone in case their buzzer was broken inside. When the office put me through to the nursery, I could hear screaming the second the phone was picked up. And not a single scream. A wall of screams. Finally the person on the other end of the phone realised what I was saying, and the door opened. A friendly woman ushered us both inside, where the screaming – unsurprisingly – was even louder.

Me:      Wow, those doors sure are sound-proof.
Thom: [raising his voice] What?
Me:      Yeah, I know.

The woman beckoned us further in, into a room the other end of the hallway, and gestured to a pair of chairs pulled up to a table in the middle of the room. As she followed us in, she pulled it closed with an exhausted sigh. The screaming all but disappeared – only the faintest noise was still audible, like a distant hand-blender.

Woman:   [sitting down with us] Welcome to Smiley Bears.
              I'm Kirsty.

Thom: Hello. Are they always that noisy?

Kirsty: Pardon?

Thom: Yes, hahaha!

Kirsty: No, sorry, what did you say?

Thom: I said . . . I was just saying, it's lovely here, isn't it?

Me: [gripping Thom's knee under the table] A lovely location, I was saying. Really lovely.

Kirsty: Sorry?

Me: [squeezing harder] It's LOVELY. It's a NICE LOCATION.

Kirsty: Yes, it is, isn't it! So nice.

Me: Do you ever take the children out?

Kirsty: Outside? Outside the nursery? Oh no.

Me: Right.

Thom: [speaking up] What do we need to know? It's our first time doing any of this stuff, and we don't know what we need to think about at all.

Kirsty: OK, first of all, will you both be working? Yes? OK, then you need to know that we run an eight-thirty to five pm day. So you have to consider whether you'll be able to do the pick-ups at five, and whether you would need to drop your child off before eight-thirty.

Me: Oh, do you offer that?

Kirsty: No.

Me: Oh. That *might* be a problem.

Kirsty: Well, don't make up your mind now: I'll give you a tour, and you can see some of the things we offer here that make Smiley Bears such a good place for all pre-schoolers.

She took us back out, through the sound-proof doors, and we were hit again by the sound of sixty screaming children.

259

Kirsty: [so loud, can only see her mouth move, gesturing around each area as she leads us from room to room, then back to the original sound-proof room] Do you have any questions?

Me: NO! IT'S LOVELY!

Thom: THANKS VERY MUCH FOR SHOWING US AROUND.

Me: WE'LL KEEP IN TOUCH ABOUT BOOKING A PLACE.

Thom: THANKS AGAIN. THANK YOU.

She showed us out with a confused expression, and with our ears ringing, we headed around the corner to our second nursery, at the edge of a bit of scrubland. In wonderful contrast the door was opened immediately by another friendly woman, with a grey smudge across one cheek. She smiled at us and said, 'Hello, I'm Noelle, come on in!' As she led us inside, I turned to Thom and whispered, 'Noelle! This has got to be the one.' And then we saw the rooms.

The first classroom had the ceiling sagging in one corner, with water dripping into a bucket. Noelle saw us noticing and smiled again. 'We're just in the process of doing a lot of this up – we're just waiting for the good weather.' The children smiled at us, though, and we gave them tentative waves in return as Noelle led us into the next classroom.

In here, a group of children were being dressed in jumpers and boots, before heading outside. 'And here,' said Noelle proudly, 'is our nursery garden!'

Through the double doors from the classroom, there was a small paved area. In the shade of the building, there was no light falling anywhere the children could reach, and a dripping pipe in one corner kept the floor littered with puddles. I jumped at a sudden movement in the opposite corner. 'Don't worry!' Noelle laughed. 'It's just one of our friendly foxes!'

I looked at Thom. He tilted his head the way we'd come – Let's *go* – and I made our excuses, taking the proffered details from Noelle as we all shook hands and edged back out the front door.

Thom: I might vote no to that one.

Me: Let's not discount it altogether. For a start, it'll definitely build Stan's immune system. And his character.

Thom: A fox attack doesn't count as a character-building experience, as far as I know.

Me: She did say they were *friendly* foxes.

Thom: The ceilings had more greenery than the garden.

Me: Snob.

Thom: Would *you* take Stan there?

Me: No *way*.

Thom: Right. One to go. Good luck?

Me: Good luck.

We were shell-shocked by our visits so far, but the final option looked very different. A converted manor house set in one of the eye-wateringly expensive streets we never had cause to walk down, the third nursery looked grand and beautiful. Before we had even rung the bell, a well-dressed woman in pearls and low heels opened the door and said, 'Mr and Mrs Sharpe?' I squeezed Thom's hand, but just smiled at the woman and followed her in.

Pearls: Right, I'm Clare, the school secretary. I'll be showing you around this morning, and you can ask me any questions as they occur to you.

Me: Lovely –

Pearls: Let's begin this way.

She led us from the enormous hallway up the carpeted stairs to the classrooms. Each was in pale shades of blue, yellow and green, with huge noticeboards bursting with paintings and pictures. In the toddler room, the children barely even looked up to see who we were, so engrossed were they by their dressing-up game. In the baby room – split into a soft play area, a messy play area, and a free play area, as Clare explained – a bubble machine in the corner was playing soft nursery rhymes and blowing out bubbles which the babies watched and clapped at. '*I* want to go here,' I whispered to Thom.

After introducing us to each of the four classrooms' teachers and staff, Clare took us back downstairs to the dining rooms and the garden.

Clare:   The older children eat in this dining room – they help themselves to seconds, but are expected in return to develop good table manners. The younger children and babies eat in this dining room, which is slightly better prepared for messiness and high spirits. [almost smiling fondly] If we head outside to the garden, we can see the chicken coop at the bottom there – the older children are allowed to feed them every day, and the eggs are collected and used in the school kitchen – and over on that side, the beds. Each class has their own area, and can grow food or flowers which, again, are used in their meals or their classrooms. Any questions?

Besides basics like opening and closing times, and what we needed to provide each day (nothing but Stan), the only question we had was the cost. She handed us an enormous, glossy information pack.

Clare:   Here are the details of the payment options, with the breakdown on the back.

Me:     And this monthly cost –
Clare:  Weekly.
Me:     No, this one. [pointing]
Clare:  Yes, that's our weekly cost.
Me:     [turning to Thom in despair]
Thom:   What would we need to do to get our son booked in?
Clare:  That's very simple – since we know there's available space for Stanley, we just require [flipping through our pack] this form completed, plus a deposit equal to one month's fees, and he can start first thing in January. We'll arrange some settling-in sessions closer to the time, and that's it!
Me:     Right. Alright. So can we give you a call?
Clare:  Well, our spaces do go very quickly, just to warn you. But you have our details, they're all in the information. We look forward to seeing Stanley in January.

Before we knew it, we were back outside, and back in our car.

Me:     I really liked that one.
Thom:   Me too.
Me:     Even though she was possibly the pushiest saleswoman I've ever encountered.
Thom:   [laughing] I know! 'Our places go quickly, get 'em while you can!' Oldest trick in the book.
Me:     Maybe we should pay the deposit, though. Just in case the place goes?
Thom:   We need to think about this. That nursery costs only slightly less than our rent.
Me:     Well then, maybe we need to move into the nursery.
Thom:   But those others . . . [both silent]
Me:     Are we just going to have to go for the super-expensive one?

263

Thom: I . . . I don't really see what choice we've got.

Me: Kirsty seemed really nice.

Thom: She was. She was lovely. And I'm sure she'll be really lovely helping our child with its ear-trumpet after several months of that deafening noise.

Me: [with empty hopefulness] The second one? That had a sandpit in the garden!

Thom: Kiki. That wasn't a sandpit, that was industrial waste from the building site next door. Even with two hundred and fifty pounds extra every month in our bank account, I really think I'd need to see a slightly better delineation between 'the place diggers and unset cement goes', and 'the place my only child goes'.

Me: But he can learn architecture!

Thom: No.

Me: No, I didn't think so either. So we're really going for option three, are we?

Thom: Either that, or one of us quits work.

Both: *Bagsie not me.*

Me: Right. Number three it is. Do you want to make the call?

Thom: No, you can do that false enthusiasm thing better than I can. I always sound slightly aggressive. Particularly since that woman knew she had us from the moment we walked in. I can't bear feeling like a sucker.

Me: OK. Making the call.

I made the call, and felt slightly sick. All they need is my deposit cheque, and they can 'begin the registration process'. His bloody *birth certificate* was only £20. Tsk.

And I don't think losing that money is going to get any less painful as the months go by. But if it means that Thom and I can both go to work, it's money well spent, I say.

June 30th

Susie took me, Stan and Frida to one of her favourite daytime haunts today, the British Museum. We'd just come into the Persian section when I saw a couple canoodling near the great lion hunt. I was making a vomiting face at Susie when the woman pulled away and looked in our direction. It was Rose, Nick's now-ex-wife, who a year ago had pleaded for me to be her bridesmaid at her wedding to my friend.

Rose:   [hesitant] Oh, hey Kiki.
Me:     Hi, Rose. [driven by terrible middle-class social conventions to give her a kiss on the cheek]
Rose:   How are you?
Me:     Fine, thanks. Do you remember my sister, Susie?
Susie:  Hi, Rose! How's things?
Rose:   Good, thanks. Oh. Is this your baby?
Me:     Yes, this is Stan. Say *hello*, Stan. [silence] God, he's so disobedient.
Rose:   How . . . have you been?
Me:     Well, thank you. Well, apart from pushing him out of me, obviously. You?
Rose:   Good, thank you.
Me:     Good.
Rose:   We'd better go. But it's nice to see you!
Me:     Sure, we'd better get going too. Take care, Rose.

We had another incredibly strained and ridiculous cheek-kiss, then she all but fled the room with her unnamed boyfriend.

Susie:  That was fun.
Me:     I wonder if Nick knows.
Susie:  Oh, don't.

| Me: | I know. I don't know which answer is worse. |
|---|---|
| Susie: | Would you tell him? |
| Me: | No way! Why would I? If he doesn't know, I don't know that he'd want to, and if he does, he clearly doesn't want to talk about it. It's his path to walk, isn't it? |
| Susie: | Alright, Yoda, get a room. |
| Me: | I choose . . . this one. [gesturing] |

Susie showed us all the most beautiful things in the museum, holding Frida up to the best stuff. When I tried to do the same with Stan, she just said, 'Really, don't bother. His range of vision is about twenty centimetres.'

On the bus home with Susie and the babies, the memory of Rose and her new boyfriend gnawed at me. Who could, a year on from their vows, be snogging in a museum with someone else? It wasn't disapproval I felt, more . . . fear, I suppose. That love can come and go, and that vows aren't really forever. Whatever the Noses' problems were, I suddenly felt that none of us were immune from the whims of the human heart.

Then we got off the bus and went to get some doughnuts for me and Suse.

July's Classic Baby

'Put them down on the floor.'

The infants were unloaded.

'Now turn them so that they can see the flowers and books.'

Turned, the babies at once fell silent, then began to crawl towards those clusters of sleek colours, those shapes so gay and brilliant on the white pages. As they approached, the sun came out of a momentary eclipse behind a cloud. The roses flamed up as though with a sudden passion from within; a new and profound significance seemed to suffuse the shining pages of the books. From the ranks of the crawling babies came little squeals of excitement, gurgles and twitterings of pleasure.

The Director rubbed his hands. 'Excellent!' he said. 'It might almost have been done on purpose.'

*Brave New World*
Aldous Huxley

July 2nd

Our postnatal class starts in a couple of days: time to find a suitable outfit. Not for me, of course (the accepted six-week look around here for mothers is plimsolls, skinny maternity jeans and an expensive jacket which used to look good but now can't be fastened over your still-giant breasts) but for Stan. For these few months in which I am invisible, he must do the talking for both of us, sartorially. I'll need something cool yet effortless, charming but not cute. I'd better start work on that now.

I took Stan to meet Eve for lunch today. When we got out of the tube station I found a message from Eve, saying she was running twenty minutes late, did we mind just killing some time? Stan was heading for a feed, squirming and squeaking in the sling I'd stuffed him into, and I knew I had to find a café, fast. There was one down the first street I turned into, thank God, so I bought a huge mug of tea for the feed and for the wait, found a table, and settled me down and him on. I let Eve know where we were, and started reading. Half an hour later, Stan was full up and I was out of tea, and Eve finally arrived. She raised her eyebrows at the jacket potato bar and the *Sun*-reading builders trying not to watch me put myself away.

Eve:     Well *this* is a novelty.

Me:      Nice to see you too, Eve.

Eve:     Oh darling, nice to see you. Can I hold him? Will he be sick on me?

Me:      There's really no guarantees, I'm afraid.

Eve:     [hesitating, taking her hands away] Well, let's wait a little while, shall we?

Me:      And do I get anything?

Eve:     Come here, you great fool [hugging me].

Me:      So what's new with you?

Eve:     Oh, Keeks, work is unbelievable at the moment. But you don't want to hear about that. How's this guy?

Me:      He's fine. Six weeks in, and he's still got all his fingers and toes. [Eve glazing over] But why won't I want to hear about work? Is that hideous woman from head office still on your case?

Eve:     [looking confused] Oh! Joyce? No, she's been gone *ages* now.

Me:      Has she? When did she go? What happened?

Eve:     Kiki, that was months ago. I didn't think you'd care about any of that. Haven't you got bigger fish to fry?

Me:      Because my brain was growing a baby? Yeah, it's a wonder I even managed to dress myself.

Eve:     I just didn't think you'd be interested.

Me:      Eve, would you suddenly lose interest in everything in life if you were pregnant?

Eve:     [uncomfortable] Well, that's half the reason I don't think I want kids.

Me:      What? Since when have you not wanted kids?

269

Eve:     Ha! Was it when my dad left Mum when I was only six, never to appear again? Or is it the way they leave you beached and sleepless, with only nappies and buggies on the brain?

Me:      What are you *talking* about?

Eve:     Kiki, you have to admit it. When was the last time you and Thom went out, just the two of you?

Me:      Oh, here we go. I'm exhausted, Eve, but I'll feel better really soon. Why do I have to prove myself to you?

Eve:     You don't have to prove yourself to anyone. But I see what having kids does to a couple: it drives them apart, it wrecks your independence, and it ruins your conversation skills.

Me:      Is this what you've been thinking about me for the last six months? Is this who you think I am?

Eve:     Kiki, you're your own person. You don't have to make any excuses to me. But you chose to marry and have kids, and I choose not to. I *like* having this life. I *like* going out. I *like* being able to hold conversations with adults. I *like* having a life at all.

Me:      I'm not trying to stop you! You can do whatever you like! I literally could not give a [covers Stan's ears] flying fuck whether you want to have a baby or not, but please don't tell me what my life is like.

Eve:     [picks up laminated menu] If you're happy, Keeks, that's all that matters.

Me:      I was happy until I saw *you*.

Eve:     Me? Or is it just having to talk about your life? You chose it, you live it.

Me:      I did choose it, and I do live it, and I *really* like it.

Eve:     Did you choose it? Stan wasn't exactly *planned*, was he?

Me:      [closing eyes, counting to ten] Do you mind if we do this another time? I don't feel great today.

270

Eve gave me a huge hug and sent me on my way with some relief, I think. I was so angry I didn't know what to do with myself, and Thom was still at school, so I stomped around to Susie's with Stan in his buggy, and Frida's birthday present.

Susie:  [opening the door, taking one look at my face] Oh GOD, was it another bus driver?

Me:  Worse.

Susie:  Eve. What's that little minx been up to this time?

Me:  Oh, Suse, I just don't understand her. She seemed so brilliant, so wonderful, so everything-I-loved-about-her, but in a new, happy version. Now she's gone all bonkers and my-life-is-one-long-party, and it's shit. But I also don't want to be some terrible smuggo, beaming at my friends with a Stepford smile saying, 'Have a baby – you'll be haaaapppyyyy.' What if she's right? What if my life is completely shit now? What if I've lost any chance of happiness for me, or for Thom, or for both of us?

Susie:  Shh, shh, there, there. [silence]

Me:  Is that it?

Susie:  If you seriously need me to talk you round from believing that bullshit, then all my years of influencing you have been for nothing. You know she's talking garbage, I know she's talking garbage, and if *she* doesn't know she's talking garbage then it's still not really our problem, is it?

Me:  I –

Susie:  Now give Stan a feed, put him down in Frida's cot for a nap, and you and me are gonna have us some *momma cocktails*!

Me:  Do they have breast milk in? Hold on, let me feed Stan. You start mixing.

271

They were breastmilk-free, thankfully; while Stan and Frida slept we had two small drinks each before Thom come by to chaperone Stan and me home again. I love that sister of mine, and she seemed pleased enough with Frida's new trainers.

When I got home, I told Thom what had happened.

Thom: Just imagine you'd had a huge operation. A lung transplant.

Me: Can you *have* a lung transplant?

Thom: Are you *actually* asking me that question?

Me: No?

Thom: Good. Imagine you'd had a lung transplant. No one would expect you to be 'back to normal' the next day – they'd all expect you to recuperate, rest, find your feet again, slowly get on the mend – but neither would they expect you to be a completely different person. No one would visit a lung transplantee and say, 'No, I didn't bring you grapes and flowers and books because that's what you used to like, and everyone knows these operations make you a totally different person.' Do they?

Me: I don't know how they would react in this science fiction universe, you're right. But lungs don't need babysitting, or wake you up all night, or require you to pay eye-watering sums of money so you can give them to someone else to enable you to be a functioning member of the workforce.

Thom: Maybe not the specifics, no. But I feel you're splitting hairs here. This may or may not be a myth: some people might find it very true, some people might find it a useful crutch to get them hobbling again, some people [gesturing to me] might find it a claustrophobic straitjacket. But *you* know this, Keeks: you can choose what you make of this. You can choose

272

for yourself whether you want to use that myth, because that's how you feel, and although it might seem scary it also seems to make a bit of sense: why wouldn't you change when you've just brought an entirely separate human into the world; or you can choose to prove what nonsense it is, and that you're the person I fell in love with, Eve befriended, Polka Dot employed, all of that.

Me:    Wow. You're so wise, Master.

Thom:  It's *Guru Sharpe*. And you get that one for free. Next one, I'm going to need your firstborn.

Me:    Hey! I actually *have* one of those!

I think – sound the lack-of-surprise klaxon – that Thom's right. It's just another absurd set of rules that we're given to live by: *You'll love your baby the second you see it. Motherhood changes everything. There are some things you can't understand until you've had children of your own.* All they do is set us up for disappointment, that we don't feel the way we're supposed to, or we do but too soon, or too late, or not exactly in the right way. It is nonsense.


July 5th

First postnatal session. There are seven of us in the class – five from our antenatal group, and two others, all of us first-timers – which is run by two health visitors. I am one of the biggest worshippers of the NHS (besides ensuring I could give birth in a safe, clean, expert environment for free, they did also save Dad's life) but I am baffled as to what *exactly* health visitors are *for*. Because giving advice on babies, it ain't. The health visitors were two nervous women, one with lank hair, a sad cardigan and a clipboard, and one with frizzy hair, glasses and a clipboard. They introduced themselves to us in that whispering, head-tilting, I'm-good-with-people voice favoured by HR people everywhere.

Woman 1: Hello everyone. Are you all OK?

Woman 2: We hope you're OK today. We'll be here over the next four weeks to run this postnatal class with you, so you can learn about caring for and living with your growing babies. Is that OK?

Woman 1: So, we can all introduce ourselves now, to get to know one another. Is that OK? Right, I'm Kate.

Woman 2: And I'm Iolanthe. OK? Who's next? [turning to me]

Me: [goggling at her name a bit] Er . . . I'm Kiki.

Kate: And what's Little One called?

Me: Oh, this is Stan, he's six weeks.

Iolanthe: Lovely, lovely. Is he well?

Me: Yes, he's fine.

Kate: And Mum too?

Me: [gritting teeth slightly] Yup. His mum is fine too.

Iolanthe: No problems at all? Delivery OK? You've been finding it OK, yes? No problems, good.

Me: [mouth open to answer]

Kate: OK, lovely, thanks Kathy, let's move on.

Me: Kiki.

Iolanthe: [turning to next woman] And who have we got here?

Besides our antenatal gang, there were two others: Leila, a single mother with a son, Charlie, and Maria, who had a daughter, Caroline.

The afternoon pretty much continued in that useless vein. It's astounding how little you can learn in two hours from people who apparently do this for a living. The seven of us learnt a) what we do when we bring our six-to-eight-week-old babies home from hospital after labour, b) how to wash our almost two-month-old infants, and c) how breastfeeding is best. We shuffled out, slightly shell-shocked, clutching one another's details in case we 'wanted to discuss anything before next week's session'.

I cannot *wait*.

After the session, Molly, Sadie, Reiko and I gathered in the café for a debrief.

Me:      That was . . . weird.
Reiko:   What's the point of these sessions?
Sadie:   According to the council's leaflet about this, 'the sessions educate and inform in an informal environment for everyone to learn about parenting and young children in a casual setting.' God, did Kate write this, too?
Molly:   This is like car-crash television. There's no way I'm missing the next one.
Me:      I have to say, I actually agree. And who knows? Some nugget of wisdom might emerge – admittedly, it's more likely it'll come from one of you guys, but still. Are you in?

We've all agreed to give it another go. If all else fails, at the end of the second session we start a riot (details to be confirmed).


July 8th

I knew I had to be out of the flat in ten minutes if I was to have a chance of making the meeting with Tony, but I also knew that Stan had to be fed in the next hour, and I'd never make it back in time. I was starting to sweat, and could feel it prickling through my clothes.

275

Me:     Thom! Where's the breast pump? I've got to express.

Thom:  Haven't you got to go in five minutes?

Me:     Ten! Shit, no, eight now. I can just do a little bit.

Thom:  Kiki, I'm only going to say this once, and you can say no and I'll never mention it again.

Me:     No, we can't fit a pool table in the living room.

Thom:  You've got just enough time to put on your shoes. Why don't I give him a bottle of formula? It's just once. You need to go. And he'll be fine.

Me:     But, I . . . but . . . it's not . . . Thom, it's not good for him.

Thom:  I'm not offering him a Big Mac. It's one bottle while you're out for the afternoon. It's not *bad* for him, Kiki.

Me:     [tearful] Fine. Why don't you just make our baby a big fat mess who'll have no self-control and the IQ of a rabbit? Why don't you just do it, then? I'm going.

I felt so tearful on the train ride to the office, convinced that I was now definitely the world's worst mother. But it was good to be back in the office, where I could clear my head for a little while and think about something other than my baby. Tony was on usual form – slightly shifty and continually giving the impression that he's doing confusing mental arithmetic while he talks to you. But our meeting, again, was brief.

Tony:  So, how are you doing? Still not changed your mind about coming back? You've got your baby now, that must be it for you? [uncomfortable laugh]

Me:     No, still not changed my mind.

Tony:  Good, good. And have you had any further thoughts about coming back any sooner? We could really do with a hand before Christmas, you know.

Me:    No, we agreed that I would come back in January. Do you remember? We wrote it all down.

Tony:   Kiki, where do you see yourself in five years' time?

Me:    At a massive desk, having published the bestseller of the century.

Tony:   [thinking] Ha! Good, good. [thinking] OK, thanks for coming in and seeing us all –

Me:    Actually Tony, I was only here to see you today. We haven't really talked about any of my ideas for January, yet.

Tony:   Good, yes, just email them over; I'm always a lot better when I've got that stuff written down in front of me. Thanks, Kiki. See you!

And he shepherded me out of his office, and closed the door.

Alice was out and everyone was busy, so I felt suddenly eager to get home and get to Stan, before his next feed was due. But my tube was delayed, and I arrived forty minutes after his meal time. I was amazed when I opened the door that I couldn't hear screaming from the baby, so I asked Thom how the feed had gone, expecting a horror story of crying, vomiting and panic. Instead, Thom reported that Stan had taken a taste, pulled a weird face, then grabbed the bottle back in his mouth and chowed the whole thing down without a pause. He saw my face. 'Don't worry,' he comforted, 'I'm sure he'll be glad to get on the real stuff again.'

He was. Or at least, he was unfazed at going between them. New thing to call bullshit on: Nipple Confusion. Any chance I will manage to get all the garbage the health visitors have fed into my brain out again?

July 10th

Susie wasn't free today, so I thought I'd take Stan for a walk on my own. I was enjoying the peace and quiet as he nodded off in the pushchair, looking around me, smiling at the summer air, when I saw her again. Like a violent flashback, she seemed to be everywhere I turned. Annie. Standing on the corner by my favourite café, pushing Grace Eva in her giant car-sized baby carrying unit. When she saw me, she began waving frantically, her face lighting up. I knew I had to do something. 'Annie! Do you fancy a coffee?' I said, as if it was totally normal for me to see her in my neighbourhood at 10 am on a Tuesday morning.

When we were at our table with drinks and snacks, I began.

Me:     Annie, have you moved here?
Annie:  No no, still over in Gerrards Cross.
Me:     Are you visiting someone around here?
Annie:  No, I just loved it so much last time I came to see you, I just wanted to get to know the neighbourhood a little more! It's lovely round here, isn't it?
Me:     Are you here to see me?
Annie:  Not specifically, of course, but it's so nice for us to bump into each other this way!
Me:     Annie, is this a coincidence? And why were you at my hospital?
Annie:  I was just curious! Your mum had mentioned to mine where you were planning your labour, and I was just wondering what other hospitals were like. That's all!
Me:     Annie . . . it's really nice that you'd still like us to be friends. But . . . maybe we just grew apart. You were a *great* friend to me then, but maybe we're into different things now.

278

Annie: But we're both mothers now! Motherhood changes you completely, doesn't it? I'm totally different to how I was a few months ago. I'm like a new person!

Me: I'm not, Annie. I'm completely the same person. It'll be really nice for us to stay in touch, but I don't think it's a good idea for you to keep coming around here to try and see me. What about the other mothers near you? Didn't you say you were in an antenatal class?

Annie: [quietly] Yes.

Me: [encouragingly] And were they nice?

Annie: [quieter] Yes.

Me: And do you think it would be nice to have those friends in your area?

Annie: [almost inaudible] Yes.

Me: Right! Well, why don't you get in touch with them, and you can email me in a couple of weeks to tell me how it's gone. Yes?

Annie: They haven't stayed in touch.

Me: Oh. Oh, well, you know how busy and distracted you get once the baby is born. They're probably all waiting for the first person to get the ball rolling!

Annie: They see each other all the time.

Me: Oh. Well. Are you sure you haven't just missed an email somewhere?

Annie: No. It's Stephen.

Me: Stephen won't let you go?

Annie: He scared them off.

Me: Oh, Annie. [silence] Are you sure?

Annie: In our first class, he told one of the women that she looked nine months pregnant already. Then he got in an argument with another couple because they drove a hybrid car.

Me: Oh, Annie.

Annie:  In our second class, Stephen declared that he didn't care what our baby was like, as long as it wasn't gay.

Me:  Right.

Annie:  And in the third class, he told two more mothers that they were stupid for wanting epidurals. After that, the teacher suggested maybe the classes might be more productive if I came alone. But Stephen said they were a waste of time.

Me:  Annie, I'm really sorry.

Annie:  I never even got a chance to get to know them. [starting to cry] They don't even know that I'm nothing like him. I'm my own person! Why won't they ask me to their stupid coffee clubs?

Me:  God, Annie, look, first of all, you can come here whenever you like, OK? Just call me, alright, and come here whenever. Secondly, I'm sorry that Stephen's been difficult with these people.

Annie:  He hasn't been difficult, they just don't understand him!

Me:  O . . . K.

Annie:  [silent] No, he has, hasn't he? What am I going to do? We've got a child now! I'm supposed to be married to him forever! What am I going to do?

Me:  Right, I think you should get in touch with those women. They'll all be too polite to refuse to meet you, and they'll probably bring backup so you can see all of them together. They'll realise within five minutes how nice you are, and how different you are to Stephen. OK?

Annie:  Yes.

Me:  They will be your friends, Annie, I'm sure of it. And you have me, too.

Annie:  Can Stephen and I come over together?

Me:      No.

Annie:   Can I come over?

Me:      Whenever you like.

What a grim time for Annie. It's hard enough feeling cut off from your real life – work, friends – without feeling that the new life you'd planned is disappearing into a baby-shaped dot in the distance. Plus, that it's basically entirely your husband's fault. Really, poor Annie. And somehow these things all feel like luck, in a way. How do nice people – and Annie is nice, despite her slightly *Fatal Attraction* tendencies – end up with such fools? And to look at the question from another point of view: what's the secret to nice people avoiding them?

July 12th

The second week of our postnatal classes. Kate and Iolanthe were there as we came in, smiling with their heads tilted on one side, watching us as six of us filed past in silence like naughty teenagers, and settled in our chairs with our babies on our laps.

Kate:      [whispering] Hello everyone! Glad to see you've all made it back.

Iolanthe:  [pointing at a clipboard]

Kate:      Oh, I see. Not quite everyone. Well, maybe they're late. Shall we just give them another ten minutes?

I knew that if I'd had any sense at all, I wouldn't have come back to this place, car-crash television or no, but I really did get bored at home and was curious to see exactly how bad it could get with these two. I was just thinking,

281

*Please don't wait ten more minutes, please let's just get this over with*, when the woman next to me, Leila, piped up and said, 'Is it OK if we don't wait? If someone's running late we can fill them in.' Kate and Iolanthe looked most perturbed at this, checking their clipboards and looking at one another – *Prisoner rebellion is not on this course list* – but the other five of us murmured our agreement. They must have felt letting us have our way was the only route to avoiding all-out mutiny, because they did begin. And oh, what a beginning it was.

| | |
|---|---|
| Kate: | OK, we're going to talk today about looking after the whole family. |
| Iolanthe: | Yes, because it's not just Baby we have to care for, is it! |
| Kate: | No, it's not. Let's think about you, and your partner. |
| Leila: | [putting up hand, eyebrow raised] Excuse me? I don't have a partner. |
| Kate: | Alright [checking list] *Leila*, you can just listen in to this one. Perhaps you can pick up some tips for the future. |
| Iolanthe: | Yes! I'm sure these tips will be just as useful with your future babies too. |
| Leila: | [turning to me, blinking] |
| Kate: | So let's think about you first of all. Are you eating properly? Have you started exercising yet? |
| Most of group: | [stifled guffaws] |
| Kate: | [hastily] Gently, of course, just a little gentle exercise. So, shall we go around and tell everyone how we're taking care of ourselves? If you want to start, Kathy. |
| Me: | Right. I . . . I walked from our flat to the |

|  | tube. And I went with my husband when he did the shopping at the weekend? And I'm definitely eating my five a day. |
|---|---|
| Kate: | Are you? Definitely five portions of fruit and vegetables? [switching to high-pitched voice, jabbing both fingers towards me] You're – not – cheating – are – you? |
| Me: | [gawping] |
| Molly: | I eat mainly Dairy Milk. And I haven't walked further than the car since I was eight months pregnant. |
| Reiko: | I was seriously considering taking up smoking again the other day. |
| Maria: | I have eaten a vegetable since Caroline was born, but I can't remember exactly when it was. |
| Molly: | A raspberry Slush Puppy counts as one of your five, doesn't it? |
| Kate: | [nervous laughter] Gosh, a lot of things to think about here, haven't we? Shall we move on to our next section? |
| Iolanthe: | Let's move on to thinking about how our *partner* feels at the moment. |
| Kate: | He's been having a lovely time with you, you've been in love, maybe you've got married – or maybe not [bowing her head to Leila] – and he's been enjoying your life together. But what's this? |
| Reiko: | Weight gain? |
| Iolanthe: | A baby! |
| Kate: | A baby. And don't we all know how babies can change things! So, I'm going to get the pens out again [passes around the box of pens], and we can all write on the big pad |

here, what kind of hurdles our partner might be facing at the moment. [room is completely still] OK, I'll kick us off, shall I? I'll put down: WORK. OK? So our partner is still having to go to work every day, even if he loves us, even if he wants to be with us, he has to head off to work without us, and leave us behind. Right, who's going to go next? [silence]

Iolanthe: I'll go next, if I may, Kate! Hand in hand with WORK, I'm going to put down: TIREDNESS. So our partner might be very, very tired at the moment, mightn't he? [Leila picks up her baby and walks out]

Kate: [referring to clipboard] So . . . it's not just us who's tired, is it? They have to get up and go to work, even if the baby's been crying all night.

Sadie: Is my husband paying you to say these things?

Kate: [nervous laughter] Ha, haha, no. Yes, I'll keep the ball rolling, and I'm going to do: SEX. [room sniggers/sighs] Oh, I – Well, we need to think about that, don't we? I won't ask you about it personally, but it's something that we might want to consider talking about with our partner, is he getting the sex he wants?

Molly: Not with me, he isn't. It's like a lawnmower accident down there.

Iolanthe: It's a very important issue with men, isn't it? So it's one of those things that's worth considering, not just how we're doing, but how our partner is doing too. OK, next,

|  | I'm going to put here: HOUSEKEEPING. Now it's quite an old-fashioned word, housekeeping, isn't it, but it just means the cleaning, cooking, and generally keeping your home in a nice state. |
| Me: | [to Molly] Is this a dream? Am I dreaming? |
| Kate: | It might not seem much to any of us, but the difference between coming home to a happy, tidy home, and coming home to a house filled with laundry and a crying baby is quite extreme for someone who's had a hard day at work. We get lovely groups like these to support and help us through these difficult stages, but what does your partner get? |
| Sadie: | [hissing] *He gets to go to work*. |
| Kate: | OK, let's break for a squash and biscuit, shall we? |

Molly was delighted, the whole thing being worse than even she could have predicted, and Reiko had tears running down her face from repressed laughter. I cannot even begin to understand how these women got this job. But you can bet that Stan and I will be back next week.

After the session, we all gathered in the café. Naturally, the conversation turned round to our labours. Everyone told their stories: Molly's stitches, Sadie's home birth, my water birth. But when it came to Maria, she wouldn't say. 'I'm sorry,' she blushed, 'I just don't really want to talk about it.' Poor woman.

After we'd left the café, Molly and I walked home together, and talked about all the possible horrible things that could have happened to Maria. We'll find out what it was, one way or another.

July 14th

As a special early birthday present for Thom, Mum and Dad had got us a night out tonight. It included an envelope with money for burgers and cinema tickets, and babysitting from the pair of them. Since we'd only be out for three hours or so, I'd expressed a single bottle just before they arrived. They gave us all hugs, and Dad picked up Stan and held him on his chest.

Dad:   Go on, you kids, go and enjoy yourselves.
Thom:  Thanks for this, it's going to be a nice evening.
Me:    And you know where the bottle of his milk is, right?
Mum:   In the fridge.
Me:    Yes. And you know how to put him to bed?
Mum:   I think we can remember. With two children and four grandchildren, we'll try to get him the right way up.
Me:    OK. OK. Thanks Mum, thanks Dad.
Dad:   Go on. You don't want to miss the trailers – it's the best bit.

We rushed out of the house – speeding out the door, hurrying back in to check Stan was still OK, racing back out, going in one more time to see that they both had both our numbers and knew where we were going, but eventually made it down the street, to the car and to the cinema. When it came to it, neither of us actually felt that hungry, so we caught an earlier screening of some popcorn thriller and settled into our seats.

Me:    They'll be fine, won't they?

Thom:  Of course they will! Who do we trust more with Stan
       than your mum and dad?
Me:    You're right.
Thom:  Just check your phone, though. See if they've been
       in touch.
Me:    Isn't yours on?
Thom:  I'm just turning it off now, but I just thought they
       might have tried to get you.
Me:    I've had nothing. You?
Thom:  No, still nothing. OK, phones on silent?
Me:    Done. Shhh, it's starting.

We sat through twenty-five minutes of ads and trailers,
and I thought I'd just give my phone one more quick check
before the film itself started. Just as I tried to move surrepti-
tiously, I caught Thom doing exactly the same, and we grinned
at one another.

The film was terrible – not the quality, necessarily, but the
content. A woman is stabbed by someone who has broken
into her home; later on, another house break-in results in
the couple who live there being shot. I squeezed Thom's hand.

Me:    [mouthing] I'm just nipping out for a sec.

Thom nodded at me, wide-eyed, and I stepped into the
aisle, down the stairs and out into the lobby. Of course, my
phone still didn't have any messages, so I sent a quick one
to Mum.

All OK? Back soon. X

To kill time while I waited for a reply, I thought of all the
things that could have happened to prevent her replying:
from a broken phone, rendering them unable to contact us

in an emergency, to plane crashes, hurricanes and gas explosions on our street.

**Stan asleep, breathing soundly. See you soon XX**

Oh. I walked back to my seat and gave Thom a thumbs up, and he nodded, relieved too. But when the house intruder stepped into the children's room, Thom leant over to me.

Thom: [whispering] Shall we go now, and miss the rush to the car park?

    I grabbed my coat and was out of my seat in a second, and we speed-walked all the way to the car, while I said over and over, 'It's fine, Mum said they were fine, she said he was breathing and everything,' and thought about our slippery kitchen floor if someone was carrying Stan, our tricky front door in a fire, and *something* from the attic caving through into our bedroom.

    When we arrived home over an hour earlier than we'd been expecting, neither of them said anything. They just took us in to see Stan, who was fast asleep after his bottle, breathing sweetly in his cot by our bed.

    We have *got* to get better at this.

July 23rd

The first day of the school holidays, we decided to celebrate by heading out to Green Park in the good weather. I had a parcel to drop off at Jacki's office before we hit the park – a care package for her, as she'd done such a great one for me; some books, nail varnish, wine and beef jerky (her secret vice) – and Thom wanted to check out a possible school-trip venue round the corner, so we agreed to run our errands and reconvene by the park gates. Stan had fallen asleep in the buggy, his head tucked right onto one shoulder in that impossible way babies have, but was still breathing, his little chest rising and falling, and looked so content. I had just dropped off Jacki's parcel with the receptionist when I felt someone's eyes on me; turning around, I noticed the security guard watching me, gesturing with his head. I looked around, trying to work out if something had fallen out of the buggy, or if someone else was trying to flag me down, but I couldn't see anything so pushed Stan back outside into the sun. I saw Thom coming down the street, his trip finished sooner than expected, and was about to wave to him when the security guard came running out of the building, calling to me. My first thought really was: What *can* I have dropped? He reached me just as Thom was a few metres away.

Security guard: Excuse me, miss.
Me:            Hello!
Security guard: It is not good for your baby to sleep like that.
Me:            [slack jawed] I'm sorry?
Thom:          [coming up to us] What's not good for the baby?
Security guard: Oh, I'm sorry, sir, I didn't realise she was with someone.

Reassured that I was in the hands of someone responsible, he hurried back into his building, leaving me gnashing my teeth.

Me:      Did you . . . *see* that?

Thom:   Jesus. Can you believe that guy?

Me:      *Thom*. It happens *all* the *time*.

Thom:   What?

Me:      It happens to me almost every time we leave the house. I'm carrying him wrongly, I'm feeding him too long, I'm not feeding him for long enough, I should be cuddling him, I shouldn't be spoiling him, he should be asleep, he should be awake, his buggy should be facing me, or higher, or shouldn't be a buggy at all, but a sling. You don't know what it's like, Thom! You leave the house with Stan and you two are the most beautiful, hilarious thing in the world: Oh, wook at the handsome daddy wiv his widdle baby, ahhhh. You could drop Stan on his head and everyone would just coo and laugh and marvel at the wonder of a man with a baby. You don't know what it's *like*!

Thom:   [shocked] Keeks. I'm so sorry. [pulling me into a hug] I *didn't* realise. I'm so sorry, Keeks.


TO DO:

Plan elaborate revenge against all the people who tell me
   how to parent better

Do nothing with those ideas

Seethe a bit more


July 25th

I had an email from Polka Dot earlier in the week, from a new 'admin' address. The email requested that I come in for a meeting today at 3, so I strapped Stan into his chair and took him to Mum's, caught two tubes and climbed four flights of stairs into the Polka Dot office, arriving sweating and psyched for a battle with Tony.

But Carol immediately came over, looking both utterly apologetic and totally furious.

Me:     Where's Tony?
Carol:  I'll give you one guess.
Me:     Not here?
Carol:  Got it in one, my dear.
Me:     So who's my meeting with?
Carol:  [looking even more apologetic] Kiki, I'm sorry . . .
Me:     You? Oh, that's OK! Let's get on with this.

Carol brought me into our meeting room, and sat down next to me at the big table. There was a big pile of papers at her place, most of which looked horribly formal.

Carol:  Kiki, I never thought I'd have to do something like this.
Me:     Like . . .? Carol. Like what?
Carol:  Tony's asked me to say that your job is officially at risk. (I can't believe he's done this.) In your absence, Tony's found that the role is redundant, and the tasks are best suited to an Editorial Assistant rather than an Assistant Editor. (It's just about money, and his ego, you know, Kiki.) You'll have thirty days in which to disprove this, and then you'll be given a month's pay, in line with your original contract. Kiki, darling, I'm so sorry.
Me:     [speechless]
Carol:  Do you want a drink? I'll get you a drink? [opens the door] Norman! Drink!
Me:     I don't . . . understand. Is this going to happen, Carol?
Carol:  I honestly don't know, Kiki. He gave me these papers

291

and told me this morning, so I've no idea about your legal rights or if he's even doing this properly. It is, of course, completely despicable and utterly wrong as a business idea, but I've no idea if it will go ahead. If I were you, once you've had this drink, I would find a lawyer, get them to look over these papers and see where you've got Tony by the short and curlies. But—

Me:      But what?

Carol:   I want you to fight this, as hard as you can, because I don't think Polka Dot can afford to lose you. But I also wonder whether, once your boss has treated you this badly, you'd want to come back here? Whether it isn't worth taking as much money as you can from Tony and finding somewhere good to work, where you're actually appreciated.

Me:      I . . . I don't know, Carol.

Carol:   Of course you don't, and you don't need to think of any of that now. All of us here will do everything to support you, whether you need written statements of your job description or references for . . . other jobs. We're all here for you.

Me:      [voice disappearing] Thanks.

Carol:   Also, Tony is a complete and total shit. [hugging me]

Then she called Alice in, who came bearing the gin and tonics Norman had made us, and who was baffled as to what was going on. When Carol told her, at my nodded request, Alice's jaw dropped. 'He did fucking what?' she roared.

Me:      [whispering] He's made me redundant.

292

Carol: Not yet, he hasn't. He's only trying.

Alice: You have *got* to be kidding me. What the living Christ is that fat idiot playing at? I don't understand. I don't . . . understand.

Carol: If he keeps Melissa on as an Editorial Assistant, he can cut the money he's spending on Kiki's wages, and if he doesn't have an Assistant Editor, it's one less person breathing down his neck, revealing how poor his own work is, how few his successes.

Me: *Great*.

Alice: If he honestly thinks he's going to get away with this, it's actually funny how ignorant he really is.

There was a lot more talking, but I wasn't taking anything in. Alice offered to take me home, but I just laughed, praying I wouldn't be sick there in the office, in front of everyone. I left soon after – I assume I said goodbye to everyone, rather than just walking out, but I don't remember. I got home in one piece, called Mum and asked if she could keep Stan until bedtime, then just waited for Thom to get back. He came through the door in a great mood, singing and calling to me, until he saw me sitting on the sofa, with a tear-stained face.

Thom: What's wrong? Where's Stan?

Me: It's OK, he's with Mum, and everyone's fine. [laughing, then crying again] Really, everyone is fine. But you're not going to believe what's happened.

Thom: [coming to sit with me] Before you tell me, do you want a drink?

Me: No, thank you, I've already had two gin and tonics. Well, you remember how you were made redundant last year?

Thom:   Yes. [waiting] No!

Me:     Yes. Carol told me today, after Tony had left her all
        the paperwork and pissed off anywhere else.

Thom:   Oh, love.


He pulled me into a huge hug, tipping us back on the sofa
and letting me cry and cry.


Thom:   [softly] For someone who doesn't cry, you've had a
        lot of causes to break your rules this last year, haven't
        you?

Me:     [laughing through tears] I know! But really . . . really
        we still have each other, and Stan, and my brain and
        my health and all of that. I'm just . . . so angry. I'm
        SO angry, Thom. I can't tell you how angry I am,
        how wrong this decision is and how poorly it's been
        handled. Poor Polka Dot! Why would Tony do this
        to them?

Thom:   At least I knew the redundancies were happening
        all over the company. It was a surprise, but not a
        shock. And although I didn't like it, I could under-
        stand their decision. But this – this just sounds crazy.
        Do you think it's worth getting in touch with his
        mother?

Me:     [laughing again] Ha! 'Please Mrs Cooper, your son
        took my job off me.' I don't how well that will go
        down.

Thom:   Poor love. Do you want me to go and get Stan on
        my own in a while?


He tucked me up in bed with a cup of tea, and went
off to get Stan, only waking me on his return home to
give the baby a feed, since my boobs were bursting,

having missed two feeds earlier while I was in town. 'Mmm, delicious gin-milk,' Thom whispered as Stan fed. 'Ah, but witness how well he'll sleep now,' I retorted. And he did.

I'm just shaking and shaking. I think I just need to go to bed.
I feel so angry and betrayed.
I'm so angry.

I just need to sleep.


July 26th

Still in shock from yesterday. All I remember from the postnatal session today was the following conversation, when I momentarily tuned in then tuned straight out again.

Reiko: When they'd slit me open like a butterfly chicken to fish Mari back out of my birth canal, the doctor warned me that the needle to stitch me back up again might hurt a bit. I asked him if he'd seen the size of my daughter's head.
Paula: [faintly] I just remember blood. Lots and lots of blood.
Molly: Of course, I'll never be able to ice skate again.

I don't even *want* to know what that last comment meant. I just can't think straight.

Got this email forwarded from Carol.

295

From: Tony King
To: Carol Martin
Re: REDUNDANCY

Carol,

I applaud your effort, but having spoken to a couple of people about this, it seems it is perfectly legal to make someone redundant while on maternity leave. That job no longer exists – and, quite frankly, I can see that it was an error to create it in the first place – and there are no other roles to offer. Because of this, the redundancy is entirely legal.

We can now consider this an end to the matter,
Tony

I was shaking with anger when I read that. Not only Tony's message, but that Carol would just send that to me – no comment, no friendly word.

Thanks, guys. Thanks so much.

July 30th

It's just all sinking in. That total fucker. Tony wants me out. Melissa isn't just some temp – Tony's been grooming her to take my place. Only not *actually* my place – my place FIVE years ago. He's found a new sucker to do all his work for no money, all in the name of being 'passionate about publishing'. *That's* what Pamela was talking about – Tony must have told her that I don't want to come back. That's why he suddenly took Ann and Charlie off me. And now he's refusing to have any meetings with me.

296

That total fucking fucker. Like all Scooby-Doo villains ever, he's not going to get away with this. If he thinks I'm going to give up without a fight, he's obviously massively misunderstood the sheer bloody brute force of my newly discovered Maternal Instincts.

Fine, I don't have an actual lawyer right this second, but I will do. And when I do, and I've explained the situation to him/her and he/she's looked through my contract (oh God, where would my bloody contract be?), and then he/she's looked into the details fully, then – *then* – Tony is going to rue the day. He's going to *rue it*.

I welcomed Thom home in a similar vein:

Me:    He's going to *rue the day*, Thom.
Thom:  [clutching his hands to his chest] Why *yes*! I have had a great day! Thank you for asking! That's really kind!
Me:    I mean it, Thom. He's going to wish he'd never been born.
Thom:  I'm assuming we're talking about Tony here. In which case he'll finally have something in common with his mother. [high five each other]
Me:    We are. And did you have a good day?
Thom:  Yes, thank you. Has something sparked this off again? Not that I'm suggesting it needs it. But have you heard something new today?
Me:    Carol forwarded me a smug hand-washing exercise from Tony, where he declared that he'd 'asked some people about it' so his actions were totally legal and the case, as far as he was concerned, was now closed. Nothing else from Carol, though. I think I need a lawyer.
Thom:  I agree. Are you happy to find one?

297

Me:     When do I have to stop asking my parents about this stuff?

Thom:   It'll probably be a bit odd after they're dead. Until then . . .

Me:     Great! In that case, I'm on it.

After speaking to Mum and Dad – Mum seemed a little distracted – they dug out the details of Mary Miller, the daughter of one of Dad's old colleagues, who now specialises in employment law on the employee side. I gave her a call straight away, but of course it's out of hours. Will try her again tomorrow. YOU *WILL* RUE THE DAY, TONY. (That would probably be more frightening if he had any chance of reading it.)

## August's Classic Baby

The baby grunted again, and Alice looked very anxiously into its face to see what was the matter with it. There could be no doubt that it had a *very* turn-up nose, much more like a snout than a real nose: also its eyes were getting extremely small for a baby: altogether Alice did not like the look of the thing at all. 'But perhaps it was only sobbing,' she thought, and looked into its eyes again, to see if there were any tears.

No, there were no tears. 'If you're going to turn into a pig, my dear,' said Alice, seriously, 'I'll have nothing more to do with you. Mind now!' The poor little thing sobbed again (or grunted, it was impossible to say which), and they went on for some while in silence.

Alice was just beginning to think to herself, 'Now, what am I to do with this creature when I get it home?' when it grunted again, so violently, that she looked down into its face in some alarm. This time there could be NO mistake about it: it was neither more nor less than a pig, and she felt that it would be quite absurd for her to carry it further.

So she set the little creature down, and felt quite relieved to see it trot away quietly into the wood. 'If it had grown up,' she said to herself, 'it would have made a dreadfully ugly child: but it makes rather a handsome pig, I think.'

*Alice in Wonderland*
Lewis Carroll

## August 1st

The first thing I thought of this morning was my redundancy – the second, that beyond Carol's early support when she broke the news to me, how quickly my colleagues – my 'friends' – had abandoned me. I wanted to just stay where I was, roll over and go back to sleep, but Stan's chirping made it *almost* impossible to lie-in. As I fed him, I thought of Carol, and Norman, and Alice, and I started crying again. Why would they do this? Carol, who had seemed so supportive in that first meeting? Alice, who had been so furious on my behalf? I wiped my face and tried to shrug: that's what happened in a recession. People couldn't afford principles, only just being able to afford the cost of living round here. They clung to their jobs and kept their heads down. I rubbed my face harder to try and stop the tears once and for all. Absurd.

I rang Suse.

Susie: [picking up] Crisis hotline, what drink can I get you?

Me:     Molotov cocktail, please. Have you got a pen for the
        address?
Susie:  Yikes. Meet at the corner in twenty minutes?

We met with our pushchairs – I can't meet someone else with
a pushchair when I'm out with mine, without thinking of all the
eye-rolling I'd done in my mind each time I saw a pair (or more)
of Mums On The Run, pushing their boring babies around town
like they were displaying an Olympic medal. Susie gave me a
hug and handed me a thermos of her delicious hot chocolate.

Me:     Thanks. You're like the witch from *Hansel and Gretel*.
Susie:  I assume you're joking. I wouldn't eat anything with
        your body fat levels.
Me:     Ooh, another pep talk!
Susie:  Tell me what happened.

So I told her about the email, and the silence from the
rest of the office.

Susie:  What does Alice say they think?
Me:     I haven't even heard from her.
Susie:  From Alice? Are you sure?
Me:     Not a peep. I understand it, Suse, I really do – they
        don't want to rock the boat, and out of sight is out
        of mind, but it doesn't mean it doesn't bother me
        and *I'm not going to cry again* –
Susie:  I can't really talk for the rest of the office, but it
        seems weird that Alice hasn't been in touch. Would
        you call her?
Me:     No. I mean, I'm sure I will, eventually, but I don't
        think I can really trust myself at the moment.
Susie:  OK. But just . . . make sure you're *sure* they haven't
        tried to get in touch, OK?

301

We stopped talking about it then, and just pushed Stan and Frida around the park for an hour, talking about other things. Then Susie sent me home to search.

Which is where it starts getting embarrassing.

In the junk folder of my email, I found a message from Carol. Not from the work address that sent me Tony's 'Case Closed' email, but from her personal address.

It was brief, and just said:

> Couldn't put this in the original email, obviously, but I think he's talking rubbish. Do you have a lawyer to check this with? Happy to provide any and all details from this end you might need. Let me know what I can do.
> C x

Oh. While I was dizzy with delight/shame at my assumptions about Carol, I noticed the pile of letters I hadn't had the stomach to open the last few days. Bills, catalogues, junk mail, and a Polka Dot envelope that I assumed just contained my P45. Guess what. It didn't.

Instead there was a card, designed by Dan, with a clenched fist in Polka Dot colours, and 'WORKERS UNITE' beneath. Inside the card, everyone (except Tony) had written messages of support and reassurance. Alice seemed to have written the final message, a long, flowing one of fury and love. At the very end, she'd written, 'We've given you a bit of space, and understand entirely if you can't face talking to any of us at the moment. But I'm coming to see you on August 1st because I am. A xx'

Tonight! Oh, my shame. My growing shame and my battling happiness. How could I have thought so poorly of them? Why would I lump them in with Tony?

I sent a text message to Suse.

Oops.

Suse wrote back straight away.

Told you so. x

Thom got back just as Alice arrived, meeting her at the front door with a hug and walking her up the stairs with his arm around her.

Me:     I thought you'd forgotten me.
Alice:   You beautiful fool.

Alice reassured me: the office was up in arms about Tony's behaviour. Carol was looking for any and all contracts and speaking to people she knew in employment law, the Art department were rebelling by refusing to put a single pair of naked legs on any jacket, despite how many times Tony asked them, and even Norman had tipped over Tony's filing cabinet, pretending to look for a mouse.

She stayed the rest of the evening, and we talked about all the things going on in the office, the books that have been bought and the latest stunts from Monica Warner and Clifton Black (suddenly around the office again now he knows he's safe from my predations) the continued mystery of erotica author Stuart Winton, and Tony's desperate attempts to get a second book from Jacki. She also said that she might have met someone. Now *that* I was interested in.

TO DO:
Find out how soon I can meet this amazing woman
Oh God, check I haven't missed any of Stan's jabs in all the
    furore

303

August 2nd

After Alice's visit last night, I felt able to hold conversations again. I gave the lawyer a call this morning, when I was sure Stan wouldn't be squeaking and squealing down the phone at her.

Me:     Hello, is that Mary Miller?
Mary:   It is.
Me:     Oh, hello, my name's Kiki Carlow and I was given your number by my dad, John Carlow. He used to work with your dad.
Mary:   Back at the law firm? Yes, I remember him. Is everything OK?
Me:     Oh, yes. Well, no, that's why I'm calling you. I've just been made redundant –
Mary:   Oh, I'm so sorry.
Me:     Thanks. The thing is, I'm not entirely sure that my role is at all redundant in the company, plus I'm still currently on my maternity leave.
Mary:   *Are* you? That *does* sound interesting.

We talked for another twenty minutes or so while she made notes, and gave me a list of everything she'd need from me: contracts, leaving dates, redundancy notice dates, formal redundancy notice letters, everything. I was delighted both for my workload and for my case that I had so few of them – Tony had run my redundancy like he'd run his bit of the business for so long: slapdash, and hoping someone else would do all the actual work. The more Mary asked from me, the more I realised that Tony, among all this missing paperwork, must have made a fatal error somewhere.

And if he hasn't? If this is it? Well. We'll just have to cross that bridge when we come to it.

Our final postnatal class. The whole thing was riddled with nonsense, but all anyone cared about was our coffee at the end, and probing Maria further about her labour.

Me:     So. What did everyone think of the course?
Molly:  Bullshit. Anyone else?
Sadie:  I'm afraid so. But I'm surprised they didn't want to talk about second labours. Labours after difficult first labours. How traumatic they can be.

Maria didn't even wait to be asked. She gave us all a shy wave and was out of there before we could even change the subject.

We *will* find out. Sooner or later.


August 3rd

Back to the doctor's yet again, this time for Stan's and my six-week check. Imagine my undelight to find Dr Moore still there, still in his burgundy bow-tie, still unable to develop any kind of bedside manner.

Dr Moore:  Right, let's have a look at him. He looks a little . . . underweight, doesn't he? Are you feeding him properly?
Me:         [sighing] Yes.
Dr Moore:—Let's weigh him. [undressing Stan and putting him on the cold scales] Oh, yes, that weight seems to be fine. Do you want to get him dressed again? And he's having all his jabs, yes?
Me:         Yes.
Dr Moore:  Alright, we'll see you for his six-month check.
Me:         Don't . . . you need to check me too?

Dr Moore: Do you feel you need checking?
Me:        [starting to wonder if he actually has a medical
           qualification or if he just dressed the part] I
           don't know. I thought you'd be able to . . .
Dr Moore: Yes?
Me:        It's fine. We're fine. Thank you.

I took Stan home again and I wondered what my alternative was – the Health Visitors? But I did feel better than the
day after I'd delivered Stan, and nothing seemed to have fallen
out of me since then, so I decided to take Dr Moore (or Dr
Less hahaha) at his word and believe I was well enough.

TO DO:
Find new doctor

August 6th

In the afternoon, Molly and I had a coffee to catch up on
our weekends. They'd just spent their first full evening away
from Patrick. I was insanely jealous, and didn't want to ruin
her buzz by telling her about my redundancy yet.

Me:    So how was the wedding?
Molly: I'm really not comfortable telling you.
Me:    Oh my God. What happened? Did you kill someone?
       Did you kill an usher?
Molly: [looking around] No. But you *cannot* tell *anyone* this.
Me:    I swear on Stan's newly-developed good sleeping
       patterns. What have you got?
Molly: OK. [deep breath] This was the first time we've left
       Patrick alone. My mum had bottles for him, and I'd
       expressed enough over the days before to have fed

him while we were out. We were due back around eleven, just in time for his night feed – we'd arranged all of this, we'd all agreed, everyone knew their part.

Me: But Patrick wouldn't take the bottle?

Molly: *Oh* no. That slugger took the bottle all right. He loved that bottle. He loved the bottle so much that when we got home at eleven-fifteen, Mum had already given our enormous baby another bottle, because he'd seemed so hungry. Meanwhile, I had the most enormous, aching boobs in the whole world, having not had them emptied for the best part of ten hours.

Me: Ouch.

Molly: It was – besides maybe actually birthing that strange giant – one of the most painful things I've ever experienced. They were like *rocks*.

Me: So did you have to express?

Molly: [silent]

Me: Mols?

Molly: In a way.

Me: I'm sure I'm now imagining something far worse than can possibly have happened.

Molly: I'd broken the expressing machine that morning. I was in a rush when I was getting the last few drops out, left it on the floor, and managed to slam the bedroom door into it. It was in pieces.

Me: So you . . .?

Molly: Craig did it.

Me: [squealing] With his *hands*?

Molly: [looking straight at me] No. Not with his hands.

Me: [mouth open, eyes wide] No, Molly. No, you didn't . . . he didn't . . .

Molly: He didn't swallow it! He spat it straight in the sink between . . .

Me: Between what, Molly? Between *what*?

Molly: Between . . . sucks.

Me: [gagging]

Molly: But the wedding itself was lovely.

Me: I don't think we're going to be able to talk for a while.

Redundancy news could wait. I couldn't even drink my latte.

August 7th

A new bit of correspondence today from Pamela: an email, which I opened with trepidation: has she heard about my legal inquiries? Is she issuing a counter-lawsuit?

To: Kiki Carlow
From: Pamela Cooper
Subject: Your departure

Dear Katherine,

I cannot tell you how sorry I am to hear about your departure, and even more so to hear the circumstances which surround it. Please be aware that steps have been taken to ensure that Polka Dot never loses an a employee of your calibre again. In refer-ence to this, please accept an increased redundancy payment equivalent to one year's salary in recognition of your valuable work over the years. You should have spoken to me about this, you silly girl.

Best wishes,

Pamela Cooper

And I should have done. It was silly of me. For all that Pamela's done for me – I should have had more faith in her, and I should have talked to her about it all. Oh lord.

As it goes, though, that is a nice chunk of change, as they say. And something else to take along to the lawyer, I suppose.

August 14th

I dropped Stan at Mum's this morning. She seemed a bit nervous today for some reason – I think it was a bump Lily got at the weekend when she and Edward were round there, although God knows it wasn't Mum's fault – and kept wanting to check she had everything, and what Stan would need when, and what she should do if he became upset. Poor Mum. With both Susie and me living round the corner and breeding like flies, she hasn't had much chance of a relaxing retirement. But I gave them both a hug and a kiss and hurried off to Mary Miller's office in Covent Garden.

When I arrived I was relieved to find it was pretty shabby. Not in a 'we're still trying to recoup our losses from the last recession' kind of shabby, nor in a 'vintage-sourced furnishings' way, both of which would suggest her bill might be more than I could manage, but just a safe, municipal, library-esque shabbiness, like a Citizens Advice Bureau without all the citizens hanging around, cluttering it up.

A receptionist who looked like Mum greeted me and showed me where to wait. Within a minute or two a woman a few years older than me came over, saying, 'Kiki? Hi, I'm Mary.

Shall we go to my office?' It took all my restraint not to say, 'Whoah, you've got an office!' and I wondered whether she'd felt that the first day she was given it. Does anyone *not* feel like they're suddenly an adult when they get their own office?

Her office was lovely, dark and wood-y, filled with authoritative-looking books and lamps on the desk and shelves.

Me:    Have you read all these?

Mary:  No, they came with the office. Well, so I heard. This isn't even my office, really. I've just borrowed it from a senior partner to impress you.

Me:    I – oh.

Mary:  I'm joking. Shall we have a look at what we've got?

We went through all the paperwork, and I confirmed that my maternity cover – now my full replacement – was doing the exact same job as me, albeit with less experience and lower pay. Poor sucker. From all accounts, she's nice enough. I don't know what story Tony's spun her, but if she had any sense she'd get the hell away from any boss who would do that to her predecessor. I also showed her the email from Pamela yesterday.

Me:    What do you think?

Mary:  I think this is an excellent deal. And as a redundancy package, it'll be tax-free, too.

Me:    Gosh.

Mary:  Quite. You can obviously shop around for advice, but I think . . . I think we could get more. This is a good deal, but it's a little late, and what they did was illegal. Would you like me to set up a meeting with them?

Me:    I think so. I'd certainly like to see what Tony has to say about the whole thing. Is that possible?

310

Mary:   Absolutely. I'll get started straight away.

Tony, you're going to wish you'd never been born.

TO DO:
Crush Tony Cooper like a grape
Also, get more wipes

August 20th

Our anniversary. What a lovely day. And what a beautiful night!

We took Stan for a picnic during the day, and met Jim and Poppy in the park for a long walk. They reported that Nick was much better – he hadn't started seeing anyone yet, but he would actually go out in the evenings, and was off this weekend with some pals from work on some kind of boating trip.

In the evening, I'd booked a table at our favourite restaurant, a French place in Soho. Mum and Dad had Stan, and I'd expressed at the very last minute, having Molly's horror story in my mind.

It was a wonderful meal, with perfect food, great service and lovely conversation with Thom. I always love spending time with him, and this evening out, just the two of us, dressed up and laughing together, felt like the best anniversary gift I could possibly have. As we left, though, Thom hung back for a minute to glare at someone, but I tugged on his arm and pulled him outside with me.

Me:      [laughing] Who were you glaring at?
Thom:  Some stupid women in there.
Me:      Did they goose you?
Thom:  No. [hesitant] They were making faces.
Me:      At what?

311

Thom: Can we go home?

Me: [feeling a bit sick] What happened?

Thom: [sighing] The stupid women in there were making faces at your cleavage.

Me: [speechless]

Thom: Let's go, Keeks. They're just jealous.

Me: Hold on. I've had enough of this.

I left Thom outside, and went back into the bar. I saw the group immediately. They went quiet when I walked in, but a few made eye contact and one looked down at her drink, raising her eyebrows.

Me: Is there a problem, ladies?

Eyebrow raiser: I beg your pardon?

Me: I was just checking whether there was a problem here. Because we've just come out for a lovely dinner on our first wedding anniversary, a dinner which was particularly special since it was the first meal out we've enjoyed since the birth of our baby, who I'm still breastfeeding, which means of course that I've rather struggled to find a dress to fit *these*. But of course, wise, intelligent, experienced and most of all *secure* women such as yourselves would understand that, wouldn't you, and certainly wouldn't be making visible judgement on someone who – more than anything – is just trying to forget about the body she left behind a year ago, and enjoy the evening with her husband.

Eyebrow raiser: [opens mouth]

Me: Goodnight, ladies. [heads outside to Thom] Right. *Now* let's go.

God, I wish I'd *really* said that, and not just glared at them through the window.


August 23rd

Thom's thirtieth birthday today. Happy birthday, my love.

He insisted he didn't want any major party, and since we'd just been out for dinner the other night, he thought we shouldn't go out either. But just letting it slip by was impossible, so I returned the hundreds of favours and brought him breakfast in bed, for a start. He ate his bacon sandwich and marmalade toast while I fed Stan, and I asked him what he'd like to do with the day.

Me:     I can offer you swimming, there's a baby cinema screening of *The Bourne Legacy*, or we can just go and read in the park with Stan. Or all three. Or two. Or something else completely.

In the end, Thom went for swimming at the open air pool, followed by a picnic in the sun. Stan wasn't crazy about the water, but dozed happily in the shade between me and Thom at the park.

Thom: This is a nice birthday. Thank you.
Me:     You're welcome.
Thom: Are you cooking tonight?
Me:     I was planning to. Any requests?
Thom: I think we need a new fire extinguisher.

Fortunately Stan didn't wake up in time to see me trying to smother his father.

## August 24th

Susie and I had a walk scheduled this morning, with a very special Special Guest. We headed to the tube, but before we got so much as a wheel inside the station, Annie came barrelling out towards us, Grace Eva cooing in her giant baby moon-unit. Annie looked like a different woman.

Me:    Annie, you look amazing! [staring] Sorry, sorry – do you remember my sister, Susie?

Annie:  Of course I do! [hugging her] Hi, Susie, how *are* you? Goodness, it must be . . .

Susie:  Don't work out how long it is. It unnerves me. It feels like only a few years, so let's just go with that. Four years. How are *you*?

Obviously I'd told Susie everything that Annie had told me and more, but she was far too discreet to let Annie know; a particularly mature decision considering she was, by these new calculations, a mere nineteen years old. Something had definitely happened to Annie – she looked fantastic. Human. Alive.

She told us that the women from her antenatal group had been completely welcoming, and had only avoided contacting her as they'd assumed Annie and Stephen didn't want anything to do with any of them. She'd had a great time with them at their regular hangout, and was now seeing them three times a week in their houses, and local parks and cafés. They were hilarious, and everything she needed right now: friends, to laugh with about everything when she was feeling her most wobbly. And Stephen hadn't said a peep. She'd told him straight away, naturally, but he'd taken one look at her and displayed a fraction of common sense for once. Who knew how long this happy détente could last, of course, but

Annie had friends and seemed happy, and I could safely put the bins out at night without fear I would find her going through them.

Annie: They're just so . . . great. We talk about everything! How to get the babies to feed, how to get them to sleep, the best slings for them, what we'll wean them on, everything!
Susie: [making puking motion behind Annie's back]
Me: That's so great, Annie. I'm really glad for you.

And I am. There's spirit in that woman yet.


August 27th

The Polka Dot meeting today. Tony insisted on hosting it at the office – thinking, what, I'd be softer if I saw the place he'd kicked me out from? – and in an even more striking misjudgement, that Carol and Alice sat in on the meeting too.

Tony: They're here as representatives of Polka Dot Books.

And Mary got started. She showed him very simply, very clearly, with all the paperwork and contractual detail he could wish for, that my redundancy was illegal, and I had a very good chance of winning my case at a tribunal. She also spelled out quite how much I could win there, and how much the case would cost Polka Dot. Tony grew pale beneath his tan.

Mary: Katherine, do you have anything to add?
Me: Yes. Tony, I will take the money your mother offered me, thank you. That will do. To take any more

315

would mean crippling, if not destroying, the company that I've given six years of my career to, and there's too many talented and hard-working people here for me to want to do that. And . . . I just wanted to say, Tony, that I'm truly sorry for you. That I really believe you can't see how, once a woman has a baby, she's still a useful, reliable employee. *Why* would you say that to me? Why would you say, 'Come on, Kiki, you've got your baby now?' I have worked so hard, and been brilliant at this job. I have always worked so far beyond my remit that – let's face it – I've been doing your job for the last two years, but without the money, the lunches or the respect. I really am sorry that you'll lose those employees who could work best for you, who keep this company afloat, and you'll be left producing boring, ugly stuff that no one cares about, because those are the only things you understand. So. Thank you for the money. I am not going to need a reference from you.

Alice:   [whispering] You hope.

After that we all went to the pub to celebrate. Tony did not come. But Pamela did, although I've no idea who told her; she confirmed I'll get my full payment in December, if that was alright – she had Norman on the case.

TO DO:
Try not to spend that money in my head before I even get it

August 29th

A coffee-shop invasion with the Postnatals today, where we finally got Maria's birth story out of her. After all those weeks of worrying about the terrible injuries she'd sustained, horror-film images of needle and thread and flesh, or a traumatic occasion with her partner, we finally learnt the truth.

Molly: I think what's hardest about giving birth —
Me: Is the tearing pain of contractions.
Sadie: The indignity?
Leila: Not being able to pay someone else to do it.
Molly: — for *me*, is how judgemental some mothers can be. It can sometimes seem like, if you didn't have some waterpool homebirth with your partner netting your placenta out of the water, that other women might judge you for it. Like, using drugs in labour is a failure. Crazy. Don't you think, Maria?
Maria: [non-committal] Mmm.
Reiko: [commencing the pincer movement] Or sometimes it's just too hard to talk about the birth. Sometimes these things can be so dreadful, it's too much to talk about them, right, Maria?
Maria: [narrowing her eyes at us] Mmmmm.
Leila: [completing the manoeuvre] Or sometimes women don't even like to say they've had a caesarean. Can you believe that, Maria?
Maria: Oh Jesus. Fine. Do you *really* want to hear about my labour?
All: *Yes*.
Maria: OK. [steeling herself] I'm going to need an espresso first. [Sadie gets up to order] Better make it a double.

We were all on tenterhooks, amazed that Maria had opened up so easily. We'd all thought it would take days of us playing that game. Sadie came back with the tiny cup and saucer, and with a, 'Sorry, baby Caroline,' Maria knocked it back in one.

We drew nearer.

Maria: OK. I'm going to tell you this once, and then we can never speak of it again. OK?

All: Of course/Poor Maria/Yes/Never again.

Maria: Right. I was due on the Tuesday. On Monday night, I felt completely fine, so we asked a couple of friends over to dinner. After the main course, I felt a twinge, so they went round to get our neighbour, who's a doula. When she came round, she took me upstairs to examine me, and found . . .

Lelia: Yes?

Maria: Well, basically she found that Caroline had been born. She just sort of . . . fell out. Then she cleaned me up and did the placenta bit, and while our friends and my husband made the dessert, a midwife was called. Just to . . . check us over, you know.

All: [silence]

Sadie: *Then* what happened?

Reiko: Was Caroline OK?

Maria: Yes, we were both fine. I didn't have to go into hospital or anything . . . That's it.

Me: *That's* your birth story?

Maria: . . . Yes.

Me: You bloody . . .

Maria: Now do you see why I didn't want to tell you?

Paula: So your baby just . . . *'fell out'*.

Maria: It does happen, you know.

Leila: Not to me it doesn't.

318

Molly said we would keep our promise if Maria got the next round of coffees in. But there is no way on *earth* that we are never going to mention this again.

When Thom got home, I told him all about it.

Thom: What, the one you all thought was super-traumatised by her terrible birth?
Me:    Yup.
Thom: It just fell out?
Me:    Yup.
Thom: You should do that one, next time.

I just stared at him.

Me:    Yeah, I will.

## September's Classic Baby

When the baby was brought I tried to amuse him with that; but poor little Arthur was cutting his teeth, and his father could not bear his complaints: sentence of immediate banishment was passed upon him on the first indication of fretfulness; and because, in the course of the evening, I went to share his exile for a little while, I was reproached, on my return, for preferring my child to my husband. I found the latter reclining on the sofa just as I had left him.

'Well!' exclaimed the injured man, in a tone of pseudo-resignation. 'I thought I wouldn't send for you; I thought I'd just see how long it would please you to leave me alone.'

'I have not been very long, have I, Arthur? I have not been an hour, I'm sure.'

'Oh, of course, an hour is nothing to you, so pleasantly employed; but to me—'

'It has not been pleasantly employed,' interrupted I. 'I have been nursing our poor little baby, who is very far from well, and I could not leave him till I got him to sleep.'

'Oh, to be sure, you're overflowing with kindness and pity for everything but me.'

'And why should I pity you? What is the matter with you?'

'Well! That passes everything! After all the wear and tear that I've had, when I come home sick and weary, longing for comfort, and expecting to find attention and kindness, at least from my wife, she calmly asks what is the matter with me!'

'There is nothing the matter with you,' returned I, 'except what you have wilfully brought upon yourself, against my earnest exhortation and entreaty.'

*The Tenant of Wildfell Hall*
Anne Brontë

September 5th

Thom back to school today. I missed him terribly, having
been spoiled by his company all summer, but I also started
thinking about the nursery we had booked for January. Later
that evening, I told Thom my plan.

Me:     That nursery was already too expensive for us when
        I *had* a job. It seems crazy for Stan to be going there
        five days a week when I'll just be at home – I think
        we should cancel it.
Thom:   Keeks, firstly, the nursery said we can postpone Stan's
        start date for as long as we want. If you don't think
        it's a good time to start paying those fees, we can just
        send him there later. Secondly, you'll have the money
        from Pamela, so we do have a bit of leeway on the
        money-front. Thirdly – you might have a job by then.
        It seems unlikely now, but even if you don't, you
        could be having interviews, schmoozing publishing
        bigwigs, anything to keep your hand in. Finally: I
        don't want you to feel trapped by Stan. No one's saying

we don't love him, but I get to go to work – admittedly to deal with other children, but still. If you think it could benefit you in any way, let's keep him there.

Me:       You had that very prepared.

Thom:   I had a feeling you'd been thinking about this.

I need to think about all of this. I appreciate Thom's kindness, but it's a lot of money to spend just so I feel a bit better. It's not like we're Lucie Martel, or something.


September 6th

When Thom came home today, I was washed, dressed and resolute.

Me:       I've been thinking about everything you said yesterday, about keeping Stan booked into the nursery.

Thom:   And?

Me:       I think you're right. I think we should still start him in January.

Thom:   What finally convinced you?

Me        Well, it was partly your well-thought out, considerate arguments. And it was partly the fact that Stan was sick in my mouth today.

Thom:   In your mouth?

Me:       He looked so adorable for once. I was doing the Circle of Life with him [mimes holding something above head, turning in a circle], forgetting I'd just fed him. I'd just started smiling up at him –

Thom:   You were singing the song, weren't you?

Me:       [silent]

Thom:   Kiki?

Me:       Fine, I was singing the song. And with the immaculate

322

timing of his mother, he threw up. Into my mouth.
So the moral of this story is: he's going to nursery in
January.

Thom:   Good. Tea?

Me:     Yes please. No . . . no milk for me. [gags a little]

TO DO:
See if I can get Susie to do Circle of Life with Stan just after
a feed


September 12th

I got a panicked call from Eve this morning.

Eve:    *You* know about babies.

Me:     [trying to respond in the right way] Are you . . .
        pregnant?

Eve:    No I'm not fucking pregnant. Alex's decided to come
        to London, so he can 'get to know me'.

Me:     He's not a *baby*, for crying out loud. He's a full-grown
        man.

Eve:    He's my little brother, and I have absolutely no idea
        what to do with him. Other than keep him away
        from you.

Me:     I don't think he'll be expecting you to take him to
        the zoo.

Eve:    Kiki, what the living Christ am I going to do with him?

Me:     Just ask him! Sounds to me like the perfect set-up
        for some *hilarious* misadventures. You should pitch
        this to MTV as a show, if you ask me.

Eve:    I wasn't asking you.

Me:     Yes you were. You just rang me to ask me.

Eve:    Not about bloody TV shows.

| Me: | Just take him to the pub. Stop being ridiculous. |
|---|---|
| Eve: | You're ridiculous. |
| Me: | I'm not the one having to babysit a nineteen-year-old. |
| Eve: | Do you think Jim will look after him? |
| Me: | No, Jim's already babysitting a grown man for me. Sorry. |
| Eve: | Damn you. |
| Me: | What about Mike? Wouldn't he be interested in hanging out with him? |
| Eve: | I'm not having Mike act as a nursemaid to my newly discovered brother. |
| Me: | Oh, but you'd ask me? |
| Eve: | I specifically *didn't* ask you. You're useless. We'll talk later. |

I don't understand quite why she hates the idea of Mike and Alex hanging out together so much, particularly considering how well Mike got on with Alex at the funeral (I think). But Eve is Eve, so there's just no saying.


September 14th

Jacki sent me a brilliant email today.

To: Kiki Carlow
From: Jacki Jones
Subject: That shit

Darling,

Have you heard about Tony's attempts to sweet-talk me? If that lunatic thinks he's getting my second

324

book, he can go whistle! And if he legally has a right to a second book, I have a perfect plan . . .!

Trust me,
Jacki xxxxx ; )

And I do. I wonder, though, what she's cooking up.

September 19th

Susie took us out for a walk today.

Susie: What the hell is wrong with you, then?
Me: How do you do that?
Susie: Older Sister Skillz.
Me: It's not Stan, but it's . . . I like it, Suse, I love being off with him. It's an incredible luxury that I know not everyone can afford, for a hundred different reasons, and it's amazing that we have this healthy baby and I'm OK, and *all* that jazz, but the fact is . . . I'm so bored right now. I'm bored, and I'm lonely, and every time I see Alice or Greta or Dan or Eve, I'm reminded of that exciting world of work and colleagues and stuff that isn't to do with sleeping patterns or how much of your nipple you managed to cram into someone's mouth – don't make a joke about Eve – and I know I'll go back to that, one day. Soon, hopefully. I know I won't always have this time with my tiny, new baby, and I should relish these fleeting moments. But what if that's me for good? What if the baby has broken me? What if I can't remember how to talk about the current Cabinet anymore, or which jacket we should go with for the

market that's developed in the last year, or which film I've just seen at the Curzon? What am I going to do, Suse? Who am I going to be?

Suse:   [staring at me] God, you are such an embarrassment.

Me:   What?

Suse:   Who are you, indeed? What *bullshit* is this? I'm sorry you're feeling lonely – that is awful. That is. If there's anything I can do about that, I will; you can come and meet the people I know, and you can go on courses, and you can leave Stan with any of us to do trips to the Curzon whenever you like (although I can't always do it if Pete's away and the Twins have any parties). But if you're going to start banging on about Has My Brain Died and Am I Any Good To Work anymore, you can just piss right off out of it.

Me:   What?

Susie:   You heard me. You're better than this, I can tell you that much. I couldn't give two shits whether you want to stay at home with Stan, go back to work after a fortnight or take the three of you off to Thailand to find yourselves – but to sit here listening to you question whether 'having a baby has broken you'. . . I can't even begin to tell you how angry that makes me. You're an idiot.

Me:   [silent]

Susie:   Are you going to cry now?

Me:   [mock-flinching] SIR NO SIR.

Susie:   Are you? Shit, have I gone too far?

Me:   No. [taking her hand] You're pretty good, sometimes.

Susie:   Alright, don't look quite so surprised.

Suse *did* make me feel better, but only when I was with her. The feeling followed me home.

September 20th

Thom didn't catch me at my best today. I was still thinking about what Suse and I had talked about yesterday, and when he got home at 5, I'd somehow slipped back into the bad old days of boxsets; I hadn't washed and was wearing some of Susie's ultra-sloppy clothes, as Stan cried and I attempted to hang up the washing.

Thom:   [giving me a big hug] Oh Kiki, do I need to ask how your day was?

Me:   Just horrible.

Thom:   Now doesn't seem like a good time to ask if it's OK to go away for Mal's stag next weekend. The wedding's not till December, though, do you remember?

Me:   From when until when? On my own? When are you going? Why are you only just telling me? Am I just supposed to stay on my own?

Thom:   Kiki, I was just kidding. Of course I'm not going!

Me:   What, so now you're not allowed out anymore? You not only have to ask my permission all of a sudden, but then you're not even going? You're just going to stop seeing your friends?

Thom:   I don't mind not going at all. You need my help more than those guys do.

Me:   So that's how it's going to be now? Whoah whoah whoah. There is a very, very simple solution to all of this. [rummaging in Thom's sock drawer] Et voilà

Thom:   The get out of jail card!

Me:   It's a Golden Ticket, actually. But didn't I say it would be useful?

Thom:   Thanks, Keeks. [thinking] It will be nice to go.

Me:   Good. I want you to have a very, very nice time. But

327

. . . Not but, but also. Also I am so *bored, all* the time. I love Stan, you know I do, and I am happy, but I'm so so so so so *bored*, Thom. I know there'll be Christmas soon – it *is* soon – but I miss work so much, and I miss my colleagues, and I am *so* under-stimulated I feel like I might go mad. Even when it's just me and Stan in here, I just feel like there's no space for anything in my brain, and it's just going to soften and trickle out of my ears and then I won't be able to read or write or speak in full sentences or anything. [gripping his upper arms] *I'm going mad.*

Thom sat me down, and we talked about whether I wanted to actually do something, or whether I just wanted Thom to know. Saying that made me realise that I did definitely want to do something, that I had to do something or I would be no good to either of them, and more importantly no good to myself. I couldn't just not have a job at all. It made me realise how much of my identity was tied up in my job at Polka Dot, and how losing it was such a fresh wound.

Thom left me browsing through courses in the area while he tidied up the kitchen. Even looking at this stuff made me feel better, like there was still a world out there for me to take, rather than this little flat – which I had always loved so much – closing in on me. Japanese? Ceramics? Something scientific? Something directly employable ?

Me:     What about Bridge?
Thom:   [coming in with Stan] Oh! That'll be perfect when we have the Major and Lady Farquhar over to supper.
Me:     Mandarin?
Thom:   Could be pretty useful, but you'd need to get to a decent level. Are you going to commit to this, or is it just for a while?

328

| Me: | Realistically, probably just for a few months. |
|---|---|
| Thom: | In which case, it's unlikely you'll reach any functioning level in Mandarin. |
| Me: | Jewellery making? |
| Thom: | Really? |
| Me: | No, just kidding. Plumbing? |
| Thom: | Ooh, that really could be useful. Keeks, of course you *can* do something useful, but when you're ready for work, you'll find something. Until then, hang out with Stan, see your friends, and do any course you like to keep your mind going. The world's your lobster. |
| Me: | Thanks, love. I think I quite like . . . this one. |

I'm tempted by Home Decoration (Practical). If all else fails, I can tile for a living.

September 30th

Thom headed off to Mal's stag yesterday morning. I really was so happy for him, happy to see him off on a good weekend with his oldest friends, and sure Stan and I would have a lovely time – in an emergency, Mum and Suse were just round the corner.

Things started well. Stan and I hung out for a while. I washed and dressed, and decided to make a run to the corner shop for weekend supplies – paper, bread, bacon, biscuits, the usual. When I was heading out of the door, tucking Stan into the sling, I noticed he absolutely stank, so came back indoors to change his nappy. But oh – it was so much more than his nappy. The recent contents of Stan's bowels had spread all the way up from his nappy, all the way up his back, and had soaked through his babygro, his t-shirt and his jumper. Fine. It took a while, but I got him cleaned and changed, and headed out again. This time, we were actually out of the front door and a few steps up the street, when I smelt it again. For a moment, I debated just keeping walking, just making my shop run and smell be damned. But I had a rare flash of conscience and took Stan back inside again.

What a fantastic performance it was. This time, he'd soaked through the new babygro, t-shirt and jumper, plus his trousers, into his socks and somehow out the back of his collar, matting into the base of his hair. *How is that even possible, Stan*? I cleaned him up again, with a vague inkling that perhaps he wasn't well, and abandoned immediate plans for the shop – we could go later, if Stan seemed better.

Three hours and almost every outfit in his drawers later, we still hadn't left the house. I didn't understand how there was still anything left for him to be soaking these clothes in, but somehow, he was managing. I'd called the doctor briefly, who just said to make sure he was getting plenty of fluids ('Good, more fluids. That's definitely what he seems to need more of,' I didn't say) and to check his temperature. It seemed fine, and he wasn't in any apparent discomfort, but I thought we write the day off, remain indoors close to showers and washing machines, and head out tomorrow.

Eventually, we headed to bed. Which is when the crying started.

On changing his nappy for the eighty-seventh time that day, I realised he had the worst nappy rash I'd ever seen. From nowhere, the smooth peach bottom had become pocked with vicious, weeping open sores that made me gag. And where was the nappy rash cream? Nowhere. *Nowhere*. By 2 am I'd torn the house apart looking for the cream, and was reduced to texting Suse in the vague hope she was still awake. Through some miracle, she was, and drove round to drop off Frida's cream (remind me not to tamper with Suse's advent calendar next Christmas after all), saying she was sure that he'd calm down soon enough.

He didn't, but the nappy rash did subside fairly quickly. By 6 am, his skin was healing and smoothing over again, like some futuristic robo-baby's. I asked him how that happened so fast, but since I was cross-eyed with tiredness I'm not sure he really understood my question. At 7, we both fell asleep for a while, waking at 8 for a feed. Hurray!

Then the fun really started. Halfway through a change, I left Stan on our low bed as I turned to grab his just-about-dry babygro from the laundry rack, and heard a soft *thunk* followed by a wild, breathless howl. I turned back to see Stan on the floor – normally not that disastrous a fall – pale-faced with pain beside our very hard, very sharp old metal toolbox, which I can only assume Thom had left out after – what? Looking for a hammer for the stag weekend? Stan didn't make much noise in his crying, which made me panic, so I stepped into my trainers, grabbed the car keys and was back off to the hospital only four short months after his birth.

At the A&E reception, I was directed to a special reception for children, and seen immediately. Stan was checked over, with careful fingers and little lights, and the wonderful doctor reassured me that Stan seemed fine, that babies were remarkably resilient. But while I was here, we might as well give him a quick X-ray, just to check him out.

Four hours later, with Stan in nappies two sizes too big (I hadn't thought to bring any out with me, and they were all the hospital had), we were allowed home again. Stan's skull was completely fine, not even the hint of a whisper of a crack, and he just had a slight bruise on one side. My skull, however, was pounding, a feeling which didn't subside when I found the parking ticket on my car. Why *thank you*, world.

We got home, washed again, dressed again, and got another hour's snatched nap before waking up to Thom standing over us, smiling, with cups of tea.

Thom: [whispering] That looks nice. Did you two have a nice relaxing weekend together?

I thought: it can probably wait. So I just said, 'It was great. How was yours?' and let him tell me all about the hideous things unsupervised adults get up to with ladles while I drank my tea and smiled at our beautiful son.

## October's Classic Baby

Tess, with a curiously stealthy yet courageous movement, and with a still rising colour, unfastened her frock and began suckling the child.

The men who sat nearest considerately turned their faces towards the other end of the field, some of them beginning to smoke; one, with absent-minded fondness, regretfully stroking the jar that would no longer yield a stream. All the women but Tess fell into animated talk, and adjusted the disarranged knots of their hair.

*Tess of the d'Urbervilles*
Thomas Hardy

## October 3rd

I thought I should probably check on at least Eve, if not Alex as well. But she seemed to mean what she said about keeping us apart, meeting me solo in the Queen's Arms tonight.

Me:     So. How's it going?

Eve:    Hang on. [drinks her pint in one] Hang on. [goes to buy another] Hang on. [checks around the pub] I can't bear it.

Me:     What do you mean, you can't bear it? What are you bearing?

Eve:    I can't bear someone else in my space. I can't bear how young he is. I can't bear how much he sounds like Dad. I can't bear how boring he makes me feel –

Me:     *You*!

Eve:    Or how much he clutters the place up. I can't bear it anymore. I want a refund.

Me:     I'm sorry, love. Do you get on with him at all?

Eve: Yeah, I suppose I do, really. He's nice enough. He's sweet, and it feels like he wants to impress me.

Me: How long do you think he'll stay?

Eve: I asked him that the other night. It's been incredibly awkward with us ever since. Not long, I suspect.

Me: Do you mind?

Eve: No. I hope we stay in touch, though. It seems ridiculous not to.

Me: Eve, this is such weird stuff for you to deal with. Have you spoken to anyone about all of this? Your mum?

Eve: No, she doesn't really want to talk about Dad at all. But Mike's been . . . brilliant.

Me: [beaming] Naturally.

Eve: Oh, stop. Don't do that face. It's not anything for you to get excited about. God, you married people are all the same – the second you get a ring on your finger, you just want to marry everyone else off.

Me: OK, I'm leaving now. This has been really lovely.

Eve: Sorry. Sorry, Keeks. I didn't mean to be . . .

Me: Marriageist?

Eve: Rude.

Me: Yes, also that.

Eve: [sighing] Am I even setting a good example?

Me: Jesus, Eve, what's happened to you? Why do you care if you're setting a good example or not? What *would* be a good example: being married with babies and living a life you neither want nor have chosen?

Eve: I just really want him to leave now. I don't want a younger version of me lying around, taking drugs and having fun. I can't bear it. I admit it. I'm old and I want to hang out with Mike.

Me: You're OLD? What does that make me?

Eve looked at me for a while, then said wearily that she'd better be off. I got a message from her later that night.

Out with A introduced him to our karaoke joint that ol' medicine still works x x

Maybe he won't go home quite yet.


October 5th

Out with Suse tonight, as she took me on a Night Without The Baby. As we left the house, she gave me this talk.

Susie:   This is a very important night for you. You'll want to go crazy, you'll want to drink every drink and dance every dance, and I am here as your Guide. I will be protecting you from your worst decisions, and recommending suitable paths for you to follow throughout the night.
Me:      You are truly wise, O Sister.
Susie:   You bet I'm wise. The first time I had a proper night out after the Twins, Pete couldn't find me for a day and a half.
Me:      [remembering] Oh yeeeaah. That was the night we'd borrowed –
Susie:   Yup.
Me:      And we met the guy who –
Susie:   Yes.
Me:      Oh. And then you got up on the –
Susie.   Exactly. And that's why *I* am doing *you* the favour of looking after you tonight. Because *I* don't want *you* to end up asleep on the last train to Diss.

| Me: | Thanks, Suse. It means a lot to me. I have already been out with Thom without Stan, though. |
| Susie: | You're welcome. That doesn't count. First round's on you. |

I remember us dancing, and I remember being on the top deck of a bus. Thom bottle-feeding Stan when I stumbled in the door.

And now my head hurts.

I see what Susie meant now.

TO DO:
Don't breathe on Stan in the morning.


October 8th

Spotted the press for *The Maltese Gherkin*, Ann Tate and Charlie Greer's latest, today. Hauled both Stan and myself out of bed and into clothes, out front door and all the way to a bookshop – I know! They still exist! – and found a great display of both the new one and *Dining with Death*, their first. Bought a copy of *Gherkin*, and through terrible, small-world-publishing habit, flicked to the acknowledgments.

Oh.

> Special thanks to everyone at Polka Dot who has helped us so much over the years, particularly Kiki Carlow, without whom this crime-fighting duo wouldn't be what they are.

Oh, you two.

I sent them a message as soon as we got back in.

From: Kiki Carlow
To: thecooks@tateandgreer.com
Subject: Gherkins and tears

Hello you two!

I just wanted to say I bought your new book this morning, and already love it. Particularly blown away by the acknowledgements.

You pair. Well done again,
Kiki x

I got a message back within the hour.

From: thecooks@tateandgreer.com
To: Kiki Carlow
Subject: RE: Gherkins and tears

Well, what else were we going to do? We wanted to show our gratitude for all the work you'd done for our books over the years. It was utter madness for Polka to lose you.

Anyway, can we have your address? We realised we haven't sent you anything for that baby Alice has told us so much about.

Charlie x

Who am I to refuse?

October 10th

Spent today redoing my CV for the New Year. After a while I do start fantasising that I could just spell out how much of Tony's work I've done for the last few years, without sounding like I was the biggest fantasist in the world. As it is, I sound like a combination of Senior Editor and Office Dogsbody – a horribly accurate depiction of my role at Polka Dot. I'm sure once (if) I get another job, I'll feel this even more strongly, but I can't help wondering – was this redundancy a good thing to happen to me?

TO DO:
Ask Thom, Carol and Alice to have a look at my CV
Delete the line about having Word skills. It's not 1998 anymore.

October 12th

Lunch over at Zoe's today, just us two and the babies. She's so excited about going back to work, and has already had a few days in the office – at her request, not Pedro's – to keep her hand in and familiarise herself with his upcoming projects. I am, of course, insanely jealous, and not just because Zac is still so devilishly handsome. I miss work, all the time, and not having that start date back in the office ahead of me leaves me unrooted and goalless.

But nothing was about to be fixed at lunch, so we just marvelled at Stan and Edith together. They roll over one another like they couldn't even begin to consider that other moving lump to be a baby like them, but they are both so adorable there's no way either of them could take offence. I do like being with Stan, a lot, and it's good to see Zoe.

Still. I miss work, though.

TO DO:

Start looking into possible jobs

Have a word with Stan about nice manners (including not
   rolling over other people's heads)


October 20th

Eve took me out for brunch today, while Stan stayed at home
with Thom. It was an enormous pleasure to see her, and we
strolled in the autumn sunshine from tube to café.


Eve:    How the hell are you?

Me:     Pretty good. Pretty busy. But only with a baby. Is
        that real busyness?

Eve:    It's more than I could manage, that's for sure.

Me:     And how the hell are you?

Eve:    Well, thanks. Listen, we didn't get round to this at
        the pub the other night – did that nervous breakdown
        ever happen? The one you thought might kick in
        after you pushed me in the lake?

Me:     I thought these were bygones?

Eve:    You pushing me in the lake is a bygone. Me being
        concerned about your welfare shall never be a
        bygone, my dear friend. But it would be nice to just
        be friends, wouldn't it? If you aren't having a
        breakdown?

Me:     I'm not. And it would. I'm sorry, Eve. What's going
        on with us?

Eve:    I didn't know anything was.

Me:     I don't know. Maybe nothing. I'm not saying friends
        have to be going through exactly the same stuff to
        be able to stay friends, but . . . we're always on such
        different paths. It feels tricky for us to have any

common interests if you always express mild disdain for whatever I'm doing.

Eve:    Maybe it's not disdain! Maybe I want that too! Maybe I want a wedding, a marriage, a baby. Maybe you've got a life that I want too.

Me:     Oh, Eve. I'm sorry. I just hadn't thought . . .

Eve:    Oh my *God*, I'm *kidding*. No offence, but . . . hhaaahaahahaaahaha . . . hhaaahaahahaaahaha [panting with hysterical laughter]

Me:     Well, it is *always* good to talk to you.

After Eve had composed herself again, we were seated inside over tea and juices. Eve reassured me that, although she wasn't jealous of my life, she would do her best to respect it and enjoy my company however it came, because us being friends was the most important thing. I couldn't help but agree, and choked up a little.

Eve:    I know I said I'd respect your life, but is this it, now? You have a kid, you cry at *everything*?

Me:     [pressing my lips together, nodding]

Eve:    Oh man. I am never having children.

For the record, I did stop crying, the eggs were amazing, and Eve is still some of the best company around.

October 28th

We were lying around in blankets around the flat – me on the bed, Thom on the sofa with Stan, when I had a sudden thought.

Me:     [shouting to Thom] Holy shit!

341

Thom: [shouting back] If you're pregnant again, I am absolutely not behind you on this one.

Me: [going to speak to him] No! Fiona!

Thom: No Fiona who?

Me: It's not a bloody knock-knock joke. Fiona! From her wedding! Don't you remember?

Thom: [vaguely] I did drink a lot of cloudy cider that night.

Me: Yeah, I know. I ended up carrying a thirty-six-week-grown baby and a twenty-nine-year-old man up the stairs that night.

Thom: Well?

Me: Well nothing. Do you really not remember? Then I'll tell you tomorrow, if that's OK. I want to speak to her first before I say anything else.

I suddenly feel . . . excited.

## November's Classic Baby

So speaking glorious Hektor held out his arms to his baby,
who shrank back to his fair-girdled nurse's bosom
screaming, and frightened at the aspect of his own father,
terrified as he saw the bronze and the crest with its horse-hair,
nodding dreadfully, as he thought, from the peak of the helmet.
Then his beloved father laughed out, and his honoured mother,
and at once glorious Hektor lifted from his head the helmet
and laid it in all its shining upon the ground. Then taking
up his dear son he tossed him about in his arms, and kissed him,
and lifted his voice in prayer to Zeus and the other immortals:
'Zeus, and you other immortals, grant that this boy, who is my son,
may be as I am, pre-eminent among the Trojans,
great in strength, as am I, and rule strongly over Ilion;
and some day let them say of him: "He is better by far than his father",
as he comes in from the fighting; and let him kill his enemy
and bring home the blooded spoils, and delight the heart of his mother.'
So speaking he set his child again in the arms of his beloved
wife, who took him back again to her fragrant bosom
smiling in her tears.

*The Iliad*
Homer, trans. Richmond Lattimore

## November 2nd

Finally, off to see Fiona today. Something tells me I should have been doing this months ago.

Fiona: Kiki, I'm so glad you came to see us.

Me: Me too. That sounds positive.

Fiona: It is, and it isn't. The thing is: things have changed a bit since the wedding.

Me: Oh. Dear.

Fiona: Wait. Listen, before you panic – we're running about six months behind the schedule we had at the wedding. We've been so picky about who we work with, we've got a couple more people on board, and it's a bit chaotic at the moment. I reckon we'll be fully on board in two months' time.

Me: Which . . . is . . . when I wanted to come off maternity leave.

Fiona: Really? Och, well that's great then! But . . . there's the possibly not-positive thing. We've been looking at the books, and from the start-up we've got, we're using a lot of freelancers. But we want *you* to come on board permanently, as a full employee, only – that means we can't afford to have you full-time.

Me:      What were you thinking?
Fiona:   [wincing] Three days a week?
Me:      In.
Fiona:   I'm sorry?
Me:      I'm in. This is a match made in heaven. I will be the very best three-day-a-week editor money can buy.

Fiona gave me a huge hug and we talked specifics – pay, my budget, how many books we'd be looking to produce each month. It sounds absolutely ideal, and I have completely free rein. And this means two-fifths off Stan's nursery fees!

Tony, have you done me the biggest favour I could have imagined?

I don't know when I'll ever be a big enough person to tell him that, though.


November 4th

Dad came round on his own today, and asked if Stan and I were free for a walk. My heart was in my mouth as I dressed Stan and tucked him in his sling.

Me:      Dad, are you OK?
Dad:     Yes, love, I'm fine. Fit as a fiddle, and doing everything the doctor tells me.
Me:      What is it, then?
Dad:     Love, it's your mother. I'm taking her for some more tests, somewhere else. We haven't even been yet, and maybe there's nothing to worry about – maybe she

just needs a few pills – but I wanted to talk to you, because I promised I would, remember? Anything to tell, I agreed I would. So, that's it.

Me:     What's it, Dad?

Dad:    Well, you've seen what she's been like this last year. It's getting worse. Sometimes she looks around like she doesn't know where she is. [voice cracking] But mostly, she's fine, you know.

Me:     Do you think she can get better again?

Dad:    I don't know, love. But we can make the most of the times we have all together, don't you think?

Me:     Yes, Dad.

Dad:    [squeezing my hand] And I'll let you know everything the experts say, alright?

Me:     Thanks, Dad.

I felt exhausted all of a sudden, so he walked me home again. When Thom came back, I finally burst into tears and told him what Dad had said.

I just don't know what to do if Mum disappears like that. My mum.


November 5th

Can't stop thinking about Mum.

My one moment of lightness today came from giving Stan some banana. My God, it was like I'd given him some deeply hallucinogenic superfood. In the mouth, out of the mouth. Staring at the banana, staring at the chewed banana spat out, trying to put the banana into his own eye. Poking his tongue out as far as it could go, widening his eyes in suspicion, calling briefly in a prehistoric language; begin again from top.

I look forward to some new colleagues. This one is such a messy eater.

But I still can't stop thinking about Mum.

November 11th

Thom had a brainwave. He suggested that, to celebrate Dad's birthday, Stan's half-birthday, my new job and his new promotion, we should have a party in a couple of weeks. I am always up for a semi-impromptu party, although at short notice it may well just be the Carlow family and associated husbands and infants. But let's do it! Sent out invitations about three million times faster than I managed for our own wedding, once Mum had offered their house for hosting. I checked with Dad after I'd spoken to Mum that it was really OK, but he said they'd both be delighted.

TO DO:
Make sure Mum doesn't have to worry about anything
Get guests
Get food
Get booze
Party like it's 1999

November 18th

Oh holy Christ. He's definitely crawling. I came in to find Stan gently sucking on my hairdryer's plug, on an entirely different side of the room to that in which I'd left him. How did he get there? Who moved him? But Stan confirmed my worst fears when he beamed up at me, rolled back onto his stomach and speed-crawled across the whole room to me, as I stood looking at him with something like horror. I know I'm supposed to beam at him, to pick him up and do a dance of delight at my clever baby's magical crawling skills, but I just feel dizzy, looking around the flat, at all the things he can now reach, at all the danger he can now get into, at all the thought we'll now have to put into making this flat safe at even the most basic level. Is there someone we can pay to make it all safe? Hahahhaha as if we could pay them anyway ahahaha. Well, maybe post-payout in December.

Thom couldn't believe it when he came home. Stan wouldn't do it at first, but I insisted we both had to turn our backs so Stan didn't get stage fright, and sure enough, he was the other side of the room when we turned back. So it's either an astounding crawling ability, or a poltergeist.

Susie and I have talked a bit about Mum, but we both feel so helpless until those new tests are done. We've just agreed to help her out as much as possible in any way.

November 19th

A long-overdue lunch with Jacki today. She wanted to hear all about my redundancy, and I was so glad to tell her about my new job with Fiona in January. Her face lit up.

Jacki: A whole new publishing house, hey?
Me: Yes, and I'll get to commission and publish all by myself – with a little help from Fiona, of course.
Jacki: Well, well, well. That *is* interesting.

348

She had a wicked gleam in her eye, but wouldn't tell me what she was up to. Instead she fed me gorgeous gossip about an interview she'd done with a very famous and very lecherous journo, and about Pedro's latest misadventures. I fell for it completely, and didn't quiz her any further.

## November 23rd

To the doctor today for Stan's six-month check. Imagine my delight when my name was called, and I saw Dr Bedford back in her room.

Me:           Hello!

Dr Bedford:    Hello to you too, Katherine. And is this the little boy I last met when he was still in your womb?

Me:           It is – Stan, say hello to Dr Bedford.

Dr Bedford:    Pleased to meet you, Stan. How have you been, Katherine? Did the birth go well?

Me:           Relatively well, I suppose. No stitches, so I'd chalk it up as a win. But I don't fancy doing it again anytime soon.

Dr Bedford:    So what contraception are you using at the moment?

Me:           A young baby?

Dr Bedford:    OK, I'm going to give you these condoms, Katherine, and I want you to think about whether you'd like to go back on the Pill, or whether you'd be interested in something more like the implant. I'll give you all the information you need – but you wouldn't believe how many unplanned pregnancies we get when babies are only a few months old.

| Me: | [gulping] OK. |
| Dr Bedford: | But other than that, are you and Stanley both well? In fact, let's get him up on these scales – if you could just take all his clothes off? |
| Me: | He's doing really well. Sleeping eight hours from his late feed. I've given him a bit of food recently – banana, that kind of thing – and he seems interested if not ravenous. |
| Dr Bedford: | That's perfectly normal, we wouldn't be expecting him to be eating a Sunday roast quite yet. And his weight and height look absolutely fine, so he's growing well. Did you feel alright after the birth? |
| Me: | Sore. But fine. Tired sometimes. Very tired. But happy. |
| Dr Bedford: | Good. Tired, I can sympathise. Will you be going back to work? |
| Me: | Yes, thank God. In January. |
| Dr Bedford: | [mouthing] Best thing I ever did. [normal voice] Any questions? |
| Me: | Is Stan able to go out to work yet? |
| Dr Bedford: | Not quite. Give him a few months. |
| Me: | Then no, that all seems great. |
| Dr Bedford: | Good. Take the contraceptive information with you, and we'll see you back here for his jabs. |

TO DO:

Do absolutely everything in my power to ensure I don't get knocked up again in the next two years at least

Maybe talk to Dr Bedford about Mum, next time

November 25th

Happy half-birthday, little Stan. The very best parcel in the world (besides you tumbling out of my birth canal, obviously) arrived this morning – a huge waxed cardboard box, tied with six different coloured ribbons, with a little card on top, delivered by a cheerful motorbike courier. I signed the screen he offered me – then the smell hit me. Donuts. And from the smell, these weren't *any* donuts.

Courier:   I've been able to smell them the whole way here. I don't know how that's possible, but I deserve a medal for not eating a few.
Me:   [hugging the box tighter] I will make sure your bosses hear about your good work.
Courier:   [pretending to make a grab for them]
Me:   NO THEY'RE MINE!

We stared at each other for a few seconds before he chuckled and walked back to his bike. I've no idea how far I would have gone to protect my gift.

Safe in the kitchen, I cut the ribbons and lifted the lid. It was beautiful. A box of fresh, sugar-dusted donuts, each one with a letter tattooed on in coloured icing sugar paste. As I looked more closely, I realised the whole box spelled out Stan's full name: *twenty-three* custard-filled donuts. There might even be enough for me to share these with Thom.

When I opened the card, I found a note from Ann and Charlie, wishing Stan a happy half-birthday (*thank you*, Alice) and hoping they might work with me again one day. The feeling, as I'm sure you can imagine, is *more* than mutual.

I spent the rest of the morning getting myself and Stan ready for the party; washed, dried and styled hair, makeup, three different outfit changes and some Ruby Woo lipstick for me; a clean babygro and a hat for him. Big day.

We headed over to Mum and Dad's, where Thom met us with all the decorations. We blew up balloons, tied up streamers and generally made the place look children's party-ish, while Mum pottered in the kitchen with Dad as her sous chef. Dad rarely let her out of his sight, but she seemed well today – happy and capable, excited about the party. Sometimes she thought it was his first birthday, rather than his half, but that was an entirely understandable confusion and no one corrected her.

Soon enough, Susie and her gang arrived. Suse shepherded Mum and Dad out of the kitchen, saying they should relax, but they just insisted on taking all the kids upstairs with them. So while they were safely being entertained by Dad and Mum, Susie, Thom, Pete and I could get on with mixing drinks and stuffing huge trays of sausage rolls in the oven. As always happens, people started arriving for the party, hours before I thought it could possibly be time. First was Annie and Grace Eva. Annie looked so different now to six months ago, and I realised that nowadays I was pleased to see her. We could talk honestly now, and I found her good company (as long as we avoided the topic of Stephen). Next was Alice and her new girlfriend, Sara. Sara gave me a big hug and grinned a bright-red-lipsticked grin: 'Let me help you with some of this booze we've brought.' How could I not love her? With tears of laughter in her eyes, Alice told me that they've finally uncovered the truth about Stuart Winton: it was Tony all along, trying to get the erotica ball rolling. His contract with himself was just what Pamela needed to finally start manoeuvering him out of the office. Then the doorbell rang again and it was Jacki.

Oh, I beamed when I saw her. She was such brightness and joy, and I had to admit: whatever miseries Polka Dot had caused me in the last year, they'd also given me Jacki. But Jacki was in her wonderful secretive mode. 'Can we hide upstairs for a minute?' she said. 'I've got something for you.' I followed her up to my old room – she remembered the way from our wedding – and we closed the door, and sat side by side on my old bed.

Jacki: I've wanted you to have this for ages, but I wasn't sure you could do anything with it.

Me: Jacks, if it's an heirloom, please hang on to it. You shouldn't give that stuff to me, non-godmother or otherwise.

Jacki: Oh yes; do I get a badge for that? It's not an heir-loom, you goose. Here.

She pulled out a flat parcel from her handbag, wrapped in white tissue paper and bound with a flamingo-pink ribbon. I pulled off the ribbon and tore off the paper, and found—

Me: Jacki, is this your book?

Jacki: Yup! And it's all yours.

Me: What?

Jacki: I'd been dragging my heels with Polka Dot for ages about what my second book would be. I've given them a different idea every week just to throw them off the scent. Last week, when you told me about your new job, I handed in the most god-awful garbage about the clothes in my wardrobe; their photogra-pher's going to take care of all the pictures, I've pretty much done what I needed. And all that meant I could save this, for you. It's all about words, and writing, and . . . well you see.

Me: Jacki, that's . . .

Jacki: The best thing to do, I think. As a business decision, I know you do a good job on my books.

Me: That's . . .

Jacki:   Plus, I like you. And I want to keep working with
         you. And it's good to be able to help people, once in
         a while.
Me:      Jacki, this is . . . God. Jacki. This is amazing. This is
         . . . amazing. Thank you. We are going to do a
         fantastic job on this, it's going to be the biggest book
         in the world. Thank you.
Jacki:   Keeks, let's go and have a nice party. And where's
         that son of yours? I could do with giving him an
         enormous cuddle.

Jacki went off to say hello to all the kids, while I rushed
downstairs to open the door again, this time to Fiona and
Mark. Jacki came downstairs just in time to hear Fiona
screaming at our acquisition, at which point Fiona switched
to a solemn business-face as Mark beamed, and we talked
briefly about formalising it all. We agreed a meeting next
Thursday to talk everything through, and I left the three of
them chatting while I opened the door again.

Pedro. 'What . . .?' He laughed, and swanned past me to
Jacki, who grinned and air kissed him. As if you would keep
me away from a Kiki Carlow party,' he laughed, one eyebrow
raised. She beckoned me over, laughing. 'I forgot the other
thing,' she said. 'Ped wants to do a book too – a high-end
look at his photography so far. And it's yours, if you want it.'

I couldn't say anything, but gave him, then her, a hug, and
left Fiona and Mark to talk to them both about what would
probably be our two biggest projects for the year.

The doorbell rang again: the whole Postnatal gang,
crowding in at once with their babies and their cakes, their
buns and their buggies, filling Mum and Dad's hallway and
speaking all at once about the walk, the babies, their
weekend, the house. I ushered them through, and left them
with Susie, who was handing out beers and mulled wine to

anyone who'd take them. Next were a whole group of teachers from Thom's school, closely followed by Rich, Heidi and baby Megan, and Malcolm and Ben from uni, plus Zoe, Zac and baby Edith, wrapped in a lumpy knitted owl snow-suit, her face peeking out from below the knobbly beak. Zoe and Zac gave me a hug, and I cuddled Edith briefly before the doorbell went once more: Jim and Poppy, Nick, and Greta, and just behind them, Eve and Mike. I gave them all hugs and sent them through, but held Eve back a moment.

Me:     Why do you look so . . . glowing?
Eve:    Guess.
Me:     [gasping] Are you *pregnant*?
Eve:    Don't ruin this moment.
Mike:   [shaking his head behind Eve's back, making neck-slashing motions]
Me:     I mean . . . pregnant with good news! Full of good news! Like you're bursting with good news! What's the good news?
Eve:    Mike's moving in.
Mike:   We're moving in together!
Eve:    Mike's moving in. To my place.
Mike:   Where we will live together, in total harmony until we die, side by side, aged ninety.
Eve:    [widening eyes]
Me:     Careful, you're losing her.
Mike:   I'm delighted to be Eve's new roomie. Better?
Eve:    [releases breath] *Better*.
Me:     Well. [small voice] Congratulations? Is that OK? [Eve and Mike nodding] Great! Congratulations! Come in, and we'll drink some kind of toast or something. I think Thom's got some breast milk on ice for everyone.
Eve:    *Kiki*! That's not OK.

355

| Me: | I'm joking! It all went in the cake icing anyway, I am all dried out. |
|------|------|
| Eve: | [retching] |
| Mike: | I'll get us a beer. |
| Me: | Good man. |

So there we all were. New friends, old friends, family from my and Thom's past, family for the years ahead. I was so glad that Mum could enjoy all this.

When everyone had gathered back downstairs again, Thom gave a short speech, about having those we loved close to us, about the tricky year some of us had had, and how we'd made it through with the support of our friends and family, and how we had so much to look forward to. I was choking up a little, and whispered, 'Rooster, *rooster.*' Dad gave a lovely speech too, about sharing his birthday with all these people, as well as all his grandchildren.

When Dad was finished, Thom clinked his glass again. 'OK, everyone. A toast, to John, and Stan, new jobs, and old friends. To the future!'

We all raised our glasses, and I looked around the room, at all these people I loved. I wondered how I could ever do without them, every day, for the rest of my life. I looked at Mum and Dad, who after his heart attack and her new episodes, seemed now so impermanent, their presence so fragile. I looked at Thom, my best friend. I looked at our son, crawling over Thom's feet to get to Frida's grinning face, and picked him up to kiss him again. We all toasted.

'To the future!'

# Check list for hospital:

*For pre-labour:*

*Elle Deco*
*Living Etc.*
CDs and player with batteries
Game Boy and games and
    batteries (yes, I still have
    a Game Boy, and no, you
    aren't welcome to judge me)
Pack of cards
Puzzle books
Jilly Cooper's *Riders*

*For labour:*

Birthing notes
Lip balm
Energy tablets
Energy drinks
Herbal teabags
Raisins
Melba toast
Jelly sweets
Cereal bars
Bottles of water
Bendy straws
Hot water bottle
An old nightdress
Socks
Massage oil
Pen and paper
Hairbands and hairclips
TENS machine
Facial water spray

*Post-labour:*

Disposable pants (4)
Breast pads
Maternity pads
Pyjamas (2)
Comfortable tops and loose
    trousers
Slippers
Nursing bras (2)
Dressing gown
Pillow
Makeup
Face wipes
Antiseptic hand rub
Hairbrush
Toiletries
Toothbrush and toothpaste
Towels
List of friends' and family's
    phone numbers
Going home outfit (2)

*For baby:*

Fold-up changing mat
Nappies (8)
Cotton wool
Babygros (4)
Cardigans (2)
Socks (4)
Sleepsuits (4)
Hats (2)
Muslins (4)
Bootees (2)
Baby blanket

Hipflask of celebratory Band
    on the Run

# birth announcement card

\* \* \*

## Thom and Kiki

*would like to announce the birth of*

### Stanley John Carlow Sharpe

BORN: May 25th, 3am

WEIGHT: 8lb 2oz

Come and meet him. He's a charmer.

# Acknowledgements

With incredulous, high-fiving thanks again to Jessie Price and Alan Trotter for all the help they've given over the months. What kind folk you are. Thanks to everyone who's fed me juicy material: Jess Kim, Thi Dinh, Roz Massey, Amelia Christmas, Lindsay Green, Hannah Beatson, the Funny-Bones, Madeleine Collinge and Rachel Tracy. A huge hug to my local PN dinner band –Jenny Fleischer Price, Karen Turner, Helen Liley and Amy Bane, for all the many, many times they've made me laugh about our crazy infants. Thanks to my sisters, Fee and Salt, for being such excellent aunts and wonderful sisters. You are the bee's knees.

Since this is a baby book and I don't get to thank them anywhere else, ginormous, enormous, whale-like thanks to my absolutely brilliant antenatal teacher Cathy Sage, a sage indeed, to midwives Marian and Denise, and of course, to the excellent NHS.

Thanks to Toby Jones for bizniz breakfasts and for making me laugh into my porridge, and thank you to Britt Iversen for being an inspirational, hilarious pal. What a gang we have.

Thanks to Clau Webb again, human laughing-gas and lovely agent-and-a-half who earns every. single. penny. To Nikki Dupin who designs such very, very nice books. To Becke Parker, wonderful publicist. And of course to Claire Bord, who works *so* hard, gives such great advice, and didn't even let me see her cry when I handed in this book a teensy bit over the deadline.

And thanks again, to my family; to my wonderful in-laws, to whom I'm grateful every day for the great times they show us, and the wonderful example they are to us all; to J, whose new glasses made me laugh so hard I couldn't see for an hour, and to those magical muses, M and F. As you two would say to me, *Make 'em laugh*. And I try.

# Babies, and all that jazz

It's something you'll probably hear again and again if you ever have a baby, but really every single pregnancy and labour is different. You may as well try and plan the weather in a year's time as plan your next nine-ish months (and the months after) from the sighting of that positive preg test. Whether you haven't had kids but want them one day, whether you don't but think of nothing else, or whether you can't think of anything worse than children cluttering up the place, hopefully there's at least one tip for you in here. But, like I say, everyone's situation is different and if nothing else, at least there are recipes. And playlists. And several instances of me hectoring people for hectoring. So let's begin this magical journey.

## — Morning Sickness —

When you're in pig, the best things in the world you can do are to eat well, get strong, find a way to sleep, get to know your pregnancy medicines (paracetamol if needs be, heartburn tablets a must) and relax. Unfortunately, when you've got morning sickness, most of those are pretty much impossible. And – *and* – morning sickness is the super-annoying cue for all those super-annoying people (you know who you are) to start raising their eyebrows and singing, 'Is someone pregnaaant?' Because that's exactly what you need when even the mention of food can make you throw up.

Morning sickness (ahhahahaa, as if it just goes away at lunchtime ahhahaha) is bad enough for your first pregnancy. But if you've avoided it in previous pregnancies and then find yourself peeling yourself off public transport one day before gagging into the gutter because someone on the bus ate an orange last night and you can still smell it on them then that's *quite* a treat. My last pregnancy introduced me to the joys of morning sickness, and here's what I couldn't eat. At all. Still can't face a lot of these, oddly:

> *Pasta* (but weirdly, only fresh pasta)
> *Butter*
> *Broccoli*
> *Bread* of any sort whatsoever

*Carrots*
*Salad* (except tomatoes sliced with finely chopped spring
   onion)
*Eggs*
*Apple crumble*

Apple crumble! What kind of cruel deity would make apple crumble off limits for someone in low spirits? And these are the only things that, depending on the time of day or the precise positioning of the spirits, I *could* eat:

*Steak*
*Cheeseburgers*
*Pork chops* (plain)
*Lamb chops* (plain)
*Burgers*, eaten plain, straight off the grill
*Mash*
*Chocolate mini rolls*
*Cheese, cheese, cheese*

Ah, the joys of arbitrary nausea. So it was a pretty exciting, very unhealthy time for me, as I stumbled grey-faced from bed to sofa to toilet, and back again. I particularly liked it when I was made the one dish I could manage the thought of eating, but a few mouthfuls in would feel violently sick and have to give it away! Hurray! Morning sickness is a really, really horrible time, and particularly when it's the first three months (the most common time for it) when you're probably nervous about the baby's wellbeing anyway. I call bullshit, our bodies. Come on.

Until pregnant bodies decide to be on the same side as their minds, here are some recipes for you that saw me through those dark, dark months.

## — MAIN —

### Easy ratatouille with pork and couscous
(Serves 2 with a bit for leftovers)

> *Ingredients*
> Onion, chopped
> Clove of garlic, finely chopped
> 400g chopped tomatoes (roughly a tin or a box)
> Jar of peppers, drained and chopped into thumb-sized
>     chunks
> Salt and pepper
> Couscous
> Pork steaks

*Method*
Soften the onion in a little olive oil over a medium heat. Add
the garlic, cook for a minute or two, add the peppers, then
the chopped tomatoes. Season and simmer. Serve with buttery
couscous, over grilled pork steak. It's so easy you might even
be able to cook it in the throes of early-pregnancy cross-eyed
exhaustion.

## — SALAD —

### Simple, fresh salad

> *Ingredients*
> Thickly sliced beef tomatoes
> Spring onions, finely chopped
> Olive oil
> Salt

*Method*
Serve on a plate – leave to soak together for a little while, then eat.

# — DESSERT —

## Chocolate tart

### *Ingredients*

**For the shortcrust pastry (alternatively, use ready-made if you don't fancy making it yourself):**

225g plain flour

Pinch of salt

100g butter *or* 50g butter and 50g lard (which makes a
    really delicious pastry)

2-3tbsp ice cold water

### *For the chocolate filling:*

300ml double cream

2tsp caster sugar

50g butter

200g dark chocolate, broken into very small pieces

50ml whole milk

Crème fraîche to serve

### *Method*

Preheat the oven to 190°C.

Sift the flour and salt into a bowl, then rub the fats in using just
your fingertips (which keeps it cool), until the whole mixture
resembles fine breadcrumbs. Sprinkle the water in bit by bit,
mixing the dough gently until it clumps together – the less
water you use, the better. Press the dough into a ball, wrap in
clingfilm and chill for at least fifteen minutes.

Roll out to the thickness of a pound coin, and place it into a
greased flan or tart dish. Prick the pastry with a fork and blind
bake for ten minutes, then remove the baking beans and cook
for another fifteen.

For the filling, gently heat the cream (being careful not to boil it). Once hot, remove from the heat, add the sugar and butter, then the chocolate. Stir until the chocolate's completely melted. Leave it to cool a little, then add the milk to the rest of the ingredients and stir through. Pour the mixture into the cooked pastry case and leave to cool for a couple of hours at room temperature. Serve with a large spoonful of crème fraîche. Continue to eat until someone wrestles the tart from you.

# ⁓ Spreading the News ⁓

Obviously, a woman's reactions to her pregnancy can – and do – vary wildly, from delight and relief and joy and fulfilment, to fear and horror and anxiety and denial. Or a mix of several of those, what with women being just normal humans with conflicting feelings about major life events. But if we go down the path of women who, either instantly or gradually are pleased about their pregnancy, we eventually come to the thorny issue of Telling People.

I keep reading mentions of women and men announcing 'their' pregnancy with a Facebook posting of the foetal scan, posts that are observed with the sort of scorn and horror usually reserved for Donald Trump's tweets. Yes, I wouldn't choose to do it, but I've seen a great deal more cloying, intrusive or boring posts on Facebook for which I'd save my horrified scorn. There's something about pregnancy that brings out the meanie in some people – complete with eye-rolling and nostril-flaring – but at the same time, there is no reason on earth to expect anyone else but the other parent to care about this pregnancy as much as you. It's your foetus, and the idea that the world will be dancing around at your positive preg test (although I'm sure there'll be friends and family who will at least high-five you) is absurd.

I've had to announce three pregnancies, and it never gets any easier. With my first, I was only 26 and had just got a brilliant promotion, and found myself telling my utterly lovely, grinning ex-boss, 'It seems I will be facing confinement next year.' What the fuck? Fortunately he just laughed, rather than asking me if I was heading towards a custodial sentence before having me escorted from the building, but even at 31, I don't like actually having to say the words. It seems so self-indulgent, so self-centred, so 'Listen to my GREAT ACHIEVEMENT', whilst I worry that everyone must just be saying in their heads, 'Oh well done, you managed to get yourself knocked up, have a medal'. It makes me feel massively self-conscious.

But announcing a pregnancy also feels fraught with danger. Is the person you're telling infertile? Have they been trying for much longer that you? Have they recently had a miscarriage? Are they or their partner going through expensive and uncomfortable fertility treatment? Or will they think less of you for having a child? Will they now dismiss you from their circle? Not to mention whether or not your boss will support you and your choices, or whether they'll try their very hardest to get you out of the door.

It might seem like I overthink these conversations (to make up for all the conversations I have in which I am utterly thoughtless, I suppose) but I'm just hopeful I won't make myself the villain with any in-pig news.

And that's why, truth be told, I announced all my pregnancies on Facebook. Just kidding. For my third pregnancy, I just got my previous children to do any news-breaking. Haha, aren't kids useful?

### In summary:

* If you're making an announcement (which is a horribly weighted word, as it's so rarely actually done with a loud-hailer), don't be disappointed by anyone's response.
* If someone's announcing at you, be a little bit kind, even if it's your ultimate turn-off.

## ⸼ Maternity clothes ⸎

Some of them are still the most repulsive things in the world, even now in this age of easy fashion at any budget. Although maybe that's just because I think anything with a waterfall hem should be taken out and shot, then burnt in case the shooting didn't finish it off properly, before having its ashes scattered across Oxford St and trampled beneath the feet of a million zombie-eyed shoppers. Waterfall hem tops, handkerchief hem cardigans, leggings with bows at the ankles – why would you do that to anyone, Designers? Why? Particularly those vulnerable pregnants who may not be familiar or comfortable with their new and ever-changing bodies? I find the biggest culprits are often the baby shops, rather than the high street fashion chains – they tend towards the 'practical', so you'll pick up a pleasant-looking top only to discover it has (not very well-) hidden breastflaps, so you can feed your baby without disrobing. (For a solution to that, see Belly Bands, below.)

But there is good news, too. There are plenty of places where, if you veer round the hideous hems and slogan t-shirts, maternity fashion does exist. As with all these places, the sizing suddenly goes a bit bonkers when you hit maternity, because they've got to design something in approximately your size, which covers a six month period when your hips may get wider than your shoulders, or your stomach goes from curved above your pelvis to bulbous below it, but as long as you're willing to try on a few sizes, you should find something worth stepping outside in.

Here are my top picks:

### Topshop, ASOS and H&M
Great for clothes of the season cut into preggo shapes. It's not my place to say whether all pregnant women necessarily suit denim cut-offs or sequinned body-con dresses, but who cares. If you want to stay on trend, these are your best affordable hopes.

### New Look and Next
Perfect for **Belly Bands**, hand-span wide lycra-cotton tubes that are great for covering that gap between your waistband and the bottom of your top. Also good for hiding the fact you're still wearing your favourite jeans, but with the zip half undone and fastened with a hairband between the button and the button-hole. *Also* great, if you're breastfeeding once the baby's born, for keeping your stomach completely covered when you surrep-titiously lift a bit of top to get the baby on. These are good shops too for basic t-shirts, leggings and vest tops.

### Isabella Oliver and M&S
Slightly more expensive, and can have a tendency towards mum-siness – a lot of plums and blacks – but Isabella Oliver in partic-ular is great quality and can be dressed up to look a bit fresher.

### Elle Macpherson
Absolutely brilliant nursing bras. I'm normally the first person to say Get Measured For Every Bra, but when it comes to nurs-ing bras, it's a ludicrous idea. If you're breastfeeding, your cup size can vary loads depending on whether it's before or after a feed, and the Elle bras are so stretchy and comfortable that as long as you get the right rib size (try a couple) you'll be fine.

## Primark

Not a fan usually, but great for your hospital things – dressing gown, nightdress, slippers. I'm still convinced that if you might be spilling placenta everywhere, there's no point buying anything you're not willing to throw into an incinerator afterwards.

## Hatch

This is my fantasy maternity wear range. Everything is so beautiful and wearable *forever* (no breastflaps here), and made of things like soft jersey, cotton and silk. *Silk*. Some of these items are dry clean only, and if there's one thing I've learnt, it's that 'dry clean only' means 'will never get round to cleaning'. So while the styles are so very lovely, real red-lipstick-and-great-shoes lovely, both the cost and the likelihood I'll never be able to take care of them means I must just look at them online during pregnancy and pull my Topshop hoodie a little bit tighter around myself as I try to stem my jealous tears.

# ~ Baby Showers ~

Yes, these can be seen as a monstrous import from the US, a nation staggering under expensive get-togethers. Or, it can be seen as an opportunity to drink beer with your friends and hang out. *Fine*, if you're preggo, you might not be able to knock back the cold ones like the good old days, but it certainly doesn't have to be all pastel cupcakes and insisting the pregnant looks glowing when she's shoulder-to-knee tiger-attack-stretchmarks, and hasn't had a good night's sleep in weeks.

As with most parties, people bringing food and drink helps out, and a theme can work too.

**Good themes:**
Round Things
Countries Around The Globe
Drinking, Eating and Having a Good Time

**Bad themes:**
Almost anything you'll find on the internet

Although they thankfully weren't cruel enough to actually play the games they found on the web, my sister and friends did read out all the games they *could* have played, including Guess The Girth and Melting Chocolate Bars Into Nappies. And I think any party

that requires more homework than your job ever will, simply isn't worth attending, so hold off on the Baby Photo Competitions that take weeks of emailing, printing, laminating, etc.

Why not just eat yourself into stasis, and play some great music instead? My Top Ten Baby Hits:

## 1 'Plump' — Hole

'They say I'm plump/but I threw up all the time.' Absolutely love this song, although how a fresh, hopeful mother-to-be might take to screamed lyrics like 'He shakes his death rattle/spittle on his bib' is unknown. I take no responsibility.

## 2 'Ice Ice Baby' — Vanilla Ice

Because any excuse to play this is a triumph for humanity. (Discuss.)

## 3 'You're the One for Me, Fatty' — Morrissey

Maybe only if the pregnant has a sense of humour.

## 4 & 5 'Push it' — Salt n Pepa *and* 'Push it Out' — Beta Band

Both great songs to warm up for your labour. Maybe even take them into the labour room?

## 6 'Babies' — Pulp

Because if you can't play a fantastic song containing Jarvis singing 'I want to take you home/I want to give you children' at a baby shower, when can you play it?

## 7 'Between the Bars' — Elliot Smith

Opening as it does with, 'Drink up baby…' I always sang this to my babies during night feeds. Turns out, it was one of the first songs to which my eldest knew all the words. It's probably they only cool thing I'll ever do for them.

## 8 'This Woman's Work' — Kate Bush

A song all about labour from the father's point of view – if you aren't all sobbing by the end, I don't know *what's* going to break you. For bonus points, make the pregnant watch the video featuring wonderful Tim McInerney.

## 9 'Don't Worry Baby' — The Beach Boys

Admittedly, the one thing babies make you do is worry forever and ever until the end of time, but it's a nice sentiment to cling to before labour kicks in. Oh, and it's a fabulous tune.

## 10 'Baby Love' — The Supremes

Because a probably-alcohol-free party ain't a party without some Wall of Sound. Just like the baby will make when it's born.

## Gifting a pregnant

I have some absolutely wonderful friends who made me the most beautiful knitted bootees for my babies. They were gorgeous – perfectly formed, with tiny little matching buttons and ribbons. I now keep them in a box, unwilling to even re-gift them as they are so handsome, even though I never, ever used them. Only you will know whether you're someone who can be trusted to take care of things, but I knew that any child of mine would lose one, eat one, throw up on one or generally negate the pleasantness of the bootees somehow. They were never worn. A hat, however – a friend knitted a deep pink hat that my eldest wore almost every day for the best part of a year. Not only was it a great, practical design, it also meant I could sing 'Raspberry Beret' each time we got dressed to leave the house.

There are some great things to give as a baby gift. But most things, I'd wager, are what in our family we call 'Shitty McCluttercrap'. Stuff that looks fine when you buy it, or unwrap it, but gradually becomes more and more obvious an example of the leaden, the ugly, the pointless, the cumbersome – in short, the Charity Shop-bound. One man's meat, and all that – someone might really enjoy a ceramic money box with a poorly painted clown on one side, and I'm sure there's a canny shopper who'll hoot with delight when they find that silver tooth box that in *no way* seems like something Buffalo Bill would keep next to his lotions – but I always feel a bit sad at a wasted present.

## Money

Cynical as it is, setting up a fund for your child is a really, really kind thing for someone else to do. It says that the giver is long-sighted enough to want your child to have possibilities in the future, not just more stuff around it now. My oldest friend Rachel, non-godparent to my son, gave him some Premium Bonds when he was born, and all I could think was, 'But I've seen you [REDACTED BECAUSE HER PARENTS MIGHT READ THIS] when [REDACTED] before they were even *conscious*. When did *you* get so sensible?' But I just *said*, 'Thank you.'

## A Hamper of Post-Baby Foods

It could be really simple stuff, like wine and ginormous bars of Dairy Milk, or an elaborate feast of all the things unable to be eaten in pregnancy: cheeses, pâté, steak tartare, smoked salmon, liver. (Oh, and the NHS says you should avoid shark during pregnancy too, so maybe put a nice shark steak in there too. You know, shark steak, that you can buy at every supermarket because everyone always eats shark. All the time). Or you could even put in a complete meal for the parents to enjoy that they won't have to cook themselves. Whatever the case, it's a really nice gift.

## A Hamper of Treats

Simple, small things here: some nail polish, a face mask, a nice candle, a pair of gorgeous hanging-around-the-house socks, bath salts (yes, that's right, I'm 80), a lovely moisturiser, colourful bracelets, a chubby lip-colour stick. I'm making it sound like as soon as one hatches an infant, one becomes a magpie-like simpleton only interested in prettifying, but it's not that. It's a friend bringing a box of things that are meant only for you, little things that have shown she or he has thought of you, thought what makes you happy, and has remembered that maybe you'd like to do something other than

feed a baby, change a baby, or give yourself a high-five if you wash that day.

## Blankets

If there's anyone even vaguely crafty in your circle, veer them away from miniature footwear and towards blankets. If the blankets are only little, they are great while they're babies, good for toys' beds as they get older, and can be made into cushions when they're older still. If they're single bed size, the baby may have to hold off using it for a year or two, but it will go with them forever. My sister has made two beautiful blankets for my children; when I think about the damage inflicted on my family-made patchwork quilt when I took it to uni, there is no way on earth I'm letting the blankets leave this house until our kids sign contracts that they don't drink, smoke, or eat any food ever.

## DVDs

An absolute necessity, whether they're for daytime sanity-keeping, or evening hanging-out time with your partner when you're both too exhausted to engage in real conversation. You'll have your own favourites of course, but in a world of *Mad Men*, *Game of Thrones*, *Friday Night Lights*, *Battlestar Galactica*, *Breaking Bad*, and *30 Rock*, why wouldn't you? Set a parent up with the first couple of series, and they'll owe you forever.

## Time Off

A meaningful, possibly *forceful* offer to babysit is a wonderful thing. To know that there are friends and family just poised for when a frazzled parent needs them can mean so much, whether they take up the offer or not (side note to parents: just take up the fucking offer – being a martyr to your child 'needing you' does not a better parent make. Having time off with your partner or friends does). Let them know when you're free, if needs be; send them cinema times, book them a table at a restaurant if you have that kind of

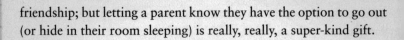

friendship; but letting a parent know they have the option to go out (or hide in their room sleeping) is really, really, a super-kind gift.

## Books

For both parents and babies. Not the same books, obviously, but books for each. Plenty of my friends said they struggled to read a book after their first baby was born, whether through tiredness, lack of sleep or inability to concentrate. I had a slight panic when, after the birth of my eldest, I couldn't get back into the book I'd been reading when I'd gone into labour, but it turns out it just wasn't a very good book. One thing that will make it easier, though, is having a light, easy, fun read. Here are my favourites.

*Hilarious books:*
*Me Talk Pretty One Day* by David Sedaris
*Bossypants* by Tina Fey
*Let's Pretend This Never Happened* by Jenny Lawson

*Childhood comfort books:*
The *Narnia* series by C. S. Lewis
*Fire & Hemlock* by Diana Wynne Jones
The *Dark is Rising* series by Susan Cooper

*Immensely readable novels at any time:*
*Love in a Cold Climate* by Nancy Mitford
*The Vintner's Luck* by Elizabeth Knox
*The Murder of Roger Ackroyd* by Agatha Christie

*Short stories and essays:*
*All Points North* by Simon Armitage
*Going Solo* by Roald Dahl
*The Man Who Ate Everything* by Jeffrey Steingarten

There should be something in there for everyone – everyone who is struggling to read because they only ever get three hours sleep at best in a single stretch, that is. Now, children are a different matter. I gag a little when I find a Mr Man book has made its way into our house; no matter how fondly they may be remembered, I find them deathly boring to read. Likewise most tie-in books – Noddy (but not the original stories), (all) Thomas the Tank Engine, almost everything featuring a character that's on TV now. God, I just thought of a children's character I dislike so much but who is so popular I don't even have the nerve to write his name down. The point is, just because something's well known, doesn't mean it's good. Conversely, something that's a household name in children's literature might be rarely read as it was written, and looking back to *Peter Pan* and *Alice in Wonderland* now, I'm dazzled by their wit, their weirdness, the complete world they created before the Disney merchandised gear I got so used to when I was young. So dig around and ask for recommendations, because if a child latches onto a book, you will have to read it approximately 17,000 times.

My favourites, roughly ascending in age:

* *We're Going on a Bear Hunt* by Michael Rosen and Helen Oxenbury
Beautiful illustrations and a wonderful story full of great sounds. Helen Oxenbury has said she based the sad bear at the end on her friend with depression – I always feel so tearful at his lonely trudge away.

* *Not Now, Bernard* by David McKee
Smart and funny. I love Bernard's parents' apathy that their son has been eaten and replaced by a hyperactive, toy-breaking monster when they don't pay him any attention. Mr and Mrs Bernard: I hear your cry.

* *The Gruffalo* by Julia Donaldson and Axel Scheffler
Probably one of the most influential children's picture books ever. Musical and funny, and you have to admire that mouse's nerve.

* *Look Out! It's the Wolf!* by Emile Jadoul
I found this in a car boot sale and it seems quite hard to track down, but it's worth it for how it made me laugh out loud in the rain. Best ending ever to a picture book, I think.

* *The Magic Paintbrush* by Julia Donaldson and Joel Stewart
Another lyrical book from the most excellent Julia Donaldson, and I cry every time I read it. Shen's good fortune, and her calm bravery and smartness in the face of a greedy emperor – just marvellous.

* *Stuck* by Oliver Jeffers
Another laugh-out-loud-er. It's a clever book with great illustrations, but there are two gags in particular that seem so perfectly timed, I laugh whenever I read it.

* *The Paperbag Princess* by Robert Munsch and Michael Martchenko
A Princess is the only obvious survivor of a savage dragon attack, and makes her way to its lair in a paper bag to rescue her betrothed. Turns out: the trip's not really worth it.

* *The Three Little Wolves and the Big Bad Pig* by Eugene Trivizas and Helen Oxenbury
A charming twist on the old tale (which I always make as bloody as possible – only one pig makes it out alive in my version), where the little wolves just want to play badminton but the Big Bad Pig keeps bringing sledgehammers to destroy their homes.

* *Princess Smartypants* by Babette Cole
Being rich and fabulous, all the princes want to marry Smartypants. She's simply happy doing what she likes, though, and with great sense battles her parents' wishes to wed.

* *A Necklace of Raindrops* by Joan Aitken
I love Joan Aitken's writing for any age, but these stories also come with the most beautiful Jan Pienkowski illustrations, lifting the whole book into a different realm. A girl has the North Wind for her godfather and can control the weather; a patchwork quilt has fantastic powers; a cat grows as big as a house. Wonderful.

* *Clever Polly and the Stupid Wolf* by Catherine Storr
I loved these stories as a child, but only reading them again to my children did I realise how immensely, brilliantly funny they are. The repartee between smart, brave Polly and the naïve, obsessive Wolf is so excellently done, I'd recommend it for anyone.

* *The Secret Garden* by Frances Hodgson Burnett
The story of sickly-faced, mean-tempered Mary and her bed-bound, utterly spoiled cousin Colin should be a bit repellent, but instead the account of how they meet and change one another, growing up and finding independence in their secret garden, is a genuine Good Read.

* *Howl's Moving Castle* by Diana Wynne Jones
I still read this now, from time to time; no-nonsense and cynical Sophie Hatter is transformed into an old woman and ends up at the castle of the murderous Wizard Howl. It's full of great characters *and* John Donne's 'Song'.

## — ❦ Choosing a name ❦ —

Nothing I say here should make any difference to what you name your child – if you want to go down the Hector Atticus route, or the Bay Bieber route, it's no one's business but yours. The only thing I will say – and I speak from bitter experience – is please, please, please: give your children different initials from everyone else in the household. Even if they're different sexes. My sister and I share an initial, and while it may have saved my parents on name tapes for uniforms, I've lost count of the number of times there's been near-bloodshed over an envelope address only to Miss S Binnie. I suppose what always made it worse was that our mother's solution wasn't to give it to one of us and ask us to pass it on if we weren't the intended recipient. No. She would open it herself, read it, and *then* give it to one us. Yes. I know. *I know*.

So please, for the sake of family harmony, ensure that a family's initials are as different as can be. Public service announcement over.

# Oh God, now the baby's arrived and it's in my house

Once your baby is actually born, it turns out there's plenty you have to do to look after it (although, hahaha, this is also likely to be the easiest it will be until it leaves home). Since the most important thing is for you to get some sleep – you'll be amazed what you can cope with when you've had more than two hours sleep a night – we need to focus on what will get you some rest.

## a) The baby being well: well-fed, well-rested, well-cared for.
## b) Some peace and quiet for you.

a)  Not-rocket-science bit: babies basically just want milk, calm and maybe a bit of love. I'm not a doctor. It's something like that. If you have any interest in breastfeeding, I think it's hugely helpful to get some breastfeeding advice – it's all well and good having lessons before you have a baby and lactating breasts, but it really becomes a *whole* different ball game – from someone who either helps people all the time, or has done it recently. I lost count of all the useless bullshit advice I was given when I struggled to breastfeed my first, but all it took for me in the end was a nice breastfeeding teacher coming to my flat and showing me the 'Shape and

Shove'. It worked like a charm, almost certainly because there was someone patient and experienced sitting with me, encouraging me and not hurrying me in the slightest, whilst I hadn't yet got to the stage of frantic panic and guilt into which the most useless Health Visitors and well-meaners can whip a mother.

Of course, there are a hundred reasons why you might not want to, or be able to, breastfeed – going straight back to work, finding it too painful, finding it emotionally hard, not enough milk, or simply not wanting to, no reason necessary – and it's not my bag to convince you that you mustn't or you'll ruin your baby. I couldn't give a hoot, and I personally don't put much worth into the belief that formula-feeding will leave you with anything hugely dissimilar to breastfed babies. There are plenty of those women out there on the internet who believe that too, should you wish to get an eyeful of tolerance and empathy at its finest *hem hem*.

I did a mixed feed, mostly breastfeeding but with the occasional bottle, either because I was away from the baby and hadn't expressed, or my husband was doing a feed when I'd fallen asleep at two in the afternoon after no sleep the night before, or that one time I made us lavender biscuits which curdled my breast milk and which, looking back, is one of the most hilarious anecdotes from that year but at the time seemed like a Shirley Jackson-esque nightmare. But overall I was glad that I could breastfeed, just because it was cheaper and slightly easier (no bottle-boiling and all that stuff).

But I think educated choice is important, and if you would *like* to breastfeed but are finding it hard, I would recommend asking for help if you can, at one of these places:

**National Breastfeeding Helpline** 0300 100 0212
**NCT Breastfeeding line** 0300 330 0771
**Local support centres** – have a look on Google
**Private breastfeeding counsellors** – prices will vary wildly, but investigate for the convenience of having someone with you in your home

I can't guarantee that any of these will work for you, but I know that when I rang up the NCT line sobbing because the Health Visitors had been such dicks and *apparently* my week-old baby was starving itself into a hospital visit, the patience and calm kindness with which they spoke to me – reminding me that I was doing a good job, and my baby would be fine no matter what I decided to do – was something I've never forgotten.

So, feed your baby however you like, give yourself every chance to breastfeed if that's what you choose, don't panic or feel guilty if you formula-feed, but mainly, just relax. Which is easier to do if you've had a little rest, bringing us neatly onto:

b) Sleep. Firstly, sleep whenever you can. Don't feel guilty about missing things, about not playing with the baby, not socialising with your partner, not staying up to hear about people's days. If you're tired, and can leave the baby safely and fall asleep, do. Just do it. Screw guilt, it's a crummy feeling. Just get some sleep. Everyone will be happier – you; your partner (because you won't drop the c-bomb when they forget to buy the particular jam you like); your baby (because you won't grit your jaw when they start crying *again*); any other children in the house (because you will be able to read them a book without getting all the words wrong and having to stop half-way through in a exhausted fury); just sleep when you can. Don't be a martyr.

Secondly, at some stage (i.e. not on day two, just whenever you fancy it) get the baby into a routine. In some circles, it's proper *filth* to mention Gina Ford's name, but the consensus from people who seem most rested and fully dressed after a baby, is that she's great for picking and choosing. Some of her advice can seem slightly extreme – don't make eye contact! Don't let the routine slip by even fifteen minutes! – but when you actually read her stuff, her overall ideas make a lot of sense. I'm not going to rehash her advice, since she's already one of the most successful authors on the topic ever, but I would recommend having a quick browse of her *The Contented Little Baby Book* and deciding for yourself. (Although ugh, that title). It's one of those books that once you understand the rules, it's easy to break them, or ignore them entirely, but still benefit from the principles.

It's basically: if you feed a baby whenever it wants, it never really gets hungry, so never takes enough to really be full, so never sleeps for long enough as it's a compulsive snacker. As with all things childcare related, this concept fires off such a ferocious, bitter feud between parents that it's almost not worth mentioning it to another mother until you know it's 'allowed', but I found it most helpful. Anything that got me closer to my lovely, lovely, wonderful long sleeps again, and kept our babies content and away from the clutches of our Health Visitors was OK by me. But you might find something *far* better.

## Conversation in pregnancy/post-natal conversation

It's stupid to imagine that conversation somehow needs to change when someone falls pregnant. From the pregnant woman's side, it's absurd to imagine this pregnancy plays on others' minds as it may play on yours, and for those in the circle of the pregnant, her brain hasn't just mashed itself up into a teddy bear shape, despite the bandying about of the *hilarious* 'Baby Brain' idea. Next time you have something squirming in your stomach like a Chestburster, can't sleep because of a crushed bladder and are constantly doing mental calculations for how you'll afford living/eating/keeping your job after the baby is born, why don't you let me know how important it is for you to remember that book you said you'd lend to someone next time you met?

So, here are some things it is OK to say to women who are pregnant, or who have just had a child:

* Anything about work
* Anything about socialising
* Anything about the world beyond their womb or the creature that's suddenly out of it

And here are some things it's probably not OK to say to those women:

* Was it planned? / Was it an accident?
* (At any point past three months) Gosh, are you *sure* it's not twins?
* You're having children *already*? / We were wondering when you two would get on with it!
* (Once the baby's born) Do you think you'll have any more?
* It's harder than you thought, isn't it?

To balance things out, here are some things pregnant women or new mothers aren't allowed to say, even though they might think them in their heads all the time or even say it to their partners who nod knowingly:

* Everything changes when you have your own.
* You wouldn't understand unless you're a parent.
* Your life changes so utterly and completely once you have a child. *Completely*.

That last one in particular, when said in a smug tone rather than a despairing one, is a bit of a bone of contention with me, mostly because I found it to be utterly untrue in any noticeably dramatic way. Yes, with a handful of kids, years after we married, my life is slightly different – the majority of the money I make goes on child-care, for a start, and… God, I'm actually really struggling to think of something else. Yes, it's different, but I'd hope my life would change from time to time. If my life was the same now as it had been when I was eighteen, I'd probably be one of the most unhappy people around, having had miserable teenage years. But having kids doesn't have to change your life – I can't really watch films where anything bad of any sort happens to a child, but otherwise I like similar music, similar books, similar food, similar people, similar jokes to those I liked three or five or seven years ago, allowing for the fact that I've got older, my tastes develop as the years go by and the world has continued to spin.

But people who say that with a feeling that *now* they're a fully developed human, and they feel a bit sorry for those friends whose lives haven't changed utterly in this fulfilling, marvellous way, just need a bit of a shove. Insisting that everything changes utterly and completely once you have a child just makes it harder for people who don't have children, and don't know happy couples with children, to see that we're still the same people, just with a car-seat cluttering up the place. But we're still in here! Look! No, behind the nappies! No no, next to the bibs. No, other side. By the teething gel. Yes! There we are. Same us, different props.

## ∽ A million dilemmas ∾

There are so very many things to decide in pregnancy. Will you have the vaccinations they offer you? Will you go to a private antenatal class, an NHS one, or none at all? Will you have a hospital birth, or a homebirth? If you have a hospital birth, will you have a caesarean? An epidural? If you have a homebirth, will it be on your bed, or in a water pool? After the baby is born, will you breast or bottle feed it? Give it a dummy? Sleep it in a cot, or in your bed? Carry it in a sling, or tuck it up in a pushchair? Will you dress your baby in pink if it's a girl, and blue if it's a boy, or will you not because that's stupid? Will you introduce food at five months, or wait until nine? When you do, will you give it solid things to chew, or make baby porridge and mashed fruit and vegetables? Will you give it a routine, or let its needs lead you?

Will you take it to Baby Signing, Baby Swimming, Baby Gym, Baby Music, Baby Massage, Baby Yoga? Or will you just let it watch Desperate Housewives with you at two in the afternoon (it's fine, they can only see about 30cm for ages)? Will you put it in a bouncer? A pen? A wheeled walker? When it starts walking, will you put it in shoes, or keep it in socks? When it's a little older and cries at bedtime, will you go back as many times as it takes to soothe it peacefully to sleep, or will you do a bit of controlled crying to teach it to soothe itself? Will you play with it every second it's awake, or will you leave the child to entertain itself occasionally? When it's older still and learns to talk, and asks for aubergine/couscous/mozzarella/chorizo in a supermarket, will you congratulate it and buy whatever it's asked for, or will you double over laughing at how pretentious and middle class your child is, but know that you're really the only person to blame and be happy that they make you laugh? Will you teach it that there are girls' toys, and boys' toys, and never the twain shall meet? Will you love it, but believe it's important for it to learn that it's not the only person in the entire universe, and if someone else requires your attention, it can wait two seconds? Will you refuse it a 'babycinno' because it makes you cold inside that it even knows that word? Will you allow your child its 'creativity and developing personality', or will you teach it that nothing in the world is as appealing as thoughtfulness and good manners, no matter how brightly coloured that drawing all over Mummy's work is? Will you help them to understand that parents are human too, and make mistakes, but show them that when you do make a mistake you apologise because you are sorry, and then you can stop feeling guilty? Will the thought of your child make you sweat, or smile?

Pretty much everything is unknowable from the moment a child is conceived, and it's never a good idea to get your thoughts down in concrete for something full of a million, million variables. Do your research, read up on the options, but be guided by what you believe to be best for you and your family. Don't feel bad about your choices. Try to make the decisions based on empathy and love, but also remember that you (and your partner, if about) are separate adults who require your own time and space. As long as you're not lighting their cigarettes for them, your loved babies are going to grow up *just fine*. Relax.

## Finally, my attempt to make this whole parenting thing easier on everyone

Whether you have kids, whether you don't, whether you're desperate for them or whether you can't think of anything worse, please don't make drive-by parenting judgments.

In a shopping centre recently, I saw a mother looking uncomfortable as her son had a massive tantrum about something he wanted her to buy him. She wasn't uncomfortable about his tantrum – she was basically just reading a magazine as he tantrum-ed himself out, but she was clearly bothered by all the glares and comments from passing mothers-with-buggies. Like some pushy do-gooder, I went over to say – and God, I really don't come out of this in a good way, but she seemed cheered and I thought it was the right thing to do – that I thought she was doing well, and it was hard but that kind of thing had paid off with my kids.

If that sounds horribly pious of me, my only thought was: Christ, all the times I felt passers-by watching and judging me (all those incidents Kiki experiences aren't a million miles away from my own), I would have killed for someone to just say, 'It's OK. You're doing OK, and you're a good parent. Carry on.' Every time you judge a mother or father, you ignore the fact that you don't know what their child is like, you don't know what the parent's situation is, and you certainly don't know what led up to the situation you've just witnessed.

My mother's favourite phrase when we're out shopping and there's a screaming child in a buggy is, 'Why doesn't their mother just *pick them up* and give them a cuddle?' My sisters and I *HOWL* with laughter at this – partly because when you're out shopping with a screaming child, the last thing you want to do is anything to prolong the trip; in, out, home, deal with the tears. And partly because, when my mum was out with her own three children, this was a more likely scenario: the youngest wanted that toy – I WANT IT I WANT IT – and would dissolve into Europe-sized tantrums, whilst my mum still had to get everything for her husband's dinner when he got home at six from his long commute from London, tights for the two older girls *and* a rucksack for the school trip. So I can probably count on my unicorn horn how many times I remember her saying, 'Alright, everyone, let's stop and cuddle this little weeping child. Group hug everyone.' It just doesn't work like that.

So next time you see someone with a child, behaving in a way you don't approve of, imagine your sweatiest, most stressful day, with someone literally screaming at you the whole day, knowing you've still got to prepare a full meal, tidy a house, and ensure the tiny person with you doesn't run in front of a bus or eat their own faeces or something, and think: would I suddenly become more patient and relaxed if someone glared at me? Or would I really, really appreciate someone smiling at me, and telling me that I was doing a good job. Quite. So: smile, guys.

If you have children, humour is your most essential tool. The whole thing is so ludicrous and riddled with so many disgusting/bizarre/scary/unbearably heart-warming/heart-breaking occasions, that humour is the one thing you need more than anything else. If you can laugh at yourself and with your child, most things seem better. Good, even. And if you don't have children, humour's still pretty good too. Just make sure you're friends with people who can see how much their new-born baby looks like a nightmarish postbox and can laugh with you.

So be kind. Laugh. And good luck, everyone.